ESTHER CAMPION

is from Cork, Ireland. She attended North Presentation Secondary School in Farranree, University College Cork and the University of Aberdeen, Scotland. Her Orcadian husband's career has taken the family from Ireland to Scotland, Norway and South Australia. Esther now lives on a small property in north-west Tasmania with her husband, youngest child, smoochy cat, second chance poodle and a couple of ageing horses. While she has settled and thrived in every place she's lived, she still calls Ireland home.

Also by Esther Campion

Leaving Ocean Road
The House of Second Chances
A Week to Remember

ESTHER CAMPION

The Writing Class

hachette
AUSTRALIA

AUSTRALIA

Published in Australia and New Zealand in 2024
by Hachette Australia
(an imprint of Hachette Australia Pty Limited)
Gadigal Country, Level 17, 207 Kent Street, Sydney, NSW 2000
www.hachette.com.au

The authorised representative
in the EEA is
Hachette Ireland
8 Castlecourt Centre
Dublin 15, D15 XTP3, Ireland
(email: info@hbgi.ie)

Hachette Australia acknowledges and pays our respects to the past, present and
future Traditional Owners and Custodians of Country throughout Australia
and recognises the continuation of cultural, spiritual and educational practices
of Aboriginal and Torres Strait Islander peoples. Our head office is located on
the lands of the Gadigal people of the Eora Nation.

NATIONAL
LIBRARY
OF AUSTRALIA

A catalogue record for this
book is available from the
National Library of Australia

ISBN: 978 0 7336 4553 2 (paperback)

Cover design and image by Alex Ross Creative
Author photograph by Michelle DuPont
Typeset in 12.1/18.6 pt Sabon LT Pro by Bookhouse, Sydney
Printed and bound in Great Britain by Clays Ltd, Elcograf S.p.A.

To my mother and father,
my first teachers

Play the hand that you're dealt.

—MAEVE BINCHY

Prologue

December 2021

Vivian wrapped together the edges of her hotel robe and leaned on the rail of her balcony, envious of the carefree surfers paddling out to catch the rollers thundering in from the South Pacific. Surfers Paradise had lived up to its name. When she returned to Tasmania, she would miss the sound of the surging waves that had lulled her to sleep each night beside her husband of over thirty years. The Festival of Singing had given their choir a goal, something to look forward to after what had felt like hiding since the pandemic. Six performances in two days had been a bit exhausting, but everyone had managed to keep upbeat, especially with the promise of a gala ball to finish the weekend off in style.

Dave emerged warbling from the bathroom, his matching robe tied around his expanding middle as he roughly towel-dried his damp silvery curls. The man had hardly stopped singing since they'd boarded the plane to the Gold Coast three days before. Lucky the other passengers had been accommodating of the group's harmonising, even giving them a round of applause after an impromptu rehearsal of 'The Bare Necessities' mid-flight. It was good to see Dave animated, a change from the past few months that had seen him so withdrawn. Choir at least had made him smile.

When he joined her on the balcony, Vivian slipped an arm around his waist, but he didn't reciprocate. Instead, he stood with his hands holding the ends of his towel about his shoulders, looking out to sea. She'd hoped the break from their routine would reignite the old spark. He'd stopped singing, and around their bubble of silence, the hum of holiday-makers, evening traffic and the rush of the light rail drifted up from the street below. Hearing Dave let out a deep breath, Vivian waited for him to say something, but instead, he turned back to the room and began to dress. A sliding door moment that took the warmth out of the balmy evening. There'd been a lot of those lately.

She went to squeeze herself into her own outfit, a full-length silky number she'd hired with her best friend's encouragement. Her phone pinged.

'Deb's on her way to do my hair. Okay if you leave us to it and we follow you down?' she asked him.

'Yes, fine.'

Vivian texted Deb back and sat on the edge of the bed. She would like to have asked him to zip up her dress, but instead she waited for him to offer, watching as he got ready. His tall frame suited the requisite tuxedo. Although it was like a work uniform to Dave, she'd always loved how distinguished he looked, striding out to take his place in an orchestra on stage or in the pit at one of the many theatre shows he'd worked on. It was nice to have an excuse to dress up all fancy. Covid, and now retirement, meant he'd been mostly at home for almost two years. Holed up in the study for hours on end, he no longer had need of his formal outfits. The two of them had become like a pair of old socks, bobbled and ragged in places, but they were still a perfect match, weren't they?

'This is the bit I hate.' He held out a black satin cummerbund. 'Give it here.'

She took the piece and stood behind him, working the fabric around his girth and fastening it in place. Coming round in front of him, she gave the cummerbund a last straighten and stepped back.

'You're handsome.'

He raised an eyebrow as he reached for his jacket and pulled it on. He hadn't noticed her zip. Pulling at the lapels of the jacket, she angled her face up toward his, but as she leaned in, he placed his hands on her shoulders and with something that couldn't quite be called a push, he extricated himself and turned away. Another knock-back? Maybe he was nervous to hear the competition results. They always had tonight, she reassured herself. A dance or two after the formalities and they could relax.

Deb arrived at the door, hair straighteners and the floral toiletry bag she took on all their trips cradled in her arms.

'I'll see you down there.' Dave hurried out of the room, nearly bumping into Deb as she entered.

'Someone's in a hurry to get to the bar,' said Deb.

Vivian gave a weak laugh. She could hear Dave whistling as he strode along the corridor toward the lifts.

Deb pushed the door closed, careful not to get her fishtail caught. 'He seems in good form,' she said.

Vivian shrugged. 'Nothing to do with me,' she said. 'But at least he's happy about something.'

Half an hour later, Vivian and Deb emerged from the lift like a pair of ageing Bond girls, as delighted as two children that had been let loose with a dress-up box and were now parading their costumes to attentive loved ones. The silky swish of her dress, the soft ringlets Deb had miraculously conjured from her limp, greying hair, the smooth touches of makeup, all had Vivian feeling fabulous. With the Christmas tree in the foyer and the festive decorations, the evening had a fairytale feel.

At the bar, Dave was holding court with some of their choir buddies. Choir was more Dave's thing than hers. She'd only recently joined as a way of ensuring he stayed connected to it. Deb's sister and the other women had made her welcome. The men too, some of them getting on in years but with voices that seemed to defy the ravages of ageing. Her contribution so far had been more to do with her organisational skills than any vocal prowess, but it gave her an outlet, something to share with Dave.

Resplendent in his tuxedo, she saw her efforts with the cummerbund were doing a great job of pulling in his paunch. A rush of admiration, pride even, surprised her. Things may not have been perfect of late, but he was still her Dave, wasn't he? Still her soulmate?

As he turned to greet them, Vivian caught a look in his eye. Something wobbly, unsure. But it was a fleeting glance. If she'd expected gobsmacked, overcome with the complete hots for her, it wasn't there.

'Espresso martinis, ladies?'

He'd already turned to order their drinks. Deb's husband, Ian, was beside them, taking Deb's hand and telling her she looked amazing. He winked at Vivian.

'You two scrub up well,' he joked.

Vivian mustered a warm smile. Ian was a good man. He and Deb had been there for most of their life in Australia, through highs and lows, birthdays, kids leaving home, family weddings and recent funerals when they lost loved ones during Covid. Yet Vivian couldn't remember the last time the four of them had spent a night out together. It had certainly been a while. She could have blamed the pandemic. Lots of people said their social lives hadn't recovered from the nosedive they'd taken in lockdowns – but she'd declined enough invites from their friends to prompt Deb to ask if everything was okay. Maybe this could be the beginning of a return to normal.

As they found their table in the vast hotel ballroom, even the discomfort of her strappy heels couldn't distract Vivian from the excitement of being with her husband and their best friends in such a grand setting. She raised her glass to her lips. *To fresh starts*, she told herself, and took a delightful drink.

Chapter One

Seven weeks later

Under normal circumstances, Vivian Molloy would never have dreamt of driving forty kilometres out of town to do her grocery shopping. With a perfectly good supermarket on her doorstep, anyone would think she was mad driving to Ulverstone. Not that she minded the drive up the coast on a good day. There was nothing quite like the view from where the highway rose out of Devonport and scooped round the downhill bend where the Bass Strait revealed itself, stretching out to the horizon in all its sparkling glory. Today, however, a low gloomy sky hung over the ocean. Rain wasn't far away. February was still summer, of course. She just hadn't got out of the habit of thinking the season came to an end with the start of a new school year.

In the supermarket, Vivian pushed her trolley round the vegetable stands. Cauliflower was on special, but she didn't need a whole cauliflower. The last one had blackened in the fridge, like a lot of things, neglected and past their sell-by date. On the radio, the presenter was asking a local author what advice he'd give his younger self. His answer was something trite about self-belief. If anyone asked Vivian right now what advice *she* would give her younger self, it would be to think hard before taking early retirement, and to know that despite what your marriage vows might say, parting could come well before death.

At the deli counter, she chose a small portion of olives and the five slices of cooked meat that would do for a week's worth of toasted sandwiches. She pressed on to pick up a loaf of bread, begrudging having to buy some preservative-packed product instead of the spongy fresh bread on offer at her local bakery. But that particular purchase would have meant running into people she knew, the conversation always coming round to the inevitable, 'How is Dave?'.

At the check-out, the lady in front had barely anything in her basket. Great. Vivian would be out of there in no time. As she placed her purchases on the conveyor, the young cashier gave her a confident smile.

'How's your day been?'

'Not bad for a Monday,' she said.

'Got much on for the rest of the day?'

She had an urge to make up some exciting event she was in a hurry to get to, a dinner party to prepare or an important meeting she would chair in the afternoon.

'A nice quiet one,' she said, mustering a bland smile. It wasn't his fault her career and social life had ground to a halt.

'Not really a day for doing anything,' he said with a nod toward the windows where she saw the teeming rain that had customers darting back and forth to their cars.

Top marks for tact, she thought as she loaded her bags into the trolley and said a polite goodbye.

Thinking she was home and dry, at least in a metaphorical sense, Vivian pushed through the automatic doors, her sights set on the shortest route to her car. *Oh god!* Cathy Shannon appeared from nowhere, grinning at her from under the hood of the rain jacket she was holding up while clutching a laptop bag to her ample chest.

'Vivian, how are you?' Cathy stopped under the overhang of the roof that offered enough shelter for a chat without getting soaked. If only she'd been another metre along, Vivian could have kept going with a passing hello.

'I'm so glad I ran in to you,' Cathy was saying while Vivian was still formulating a response as to how she was.

Cathy rested her bag on Vivian's trolley, pushed down her hood from her mop of bottle-blonde hair and leaned in. Vivian had known Cathy for years. They'd taught at the same high school until relentless crowd control, or the lack of it in Cathy's case, became too much and she'd taken a transfer to a much calmer number at the community library as an outreach officer. In fact, Vivian realised, Cathy was probably on one of her jaunts up the coast to the outlying libraries right now and, if her relaxed demeanour was anything to go by, thoroughly enjoying it. Why couldn't *she* have kept her own good job? Early retirement was hardly what she'd expected.

'I haven't seen you since your leaving do,' said Cathy.

Vivian could picture them now, chatting over a cuppa in the staffroom of the school she'd given half her life to. Cathy had been invited to the afternoon tea, where teachers and admin staff, past and present, told her how much she'd be missed. At the time she'd given a wry laugh and joked about how she'd be thinking of them all, especially on the Sunday afternoons she'd no longer spend preparing for the working week.

'Gee, they must miss you,' said Cathy.

Vivian shook her head. *Not as much as I miss them*, she wanted to say, but Cathy didn't need a response.

'I'm so glad to be out of it,' Cathy continued. 'Those rascals in Year 9 made it easy to leave.'

Vivian smiled. 'We sure had some wildcards. Kept us on our toes, all right.'

'But you had a gift,' said Cathy. 'You didn't let it faze you. Best English teacher that school ever had.'

Vivian blushed.

'Been doing much lately?' Cathy asked.

The question shot through Vivian like a poisoned arrow. How to go from boosting one's ego to laying it flat on the ground and stamping on it. No, she hadn't been doing much lately. She shrugged.

'Probably still getting used to the new routine,' Cathy answered for her.

In the awkward silence, Vivian glanced round to where a northerly gust blew the rain directly into them. When she turned back, Cathy was looking at her with new intent.

'There's actually something I'd like to chat to you about,' she said, moving in closer. 'I'm planning to run a writing class.

You'd be perfect to lead it.' A broad smile spread across her face like she'd just been inspired. 'Come see me Friday at the library. Morning works for me. Say ten?'

Vivian was about to protest, invent a prior engagement, but Cathy lifted her bag from the trolley and made toward the supermarket door, talking as she went. 'Best get in here and grab some lunch. Interviewing all day. Casual staff. Bet you're glad to be free of all that hassle.'

By the time Vivian got to her car, she couldn't recall actually agreeing to a meeting with Cathy, but neither had she put her off. As she shoved her shopping bags into the boot of her ageing Subaru, a tear slid down her cheek. She slammed the door shut and plonked herself into the driver's seat.

With raindrops pooling on the windscreen, she sat for a moment to gather herself. Why the heck did Dave have to be away, 'sorting himself out'? Couldn't he just come home and let them get on with the next phase of their lives? In the privacy of her car, she swore aloud. *Fuck you, Dave!* Tears poured as the rain occluded her view. How could she possibly entertain the idea of teaching a writing class? Did Cathy have any idea how bad things were? No, only one person could possibly know. She'd give Deb a phone once she got back to the safety of her four walls.

Chapter Two

Deb had been there the night Vivian's life had been turned upside down. And the next day when she'd had to show up for the flight home alone, everyone bearing witness to the fracture in her marriage, which, in hindsight, had been looming since Dave retired. It reminded her of a glacier she'd seen on television, underlying stress in the ice building up to form a crevasse. Were there warning signs? Things you could know to avoid falling in? As she drove home, almost on automatic pilot, the sequence of events played out in her head like a movie she couldn't rewind.

When the pandemic hit, Dave had joined the ranks of artists and musicians locked out of their normal environment. With no sign of borders reopening, his lifeline had been severed, his travels on indefinite hold. He'd begun to talk about retirement. At sixty, he was old enough to tap into his Super. They'd been careful with finances, their one splurge a third-hand Winnebago to practise for their dream of taking a long, slow road trip around Australia. But instead of hitting the road, she'd watched Dave retreat to his study.

At first, he'd spent hours practising his beloved music. Two hours on sax, a brief trip to the kitchen to grab lunch, another two hours on piano, playing, singing. The routine seemed to fall off almost without her realising. She'd spent months at their kitchen table, immersed in learning to teach online, putting in extra hours to ensure her students stayed connected and on track, especially the older ones who needed top grades to win university places. Over dinner, she'd tell him about her busy day, the frustrations of her new normal: tech issues she'd had to troubleshoot, the conversations with parents of kids who were holed up in bedrooms, too anxious to turn their cameras on, withdrawing into themselves and unable to keep up with their learning. When she'd ask what he'd been up to, he'd say he was composing. If there were a few extra grog bottles in their recycling, she didn't nag. She'd felt his loneliness. He'd gone from a life of travel and theatre to being home full time. No preamble, not even a period of working some day job which brought him home at night. She'd persuaded him to keep the local choir going via Zoom. It buoyed him a bit, but when she returned to the physical classroom, it felt like leaving him behind. She'd watched enough live-streamed funerals to feel her mortality. Fifty-eight wasn't too early to retire. She gave the department notice. They'd navigate this retirement thing together.

It hadn't made an awful lot of difference. Dave still spent hours locked away in the study. Still drank too much. She'd insisted they get out for a brisk walk every day. They went for coffee at the local cafés, but they didn't talk like they used to, always busting to update one another when Dave came back from a gig somewhere on the mainland. Even the subject of taking off in their camper van had been dropped. When he missed a couple of choir practices, she decided to join to ensure he kept going, give them something to talk about. She'd had such high hopes that night on the Gold Coast. He'd seemed to come out of himself, still a little distant, but there were glimpses of her old Dave, the whistling and warbling in their bedroom as they'd dressed, the enthusiasm about going down to the gala ball. Over dinner he was animated, speculating with the others about what the competition's results might be.

When the waiting staff cleared the main course dishes and began to serve dessert, the room grew quiet. Vivian's tummy did loop-the-loops as the adjudicator approached the lectern on the low stage at the front. He was all drama, taking them through the list of categories with the requisite pauses between places: winners, runners-up, highly commended. She'd always been a 'taking part is what's most important' kinda gal, but tonight there was more at stake. A win just might keep Dave on the up. Yes, they could do with a win.

And finally, their turn came; they'd won Best Arrangement for what their host called 'a sublime performance of Eric Whitacre's "The Seal Lullaby"'. It had taken all Dave's patience to get right, but it had paid off. There was no mistaking where the north-west Tassie crew were situated in the room, such was the whooping and clapping around the table. The Queenslanders were generous in their applause. With so many borders still closed, only Tasmanians had been allowed to join them. Vivian had turned to give Dave a hug, but he was already on his feet and making for the stage. It had been decided earlier that if they were placed, that as conductor, he would be the one to accept the trophy. Besides, none of the women wanted to trip on their heels and the men deemed him the best looking. Vivian had to agree. As he strode up to the podium, buttoning his jacket, she fancied him as much as she had in her twenties. She shrugged off his hurry and hugged Deb instead.

Sometimes she wondered how the night might have ended differently, happily, with the two of them falling into each other's arms between the crisp white sheets of the hotel bed, mustering the energy to make love there and then, or in the morning, waking without speaking, their mouths finding each other's as they moved in close under the covers.

Once the host had presented the prizes, thanked the sponsors and introduced the band who would entertain them once dessert was cleared away, the convivial chat resumed around the table. Halfway through the best chocolate mousse she may ever have tasted while listening to Deb's take on the winning performance in the male voice category, Vivian noticed Dave getting out of the seat beside her again. Glancing sideways, not wanting to lose the thread of what Deb was saying, she saw Dave reach out a hand to greet a man she didn't recognise. She turned back to continue her conversation with Deb, half-wondering if the bald sixty-something was an old friend of Dave's she didn't recognise. A work colleague she'd never met?

'Viv,' Dave called, extracting her from Deb's commentary. 'This is Rory, an old mate of mine. A Corkman . . .'

She held out her hand and smiled. 'Hi, I'm Vivian, Dave's wife.'

The cheery man took her hand and shook vigorously. 'Nice to meet you . . . I'm a baritone with the Gold Coast Gospel there.' He gestured with a thumb to indicate a table somewhere behind him.

She'd seen them perform. Dave hadn't mentioned knowing one of them, let alone someone from home.

'You guys were brilliant . . .' Vivian was about to congratulate Rory on his group's stirring rendition of 'Oh Happy Day' when Dave gestured with a thumb over his shoulder.

'We're just going to get a drink, catch up. It's been years . . .'

'Lovely to meet you,' said Rory with a smile that made him look like the kind of fella you couldn't dislike.

She wanted to tell them to bring back a bottle of bubbles for the table in celebration of their win, but she'd get it herself in a minute. Best to leave them be. It wasn't often Dave got a chance to get out and enjoy himself these days, and how good would it be for him to chat with another Corkman. She'd join them later. Although Vivian loved where she lived, there was always that longing for home that came over her when she heard the Cork accent. She spent lots of time listening to Dave, of course, but that was different. Her friends always talked about his sexy Irish accent, but she took it for granted now. When they'd finished dessert and the bottle of house wine they were sharing, Vivian enlisted Deb to come to the bar with her. As they waited for their bubbles, they looked around for Dave and Rory, but there was no sign of them.

'Probably gone somewhere that serves better Guinness,' said Deb.

Vivian agreed, but Dave could have told her. When he hadn't returned by the end of the evening, she'd sent a text.

Everything okay? We're all heading to bed.

I'll be late, he replied.

Deb asked Ian to text Dave too, but Ian had been his usual laidback self.

'I'd say he's having a few beers with the competition to commiserate.' After a big meal and lots of wine, Ian thought that was hilarious. Deb rolled her eyes.

'Phone me if you're worried,' she said, 'but Ian's probably right.'

Vivian had lain awake until the early hours, but still there was no sign. When her alarm went off at seven, she woke up alone, torn between wanting to scream down the phone at him to demand an explanation, and treating him like a grown man who could do what he liked. Should she involve the police? What if he'd gone missing? Her phone pinged.

I'll stay on here for a bit. Explain later.

She pressed Call.

There was a muffled sound in the background when he answered. A fan whirred, a door clicked closed.

'Sorry, Viv. I crashed at Rory's place. Not too good this morning.'

She could tell he was still pissed. 'What the heck are you doing, Dave? Staying where for a bit?'

He sucked a breath in through his teeth. She knew the face he was pulling; it was the one he always pulled when considering an argument, especially one where he was planning to do something whether or not she approved. They weren't good at conflict.

'Rory and I go back a long way,' he said. 'He's had a diagnosis. Prostate. I'd like to spend some time with him. Maybe sort myself out as I'm at it.' He said the last bit with what sounded like mild frustration.

She stayed quiet, trying to process what exactly he meant. If it were Deb, she'd drop everything to help. Of course, she would. But this friend she'd never heard of before last night . . . And this business about sorting himself out. She knew he'd been down, but wouldn't a bit of therapy or a course of SSRIs fix that? She hadn't been able to convince him to go up the road to the GP, yet here he was telling her he'd be staying in another state.

'I'm sorry about your friend,' she began, trying to sound sincere. Perhaps Dave was in shock. Maybe the guy had no support. 'Am I allowed to ask how long you'll be away for?'

'I'm not sure. I'll keep in touch.'

It was on the tip of her tongue to say, 'And what am I supposed to do?' but she rallied her self-respect. There'd been so many things she hadn't been able to say.

'Right so.'

She let the phone slip onto the bed covers and put her face in her hands. Thirty-odd years of getting to know him, and he'd sounded like a stranger.

'Oh, Viv,' Deb said when Vivian had managed to get into their taxi to the airport. 'I'm sure he'll only be away for a few days.'

If only she could call round for a coffee and vent to Deb now. The pain of Dave's absence wouldn't go away, but it would ease. A problem shared and all that. A phone call would have to suffice.

Deb answered in the Hobart suburb where she and Ian had moved to look after grandchildren. It was the other end of the state, not exactly the other side of the world, but some days it may as well have been. The timing of the move couldn't have been worse; a week after the trip to the Gold Coast. Vivian had seen them over Christmas when she'd gone down to spend a week with her daughter, but they had lives to get on with, new friends to make. She'd come home bereft.

'How are you coping?' Deb asked.

Vivian took a long breath and shrugged. 'Ah, you know, plodding along.' At least she wasn't sobbing inconsolably as she'd expected to.

'Any news from Dave?'

'I've stopped texting. There's not much point.'

'Oh, Viv, he'll come to his senses eventually.'

Vivian sighed. She and Deb had spent hours explaining away the difficulties of her marriage, but Vivian couldn't shake the feeling that Dave hadn't wanted to be around her. The hours he spent in the study, the turning away from her bids for affection, the stonewalling . . .

'Have you gone back to choir yet?' Deb asked.

'No, not yet.' And she wasn't planning to. After the humiliation at being so publicly stood up, there was no way she could face them.

'One day at a time, I suppose,' Deb was saying.

'That's it.'

There wasn't much else to say. She could wish Deb hadn't moved away, she could wish Dave hadn't gone AWOL, but the wishing wouldn't bring them back. *Ugh!* Life could be so unfair. Dave used to tell her how lucky she was to be a woman because they outlived men. Washed up by sixty? Beset by fluctuating hormones from forty? Abandoned by men in mid-life crises? Ending up in care homes with brain disorders like dementia and Alzheimer's, on top of failing bodies? Oh yes, so lucky.

'How are the grandchildren?' she asked Deb before she could be swept away by a flood of self-pity.

Deb could talk about her grandchildren all day, such was the love and delight they evoked in her. But even bringing up that subject felt disingenuous. Grandchildren might have provided a welcome distraction, if it weren't for her son's allergy to settling down and her daughter's paranoia about her only child.

'Has Clodagh calmed down at all?' Deb asked, having told her the latest on the babbling baby and preschool cherub she and Ian had the pleasure of seeing every day.

'I wish.' Vivian sighed. 'Calm and Clodagh never went in the same sentence, as you well know.'

That Christmas had been the worst of her life. Her first in thirty-five years without Dave. It should have been a joy to spend it in Hobart with her daughter, son-in-law and two-year-old grandson, but Clodagh's helicopter parenting and insistence on over-the-top hygiene rituals only compounded the pain of Dave's absence. Finn, Clodagh's more sensitive younger brother, was also missing, with borders still to open in New South Wales. Whenever Vivian brought up the subject of her and Dave's sudden separation, Clodagh insisted they'd sort it out. She loved them both. She wouldn't take sides, she'd said. Between that particular elephant in the room, and the way Clodagh went on about little Max, it had been an exhausting few days. Vivian had been glad to get home. She could only hope that one day she and her grandson could spend time together without Clodagh hovering over them, lecturing her on the dangers of everything from screen-time to salicylates. Not that she had been the model grandparent either. To say she hadn't been herself was an understatement. She suspected the toddler was a little afraid of her.

'Oh, I'd better go,' said Deb. 'That's the baby waking up for his lunch. Talk soon, Viv.'

After hanging up, Vivian realised she hadn't told Deb about the writing class. Not that there was much point, as she had no intention of doing it, but it might have made her sound like less of a broken record. In the lounge room, she slumped into an armchair and allowed herself a mournful tear for the loss of Deb in her everyday life.

In the silence, she thought again about her plans, the dreams she and Dave had shared when they'd emigrated from Ireland. What did she have to show for all her years away? A marriage in some kind of strange holding pattern, a daughter caught up in her own concerns, a distant son, and a best friend at the other end of the state. *Uaigneas.* The Irish word came to her as it had in recent weeks when a slow, insidious cool had come over her. *Loneliness.* Like fog creeping across her skin, burrowing into her pores, settling between the layers of tissue, a squatter she couldn't evict.

Chapter Three

Marilyn tucked her book bag under her arm and stepped onto the small ferry that bobbed at the edge of the Mersey River. She was the sole passenger today, but that made no difference to the skipper, whose days were spent traversing the short stretch of water between Devonport and its eastern suburb. With no timetable as such, passengers would just stand on the gangway, press a button to summon the boat, and it would come. The three-minute crossing allowed for the casual arrangement, and it was quicker than the bus over the bridge.

Tuesday was the only day Marilyn crossed the river. She tried to make the most of it. From her usual seat at the stern, she watched trucks drive onto the *Spirit of Tasmania*, the red and white sea giant looming over their miniature version, like a Dinky toy in comparison, ploughing through the chop stirred up by the fresh summer breeze. Her mind drifted to where the trucks might be headed once they'd crossed the Bass Strait. West across Victoria? Or maybe all the way across

the Nullarbor, carrying Tasmanian-grown food to the fancy
restaurants of WA? Or would they head east into New South
Wales? She'd been to Sydney and the Blue Mountains once,
but that was a lifetime ago.

Today she had jobs to do. She'd look in a few op shops
for a doona set as a welcome home present for her middle
child, who she hadn't seen in almost a year, but first she'd
give herself a half-hour in the library to swap her bagful of
books for some new ones. This was her favourite part of the
week . . . that and catching up with her friend, Georgie.

With a nod to the skipper, Marilyn disembarked, pulled
the straps of her bag tight, and made her way toward town.
Anyone looking at her would think she was a woman on a
mission, with the clap-clap of her thongs against the concrete
as she crossed from the riverside to the CBD. She didn't care
what they thought. Getting off that boat just had a way of
putting a spring in her step.

Devonport was hardly Melbourne, but with the new
hotel and the glass-fronted building that housed the library
and the council offices, it had the look of a place that was
on the up. People were always complaining about the waste of
taxpayers' money that was the paranaple building. It had been
a long time since she'd paid tax, but she disagreed. The name
alone was worth every cent, in her opinion. It was the local
Aboriginal term for the mouth of the river. She'd read as much
in the newspaper upstairs in the library.

Inside the building, she made her way to the first floor
and emptied her books onto the service counter.

'Hello, Marilyn!'

'Cathy. Haven't seen you in a while.'

'Oh, been getting out of the office. How're you going? Read anything interesting lately?'

Marilyn knew most of the staff by name. Cathy hadn't been there long, but she was good. Liked to talk about books and knew the kind of authors Marilyn preferred to read; Australian women who wrote stories about the land, the outback, and who could always come up with a romance between the main characters that made you feel you were right there in it with them. She eyed the cover of the latest book she'd devoured partly by the light of her phone in bed under the covers, so as not to disturb Frank, and partly in the bathroom where she did most of her reading. Not something she'd care to share with Cathy, but she'd tell her about the story.

'That's a good un.' She tapped the nail of her index finger on the embossed title. 'Trouble in Hayville,' she read.

'What's it about?' Cathy asked as she scanned the books and piled them up beside her.

Marilyn cocked her head to one side, leaned an elbow on the counter and lowered her voice.

'Chick from the city comes back to her hometown, set on selling the family farm after her parents get killed in a horrible accident.' She paused, not wanting any judgey types over-hearing, but Cathy's nod encouraged her to go on. 'Can't wait to get the hell out of the place in the beginning, but then she meets the fella who's running it . . . That's when the fun starts.'

Cathy's eyebrow raised in anticipation.

'Best stop at that.' Marilyn stood up straight and smiled. 'Don't want to spoil it for ya.'

Cathy gave a tut. 'Good writing?'

'Yes indeed. Had me turning the pages all the way to the end, that one.'

Cathy scanned the barcode and held the book a little away from her, looking at it for a moment longer before adding it to the pile. 'How many stars would you give it?'

Marilyn didn't need to think. 'Five,' she answered. 'A real good Aussie read. Ticked all the boxes . . . for me anyhow.'

'You should be writing reviews for the library newsletter,' said Cathy.

Marilyn gave a chuckle and was about to go, but Cathy came around to the side of the counter and gave her arm the lightest touch.

'You could enrol in the writing course I'm running,' she said, her voice low. 'Hasn't started yet. Every Friday for ten weeks. Do much on Fridays?'

Marilyn shook her head.

Before she could say anything, Cathy returned to her computer and started to tap at her keyboard, eyes shining with enthusiasm.

'There! I've added your name to my list. I'll give you a call with the exact dates. Have a think about it.'

Marilyn gathered her empty book bag and made for the lift. She wouldn't borrow any more books today or possibly ever. Frank would have a fit if she announced she was going into town every Friday. Should have kept her big mouth shut.

Shrugging off Cathy's proposal, Marilyn walked along the mall to the nearest op shop. In the cool of the air con, she smoothed down her t-shirt over a pair of too-hot trackpants and flicked forward her fringe to obscure the grey hairline that had begun to annoy her. A lady with one of those lanyards asked if she needed help.

'Just havin' a look,' she told her, but she didn't stay long. Cathy's assumption that she could waltz in and out of town whenever she pleased irked her. She gathered her fabric bag, empty now apart from her house key and wallet, and left. Jamie and his doona set would have to wait.

Outside in the sunshine, she took a breath and wished she had a cigarette. All her hard work, giving up the damn things to save money she couldn't even get her hands on. No point crying over it either, she told herself. She turned off the main drag and trudged up the hill to Georgie's shop.

Marilyn found her friend restocking the back shelves with the vibrators she'd been moaning about being overdue.

'Put the jug on, will ya, darl?' Georgie didn't look up as she rustled in the box of plastic packages and let out a loud sigh. 'They haven't even bothered to separate the sizes.'

Marilyn didn't comment but rolled her eyes as she skirted round the delivery with its questionable contents. She went to the small back room where a kettle, microwave and rusty bar fridge allowed Georgie some respite from the shop and its adornments. *To each their own*, Marilyn had decided after trying to dissuade her friend from taking the low-paid job from the shop's dodgy owner. At least it had given Georgie a few dollars and a break from that crazy family of hers. Not that Marilyn could talk. That morning, she'd walked out of her three-bedroom house that was technically the government's, leaving her partner and the youngest of their three sons in the middle of a heated argument about when Ethan was going to move out and get a place of his own. 'Lazy bastard,' Frank would grumble, regardless of whether or not the boy was in earshot. Another father would have taken pride in a son that had scored an apprenticeship. Not Frank. But it didn't serve her to argue. Marilyn had learned to take deep breaths and let it wash over her like most of the domestic dramas that played out in their home of twenty-five years.

Georgie shuffled in, hitching her bad leg on every step, and slumped into one of a pair of plastic garden chairs they'd procured from the tip shop for a dollar. Marilyn poured milk into two mugs of tea and handed one to Georgie with the teabag still in, just how she liked it. They'd been friends since high school. Even spent a couple of years travelling a bit on the mainland. Their catch-ups always took Marilyn back to those days when she and Georgie had run amok, left Tassie behind and worked in bars and clubs, barely making ends meet but living on their own terms. She sometimes wondered if they wouldn't have been better off if they'd stayed away, but word of Georgie's father's stroke meant their carefree days were over. Within two years they'd both buried fathers and had kids on the way. Neither of them ever left Tassie again.

'I seen your Brad coming out of my neighbour's in the early hours.'

'Did ya?' Marilyn responded in that disinterested way she'd perfected after years of being on the receiving end of announcements as to her children's embarrassing behaviour.

'Woke me up with their drinkin' and music blarin',' Georgie went on. 'Should have been home with Brooke and the kids instead of carrying on like a teenager.'

News of her eldest son, Brad, staying out all night didn't surprise Marilyn, although she would have preferred not to have heard about it. Started too young, those two. Brad and Brooke were only kids themselves when Keisha came along, and then the twins. She wasn't making excuses for him, but it wasn't like she could make her son stay home and mind his kids.

Georgie eyed her over her tea. 'Too like his father,' she said. 'Thinks he can do what he likes.'

Marilyn shrugged. 'I wouldn't like to have heard the earful his missus gave him when he got home.'

'Might take a leaf out of her book yourself.'

Marilyn didn't respond. How she'd survived to nearly fifty and stayed in a relationship with the same person for more than half her life she didn't know. Georgie always told her to stand up for herself, but it was like she didn't know how. Her own mother hadn't exactly led by example. Marilyn lost count of the number of boyfriends she'd had once her dad walked out. After that lot, Frank had seemed like a safe bet when they'd met. The fact that he was divorced and twelve

years older didn't matter to her twenty-two-year-old self.
By the time she worked out why his wife left him, she was
pregnant with their second child. He'd come home drunk,
going off about some bloke who'd crossed him in the pub.
Angling for the fight he should have had there, he'd taken a
swing at her. Stunned, she didn't even duck as he went in for
the second punch and the third. Full of apologies the next
day, she'd forgiven him. Over a cuppa at her mother's, she'd
bawled her eyes out.

'First time's the worst,' her mother said.

She'd never forgotten those words. Just got smarter about
avoiding him, like sleeping in the kids' room and locking
the door. He was always contrite in the morning, blaming the
drink.

'You not been to the library yet?' asked Georgie, nodding
toward the slack bag at her feet.

Marilyn blew over the hot tea. 'Oh, I've been there all
right.' She set the drink down to cool and clasped her hands
together on her midriff. As Georgie waited for her to go on,
Marilyn looked down to where she'd begun to turn her thumbs
over one another.

'You plannin' on going back after?' Georgie asked.

'Nope.'

There was silence as Georgie held out for more information. Marilyn knew that no matter how much she'd prefer
to put the whole library incident behind her, she'd never get
out of the shop without telling Georgie what had happened.
But that was why they were still friends after all these years.

They mightn't be able to solve one another's problems, but they could listen.

'That lady I talk about the books with, she's gone and put my name down for some writin' course.'

Georgie's eyebrows arched as her mouth opened in surprise.

'Wants me to write book reviews for the newsletter or some such.' Marilyn shrugged, but Georgie leaned forward and slapped her on the thigh.

'Good on ya!' she said, genuine excitement in her voice. 'You were always the smart one. Got us out of a few tight spots on the mainland.' She gave a cackle. 'I'd never have got a job if it wasn't for you writing those applications for me, remember?'

Marilyn waved a hand to dismiss the remark. 'You were plenty smart yourself, Georgie. Head for figures, you had.'

Georgie looked toward the main shop. 'Lot of good it did me.'

'You've done more than me,' said Marilyn.

Georgie screwed up her face. 'You only never worked because Frank didn't let ya. If I had a dollar for every time I wondered what would have happened if we'd stayed on the mainland . . .'

As her friend went on about their relative talents and what they might have done with them, Marilyn mused over how neither one of them had lived an easy life once they'd returned to Tassie. Frank had convinced her he was between jobs when one of her brothers had introduced them at a party. Said he'd had a bastard of a boss and had to leave the carpet laying business for his sanity. Marilyn began to doubt the story when he'd go off at her for suggesting he give their friends a hand when they were buying new floor coverings. Mates' rates, cash in hand might have supplemented his dole, but he wouldn't have a bar of it. Whenever she mentioned the possibility of looking for a job herself, he saw red. No, he wouldn't be humiliated by having a wife who went out to work every day while he became a house husband. Eventually, his smoking and drinking habits made his health deteriorate so much as to render him unfit for work, and while his welfare payment increased, any hopes Marilyn held of working outside the home were dashed by having to be his carer.

In a way, Georgie was lucky in that she'd always found work. But she'd never been without someone to look after either; wayward kids, her partner before he'd passed away, her parents, aunties. What had Georgie ever done to deserve such a lousy hand of cards? What had either of them done? She drained her mug and made to get going.

'Anyway, I think you should give that library course a go,' Georgie was saying. 'Get you out of the house doing something besides bingo and visiting me.'

They both knew she'd need Frank's approval and how slim her chances of that would be.

Georgie read her mind. 'Tell Frank you're helpin' me if you don't want to tell him the truth.'

'And risk him coming to check up on me? He still thinks you're running a dress shop, ya know.'

'Make him something, then, butter him up. Something for that sweet tooth of his.'

Georgie stared into her eyes, willing her to agree.

What was it with these women trying to run her life today? Marilyn took her mug to the sink and gave it a rinse.

'You really think I should do that course, don't ya?'

'Absolutely!' Georgie got up and took her mug with her as she walked Marilyn to the door. ''Bout time you did something for yourself, darl.'

'You right for next Tuesday?' Marilyn asked, uncomfortable with the attention she'd drawn to herself, even if it was from her best friend.

'I'll be here . . . unless I get a better offer.' Georgie laughed. 'Tell your Brad to stay out of that whorehouse.'

Marilyn shook her head as she ambled out of the shop, wishing again her friend hadn't told her about her son. She didn't need to be reminded of her less than perfect parenting.

On the bus home, Marilyn thought about their conversation. Not one to say things lightly, Georgie's words settled like pebbles in the bottom of a stream, unmoving despite the current's efforts to wash them away. She *had* been the smart one, but that was way back in high school, long before life had taught her that brains didn't guarantee you'd get on in life.

As the bus rumbled over the bridge, she looked down the mouth of the Mersey where boats, big and small, held position in the picture postcard scene she loved. At the quayside, tourists filed onto the *Julie Burgess*. A favourite teacher had organised for them to have a trip on the old fishing ketch once. The same teacher had tried to encourage her and Georgie to complete their last two years of schooling, but they'd already planned their escape. With an alcoholic mother and two brothers who didn't exactly bat for her, she couldn't get away quick enough.

Frank would never agree to her going into town two days a week for weeks on end, but she hated the idea of letting Georgie down. Her friend knew her better than anyone. If Georgie thought she should do that course, she was only speaking the truth. Frank went to his mate's on Fridays. She'd tell him she'd be back in good time to look after him.

As the bus neared her street, the familiar knot tightened in her stomach. Marilyn checked her phone and gave an inward sigh of relief. She'd be home in good time to prepare Frank's lunch. He'd only be grumpy if she didn't. She missed the old days when the boys were young, and she had a whole family to feed. They might have had to have gone without other things, but she always made sure they were well fed. The only times she cooked for all of them now were Christmas Day and on their monthly Sunday catch-ups. Not that they always turned up. She could make a huge cottage pie full of lean mince from the butcher and lots of fresh veggies from the garden, only to see herself with a fridge full of leftovers when her children had been too busy or hungover to visit.

She'd hardly reached the front door when she heard the raised voices. It was as if nothing had changed since the moment she'd left that morning; only this time it wasn't Ethan, the youngest, that was sparring with his father. She dropped her bag on the hall table and rushed into the kitchen. The argument stopped when they saw her, the two men frozen for a second that gave Marilyn time to arrange her face. *Always a home for you here, can't wait to see you,* she'd told her middle son who was standing in front of her after a nine-month absence. As she smiled through the dread, his face crumpled like it had when the magistrate had handed down his sentence. Jamie came to her – remorse, regret, shame written in the lines around his eyes.

'Good to see you, Mum.' He whimpered as he bent down, more to fall into her than to gather her into his arms.

With his shoulder bone threatening to cut off her air supply, she looked at Frank, reading the anger in his clenched fists and the blood vessels throbbing at his temples.

Jamie stood back and ran a grubby hand over his face.

'Will you be staying, son?' she asked.

Frank shot her a firm 'not on your life' glance before grabbing his cigarette packet from the worktop and storming into the yard.

'I'm movin' in with the missus,' said Jamie.

'New missus, old missus?' she asked.

'A girl I met online.' He looked away as he spoke.

'Is that right?' Marilyn mightn't be fifty yet, but sometimes she felt as old as the hills. This was one of those times. 'I thought you had no wifi in the lockup,' she said.

'I was talkin' to her before I got put away,' Jamie explained. 'Nice chick. You'd like her.'

He'd do well to keep his assumptions to himself, she thought, but she'd humour him. She switched on the sandwich press and started to butter slices of bread.

'So what would I like about her?'

'She's smart, Mum,' he said, a look of what she knew was probably misplaced lovesickness in his eyes. God, he was hopeless. Her lost lamb. It's how she'd always thought of Jamie, whenever he'd break up with a girlfriend or end up in the police station for a botched burglary.

'Even wrote me letters when I was down south,' he added.

Down south! You'd think he'd been away for all those months on an Antarctic expedition.

'Letters, eh?'

She listened as Jamie told her about the girl, how he'd had time to think things over in prison and how he was a different man to the one who'd gone in. Sounded better than getting back with that crowd he hung around, she thought. They were bad news, but ever since he was a kid, he'd been impressed by the naughty boys. When he played up, he'd get a hiding from his father but to no avail. Marilyn reckoned it drove the boy away, made him easy pickings for the drug dealers, but she'd only have copped the same if she'd said anything.

She served up his sandwich and watched as he ate greedily at their small kitchen table.

'This is good, Mum,' he said, wiping at the side of his mouth and sucking a morsel back in.

She smiled, grateful for a moment with just the two of them.

∾

'Your bloody timer's goin' off!' Frank roared as she sat on the toilet re-reading one of her rural romance books.

'Be out in a minnie,' she called.

Setting the book down and fixing herself, she basked in the scene where the jillaroo had finally got the attention of her neighbour over a ranch-style fence between thirsty drought-hard paddocks. The flushing sound broke into her dreamy musings as she tried to hold on to the image of the girl with hair the colour of parched earth.

Taking a little longer than necessary to lather her hands with one of the soap bars she stockpiled in the vanity cupboard, she smiled at her collection of dog-eared romances. The shelves either side of the toilet that used to house the children's bath toys and toiletries were now home to her favourites; some she'd read and re-read, the ones she hadn't given back to the op shop. Ethan sometimes let her use his tablet and showed her where to find the kind of books she liked and reviews that told you what the stories were about.

'Could do a better job than some of those sheilas who put themselves out there,' Georgie had said.

In the mirror, Marilyn stared at the daggy middle-aged woman with limp hair and suitcases under her eyes. But there was a glimpse of that jillaroo she'd just read about too, and for the briefest moment, she felt much taller than her shrinking ageing self. She dried her hands on the fresh tangerine towel she'd put out that morning. Nothing ventured, nothing gained, she told herself. Taking a last look in the mirror, she straightened her shoulders and willed herself to be strong. Maybe she could be more than the family peace-keeper. She'd spent enough time in this madhouse.

On her way to the kitchen, she caught the warm homely smell of the apple tart she'd put in the oven. She turned off the timer and opened the oven door, allowing herself a moment's satisfaction as she saw the golden crust with the sugar she'd sprinkled glistening on top. Perfect. She pulled on her oven gloves and set the tart on a wire rack to cool.

In the lounge room, she found Frank sitting in his usual spot on the sofa, reading the sports pages of the daily rag. She straightened her t-shirt and rubbed the hem between her thumb and forefinger, weighing up whether to lie about giving Georgie a hand or just come clean about the writing course. Neither excuse for a second weekly excursion to the other side of the river seemed likely to gain approval.

'Want a cuppa and some of that apple tart I made?' she asked.

His response was a grunt.

'There's a thing at the library I was thinkin' of goin' to,' she went on.

He didn't look up, but she knew by the way his eyes had stopped moving across the page that he was no longer reading.

'It's on a Friday mornin'.' The weight of his silence threatened to make her unravel, but if there was one thing she'd learned in twenty-five years, it was to work around him. 'I'd be home well before lunch.' It was a white lie. In truth she'd have to figure out lunch in advance, but right now, this had to sound easy.

There was another grunt as his head bobbed in a single nod before his eyes tracked the lines of the racing news again.

'I'll put a dod of ice cream on the tart for us.'

'You trying to kill me, woman?'

He still hadn't looked at her, but she turned and smiled to herself. In all their years together, she'd never known Frank to say a simple 'yes'. But it wasn't his usual straight out 'no'. It was all the permission she needed and about as much encouragement as she was likely to get.

Chapter Four

At his sister's house in their leafy suburb, Oscar let himself in and disabled the alarm. Before he could stop him, Dog barrelled past and left a trail of sand across the otherwise sparkling tiled floor.

'Out, Dog!' he shouted, going straight to the laundry to let the retriever out the back before he could deposit any more of the beach in his sister's million-dollar home.

At the end of a built-in cupboard that could hold the linen for a small hotel, he found the vacuum and plugged it in. He'd hardly vacuumed to the front door when he registered the soreness in his wrist and the shortness of breath. *You're on holiday*, he thought. Returning the vacuum to the cupboard, he searched for something to wipe Dog's paws. The cloths were neatly folded in one of a set of matching baskets. At least he wouldn't have to do much cleaning here. They had someone to keep the place spick and span. He'd met their cleaner once: Angie, a scary woman who scowled at him from under a pair of over-plucked eyebrows as if he wasn't meant to be there. Geraldine said Angie made Robo-maid look like a slacker but tried to make sure she and Malcolm had somewhere to be when she came round, preferring to let her get on with it. Friday was her day if his fuzzy memory served him correctly. Maybe he could find something to do on Fridays to make himself scarce.

From the garden, Oscar heard a low growl. His first thought was that Dog had found a snake, but an eerie creaking sound from the side of the house made him stop. As the sound grew louder, he roared at Dog.

'Get here!'

With a whimper, the dog came to him, and together they legged it toward the front of the property, away from the noise. Oscar didn't need to watch to know it was one of the old gums crashing through bush. With his heart pounding in his chest, gasping for breath, he kept hold of Dog's collar and waited for the thud.

'Jesus Christ!' Surveying the scene, he took in the tree that lay across the pool that wasn't far off the size of his flat in Melbourne. Leaves floated on the water's surface and strips of bark gathered at the filters. Hands on hips, Oscar leaned forward to steady his breathing and wondered how the hell he was going to move the monster.

~

As much as he hadn't wanted to ruin their trip, he'd had to let his sister and brother-in-law know what had happened. He'd hardly sent the voice message when Geraldine video called him from Vanuatu. The poor woman was beside herself. He went outside to show them the damage.

With shock turning to anger, Geraldine screamed at Malcolm, 'I told you months ago we needed to chop down that widow maker!'

Oscar listened while a red-faced Malcolm took him through the drill for dealing with repairs and insurance. He'd have done anything for his sister, but as he scoured their study for the necessary paperwork, he imagined running over hot coals might have been an easier way to show his brotherly love.

Sure, he'd been at the house many times, knew where they kept their sharp knives and shot glasses, but paperwork . . . he had no clue. Geraldine sent a long text he struggled to read, but he eventually located the insurance policy in a drawer of the filing cabinet he'd never even noticed before. At least their files were clearly labelled. *H for House Insurance*, he told himself. Second or third drawer, Malcolm had said. Should be easy to find. But it took three goes before he saw 'House Insurance'. Pulling the file out, he felt the weight of the wad of papers inside and prayed to God he wouldn't have to try and read through it all.

'Useless prick,' his Year Four teacher had called him when he couldn't spell *Australia*. Lived here all his life and couldn't even spell his own country.

In the background of their phone call, his sister had told Malcolm to say the documents were ordered by date, the most recent correspondence at the front. But as he tried to decipher the headings on the different letters, he was filled with frustration and regret. If only he'd tried harder to get his ex-wife to help him, include him in his own affairs, insist even. But their finances weren't the only affairs she'd kept from him. In the finish, it was their one child turning eighteen that brought it all out in the open. Said she'd done her bit, Bobby was off to university, time to move on. Whenever he thought about it, and he tried not to, he knew he'd gotten a raw deal. She'd asked him to move out and promptly moved the latest fella into the house he'd put his heart and soul into renovating to keep her happy. He bit down on the bile that rose in his stomach. Bitterness wasn't a feeling he'd wished to entertain.

Taking the file over to the desk, Oscar sat down and took a deep breath. With the company name in Geraldine's text message on the phone beside him, he scanned the letters with the name at the top and concentrated on finding dates. At least he knew his numbers. Grateful for their careful record-keeping, Oscar found the current policy. 'Bui . . . l . . . dings and c . . . on . . . tents. Whoah!' He gaped at the figure on the right of the page. He knew the house was worth a lot of money but what they paid to insure it would nearly keep him in food for a year. Embarrassed to be poking around in his sister and brother-in-law's private affairs, he scanned the page to find the phone number they'd asked him to call.

In the paranaple centre, Oscar ordered a large triple-shot coffee at the small café and asked the barista if there was a community notice board. Not yet midday and he'd already packed in enough stress and exertion to make him rethink the decision to come to Tassie. He'd phoned a couple of local companies to come and deal with the tree, but their estimates were exorbitant and availability limited. If it had been last year, before Covid had got a grip of him, he would have hired equipment and added a decent stack of firewood to his sister's woodstore. He would even have relished the task that would have given him something to do and a way to repay Geraldine and Malcolm for the run of the house, not to mention the freezer full of the meals they'd left him. Some days he had to remind himself he was still only forty-five, not the eighty year old his body made him feel. Hating himself for being a lesser man, he took a sip of his hot drink and made his way to the notice board.

'Be out of your way in a moment.' A woman was pinning up a sign, blocking his view with her broad frame and unruly mop of blonde hair. When she turned from her task, she smiled at him like she was pleased with herself for performing some great feat. 'New writing course starting,' she said.

'Really?' He had it out before he could think.

The woman took a bunch of flyers from under one arm and thrust one at him. When he accepted it out of politeness, her eyes took on a shine like lasers scanning him.

'Are you local?'

'No, no.' He stepped to one side, hoping to have ended the conversation, but she took a matching step.

'What brings you to Devonport?'

'I'm on holiday . . . house sitting, actually . . . for my sister.'

She pressed her lips together and considered him. 'Over from the mainland?'

'Melbourne.' Something about the way she looked at him made him think he could hear the cogs turning in her brain. To avoid awkward eye contact, he looked down at her badge. *Cathy*. Maybe she could help him navigate the busy notice board. 'I'm actually here to find someone who can move a fallen tree.'

Her smile didn't abate. 'If it's a tree doctor you're after, we've got just the thing.' She'd turned back to the board and let a brightly polished fingernail trace the notices. As she searched, he took his battered glasses from the breast pocket of his shirt and had a quick look at the flyer she'd given him.

W-ant . . . to . . . white-write best . . . better?

'Here!' From an advert with a fringe of phone numbers, the woman ripped off a slip of paper and handed it to him.

'Thank you so much,' he said. 'I'll give them a call.'

'Not a handyman yourself then?' she asked.

He shook his head. 'Not anymore. Worked in a printers' all my life . . .' He shrugged, not sure he wanted to tell the woman, but he had her full attention. 'Got retrenched with Covid.'

Her eyes dropped to the flyer in his hand. 'The writing course . . .' She looked up at him again. 'It's for anyone who wants to improve their skills. Doesn't matter what level you're at. Might help you to write a good resume.'

'Oh, I don't think . . .'

She gave a wave of her hand. 'I'm sorry if I've offended you. It's just when you mentioned printing experience . . . I got ahead of myself.'

His face betrayed the fact that he wasn't following. She lowered her voice as if to let him in on a secret.

'You see, we're going to write a little book.'

He nodded but kept his focus on the slip of paper with the phone number for the people who could move the tree.

'They cover the whole north-west coast,' she told him, following his eyeline. 'No job too small.'

He was grateful she'd switched topics from the sales pitch. Putting away his glasses, he took a couple of steps back and gave a wave of the papers clutched in his hand.

'Thanks again for these.'

As he made his way back to the car, relieved the caffeine was kicking in, he considered the insistent woman and her offer. Geraldine would say it was fate. She'd been trying to get him to do a course since he'd been retrenched. Said it was the only way he'd get work if the long Covid continued to hang around. It was a thought he didn't like to entertain, but he knew she was only speaking the truth.

The welfare payments helped, but finances were only part of the problem. He was starting to go stir crazy. If it weren't for Dog, he'd have hardly left his flat in Footscray for anything apart from grocery shopping. He could only hope the fresh Tassie air might be good for his health, boost his immune system, help build the kind of strength he would need if he were ever to get back into work. But the nagging voice in his head reminded him that the odds of returning to something like his old job were not in his favour. Been at the printers' since he'd left school at fifteen and his father insisted he follow him into the trade. All a bit ironic for someone who couldn't spell, but he got by. Knew his way round the machines. Was smart enough to learn the basics, make himself useful with the manual jobs others thought beneath them. But it wasn't enough. When he'd tried to go back to work, they could only offer him an office job.

'Only way we can have you back, mate,' the boss told him. 'Should have promoted you a long time ago.'

Oscar wasn't ungrateful, but he'd managed to avoid promotion for years, kept telling them he was happy on the floor. It was all the writing they wanted him to do – filling in forms, running reports, responding to endless emails. Gone were the days when if you had something to say to the bosses, you knocked on their door. In the end, they'd offered him a small redundancy package. He'd taken it, but it would hardly last him to retirement. It wasn't like he didn't want to work. But he was running out of options. If he couldn't read and write like normal people and he couldn't go more than an hour without needing a caffeine hit or a nap, his chances of earning his own money again were looking slim.

Fed up with feeling deflated, he looked again at the flyer. The classes were on Fridays. *Keep me out of the way of the cleaning lady*, he thought. He had nothing to lose. No one knew him here. Besides, if this Cathy woman was genuine about that book, he might have something to offer in return for getting help. Make a change from feeling completely useless.

Chapter Five

In their small weatherboard home, Sienna lay curled up in bed beside her daughter, only one of them able to sleep. It was the early hours when she heard the suite of sounds she'd come to dread, familiar but still terrifying: the rumble of a car approaching, its stereo blaring despite the late hour, the screech of brakes as it came to an abrupt stop, the slam of the driver's door, the heavy tread of footsteps, the jangling of keys, the f-bombs. It was the same routine every weekend. Sienna shut her eyes and let herself imagine that tonight he'd let her be, that like another partner he might tiptoe past, pull the covers up over them perhaps, place the lightest kiss on their baby's forehead, even one on hers.

Instead, he almost pulled her arm out of its socket. Her legs tried desperately to keep up, but it was no use, they buckled under her as he dragged her body across the carpet like a refuse sack. She would have the burn marks to prove it tomorrow. Sure, she wanted to scream the house down like she used to, but poor Daisy had cried herself hoarse enough times to make her bear what Cole did in silence. She flopped onto the floor like a ragdoll. Fighting only made it worse.

The stench of him made her want to vomit; base notes of beer, overtones of weed, stronger with every gasping grunting breath. As he thrust himself inside her, she turned her face away and waited for it to be over. Biting down on all the hurt and fear, her eyes landed on the pair of scissors she'd left on the tallboy beside the pair of jeans she'd cut into shorts that afternoon.

When he finished, he let out a loveless laugh.

'Thinking of using them on me, are you babe?' His sly eyes had followed her gaze.

She pushed herself up on her elbows and made to scoot away but he reached up to grab the scissors and pinned her down again.

'Maybe you'd like a haircut, babe? Be all cute like when I met you.' He licked his tongue along the sweat on his top lip, opened the scissors and began to trace the blades across her cheek. 'You're too damn pretty, babe.'

As he pressed down, she tried to stay his wrist. 'Cole, Cole please . . .' Her mouth moved, tongue, lips all engaged, but there was no sound. 'Cole, please,' she begged, louder this time, but again it was like she was miming the words.

The blades tracking over her face, grazing the tip of her nose, blood starting to drip, she tried again, 'Cole, I'll do anything . . .' Still no sound. She tried to sit up, her body a lead weight, pushing . . .

There was a loud knocking sound. A neighbour shouting, a siren. The police?

Her eyes opened. Mouthing a last silent plea for help, she took in the room. Bright sunlight shone through thin yellow curtains. Daisy slept beside her. Her hand shot to her face. No blood. She touched her hair. Dark silky strands covered her shoulders. She checked her legs. No burn marks. A gasp escaped her lips. The sound real. She wasn't in that house. They were safe.

∼

It had been weeks since they'd left but that didn't mean the nightmares had stopped. She began to sob, tears streaming down her cheeks. Lying back against the pillow that smelled of cheap washing powder, Sienna willed herself to calm down. She wasn't going mad. They were only dreams. She had her baby to care for. Somehow, she had to get through this, find her way back to normal. Right now, she had no idea what that was. She was in a women's shelter, for god's sake. About as far from normal as you could get.

Through the wall, she heard the shuffling of feet as the three children in the next room got out of bed and dressed for school. Well-behaved children, their mother a beautifully turned-out woman, black like the kids, with brightly coloured clothes Sienna found at once strange and appealing. She'd tried to strike up a conversation over the washing line, but the woman was guarded, not reciprocating when Sienna introduced herself and Daisy. She surreptitiously looked for bruises but didn't see any on the woman or the kids. That was the thing about abuse; it happened to all kinds of people and didn't have to mean you got knocked around.

She watched as Daisy stirred. Locking eyes with her, the little one reached out and touched her face. The tiny fingers pushed at Sienna's cheeks. As her small face lit up with a broad smile, a dribble ran over the gummy space where Sienna desperately willed a pair of incisors to cut through. Nine months and still no teeth.

'Ma-ma!'

Sienna's eyes widened. 'What did you say?' She backed a little away, but seeing the child's eyes darken at the sudden movement, she snuggled in close again and smiled at her.

'*Ma-ma*, eh? Good girl.'

After months of 'Da-da' this and 'Da-da' that, it had finally happened. A fresh lot of tears threatened to spill from the corners of Sienna's eyes, but she sniffed them away. Daisy had already witnessed too many of her tears, heard too many of her screams, way too many shouted obscenities, objects crashing against walls . . . *Stop! Focus on this beautiful gummy smile and the sweet sound of the word you have been waiting for all these months.*

Sienna didn't want to get out of the warm bed. Some days she woke wishing she never had to get up again, but then she would see Daisy and resolve to try harder. She reached for her phone on the nightstand. It would have been nice to take a photo and put it on Facebook, tell friends about the morning's surprise word, add her little one to the millions of babies on Instagram. But friends were part of the problem. After losing her dad, she'd become withdrawn. A few tried to include her, invite her to parties, trips to the cinema, but somewhere in high school, it became normal to leave her out of things. She'd always wanted a bestie, but the crew she tried to hang out with kept her at a distance. In Tassie, Cole made sure she never got close to anyone. Instead of posting, she checked for the kind of messages that had driven her to this shelter in the first place.

'Oh fuck! It's Friday!'

She covered her mouth. She should calm down. It was only an appointment reminder. Swearing was another thing she needed to rein in. This was not how her parents had raised her.

She wondered what her dad would make of all this. Sometimes she imagined him pinning Cole to the wall and putting the hard word on him until he begged for mercy. But that would've probably breached the army code of conduct, abuse of power or something. Her dad would never have done that, but he'd have been strong and dependable. If he hadn't been unlucky enough to have been killed in the line of duty, he would have rescued them ages ago, taken her and Daisy home and looked after them. She knew there was no point trying to envision the man she'd lost when she was thirteen, no matter how much of a hero he was. But it wasn't like Gary Stone would stand up for her. She'd been trying to steer clear of him ever since her mother had met him. In fact, he was probably sitting in the sunroom of their Queensland home reassuring her mother everything was fine over smashed avocado and filtered coffee, without a shred of concern for her welfare. If her mother harboured any doubts, he'd only tell her she was overreacting. Michelle would most likely pop a Xanax and convince herself he was right. Her father would be rolling in his grave if he knew how Gary had treated her.

As Daisy started to grizzle, Sienna lifted the baby onto her hip and padded to the communal kitchen to heat a bottle. At the dining table, the kids from the next room clambered onto chairs as their mother shook cereal into bowls. The eldest, who couldn't have been more than six, poured milk for each of them. Had their father been kind to them once, as she thought Cole had been to her? Was it only the mum who'd been abused? Had she loved him? As the bottle warmed in the microwave, Sienna remembered how Cole would sometimes cradle Daisy in his arms and feed her. He'd tell her to get some rest. She'd trusted him then. Loved him for looking after them.

Back in the comfort of their warm bed, Daisy drained the bottle with a loud suck. Time to face another day, whether they liked it or not. There was a pink polka-dot dress with matching sunhat in a bag someone had donated. It would look great on Daisy if it fit. She tossed her short pyjamas onto the bed and pulled on the clothes she'd worn yesterday. There was no point wasting money on the washer-drier. Maybe she'd handwash tonight and hang a few things out in the courtyard at the back in the morning. She changed the baby, careful to run a wipe between the folds of her chubby legs. They'd bathe together later, play and wash at the same time. Daisy loved her bath. Hated getting out. When the shelter kids were at school, they could take their time, stay in there as long as they liked.

The dress was a little tight, but they only had ten minutes to be ready for their appointment. She didn't even know who it was with. Those workers were like horses on a carousel. She'd met a different one every week. Gary had probably convinced her mother she was living the life in Tasmania. If they knew what had happened to her since she'd left home, they'd be mortified. Definitely not the kind of thing her mother could discuss at her book club or her stepdad at the bowls. But she had no idea what they thought. Any contact with them had been cut after she'd phoned to tell them she'd decided to stay on in Tassie.

'Try not to blame yourself,' the shelter counsellor had advised. But she was the one who had let someone into her life and do exactly as he pleased.

~

Downstairs in reception, Sienna and Daisy sat in the corner on a playmat that had seen better days. Daisy chewed on an orange ring Sienna hoped had been sterilised after the last mini monster. Kids could get so many sicknesses from each other. At least that's what Cole had told her. It wasn't that she wanted to develop any of Cole's paranoia, but she had to do right by the small helpless child, even if she sometimes sapped her energy like a sponge absorbed water.

As they waited, she watched Daisy play, oblivious to everything that was going on in their lives: the upheaval, the threats, the question marks that hovered over what would become of them. That's what the case worker is for, Sienna reminded herself as she pulled Daisy onto her lap for no reason other than to keep her close.

From the window, she saw an unfamiliar woman with a leather workbag come through the security gate and make her way to the front desk.

'I'm here to see Sienna,' the woman told Mandy, the receptionist.

Sienna gathered Daisy to her hip and stood up from the playmat, letting the child hang on to the chew toy.

'Another new face for you, dear.' Mandy addressed her in a voice that made no secret of her exasperation at the turn-over of workers that came through the door.

Sienna smiled. It wasn't this newbie's fault. Helping women and children escape from scary situations day and night struck her as the kind of tough station that might involve a fair bit of stress leave and burnout. Not that social work was some-thing she'd ever aspired to. In Year 12, she'd applied to train as a teacher, but remembering those distant aspirations only stirred the shame of wasted opportunities. Cole had told her she had nowhere near the brains to go to university. Even though she'd been accepted, he assured her she'd never have gone the distance. He was right, really. Wasn't he?

In the little interview room, Sienna set Daisy under a baby gym and took a seat in a faux leather bucket chair at a small table. She watched as the woman let the strap of her bag slide off her shoulder, push a strand of barely brushed blond hair off her face and settle into the seat opposite. She was younger than Sienna had expected, rings on every other finger, a sequence of stud earrings following the curve of her ear. A nose ring made her stare. She couldn't remember when she'd stopped wearing her own jewellery.

The woman reached out a hand. 'I'm Jess.'

Sienna shook her hand, the heat rising in her cheeks. 'Sorry for staring . . . It's just . . . you don't look like the other . . .'

'Not as cool you mean?' The woman cocked her head to one side, her face serious.

Sienna struggled to respond, but Jess gave her a wink that told her she was kidding.

'So . . .' she took a long look at Daisy who was bashing a cloth book with the orange ring. 'This must be the cutest baby I've seen in at least a couple of weeks.'

When their eyes met, Sienna realised she was kidding again. She smiled and let her shoulders relax a little.

'Well, I won't keep you all day,' said Jess.

She reached into the bag she'd set on the floor and took out a bunch of papers and a cereal bar.

'Sorry, Sienna. Didn't have time for brekkie. You want one?'

Without waiting for an answer, the woman took out a whole pack and offered it to her.

On cue, Sienna's stomach gave a low growl.

'You not had breakfast either?'

Sienna shook her head. Feeding herself hadn't crossed her mind. 'We were in a bit of a rush.'

The comment seemed to eject Jess from her chair. Sienna looked on as the woman abandoned the package on top of her papers and headed to reception where she could hear her ask, or rather instruct Mandy to make them two coffees. With a flick of her surfer chick hair, she turned to where Sienna sat stunned in the interview room.

'Milk? Any sugar?'

'Yes, and no . . . sugar.' Sienna couldn't believe this woman. Most of the others were in fear of the receptionist. Jess was certainly different.

When Mandy came in with the coffees, they were deep in discussion about housing options and how Jess could help Sienna and Daisy find a place of their own. Jess said thank you but barely looked up. Sienna slapped on her best beam to show her gratitude, but Mandy rolled her eyes and sashayed back to her post, giving the door a good slam as she went.

Jess seemed not to notice.

'I've spoken to our housing officer . . . a one-bedroom unit's become available . . . hen's teeth, but you only need somewhere small.'

Sienna held the mug with both hands and nodded. As strange as it had been to spend the past four weeks living with a bunch of strangers, the thought of taking the big step to independence scared her witless. She knew how to take care of her daughter: feeding, washing, changing . . . that wasn't a problem. But what if Cole found them again like last time? As Jess sat back against her chair and took a drink, Sienna wanted to say something, but the words wouldn't budge.

'I know you're worried.' Jess set her papers to one side and leaned forward. Sienna took in the sun-baked tips of the woman's hair, the faded fabric of her fitted denim jacket, the crinkles in the white shirt with its strings tied loosely at the V, her flat chest. If she agreed to give the property a go, she would be placing all her trust in this stranger. And yet, it had been strangers who had helped her the most.

So-called friends, on the other hand, had been the ones to let her down.

They'd been living up the coast in Ulverstone when, after one of Cole's weekend rampages, she'd fled to his friend Josh, banging down his door at 2 am with Daisy in her arms. He'd let her in, made her a cup of tea, given them a bed in his spare room, but he'd let Cole in the next morning. She was hardly awake when she heard voices coming from the kitchen, Josh agreeing she should give his mate another chance. Cole had started off all apologetic, promising things would be different. With nowhere else to go, Sienna had gone back and put up with months of more abuse until someone unexpected came to her aid.

At a routine vaccination for Daisy, Cole's phone had launched into its aggressive ringtone. Annoyed, the nurse asked him to take the call outside. Reluctantly, he'd done so, but not before he'd shot Sienna a threatening look. The nurse clocked it. When he left, she asked if he was a good partner. Sienna glanced at the door and considered the consequences. The woman told her that if she needed her help, she would need to be quick. Sienna remembered how the nurse had locked the door and asked if she wanted to talk about it. As she'd shown the nurse the marks where he'd struck her, the woman's concern had given her the kind of empowerment she hadn't remembered feeling since her dad had been alive. She told the nurse about the abuse, the rapes, how Cole would apologise, saying he couldn't help himself, how she was so hot he couldn't wait, he was a bad lover, he'd try harder to be good.

When Cole tried the door and rattled the handle, shouting at her to let him back in, the nurse phoned reception instructing them to keep Cole talking while she got the police. If it hadn't been for that woman's intuition . . .

With her hands shaking, the coffee dripped down onto her jeans. Jess was on to it, searching her bag and producing a crumpled serviette. Taking it from her, Sienna registered the cheap texture of the fast-food outlet napkin. Her stomach rumbled again at the thought of an easy meal, but she had to focus on the decision she was being encouraged to make right here, right now.

'Wouldn't it be nice to have a place of your own?' Jess was saying. 'We'd be looking in on you. I'd organise a support worker to help you settle in, get your groceries, banking sorted . . .'

Sienna shook her head. When she finally found her voice, it came out in a whisper, as if Daisy might overhear and understand. 'What if he finds us?'

Jess set down her drink, crossed her legs and grasped one knee with her hands. 'There's a Family Violence Order out against him. He'd be foolish to breach it.' She gave a sigh. 'Look, all our houses have locks on both windows and doors . . .'

This might have seemed like any other day's work to someone like Jess, but Sienna was only too aware of the risk she would be taking by signing up to a new home. What if Cole found them? There would be no fenced shelter and trained staff to protect them. She'd managed to keep Daisy safe in the past, but what if he broke into this new home Jess was so keen to get her to move into, bash them both, or worse . . .

Daisy smiled at her from where she'd rolled onto her tummy. One of her sleepy smiles, the ones that came just before the frown and face-rubbing that meant she needed a nap, always followed by a scream if she didn't pick her up. Sienna went to her and bent down to lift the tired girl into her arms. She looked at Jess.

'You can't let anything happen to her.' Cuddling the baby in close, she rocked her back and forth.

'I'll do my absolute best.'

Sienna hesitated, but right now, it was all they had.

'I think I might go mad if I stay here,' she said quietly.

'Is it Mandy or the coffee?'

Sienna laughed despite herself. She was beginning to like Jess. There was none of the sad, sympathising faces of the other workers she'd dealt with. None of the frowns or tut-tuts that had made her want to cry her eyes out. She didn't need anyone's pity. She found herself smiling, the weight of intense dread lifting, at least shifting onto one shoulder instead of two.

Jess shuffled forward in her chair and leaned over the table. Holding a blue pen, she pinched at a sheet of paper, turning it over to its blank side. With her head cocked and lips pressed together, she began to draw.

'I know,' she said, going over the shape with her pen to give it a more definite appearance. 'You're thinking, *What the hell is she drawing?*'

'Looks like a three-legged stool,' Sienna offered, as she sat back in the bucket chair with Daisy in her arms.

'That's exactly what it is.' Jess looked pleased with her artwork, but Sienna was at a loss as to what it meant.

'A wise man once told me that life is like a three-legged stool.'

Sienna waited. Any moment now, some wisdom would be revealed.

'So, according to my friend the wise man,' Jess began, 'in life, we need . . .'

Sienna watched as Jess wrote in the space in the first leg.

'Something . . . or someone . . . to love.' Jess moved on to the second leg, writing in neat deliberate print. 'Something to do . . .'

Sienna noticed a lone fine hair growing out from under Jess's left cheekbone as the pen moved to the third space.

'And something to look forward to.' Jess looked up, her cool blue eyes searching for understanding in Sienna's. 'Make sense?'

'I suppose.' Sienna looked back at the paper between them. Jess let out an audible breath.

'You have a lot on your plate just now, Sienna, but things will get better. I'd like to help you and Daisy rebuild your lives, put Cole behind you.'

At least she'd stopped short of saying anything so patronising as 'You're so young, you've got your whole life ahead of you,' like another worker had done. Sienna wasn't ignorant of the statistics around family violence. She'd seen enough

TV news reports to know hers wasn't the only life in danger of being cut short by an ex-partner who couldn't keep a lid on his anger. She shivered at the thought and looked back at the drawing. Was this another way of oversimplifying the challenges she was facing, or could it really help her?

'Safety is our number one priority.' Jess read her thoughts. 'But we want you to have a life.' She pointed to where she'd written, *Something to love*. 'So this is Daisy.' She smiled at the baby who was dropping off in Sienna's arms and moved her pen to the second leg. 'Something to do ... Before you met Cole, what were your dreams? Was there anything you thought you might do – for work or study, maybe?'

Sienna sucked in a breath, stroking Daisy's fine hair as she exhaled. 'My mum thought I'd go to uni.' She shrugged. 'Cole said I was no way smart enough to get through it.'

Jess didn't jump in with an argument, but listened before asking, 'And what does *Sienna* think?'

Sienna kept her gaze on Daisy. It was easier than looking into this woman's eyes and seeing disappointment.

'I did okay at school ... I finished Year 12.' Sienna shook her head. She didn't want to talk about her interest in languages and how she'd been dux of Japanese. None of that mattered anymore. Images of Cole loomed large in her head as she went on, 'I was meant to start uni a month after we came to Tassie.'

That was when it had all turned sour. The holiday Cole had promised to be a 'nice break' for them had turned into what seemed like a nightmare she couldn't wake up from. When he'd announced he'd got himself a job, she'd agreed to defer her university place. She'd phoned her Mum and Gary to tell them. Gary sounded like he'd won Tatts Lotto. 'That's great news,' he'd said. 'See a bit of the country before you get back to the bookwork.' But her mother had sounded concerned. Sienna knew she was trying her best to sound calm, but when she'd asked her about where they were living, what their house was like, Cole – who'd made her put them on speaker – had gestured for her to hang up. She quickly finished the call. She never got a chance to tell her mum where she was.

'Give them time to get used to the idea,' Cole had urged. 'Mum's little girl is all grown up. *We're* family now.' He'd placed a hand on her belly where the person who would bind them for the rest of their lives was starting to grow. He hadn't given her a chance to tell her mum she was pregnant either. The next day, Cole produced a brand-new phone. It had a different number. She never could find the old one.

The shame of how she'd let her plans and dreams be crushed by him hit Sienna hard. Tears welled in her eyes and made her nose itch, but she sniffed them back. There was no way she was going to fall apart in front of this case worker. They'd said over and over it wasn't her fault, he was a manipulator, yet she was the one holding an innocent child in her arms with no clue as to how she was going to protect and provide for her. Jess seemed nice, but Sienna needed to be careful. She couldn't give them any excuse to take Daisy away from her.

'Would your parents help look after Daisy if we get you back there . . . ?'

Jess made it all sound so easy. Sienna bit down on the mix of dread and disgust at the thought of Daisy being left in the care of Gary Stone.

'My mother's partner isn't exactly what you'd call . . .' She searched for a word to describe the man who might make her mother happy but could never take the place of her father. 'Trustworthy.' She wouldn't elaborate. It was enough to have had to think of him at all. 'I can't go back.'

With Jess waiting for an explanation, Sienna looked at the three-legged stool again, sitting between them like a map of whatever it was this woman was trying to help her navigate.

Jess smiled. 'The wise man I mentioned once helped me out of a dark place.' Sienna couldn't imagine what this confident woman meant but she let her explain.

'We all need something to do . . . something that gets us up in the morning.'

Sienna remembered the word *ikigai*. Her Japanese teacher had given the class a list of words that would have taken a whole sentence to say in English.

'And then there's something to hope for, look forward to,' Jess was saying. 'I want to help you find a reason to get up for you and Daisy, have a bit of a plan, you know?'

'Like besides staying alive and finding somewhere safe to live?'

Jess nodded. They eyed each other over the drawing.

'Tell you what . . .' Jess gathered her papers and returned them to her bag. 'Let's take Daisy for a stroll across to the library. There's someone I'd like you to meet.'

It wasn't like she had anything else on. Besides, there was something about this young woman that made Sienna want to hope that somehow things could be okay. She settled Daisy into the pram the shelter had given her, took her baseball cap from the change bag and tucked in her hair.

Chapter Six

That morning, Vivian had woken to the unfamiliar sound of her alarm clock. She'd had to wipe the dust off it the evening before, when she'd set it out of fear she would sleep through her appointment with Cathy Shannon. Now, part of her wished she hadn't set it at all, and that she could drift back into the deep sleep she'd finally managed to fall into somewhere after 5 am when the ruminating abated.

Sleep was not Vivian's friend. They'd fallen out long ago, in a time she learned was called perimenopause. How she'd survived her forties on five hours a night, six at best, was a mystery. That she'd been made head of the English department by the time she'd turned fifty on almost a decade of sleep deprivation was nothing short of a miracle. The coffee machine she'd installed in her office might have been popular at meetings, but its primary purpose was to keep her awake. Little had she known it would take more than caffeine to combat the effects of middle age.

She'd been up twice in the early hours, once to pee and again to wander through the house to locate her earphones so she could listen to her sleep app. Dave had always said they gave a better quality of sound. *What a stupid habit*, she thought as she untangled herself from the wires that were lodged under her neck. At least she'd managed some sleep. A dull light filled the room, the blackout curtains belying the forecast sunshine. The air held a summer weight that had her lying with one leg outside the duvet and an arm resting where she'd pushed at the covers to keep them away from her chin. As had become ritual, she turned to consider the neatness of the pair of pillows and smoothness of the stretch of fabric along Dave's side. She kicked the cover into the air, but when her legs came to rest, it hardly made a difference.

'Ugh!' she huffed, the feelings mixing in her stomach like a stew.

As far as Vivian knew, Dave was still 'sorting himself out'. He'd been in touch with the kids more than her. Clodagh never spent long on the subject when she called. Finn had at least been kind, reassuring her that his dad just needed some space, time to come to terms with retirement. What had happened to 'they' and 'we' in all of this wasn't mentioned. Dave was on the other side of the country for pity's sake. Although she hated to admit it, some days were so bad, she felt he may as well have died.

Didn't grief have five stages? For Vivian, all five seemed to be hanging around, jostling for position. She pulled the duvet over her head. Denial, right there. Stay in bed. If you don't get up, you can pretend it's not happening. Throw in depression for good measure. Why not? It's not like anybody cares. Ha, there's the anger. As the minutes passed, she mulled over the decluttering job she'd promised herself to take on. Bargaining with herself, another stage.

She'd heard about the 'doorstep mile', a Norwegian expression about the first small part of anything being the hardest, like the first steps in a long walk. Getting out of bed was hers. She threw back the duvet and went to the window, pulling open the curtains to let in the light of a new day. What the hell was Cathy Shannon thinking? She was a long way from being capable of leading a writing program.

Feck it, she was up now. She'd press on. There it was, the fifth stage, acceptance. Before she could change her mind and slip back under the duvet, she went to shower and make herself presentable. *The apparel oft proclaims the man*, she quoted Shakespeare as she chose a pair of capri pants and a linen shirt. Things were bad enough. If she had to be seen in public, she wouldn't give anyone an excuse to think she wasn't coping.

⁓

Downstairs as the kettle boiled, the doubts and negative thoughts started up again like an orchestra coming back after intermission, the players eager to make their mark with renewed energy and vigour. She had to get out of her own head. The deafening silence in the house was driving her mad. She searched her phone for something to play on Spotify, a podcast maybe, hoping to drown out the internal din. Jack

Johnson was first on her playlists. Her finger hovered for a second. She pressed shuffle play, the mellow tones shifting her thoughts to a morning when they'd been right here, making brunch together, singing along in snippets of familiar words, brushing past each other in that playful way they had. The memory of what used to be, the easiness between them, melted over her. She held it like a tiny feather that might land in your hand for a moment before being picked up by the breeze and swept away.

Leaning against the sink, Vivian looked out over the back garden to where a kookaburra sat on the lowest branch of a white gum watching something in the leaf litter. Dave used to leave scraps there for opportunistic natives. She wondered if they missed his rotting offerings. She crossed her arms at her waist and turned from the scene. Pressing pause on Jack Johnson, she knew there was no way she could run this writing class.

She'd have to phone Cathy and apologise, say it wasn't possible, make some excuse, suggest someone else. She thought for a moment, but instead of possible candidates to take her place, she could only think of Cathy and how generous she'd always been to them. When Dave had been in hospital once, she'd made quiches and left them at the door. That was the type of person she was. She deserved to be told face to face. And besides, Vivian reminded herself, she wasn't a coward. If this was how her life was going to be for the foreseeable future, fending for herself and doing her own heavy lifting, she would sooner accept and get on with it.

By the time she'd parked her car at Victoria Parade and walked the short distance to the paranaple centre, she'd rehearsed the cop-out speech she'd give to Cathy. She wasn't ready for another teaching role. It would be a lovely project, she was sure. Someone else would do a much better job. No, she wouldn't do it justice.

As she rode the escalator to the first floor, she could hear Cathy's cheery voice. Stepping off, she spotted her coming along the corridor, pushing a pram for a young girl wearing a dark baseball cap and carrying a baby. The girl reminded Vivian of her high school students, more teenager than adult.

Cathy beamed when she saw her. 'Ah, great timing!'

Oh god, this was going to be painful.

'Vivian, I was just telling Sienna all about you.'

With her legs threatening to go to jelly, she noticed the girl reposition the baby on her hip and wondered why she wouldn't just put the hefty bub in the pram.

'Beautiful outfit,' was all she could think to say, even though the poor child looked a bit squashed in that polka-dot dress.

'Sienna will be joining our writing class.' Cathy introduced the young woman with a pride Vivian recognised. She'd always had a knack for promoting people. While others would despair about wayward students in the staffroom, Cathy would find something positive to say.

'Vivian is a wonderful teacher,' she told Sienna. 'I'm sure you'll get on well.'

There she went again, voicing what might have been close to the truth in the past, but now sounded like an out-and-out lie, irrelevant to the present.

'Sienna's from Queensland,' said Cathy. 'That lovely place you went to with the choir, Vivian . . . Surfers Paradise?'

Sienna nodded, her head low, the colour rising in her cheeks.

Vivian imagined Cathy's good-intentioned jabbering was embarrassing the girl, but the mention of her hometown made her think of Dave. Like him, this young woman was a long way from home.

'We've agreed that Sienna will bring Daisy with her to our sessions.' Cathy gave the girl a gentle nudge. 'Vivan's a grandmother. She'll love having a baby in class, I'm sure.'

As Vivan watched the baby turn her face into the girl's chest, something stirred deep inside of her. If Sienna was anything to go by, Cathy's project was going to be very different from any class she'd ever envisaged. And there was Cathy now, smiling, fully present for this young person and her baby, assured that she, Vivian Molloy, would do a great job. How could she let them down?

⌒

For the next hour, Vivian mostly nodded and made scant notes in a small notebook she carried in her handbag. Had she been prepared to agree to this project, she might have brought her laptop or at least her paper diary. Cathy was trotting out a list of possible themes and topics that would form the basis of the course and the small book they would ultimately produce. *A book!* Her face must have betrayed her.

'Oh, don't worry about the book just yet,' said Cathy. 'It will be nice to have something at the end to share with our stakeholders and give the students something to remember, be proud of . . .'

Cathy carried on with details about how the course would run over ten Fridays, so as not to clash with other educational offerings in the city. Mornings, three hours each week, so as not to interfere with school drop-off and pick-up for parents. Cathy would look after initial assessments of the students and pass on the results of course. She'd make arrangements for a couple of excursions to local attractions. Might inspire the students to write about where they came from, she said, insights about where they live, little articles they might want to put in the book.

'So, is it a literacy-cum-English language program you have in mind?' Vivian interjected at one point. 'Or more of a creative writing course?'

Cathy took a rare breath and paused before responding. 'I'm hoping this project will be more about building confidence than any kind of prescriptive writing course.'

Vivian could only nod as she considered the irony of putting a woman who could hardly leave her own home in charge of a confidence-building initiative. In any case, Cathy was back in full flow. They already had six candidates signed up. A couple more would keep the funding body happy and make a nice number for interaction, group work, that sort of thing. Didn't she agree?

Whether she agreed or not seemed irrelevant to Vivian. She would be committed to show up here Friday after bloody

Friday. If it hadn't been for that young mum she'd met earlier, she could have cut this meeting short and given Cathy some line about the timing not being good for her. Oblivious to her misgivings, Cathy rattled on. They would meet again before classes started to nut out the details, but it was up to her what the sessions entailed. And the students were lovely. A few from culturally and linguistically diverse backgrounds, a man with long Covid who'd lost his job, that bright girl from interstate she'd met . . . 'Nineteen, god love her, she's found herself in dire straits . . .' Cathy had stopped there, before any doubt or darkness could settle over their conversation. Regaining her positivity, she said the girl might prove a great help. Vivian wasn't sure whether to be grateful or even more worried, but managed to leave with assurances that her old colleague was feeling much more confident about the project now that they'd had a proper chat.

⌒

'Jesus, Mary and Joseph,' Vivian whispered as she stepped back onto the escalator that brought her downstairs to the revolving door and out into the fresh air. It was a done deal. Ten weeks to improve people's writing and produce a book to prove it. She'd expected to walk out of there with a plan, but instead had been given free rein for Cathy's ad hoc notions about excursions and confidence building. Where was the structure? In high school she'd had a curriculum, a solid frame-work like rungs on a ladder that marked out the progression from A to B. But then, hadn't she thought of her marriage in similar terms? Milestones like children, special birthdays, anniversaries, grandchildren – all setting the path from youth to retirement, then old age, enough to look back on, feel fulfilled. Not this curvature that had hijacked her life.

At the coffee shop on Oldaker Street, she caught herself glancing in the window to where a couple sat with large mugs of coffee and plates of plump scones. She could really do with a regroup after the meeting. She'd been so uptight that morning, she hadn't been able to eat. It wouldn't do to drive all the way home with her stomach out to her backbone, and if she sat amongst those large cheese and umbrella plants, she'd be screened from view and hopefully not run into anyone. She stepped inside.

'Could I order a coffee and . . .' *Food* about covered it.

The girl behind the counter had seen her swithering type before.

'Take a seat and I'll send Caitlin out to you.'

Her bottom had hardly touched down in the chair when a girl appeared beside her, a smile spread from cheek to rosy cheek like a sunbeam.

'Mrs Molloy, what can I get for you?'

Taking off her sunnies, Vivian took in the young woman who couldn't have been more than twenty.

'It's Caitlin,' she said. 'From college.'

Of course. Vivian sat back a little. 'Caitlin, you lovely girl. How are you doing?'

'I'm good, Miss.'

'Are you working in here all the time?'

'Oh no, Miss. I do a couple of days a week when I don't have uni.'

Vivian could see the girl now, a shy, mousy thing, an earnest student, not at all cocky like some of the brighter ones with the kind of god-given talent that made getting through school a walk in the park. Yet here she was, all blossomed into a confident young woman.

'Good on you,' said Vivian. 'You were always a hard worker.'

The girl gave a slight bend like a curtsy. 'Wouldn't be in uni without you, Miss.'

Vivian's eyebrows gathered as she tried to remember how she might have helped the girl.

'You were my favourite teacher,' Caitlin went on. 'Probably because *you* didn't have favourites, actually.' She laughed at her cleverness, hugging the menu into her.

Something seemed to lodge in Vivian's throat, preventing a reply. The girl stretched out her arms and set the menu down in front of her.

'The scones are great if you're after a treat.'

'Scones and a skinny cap then, please.'

As Caitlin went to prepare her order, Vivian took out the notebook and opened the page at where she'd been mind-mapping with Cathy. A clutch of English language learners, some older adults who wanted to improve their skills, a young single mum who should be in university . . . ten weeks . . . carte blanche. What a mixed bunch. She sighed at the thought of how she'd even start but reminded herself she'd had two votes of confidence already today. Maybe it was a sign.

She remembered what she used to tell her students toward the end of the school year. Beset by exam stress and writing anxiety, she'd tell them she had the utmost faith in them, that they'd worked hard all year, handed in all of their assignments, done everything she'd asked of them. It was time to shine and let their hard work pay off. She would say that if they didn't have faith in themselves, they could lean into the confidence others had in them. Perhaps she could take a little of her own advice.

Chapter Seven

By the following week, Cathy had sent through the student profiles she'd promised. Vivian cleared a space on her kitchen table and read the email on her laptop. The range of levels looked daunting, but she'd taught plenty of mixed ability classes to know she could handle that aspect. What interested her most were the reasons the prospective students gave for wanting to do the course in the first place. A couple of them wanted to improve their writing so they could apply for jobs or courses. There was a new Chinese migrant who had set a goal to learn to write in English so she could write about her life in Tasmania and share it with her English-speaking in-laws. A local woman who Vivian noticed wrote quite well, albeit with little regard for punctuation, wanted to write book reviews. The insights spurred her on enough to make a start.

An hour later, she sat back in her chair and stared at the screen. With lots of ideas captured and the first session at least outlined, something about the order she'd been able to bring to Cathy's ideas gave her a small but definite sense of achievement. Beyond the first session, she thought to divide their mornings into two halves where she could cover the rudiments of writing in the first half and allow time for more personalised writing after morning tea. Although the book idea was a bit daunting, the title was starting to grow on her. 'Special Spaces' would surely give her a broad scope. She would see what the students brought to the table.

As she packed her notebook and laptop away, she looked around at the clutter that had begun to creep into her home without her even noticing. Papers, opened and unopened envelopes on the table, not even in her usual neat piles. The kitchen bench had that neglected look, like no one cared if it hadn't been wiped down or what was left on it.

Upstairs, her washing basket was full to overflowing. Her walk-in robe resembled a teenager's floordrobe. She'd been thinking about having a clear-out for weeks, but as she used to tell her kids, thinking about something wouldn't get it done. Before exhaustion could get the better of her, she grabbed the basket of clothes and put a load on to wash. Outside, she pulled up one of the roller doors of the garage. The camper van took up half the space, cobwebs gathered at the windows and mirrors where spiders had taken up residence. Steeling herself, she set about retrieving the boxes and large refuse sacks she'd come in for and bolted back to the house before sentiment could derail her productivity.

With a box for recycling, a bag for rubbish, a cloth and a spray bottle of detergent, Vivian went through the kitchen like a dose of salts. She'd never begrudged tidying up after

Dave. When they'd become empty-nesters, she'd found herself waiting restlessly for a full load of washing or enough dirty dishes to warrant turning on the dishwasher. It was strange how being alone had had the opposite effect.

As a father, Dave had been hands-on, never shirking child-minding or domestic responsibilities. When he wasn't away, they both cooked and cleaned, his cooking better than hers, her cleaning definitely of a higher standard than his, but it worked. Or at least it had. Looking into the study, cardboard box in hand, unease pricked at her insides. Perhaps she should put on some music, one of those housework playlists, something to speed up this awful process. But music was at the very heart of her problems. Sometimes she wished they'd never gone to that Festival of Singing.

A framed photo on the piano was a reminder of happier times. If the best parties usually ended up in a kitchen, theirs would find their way to the study. In the photo, she and Dave were laughing with a group of friends. A typical night when, after a shared meal and several bottles of wine, Dave would be persuaded to play, and their friends would sit, squashed together on the old leather lounge or lean against the piano or the desk she'd insist they clear before anyone showed up. Dave would have them lifting the rafters with raucous renditions of songs from their teens and childhoods. The soundtrack of their lives had been played and replayed in there. Anything from lyrically innocent if vocally challenging numbers from the likes of *The Sound of Music* to pop hits from icons like Billy Joel, Stevie Wonder, Elton John. And then there was always the raft of Irish ballads to finish the night off, Dave doing a reasonable 'Danny Boy' or something from Christy Moore, 'The Voyage' perhaps. One of their favourites that always saw him turn from where his fingers glided over the keys to find his wife amongst the guests and give her the look that made her tingle. Vivian gave herself a mental shake, strode across the room to the piano and closed the lid.

It wasn't long before she'd filled two boxes with CDs and organised the papers in the cupboards that she and Dave had promised themselves they'd sort through as one of their many retirement projects. She dispensed with the old jigsaws and books that should have been passed on years ago. Her folders from school would have to wait until another day. That was too raw.

Armed with a refuse sack, she continued upstairs in her bedroom where the large walk-in wardrobe had gone from a place she would spend hours arranging, to one she merely dashed in and out of. With her back to Dave's side of the wardrobe, she flicked through her clothes rail, choosing a couple of jackets she hadn't worn in years. Padded shoulders would hardly come back into fashion, she reasoned, but they might do someone for a retro night. On a roll, she went to her winter shelves and discarded a couple of jumpers in colours and styles that no longer held their appeal. Somewhere in her early fifties, she'd become a linen lady, favouring single coloured clothing from quality brands, preferably when they were on sale.

With the clothes in the bag, she was ready to get out of there. But as she bent to tie it, her bum brushed against the long overcoats on Dave's rail behind her. She stood up and, letting the bag slouch and gape open, turned to touch the row of sleeves: suits he wore for work, warm fleeces she liked to link her arm through as they strolled around the block on cool nights, shirts in plain and flamboyant fabrics he'd choose to match an occasion or indeed his mood. She pushed at them just to hear the sound the metal hangers made when he'd be trying to decide what to wear or what to pack for a trip. She could almost hear the tuts and sighs before he'd emerge with something. A tear leaked from the corner of her eye. She could text him right now and ask if he wanted her to chuck anything, pass it on to charity. An innocuous enough question. But the tightness in her tummy that had begun to show up whenever she thought to call or text stopped her from reaching for the phone.

She chose a few threadbare items he no longer wore. He'd always taken her wardrobe advice. She wondered what he was wearing now. They'd only brought carry-on cases and his suit bag to the Gold Coast. She could still see his case lying open inside the door of their hotel room, his toilet bag unpacked in the bathroom, a light jacket hanging over a chair. He'd said he'd go back later and check himself out. It was as if he'd pressed pause on their life together.

The scent of him intensified with each deposit into the bag. When the children moved out of home, it had taken months for their rooms to stop smelling of them. First Clodagh, then Finn – their unique aromas dissipating until one day she would walk in to open a window to air the place and find that the old familiar smell had disappeared. The thought of the same thing happening here filled her with something she didn't want to name as dread. Tying the bag tight, she hauled it out of the room and down the stairs.

As she deposited the bag in the hallway beside the boxes she'd filled earlier, she registered a soreness in her shoulder. *That's what you get for pulling and hauling,* she thought as she wound her arm like a wheel in need of oiling. *What was the expression? Age doesn't come alone?* Whatever it came with, she might well have to deal with it on her own. She would do well to look after herself. She tramped downstairs to the memo pad on the fridge and wrote, *See physio!*

About to return to her task, she heard a car pull up outside. She wasn't expecting a visitor. Like a dog who knew their owner's vehicle, she stood and listened carefully before relegating the arrival to the 'Anyone But Dave' list and went to the door.

⁓

Petronella had not so much parked her Porsche as left it in the middle of the driveway, ensuring no one could get in or out of the property until she saw fit to leave. Vivian sighed at the sight of her, looking fabulous as usual, tottering over the uneven pathway in the pair of wedged sandals she wore to give her diminutive stature an extra couple of inches. She wished she was in something respectable instead of the faded Bermudas and one of the four t-shirts she lived in these days.

'What a lovely surprise!' Vivian wasn't surprised at all, but her pride made her dismiss the near certainty that Deb had put her sister up to this impromptu visit.

'How're ya goin'?' Without waiting for an answer, Petronella shoved a posy of fresh-cut flowers at Vivian who held them out to one side as the woman thrust her skinny frame in for a kiss on the cheek. As Vivian bent down to accept the embrace, she thought she might keel over from the strength of the perfume that hung around Petronella like something from the eighties.

'I was just passing,' she announced, rebalancing on her sandals, 'and said "Ah, I'll swing by Vivian's and see if she's got time for a cuppa".'

Yeah, sure you did, thought Vivian, but then no one else was likely to call on her today.

Petronella was the kind of friend who kept your standards high, but your bank account low. Technically, she wasn't even really her friend, more of an inheritance. Before Deb had moved to Hobart, she'd asked Petronella to look out for her. Vivian didn't need to have heard those exact words to know she'd said them. Up until now, she'd managed to avoid Petronella, replying to her texts about catching up or coming back to choir, saying she was busy. Deb and her sister might have been like chalk and cheese, but they were equally caring. The problem with Petronella was her permanently cheery disposition that reminded Vivian of someone with one of those Botox smiles, constantly willing you to see your glass as half full even on those days you'd happily hurl any unsuspecting glass at the nearest wall.

Vivian considered mentioning that she was about to go out, lie about an appointment perhaps, but Petronella had the eyes of a pleading puppy dog, and the flowers were such a beautiful gift. She would have stopped specially at one of the brightly coloured side-of-the-road stalls on her way back from town. Or worse, she might have gone out of her way to get them if Deb had asked her to stop by.

'Would you like to come in?' Vivian stepped aside and gestured along the passageway. Not needing to be asked twice, Petronella popped her keys in her posh handbag and launched herself into the house, leaving Vivian standing in a waft of airborne luxury.

In the kitchen, she perched herself on a stool at the bench and took in the bags and boxes.

'Having a clear-out?'

'Long overdue.' Vivian went to the pantry and took out the good coffee she'd begun to ration. Finances were another thing that needed attention, but she was far from ready to take that on.

'We should get the girls round to help you,' Petronella was saying over the noise of the kettle.

'That's kind of you, but I think I'd . . .'

'Oh, I know. Some things are better done on your own.'

The girls were the well-meaning group of retirees from the choir who enjoyed the kind of coffee mornings and theatre outings that Vivian had looked forward to in the lead-up to leaving school. When a particular Year 9 cohort gave her the kind of grief that might have had a lesser teacher out on stress leave, Vivian had merely looked over the heads of the hormonal youngsters to where the clock at the back of the room ticked out the remaining minutes of her career and thought about all the concerts and long lunches she and Dave would soak up once she'd retired and started a new chapter. When and whether that 'chapter' as she'd called it would ever play out, she honestly wasn't sure. It was a prospect she tried to avoid thinking about, but if she didn't know what her husband had to sort out, how could she be sure he didn't want a divorce?

Vivian spent the next half-hour mostly listening to Petronella until *the girls'* exploits had been exhausted and their coffee cups were drained.

'We're trying out that new café in the village on Friday,' said Petronella, with no sign of moving. 'We'd love you to join us.'

Oh god, the woman was giving her that expectant look again, the tinted eyelashes batting over the twinkling topaz irises. Between Cathy Shannon and Petronella, she felt like a project for the benevolently inclined.

'I have a meeting on Friday,' she said, setting down her cup in the hope of drawing the awkward conversation to a close. For once, at last, she wasn't making something up.

'Morning or afternoon?' Petronella persisted. 'I'm sure the girls would . . .'

'All day, I'm afraid.' She hated hearing herself fudge the truth, but how else was she to guard her privacy and avoid the kind of 'group therapy' Petronella no doubt had in mind?

'No worries.' Petronella smiled sweetly at her without a sign of being offended. There was a moment's silence before she spoke again. 'I suppose there's no chance of you coming back to choir yet?'

A thousand words backed up against Vivian's tongue. *Are you freaking mad, have you any idea . . .* but she shook her head.

'Rightio.' Petronella set down her cup and gathered up her handbag, slipping it over the tanned leathery skin of her arm. 'It's a bit of a shambles without you and Dave,' she said. 'Old Tom Simmons is hopeless as a conductor, and no one's capable of organising things like you.' There was a hint of something like hope in her eyes as she hesitated to leave. 'Dave still away on the mainland?' she asked.

Vivian murmured in the affirmative, not wanting to make this a topic for discussion.

'Men and their mid-life crises!' Petronella laughed and hopped off her stool. 'How do you think we ended up with a Porsche?'

Vivian gave a weak smile in response. At last, her visitor turned and began to click-clack back down the hallway.

'We'll catch up another time,' said Petronella. 'I'm sure there's a couple of good movies coming to town.'

Vivian watched as the Porsche disappeared down the driveway. *Mid-life crisis*, she mused.

With the door closed behind her, she stared at the bags and boxes she would have to take to the charity shop. After Petronella's chatter, the house felt suddenly quiet. Shouldn't she have grown used to it by now? But she didn't want to grow used to it. Exhausted, she closed every curtain in the house and climbed into bed.

Chapter Eight

Week One

Vivian stood at the front of her new classroom, eyes darting about, willing herself to calm down. This wasn't even a rowdy bunch of school kids high on summer and hormones. A quick headcount gave her seven students, all seated around two long communal tables. She'd faced hundreds, possibly thousands of much larger classrooms in her time, and yet it might as well have been her first student prac. As she smoothed down the loose teal kaftan she'd chosen to wear with her cream linen trousers, she noticed Cathy smiling at her from where she was manning the door. At least someone had faith in her ability to do this.

Swallowing hard, Vivian took a sheaf of coloured A4 papers she'd found in her clear-out and tapped them on the table at the front of the room to neaten the pile. The noise was enough to turn down the volume of the chat and make her charges sit a little straighter in their chairs. Their collective expectation tangible, she held the paper to her tummy, ran her fingers around the edges and said a silent prayer she could get through the next three hours.

'Hello, everyone. I'm Vivian.' It was an effort to smile, but she reminded herself how hard it must be for some of the people in front of her to come over the door at all. She took a step forward and began handing out the paper. 'We'll get to the introductions a bit later, but if you could all take a piece of paper.'

As she walked around, she thought about the positives, how fortunate they were to have the spacious modern room, the comfortable swivel chairs, and state-of-the-art tables with tastefully hidden cables that would let them use laptops later in the program. There was even room for the prams, she thought, as she took in the two babies and prayed they wouldn't cause too much disruption.

'Can I grab a pink one?'

The voice came from a girl whose hair had been dip-dyed a shade like fuchsia. There was always one, thought Vivian, as she watched the girl unzip a pencil case that was fit to bursting. If nothing else, she'd come prepared.

Beside the girl, a man in his forties took a sheet and thanked her quietly, his hand shaking as he did so. Vivian noticed the tall coffee cup he must have picked up from the downstairs café and hoped she'd get them through to morning tea without either of them unravelling.

'If you could all fold your paper, we're going to use them as name cards.' She demonstrated how she wanted the papers folded in three so they could stand like Toblerones on the tables in front of them. 'I've got thick pens for you to write your names.' As she went round distributing the stationery, the hammering in her heart began to slow.

'What's your favourite colour?' Miss Pink gestured with one of her own textas and looked at Vivian with a wide-open expression that made answering unavoidable.

'Oh!' Vivian had to think. 'Blue,' she said. Why on earth had she given Dave's favourite colour and not her own?

'Mine's pink,' the girl said without looking up from her page, where she was drawing big bold letters.

As she caught Cathy's eye, Vivian's old colleague gave her a wink. But any shared amusement at the girl's comment was short-lived when Vivian realised Cathy was helping the young single mum who'd been trying to organise her name plate one-handed. So preoccupied with her own nerves, she'd just left them to get on with it without even considering that the mums holding babies might struggle. After helping the other mum, she returned to the front desk, took her folded sheet and wrote *Vivian* in bold blue letters. Turning it toward the group, she tried not to think about whether she would soon have to relinquish the title of *Mrs Molloy*.

'I have an auntie called Vivian,' a mature woman piped up from the back. 'Spells it different . . .'

Vivian smiled and waited for her to recall the spelling, but the woman's cheeks flushed at the attention she'd drawn to herself.

'Is it the French way, with *enne* at the end?' Vivian asked.

'That's the one,' the woman answered.

'My mother wasn't a great speller, I'm afraid.'

The woman nodded. 'My grandmother weren't neither. Got it off a magazine.'

While they completed their first task, Vivian went around the two tables and handed out the official library pens and spiral-bound notebooks Cathy had purchased for each of them. There were murmurs of gratitude from some, a grumble from the woman at the back, but she pressed on.

'Okay. I'd like you all to put everything you write for the class into these notebooks, so you each have a collection of writing in one spot, okay?'

She opened her own book to a blank page and turned it toward them. It served as a good prop as she went on.

'This course is about giving you lots of writing skills and time to practise them.' She paused, aware of how long it had been since she'd been in charge like this, but she pressed on. 'All of your efforts, no matter how good or not so good,' she said, managing a smile, 'will go into these books. You'll be able to see yourself improve over the weeks.'

The theory sounded plausible. She said another silent prayer.

'By the end, we will have a book to show for ourselves. We want to call it Special Spaces. It will be up to you what goes in there, but that's a while away.' She looked over at Cathy and asked if there was anything she wanted to add. As Cathy told them about the excursions, Vivian took a mental moment to breathe.

'Well, I'll leave you in Vivian's capable hands,' said Cathy when she'd finished. Vivian watched her leave and turned back to the class. It was time to dive in.

'First up, I think we should get to know each other a little better,' she said. 'Can I ask everyone to write two truths and one lie about yourself?' There were a couple of laughs and some confused faces. 'Please don't worry about what your writing looks like. Just get your ideas down on paper. I'm happy if you draw pictures.'

Taking the pen from beside the smartboard, she put up a list: *true, true, lie.* Turning back to the group, she explained, 'Two things about you that are true and something that's not true but may be still believable. It might be something you like to do, a sport or hobby, a place you've visited, something you're afraid of . . .'

The mum she'd helped, who Cathy had told her was South American, jiggled her baby on her hip and nodded. 'Si, I think I know what means . . .'

Vivian gave them a few minutes, quickly writing down the three things she'd thought of in the car on her way in. Icebreakers were not her strong point, but she'd been to enough staff training sessions to have a few up her sleeve. When most of the pens had stopped moving, she asked everyone to join her in a circle at the front of the room.

'I'll go first if you like.' She held her paper so they could see, took a deep breath and read, 'I'm from Ireland, I'm vegetarian and I love gardening.' Looking around the group, she asked, 'Which one is not true?'

'You're definitely from Ireland.' It was the short middle-aged man with the coffee who looked as nervous as she felt. At least he was helping her out. She checked his name plate.

'That was the easy bit, Oscar.' There were a few laughs as most of the group had no doubt suspected her origins. Oscar smiled then, an embarrassed smile, but the ice was broken. 'Would any of you have a guess at what I was lying about?'

A slip of a thing whose real name she was almost certain was not Robyn beamed at her, 'You love gardening?'

'That's it! Well done. I hate gardening.'

The woman with an Aunt Vivienne looked disappointed. 'I love me garden,' she said. 'All them fresh veggies . . .'

Not wanting to stall on the gardening issue, Vivian moved the exercise along. 'So what did *you* have? Marilyn, is it?'

The woman took a pair of metal-framed glasses off the top of her head and popped them on. Folding one arm across a pair of low-slung breasts, she held out her notebook.

'Marilyn's me name. I have three sons. I love me romance books. I used to be a model.'

Someone giggled, but most of them, much to Vivian's relief, managed to keep straight faces.

'That has yous stumped!' Marilyn gave a cheeky grin.

'You could have been a model when you were younger.' It was Sienna who had lain her sleepy baby in her pram and was now pushing it back and forth as if her left arm was on autopilot.

'That's kind of you to say,' Marilyn replied, 'but none of yous believe that.' She shrugged. 'What the rest of you got?'

Vivian was grateful to a ponytailed man in his thirties who offered to go next.

'Johnny. I own a Harley. I got two kids. I'm from Baghdad.'

'How come you don't have an accent?' the pink-haired girl asked.

Before Vivian even had time to be mortified, the man responded with a string of what sounded like Arabic that was met by applause and whoops of delight.

'Okay, you lied about the Harley.' The girl laughed, but Johnny shook his head.

'No kids?' Vivian asked.

'No missus, no kids.' He held out his palms.

'How long you been in Tasmania?' Marilyn asked.

'We moved from Iraq to Melbourne when I was a teenager. Came down to Tassie to work for a friend, couple of years back.'

Vivian noticed the dimple in the middle of his chin. A rather good-looking individual, she decided, not that it was anything to her. Eye candy couldn't have been further from her mind when she'd agreed to take this class.

'He had a restaurant. Went bust in the pandemic,' Johnny was telling them. 'That's why I'm here. Thought I'd get better at writing so I can do a course in aged care or something, get a job . . .'

'Good on you,' said Vivian. 'If you need help finding a course, we can certainly help.' She was rewarded with a nod and a warm smile. 'Who's next?'

'I will go.' Rosa had her hand up. Vivian made a mental note to let her know it wouldn't be necessary to do that in this class.

'What have you got for us?'

Rosa began to read without disturbing the tiny baby who was sleeping over her shoulder. In that beautiful Latino accent, she told them she was from Peru, that she liked to dance and that she was divorced. Her deadpan expression had the group guessing.

'You've just had a baby, so unless you were married before, I don't think you're divorced.' It was Marilyn. Her matter-of-fact tone seemed to have no impact on Rosa whose face broke into a smile that lit up the room. To their surprise, she began to take quick steps forward and back in an elegant salsa.

'Who would be my dance partner if I was divorced?' she joked. 'I am lucky girl . . .' She stopped dancing and secured the sliding baby back on her shoulder. 'My Enrique is handsome, good father *and*,' she drew out the word before adding, 'excellent dancer.' The pride in her eyes wasn't lost on Vivian. There'd been a time when she'd have felt the same about Dave.

'Maybe I teach you a little Latin dancing one time,' Rosa suggested.

There were murmurs of enthusiasm. Marilyn huffed and muttered something Vivian didn't catch but suspected ran along the lines of them being there to learn to write, not dance. Although not super keen to make a spectacle of herself and her two left feet, Vivian couldn't let Marilyn bring down the energy of the group.

'Don't worry, Marilyn, we'll get to know each other a bit better before we try anything that adventurous.'

The woman did not look convinced.

With her focus firmly fixed on getting through the morning, Vivian proceeded with the name task she'd made up earlier in the week which she'd hoped would give a few insights about her students and give them a little confidence to talk about themselves. She began by modelling what she was looking for, putting her name on the smartboard and drawing a spider diagram, lines fanning out with a nugget of information at the end of each. *Who you were named after.* An uncle in her case, which raised a few eyebrows and started the conversation about names that could be boys' or girls'. *Surname(s)*: that was tricky, but she kept to Molloy and didn't make much of it for fear she would wobble. Rosa saved her with the story of her three surnames: Mendez for her father, Gonzales for her mother and de Silva for her husband.

Encouraging the students to make a mind map of their own names, she took a couple of deep breaths and let them settle into the task. Although she'd been worried sick it might bomb, by the time they were finished, they all amazed her with the stories behind their names and their willingness to share.

When she'd asked for a volunteer, Robyn came straight to the front and addressed the group. From southern China, her Cantonese name was Kam Fung. It meant 'golden phoenix'. Her father had given her the name as a mark of good fortune. She'd chosen *Robyn* because it would be easy for people to say, she told them. Vivian thought of Lucky and Sunny, two Chinese boys she'd taught at school. It saddened her that those names, chosen for ease of pronunciation by the average white Australian may have been a far cry from what their parents had called them. In any event, she was glad Robyn had been comfortable enough to share and had led the way for others to follow suit.

Marilyn had been named after the actress, which had the whole class in danger of erupting with laughter. Except for Robyn, who had to ask who Marilyn Monroe was. Miss Pink, who turned out to be called Amalia, asked her smart watch to provide the meaning of her name. When it said, 'hard-working girl', she'd flicked her pink locks over one shoulder and told them she'd been well named. Vivian hoped she was right. Only Sienna gave her any real cause for concern. She'd been hesitant to share, started to tell them she'd been named after the city in Italy where her parents had married, then trailed off with her eyes looking toward the floor. Vivian had thanked and praised her before suggesting they take a well-earned break for morning tea.

After the break, Vivian had talked about daily gratitude jour-nalling, hoping they'd view it less as homework and more of a practice that would help get them writing for themselves. They'd talked about their writing goals. For one or two it was to be able to write better job applications, for others it was to improve spelling or to be able to write something crea-tive. She would have to cover all of it over the coming weeks.

When it was time to leave, many of the students came and thanked Vivian for the session, promising to see her the following week. Even Marilyn gave her a nod before making an exit. Vivian hoped it meant she'd be back.

'I had a phone call from the older gentleman who couldn't join us this morning,' Cathy told her when the students had left. 'He'll be here next week.'

'Oh, that's fine.' Vivian didn't think it was fine at all. Missing the first day meant she'd have to introduce everybody again, but she couldn't think about that now. All she wanted was to get home to her own four walls. Was it too early for wine?

'Any plans for the weekend?'

Vivian wished Cathy hadn't asked. She didn't care if she stayed in her house until next Friday, such was the effort it had been to get herself here.

'Clodagh's talking about coming up with Max.' The lie rolled off her tongue, but she'd become adept at making up stories as to how she filled her days.

'How lovely,' said Cathy. 'Well, enjoy! See you next week.'

'See you then.' Vivian gave her the most reassuring smile she could muster. It had gotten Cathy off her back, which was exactly where she wanted her and everybody else who harboured the kind of unspoken sympathy she'd come to hate.

Chapter Nine

Sienna found Jess working on her laptop in the foyer café, waiting as promised.

'How'd you go?' Jess beckoned for her to take a seat.

'Yeah. Good.'

Keeping one hand on the pram, Sienna set her bag on the small round table and pulled out a chair.

'*Really* good or just good?'

Sienna smiled. Apart from almost having a mini-breakdown when the teacher asked them to share the story of their name, it *had* been good to think about something other than the horrors of the past few months, but it didn't mean she could drop her guard. Glancing round, she scanned the collection of café customers, library users she could see through the glass partitions, and a queue of people gathered at the local government service desk. A couple of guys sat at computers where you could take the theory test to get your licence. For a terrifying second, she thought the one with dark hair and a varsity jacket might be Cole until he stood to reveal a much smaller frame. Lots of men looked like Cole these days.

'Good enough to come back again next week?' Jess cocked her head, bringing Sienna back to the conversation.

In truth, Sienna hadn't been at all sure what to think as she'd wheeled Daisy into the library room and watched it fill with the strangers she'd be spending another nine Fridays with, if she could survive that long. The friendly woman who Jess had brought her to see had shown her to a seat at the front where she could park Daisy beside her. She'd wished Daisy hadn't decided to take a nap when she could have done with a cuddle to not feel like a complete fish out of water. The room itself had felt like a fish tank, with large glass walls. At first, her only thought had been, *What if Cole walks past and sees me sitting here?* But they were on the first floor, and if she could guarantee having the same seat each week, anyone coming off the escalator would be within her line of sight.

'I met some nice people,' she told Jess as she thought about all the names and the unexpected stories behind them.

'Daisy cope all right?' Jess asked.

Sienna nodded.

They were a mixed bag, Sienna thought, still unsure of how she'd go in a class with people of different ages from so many places. On the plus side, she'd managed to get out, do something different. Cathy had talked about excursions to the gallery and some famous house in the town. She wasn't too crazy about the idea of going to new places, but she tried to be rational. They didn't sound like the kind of places where she'd run into Cole.

'There's stuff you can put on that,' Jess was saying.

Sienna realised she'd been chewing at a piece of skin sticking out from the side of her nail. She bent her head and hid her hand in her lap.

'I'm not judging you,' said Jess. 'Just don't want you getting a nasty infection.'

Sienna shrugged. 'That's okay. My brother used to do it all the time. I hated it.'

'Do you contact him?'

Sienna pulled her phone out of the pocket of her hoodie.

'That's Hugo.' She held the phone out to show Jess her favourite photo of them both. Their father had taken it at a surf comp a few months before he'd been killed. Arms around one another, boards either side, pissing themselves at how long it had taken their dad to work out how to take the photo on Sienna's first phone.

'You look close,' said Jess.

'We message once in a while. He thinks I'm still with Cole, living the idyllic Tassie life.'

'Why don't you tell him the truth?'

The truth about Cole, the truth about Gary Stone? What good would any of it do? Have Hugo fight her battles, bring more upset on their mother whose only happiness in life was finding love again after the tragedy of losing her husband?

'He's in the army, in the Top End. No point getting him all stressed out about me and Daisy.' She shrugged. 'At least one of us won't be a disappointment to our parents.'

She watched Jess take in what she'd said. Another worker had urged Sienna to let her brother know what was going on, but Jess didn't comment. Sienna was grateful when instead she changed tack.

'I got keys to the unit I told you about. Would you like to have a look?'

A nap back at the shelter would have been nice, but she knew she should take the opportunity. There would be other women waiting for her room. There would always be other women and children in need. She pulled on her small backpack and let the brake off the pram

'Won't hurt to look, I guess.'

⁓

As they drove up the steep hill out of the centre of town, Jess assured Sienna that regular buses would mean she and Daisy could get around easily. Sienna hadn't ventured far from the shelter since she arrived. Without a car, she'd been too afraid to take Daisy anywhere other than the shops. So many of her old classmates already had full licences and cars of their own when she'd left Queensland. Her mum had taken her driving once she'd got her learner's licence. That was another photo moment she'd stored away; the day she'd got her Ls and posed beside her mum's car. If only she'd stayed at home, she'd have her Ps by now. Maybe saved enough to buy one of those Wrangler jeeps she used to dream about. Cole had promised to take her driving once they moved to Tassie. Said the roads were quieter. Better for a nervous driver. Her mum had never called her that. But numbed by meds, maybe she hadn't taken too much notice.

When Jess turned off the main road and into a driveway with speed humps, Sienna thought she'd come to a retirement village. The quiet crescent was lined with tiny red-brick bungalows with neat front yards and those windows that had lots of small panes. Net curtains and venetian blinds made it impossible to see inside. It was a far cry from her parents two-storey with its own stretch of beach right on the waterway. As they rounded the bend, Jess slowed to let a little white Getz back out of one of the single garages with funny archways. Sienna thought of her dream jeep. She'd been so naïve.

'Here we are!'

Jess had to pull up onto the square of lawn to park her Land Cruiser without blocking what Sienna imagined was next to non-existent traffic. She gathered Daisy onto her hip and followed Jess to the door. Compared to the other units, it looked like an empty shell. Vacated by someone who had died or moved into a care home, she thought as she stepped over the threshold and breathed in the stale smell. Cigarettes? Her grandmother had been a smoker. This was definitely the telltale sign.

'We'll get the walls washed down for you,' Jess was saying as she too registered the stench. 'It's not bad, though.'

With Daisy weighing heavy in her arms, Sienna trooped after Jess through to the bedroom where an old stained carpet made her want to vomit.

'That will have to go,' said Jess, her eyes following Sienna's gaze.

In the bathroom a line of rust ran from the showerhead down the curve of the bath to a drain blocked with all sorts of detritus. She would never be bathing Daisy in there. Her silence must have spoken volumes.

'Don't worry,' said Jess, 'we have an upgrade budget. You won't know this place once we've finished with it.'

Sienna wasn't sure if her case worker was trying to sell the place to her to make her agree to move in, but it wasn't like there was anyone else she could trust. She held Daisy a little tighter, let her cheek soak up the feel of her soft downy hair, and tried to imagine this place as the home they desperately needed, tucked away in a quiet corner of Devonport, hopefully out of Cole Sutton's reach.

Chapter Ten

Vivian shut her front door behind her and trudged to the kitchen where she shoved her laptop bag onto the bench and slapped the parking fine down beside it on the cool granite. As she filled the kettle, water gushed over her hand and splashed her sleeve.

'A fecking parking fine!' She was sure she couldn't have been more than ten minutes over. 'Those people!' As if the stress of getting to the library and delivering her first class hadn't been enough.

She put the kettle on to boil and pulled the kaftan over her head. In her walk-in robe, she found a spare hanger. She'd hang the garment up to dry. It didn't need a wash. A sniff at the underarm seams of her camisole confirmed that, despite working hard that morning, she hadn't even broken a sweat. *Pity calories aren't burned as much by thinking as exercising*, she thought, unable to avoid the sight of her muffin top in the full-length mirror. She'd be an Olympic athlete by now if overthinking had anything to do with fitness.

Popping an Earl Grey teabag into a mug, she poured the boiling water over it and sat on one of the stools at the kitchen bench. She took her laptop from her bag and logged in to her bank account. Despite not having spoken to her husband in weeks, she could see exactly where he'd been. Sixty dollars at the bottle-o, two hundred and fifty-six dollars at Woolworths . . . that was an awful big shop for one person, unless he'd taken cash out . . . Six hundred dollars at Kathmandu! He could nearly get to Nepal for that money. She knew he liked Kathmandu's outdoor clothing, but six hundred bucks . . . She took a deep breath and clicked on Payments. The parking fine was only thirty dollars, but this week already the car registration had been due, the mortgage had come out, and she'd only just paid the speeding fine for the time she'd driven down the highway, railing at her predicament, oblivious to the 80 sign.

She took a sip of her tea. A string of expletives were on the tip of her tongue, but she suppressed them. Getting het up about her situation was both futile and expensive. She had to take responsibility and put on what her nail tech called 'her big girl's pants'. Her regular manicure was probably something else to cut back on. With no sign of Dave coming back, perhaps it was time for separate accounts. He'd always taken care of the bills, but the mail came to her.

Vivian glanced at the pile of unopened letters in the basket near the kettle. One by one, she opened them. Just as she'd thought: an electricity bill you wouldn't get in Alaska, an insurance reminder she couldn't avoid, especially now that ringing Dave in the event of any vehicular or domestic mishap was no longer an option. Not to mind the series of donation requests for a multitude of natural disasters and charities they would have happily supported on two good salaries. The only donating she could afford right now was to the local op shop. In fact, the bags and boxes she'd filled were still in the boot of the car, waiting for the moment of supreme confidence it seemed to require for her to walk over the door. *This afternoon*, she promised. She'd reward herself with a stiff gin and one of those Netflix shows Deb kept texting her about.

As she clicked her way through the payment process, transferring money from the savings account that should have seen them road-tripping around the mainland, she remembered her mother's expression about robbing Peter to pay Paul. She wished she'd inherited her mother's talent for handling money. But her family weren't the kind she could call on to help her through the quagmire of her relationship. Her mother had never forgiven her for moving to the other side of the world in the first place. Phone calls were painful. Even the weather was off limits. If Vivian mentioned a storm or a wet winter, she would be cut off. 'Rain? Don't talk to me about rain,' her mother would counter. 'We've had the mother and father of a storm!' It was as if the weather had turned into a competitive sport or a high stakes card game. *You play a shower of rain, I'll raise you two floods.* Maybe her mistake had been inviting her family for Christmas one year when the gods spoiled them with an unusually steady run of beach weather, reinforcing their belief they had it good.

In a recent phone call, her mother had asked after Dave. 'He's still on the mainland,' Vivian told her, knowing her mother's declining mental faculties wouldn't remember from one week to the next the details of her family members' whereabouts. Vivian had told her he was grand. Visiting a friend. 'Is he still up there with that Cork fella?' she asked. Vivian was taken aback. The woman could hardly remember her grandchildren's names and yet that detail about Dave had stuck. 'I always thought you were mad to go all that way with him,' she said. 'A bit late to come back now I suppose.' Vivian wasn't sure if this was one of her mother's lucid moments or whether she'd lost the plot completely. In any case, she may have had a point, but Vivian *was* here now, Dave or no Dave. This was where she'd built her adult life. Her mother had been right about one thing. There was no going back. Not much in the way of going forward either. *One day at a time*, she reminded herself.

An email popped up from Cathy Shannon. *Thank you so much for this morning's session. What a great start to our writing project!*

Vivian sat back and re-read the message. Her shoulders dropped as she let the much-needed praise settle over her. The morning had gone well. All the nerves, the churning stomach, the tossing and turning the night before, imagining all sorts of shortcomings in her delivery had been unnecessary. But could she repeat it in a week's time? Perhaps if she prepared now, she could park it for a few days. Taking the notebook from her bag, she looked over the plans she'd made with Cathy. Then she opened a blank document on her laptop and typed: *Session Plan Week Two.*

She began by listing the names of her students together with a short piece of information she'd gleaned about each one, then she typed *Find Someone Who*. A quick get to know you exercise would hopefully build on connections made the previous week and give the new student a chance to mingle. After that they would look at different types of texts. She brainstormed ideas, listing all the reasons they might have to write in their everyday lives. Their trip to the gallery was booked for Week Three. There would be vocabulary to pre-teach to ensure the non-native speakers could keep up with the guide. They could have a look at the website on the smart-board before they went across. She'd walk them through how to write a recount . . . As the ideas came, so did the flow. Almost an hour passed before Vivian registered the time. She was two weeks ahead and feeling much better. Maybe Cathy's idea of taking an organic approach and getting to know the students before doing too much planning wasn't a bad one. It wasn't how she'd normally work, but lately, everything else had steered well clear of normal. Why not this?

Instead of the possible visit from her daughter she'd mentioned to Cathy, Vivian spent the weekend alone. With the house decluttered and cleaned to within an inch of its life, she turned to the garden that threatened to become a jungle if she didn't get a handle on it. She was bent over a row of fat zucchinis, wondering what Marilyn from the writing class would make of her gardening skills, when the phone chimed in her pocket.

Careful not to cover it in soil, she shook off one of her gloves before taking out the phone and opening the text.

Just checking in x

She sat back on her haunches, took off her sunhat and set it down beside her. Pulling off the other glove, she looked at the message again. *Checking in?* As her shoulders slumped, part of her longed to tell Dave about the writing class, how stressful it had been to even consider, but how she'd managed to get through the first session. She might cry down the phone and wait for him to offer encouragement and tell her how proud he was of her. He would soothe and comfort her, promise to come back that evening and take her to bed . . . But what was the point of letting emotion into the mix when he'd clearly decided to stay away? She tossed the phone into the sunhat and turned to hack away at the bristly zucchini stems, severing the green lengths with her Stanley knife and casting them into the gardening bucket.

A photo would have shown him how the silver beet they'd planted together had overtaken the top half of the plot they'd carefully laid out two summers before. She was sure he'd love to see the tomatoes turning from green to red on the stakes he'd driven in with that old mallet he used for everything that wouldn't budge. The carrots, tiny wrinkly looking things, but recognisable nonetheless. He would be so pleased. If he never came back, it would be *her* veggie patch, every sodding inch of it. The plants hers to harvest, the weeds hers to dig out. She hadn't even wanted a veggie patch! It had been another one of the projects she'd gone along with out of love. Yes, love. She gathered her bucket and tramped to the back of the house. No, she wouldn't respond to his text. If he needed space, she'd give him space. Didn't he know how she was anyway? Half the community was probably in touch with him, mentioning her in dispatches. He'd know fine well how she was. There was no need to be checking in.

Chapter Eleven

Marilyn took the roast lamb out of the oven and set it on the large serving plate she'd run the hot tap over to warm. Into a measuring jug she poured the excess juice from the meat and mixed it in with the gravy she'd made up from the tin she always kept in her pantry. The boys were going to love this dinner, she thought as she hummed along to the radio. First time in nearly a year, she would have the whole family sitting down together for Sunday dinner. She'd been up since dawn cooking, cleaning and setting the table just so. Frank's contribution had been to help drag the trestle table and extra chairs out of the shed when Marilyn convinced him they'd have more room outside. He'd grumbled the entire time, despite her taking most of the weight of the table and shifting most of the chairs. If he had his way, they'd all be in the lounge room, telly on high volume while they ate in near silence from dinner plates on their laps, the grandchildren sitting on the carpet around the coffee table, all on their parents' phones. When he'd left her to wipe the cobwebs off the table, he'd returned to his usual spot, wearing out the far end of the sofa where he watched endless television.

'Smells like Christmas in here!' Ethan appeared, bed hair at all angles around his stubbly face.

She gave his hand a gentle swipe as he reached for the chocolate Flakes she was planning to sprinkle on the pavlova.

'Don't even think about it,' she said. 'Get and have a shower before they arrive.'

He gave a resigned sigh but did as she asked. Although he'd wasted half the day lying in his bed, she knew he'd be the one to lend a helping hand later when it came to washing up after the family gathering.

At the sound of the doorbell, Frank shouted from the lounge room, 'Who the fuck is that?'

Wiping her hands on her apron, Marilyn went to see who was calling at this most inconvenient time. Any family members would have walked straight in or come round the back. But she needn't have worried. Through the frosted glass panel to one side of the door, she saw Jamie and the shape of someone she didn't recognise beside him.

'Since when did you ever ring the bell?' As she pulled open the door, she took in the small Asian woman beside him.

'This is Neha, Mum.'

Marilyn wasn't sure if she might be dreaming as she took in the sight of her unusually scrubbed-up Jamie and the cheery creature who held her hands like she was praying and bowed her head of jet-black hair. Frank was going to love this, *not*, she thought as she forced her mouth into a smile.

'Why didn't you come round the back?'

'Wasn't sure if Dad would be okay with me bringing . . .' He gave a sideways nod of his head toward the woman Marilyn took to be the pen pal he'd told her about. She stood to one side to let them in.

'Only one way to find out.'

Before she could follow them, Brad's car appeared in the driveway. It had hardly stopped when her two grandsons jumped out and barrelled in past her, shouting in an argument they weren't about to finish just because they'd entered her home.

'Boys!' Brad barked.

Her daughter-in-law emerged from the vehicle with a face that could turn milk sour.

'We can't stay long,' she told Marilyn. 'The boys have a birthday party . . .'

'That I wasn't told about,' Brad rounded. He shot Marilyn a look she read as half smouldering anger and half apology. She sucked in a breath.

There was always something with those two. Julie used the kids as a bargaining chip. Her son would promise to bring them over, and at the last minute, he'd text to say Julie had them at her folks' or that they had something on. Frank would go off at him about giving his mother more notice and showing her respect, but it wasn't as if he'd been a great role model in that regard. Marilyn didn't hold it against Julie. It wasn't her fault her husband chose to stay out all night getting up to mischief.

Ignoring them, Marilyn went to the car window. 'Where's Keisha hidin'?'

Her granddaughter sat sobbing into the comfort blanket she should have long grown out of.

'What's up, hun?' Marilyn pulled the door open and stepped aside to let the nine-year-old out. The sobbing didn't abate.

'Oh, suck it up, princess.' Brad tugged the blanket from the child's arms and threw it on the back seat before slamming the door.

Marilyn put an arm around her granddaughter's shoulders and bent to kiss the top of her head.

'Those boys been playing up?' she asked.

Keisha nodded. Marilyn wanted to wring their necks at times. Brad and Julie were far too tolerant of their behaviour, but she risked seeing even less of them if she caused any more drama. She led Keisha toward the house. 'Nan's got a special lunch ready 'cause Uncle Jamie's home.'

Brad let out a snort, but she shot him a glance and took the child inside.

'Keisha!' Jamie met them at the back door and squatted down to be at eye level with the girl. 'You been missin' your favourite uncle?'

'As if!' Ethan gave his brother a playful push that made his backside hit the deck and sent Keisha into a fit of giggles.

Marilyn was grateful her sons' antics made the child forget whatever had upset her. She went back to work on dinner, keeping one eye on proceedings outside through the kitchen window. Jamie's date looked so out of place. 'Won't last,' she murmured to herself as the two young boys chased each other round the table, bashing past Neha's chair without noticing or caring; it was exactly the behaviour that would convince the young woman she was dating a bloke from the wrong kind of family.

'Frank around?' Julie asked, hands in her pants pockets like they were hoping they wouldn't be called upon to help. Julie never helped. She probably thought it was Brad's job as it was his mum's place, but Marilyn gave her a job anyway.

'Go and tell him dinner's nearly ready, will you, darl?'

Julie's eyes scanned the kitchen bench where Marilyn had begun to set the serving dishes she'd loaded up with crispy roast potatoes and steamed veggies she'd plucked from her garden. Without a word of praise or interest, Julie turned on her heel and headed in to the lounge room.

'Who's that with Jamie?' Frank's too loud voice caught her off guard as Marilyn hefted the meat dish toward the back door. As she turned back to face him, the hot juice splashed, seeping through her apron and t-shirt, into her skin where she registered the burn. Had Jamie introduced the woman to his father or had Julie just broken the news?

'I . . . I didn't invite her.' It was the only thing Marilyn could think to say in her own defence. With the skin smarting under her shirt, she hurried out the door and set the roast lamb at the closest end of the table. 'Brad, can you look after that? It's super-hot.'

In the bathroom, she scrunched up the end of her shirt and ran the cold tap. Holding the wet fabric to the burn mark, she searched the vanity for aloe vera. Even before they sat down, she knew the dinner would be a disaster.

Apart from her grandsons pushing and shoving one another and making the mean remarks Marilyn wished their parents would put a stop to, there was a quiet around the table. She told herself it was the good meal she'd served up as they all tucked in, passing round the gravy boat she'd already had to replenish. First to finish, Jamie pushed his plate a little away from him. As he leaned back, placing an arm around the back of his girlfriend's chair, he had that naïve look about him Marilyn knew only got him into trouble.

'Anything new happen since I was away?' he asked.

Frank gave a mocking grunt as he shovelled a forkful of meat into his mouth. Marilyn wished he'd chew with his mouth shut, at least when they had company.

'Mum's doing a course at the library.' It was Ethan. He looked at her with admiration.

'And who said you can't teach an old bitch new tricks?' Frank gave a raucous laugh that sent him into a horrible phlegmy coughing fit.

Mortified, Marilyn could only hope Neha didn't get the reference. She knew the boys weren't impressed by the put-down, but they did what they'd always done and let the comment pass.

'Come on, boys.' Julie jumped up from the table and held out a hand to indicate to Brad she wanted the car keys.

'Won't you stay for the pav?' asked Marilyn.

'If you'd invited us earlier, we could have stayed longer,' said Julie.

Marilyn could hardly believe the cheek of her daughter-in-law but wouldn't cause a scene by saying so.

'Can I stay?' It was young Keisha who was giving her mother a pleading smile.

'No.' Julie cut her off. 'See you, Frank.' She said it as if her father-in-law was the only person at the table.

'Say goodbye to Nan,' Brad told the kids.

But only Keisha came and gave Marilyn a cuddle. The boys barrelled back through the house, just as they'd come in, already focussed on the next event in their social calendar. When she went to serve her pavlova, Marilyn noticed the Flakes were missing from the counter and fingermarks had scored the edges of the cream. Still smarting from Frank's comment, she ran a knife over the pav to hide the damage and put some icing sugar through a sieve to tart up the mango and strawberry topping. In the garden, Frank was downing his fifth can of beer while their two younger sons and Neha tried to make the conversation he was refusing to be part of. Why had Jamie brought that girl home? Being in a class in the library with her kind was one thing, but a girl like her didn't belong under their roof. She was never going to hear the end of it from Frank if her son didn't break up with her.

Chapter Twelve

Week Two

On Friday, Marilyn stepped onto the ferry boat and left her life in East Devonport behind for a few hours. Whatever drama she might return to, she could put to one side to focus on what faced her in the library. To say she'd been somewhat overwhelmed the week before would have been an understatement. She'd told Georgie about all the accents and introductions. She'd had to concentrate to keep up, given her brain a right workout, and that was before any of the actual work got underway. But her friend only encouraged her to keep going. She was there now and would give it at least another go.

In the library, she found Cathy all smiles, speaking to a big man with a cane she didn't recognise.

'Good morning, Marilyn!' she said as she greeted her at the door. 'Nice to see you've come back to us.'

Marilyn huffed and carried on into the classroom where their teacher was deep in thought, reading from a notebook like the one they'd all received the week before. The tall, elegant woman looked immaculate in a pair of linen trousers and another one of those kaftans Marilyn sometimes touched in shops. Light, airy things, she imagined would feel all stylish and floaty on. Not that she'd ever wear one.

When she sat down, Marilyn saw Vivian turn to speak to Cathy and the man she presumed would be joining them and took in Vivian's classy jewellery: the black necklace with a small silver ball that sat between a decent pair of collar bones; the matching drop earrings with the same balls that swung back and forth as she spoke. Frank would think she was losing her marbles if she brought home any of that gear. It would be enough to give him a heart attack. He'd already had one too many of them and all.

From the doorway, the short grey-haired man about her own age caught her eye as he entered the room. He smiled like he was genuinely glad to see her. Oscar, if she remembered rightly, but there was no point getting too friendly if she wasn't entirely sure she wanted to be here.

'That one free?' the man asked, gesturing to the spot beside her.

'Sure is.' Part of her wanted to dash out through the open door, but she'd spent that long going over the whole prospect of coming here with Georgie that she knew her friend would be sorely disappointed if she pulled out. If nothing else, it had given them something to talk about other than their dysfunctional families and the comings and goings of the sex shop.

The younger bloke with a ponytail came in and took a seat opposite her. Marilyn gave him a smile as he sat down, thinking he might need bit of encouragement too. When he smiled back, she noticed the John Travolta dimple in the middle of his chin. But instead of Danny in *Grease*, she found herself likening him to the hero in one of her books. In her mind she was fitting him out in denim jeans and one of those flannies, the check shirts worn by Australian cowboys, and an Akubra of course. He had the face for an Akubra, the jawline anyway.

'Had a good week?' he asked as he took off his worn leather jacket and hung it over the back of his chair.

'Yeah, mate,' Oscar answered. 'What about you?'

Marilyn took in the tobacco-stained fingers and each tattoo that appeared as he rolled up the sleeves of his faded shirt. Her boys all had tattoos. Brad even had Julie and the kids' names done on his arms. She wondered if the surgery to remove them had come far enough in case Julie ever decided to leave him. She didn't mind tattoos, but she'd always insisted her sons look after their appearance. Only Brad took any notice. His brothers called him a babe magnet, as if keeping yourself neat and tidy had the sole purpose of getting women into bed. She gave a mental shake of her head. Those boys had pushed her to her limits. But what was done was done. She was here now, trying desperately to do something for herself. With fifty calling, her life was in danger of grinding to a halt with nothing to do except cook and clean for Frank and the rest of them whenever they cared to call round.

'Good morneeng!'

At the sound of the accent, Marilyn glanced sideways past John Travolta to where the stunning woman with the long dark hair was manoeuvring one of those running prams between the tables. Cathy waved her laptop out wide like a traffic cop to indicate where they should park as the other mum-and-baby team came in behind them. Marilyn had hardly seen the light of day when her boys were babies, let alone attend a course with any of them.

With prams parked and everyone who'd been there last week present and ticked off on Cathy's device, Marilyn hoped they could get on with it. The noise in the room subsided. Only the Asian woman was still milling about at the front, fussing over pen and paper supplies, asking Vivian if she could help by handing them out now or if she might wait until later. When the teacher politely declined the offer, the woman's eyes shone with undeterred enthusiasm as she turned and took a seat. *A coiled spring*, thought Marilyn as she hoped she wouldn't get landed with her on any group tasks.

'Good morning, everyone,' said Vivian. 'If you have your name card from last week, can you put it in front of you?' There was some shuffling of bags and notebooks as they all retrieved the name plates they'd made the week before. 'Okay, has anyone done any writing since I saw you last?' she asked. 'Any journalling maybe?'

There were a couple of mumbles. Marilyn said a silent prayer she wouldn't be picked on to answer, but the lady from South America was onto it, multitasking with her baby squirming at her breast.

'Rosa, what have you got for us?'

'I write something every day. About my kids, my house-work, just trying you know?'

'That's wonderful, Rosa,' said Vivian. 'Keep at it. Anyone else?'

Beside her, Oscar began to shift in his seat. With no one else forthcoming with a response, he offered to go next. Reaching into a breast pocket, he unfolded a pair of battered-looking glasses that only had one arm. They looked a bit lopsided when he put them on, but it didn't seem to bother him. He cleared his throat and held his notebook a little away from him.

'I wrote about my dog,' he said and began to read, 'I am grateful for my dog as he gets me out of the house. He is a good dog, gives me no trouble, and barks his head off if someone comes near the house.'

There were a few laughs, then gasps as a lens fell out from the side of the glasses with no arm. Oscar caught it in a practised move that had Marilyn wondering why he didn't just get them repaired. As he went on about the dog alerting him to a tree falling at the property where he was house sitting for his sister, Marilyn saw that Oscar had written far fewer words than he'd actually 'read'. When their eyes met, he looked like he might die of embarrassment.

'Ah, that's great, Oscar,' Vivian was saying.

Regardless of what he'd written, Oscar had kept the ball rolling and, one by one, the rest of the class spoke about being grateful for things like living in Tasmania, their children's health, supportive partners, the library itself. Even Vivian added from her own list, which she told them she'd only jotted down on a sticky note when she got in. At least she was honest.

'I'm grateful for my children's health too,' she read, 'and for a lovely bit of sunshine today.'

Marilyn looked out of the room's extensive windows where a cornflour sky stretched high above the buildings. Gratitude hadn't come easy of late. Worry in spades, but gratitude not so much. She didn't volunteer to contribute. Vivian locked eyes with her for a moment, but instead of pushing it, she spared Marilyn with another of her own reflections.

'I'm also very grateful that you all came back,' she said.

Marilyn wanted to shrink into the seat with the guilt of knowing she may not be there the following week.

'So, let's do a quick get to know you exercise to recap from last week and bring our new student up to speed,' said Vivian.

Marilyn stood up and shuffled to the back of the room where the Asian woman was handing round papers and pens. *Here we go*, Marilyn thought, she grumbled only half under her breath.

She pulled the glasses down from her head and tried to follow as the teacher explained how they needed to get a signature to match each description on their sheet.

Marilyn glanced round to see who she could buddy up with. The quiet young mum was closest. With the baby asleep in the pram, they might even get this done without any caterwauling.

'You want to do this together?' she asked.

The girl nodded. 'That would be great.'

At least she looked and sounded Aussie, thought Marilyn. She'd be able to understand her.

'Righto.' Marilyn began to read the first entry on the sheet. 'Find someone who is hardworking and diligent.'

She spotted Amalia, but others were already beside her getting her to sign their sheets. Scanning down the page, she turned to Sienna. 'Why don't we work up from the bottom?'

'Sounds good to me.'

'. . . name means golden phoenix.'

'I remember that one,' said Sienna. So did Marilyn.

'C'mon,' she said and led the way to where Robyn was standing, looking confused. 'Hi. Will you sign there?'

'Oh, I can't remember anything from last week,' Robyn began, but took the pen and drew what looked like the shape of a house. Seeing Marilyn's confused expression, she explained, 'It's Cantonese.'

Marilyn thought of all the lovely food in the Chinese restaurants she and Georgie used to frequent on the mainland, but she focussed on the task. 'Here, I'll sign yours as we're at it.' They swapped sheets.

As Sienna enthused about the Chinese lettering, Marilyn signed opposite *named after a movie star.* She was glad she'd never been a movie star with all this autographing business.

'What a great way to get to know everybody,' Sienna was saying to the older man Marilyn hadn't spoken to yet. 'Does your name mean *bear*?'

'Yes. Bjørn is Norwegian for bear.'

At the sound of the deep voice and strange accent, Marilyn looked up from her paper. He wasn't from here either. She took in his longish grey hair and piercing blue eyes. Bear? In her view, silver fox suited him better. She allowed herself an inward smile.

When she and Sienna had filled their sheets, Marilyn flopped down and set her paper and glasses in front of her. Rubbing a hand across her face, she felt the heat in her cheeks. A nana nap might be in order this arvo. As Rosa's baby started to bawl, she looked away. The South American woman had whipped out the boob and stuck the child on with no sign of embarrassment. This place was almost as much of a mad house as her own.

When they'd compared sheets, the teacher finally set them some real work. They were going to learn about forms. Vivian put them in groups and gave each group a drawstring bag. Marilyn wasn't unhappy to be put with Bjørn and Oscar. At least there wouldn't be any crying babies at their table.

'In these bags,' the teacher began, 'is a collection of words we come across when filling in forms. Maybe a form for a driver's licence or a passport, or like the one Cathy gave you when she chatted to you about doing this course . . .'

'Those Centrelink forms are a nightmare,' said Johnny. He wasn't wrong there, thought Marilyn.

'Exactly! Thanks, Johnny,' said Vivian.

Marilyn had her doubts about their teacher ever having to fill in a Centrelink form, but she kept the thought to herself.

'I'd like you to take turns pulling out a word from the bag and talking about what it means on a form and what you might put down.'

When they suggested she go first, Marilyn wasn't sure if Oscar and Bjørn were being gentlemen or just plain chicken. She huffed and drew the first card.

'Marital status,' she read.

Bjørn poked a finger at the card and turned it to get a better look. 'Status, I know,' he began. Marilyn noticed the swollen knuckles, recognising the arthritis she knew all too well. With no contribution from Oscar, she took it upon herself to explain.

'Are you married, single . . . ?'

'Divorced,' said Oscar, his voice quiet.

'We're de facto,' said Marilyn. Frank had asked her time and time again to marry him. Saying no had felt like a kind of insurance, a way out if she was ever desperate enough. So far, she'd never managed to leave. She had Ethan to think about. As long as their youngest was under their roof, someone had to be there to keep the peace. Besides, the prospect of ending up sleeping on a sheet of cardboard in a park didn't fill her with enthusiasm. At least they *had* a roof over their heads.

'I'm a widow,' said Bjørn.

'No, you're not.' She turned and smiled at him, realising she may have sounded rude. 'Sorry for your loss, Bjørn, but if you were a woman and your husband died, you'd be called a widow.'

'Ah,' he said, the explanation dawning on him. 'Is there a word for a man who loses his wife?'

'Widower,' said Oscar. 'Just don't ask me to spell it.'

'That's right,' said Marilyn. 'Not a word you hear very often, is it?'

She passed the bag to Bjørn.

'Dep-end-ents?'

'That's kids, isn't it?' asked Oscar.

Vivian had come to see how they were getting on. 'I think it can be a spouse too,' she said. 'Anyone who relies on someone for support if they're not working.'

Oscar looked nervous as he took his turn and pulled a card from the bag. He hesitated before sharing,

'Ab . . . ad . . . address.'

Marilyn waited as Oscar stuttered over the word, a little taken aback at the hesitancy in his voice.

'What else we got?' She reached into the bag to get past the cringe-worthy moment. 'Given name.'

Beside her, Bjørn shook his head. Leaning closer to see her card, he gave a tut.

'So many names,' he began. 'First name, middle name . . .'

'Family name, Christian name,' Oscar added. Marilyn was relieved to hear his confidence return.

'Not just me!' said Bjørn, smiling.

'My wife did all our paperwork,' said Oscar. He gave a regretful sigh. 'Now I wish she hadn't.'

Marilyn raised her eyebrows at the candid remark. She thought how frustrated Frank always got with bills and forms, swearing and carrying on about the stupid government and their endless documentation. Thinking about it for the first time, she considered whether the bullish behaviour was a front to cover up a weak point. She doubted Oscar would have carried on like that. He struck her as an honest ordinary bloke, but who knew what anyone went through behind closed doors? Like that young girl with the baby; looked well brought up, sounded it too, yet here she was with the rest of the motley crew. Marilyn wondered what *her* story was, but she wouldn't get involved. Mightn't be here long enough to find out.

Their next task was to have a go at filling in actual forms. Vivian instructed them to use block letters. Marilyn always did the newspaper crossword in capitals. Easier to make out, she reckoned. The forms were easy for her, been doing them all her life, for her and Frank, for the kids. But as she glanced over at Oscar's paper, she could see he'd barely written his name. Bjørn was having a red-hot go, making deliberate marks in the boxes and on the lines provided. Something told her he enjoyed the challenge. Oscar on the other hand looked in pain. She noticed he even had to check his phone when filling in his phone number. Perhaps it was a new phone, but he'd crossed out his address twice and his email didn't look real. Marilyn was grateful when Vivian came round and gave him a hand. The woman was patient, not putting him down. They talked about how he could use something called 'speech to text' on his phone to see how the words looked. Vivian helped Bjørn too. Even asked Marilyn if she agreed with some of the suggestions she'd made about his work. For once in her life, she was the best at something.

❧

Any satisfaction was short-lived when Vivian asked each of them to collect a laptop from a little trolley that had appeared at the front of the room. Marilyn hung back as others went to retrieve the computers that stood on one end like books with wires plugged in to them. When Marilyn sat back down with hers, she kept an eye on what Johnny and Oscar were doing, her palms clammy at the thought of making a fool of herself. Up to now, she hadn't done too badly. Computers, however, were not her thing.

'How're you going, Marilyn?' Johnny leaned toward her, cheery as ever.

'Ugh! I could throw it!' She felt the heat rising in her cheeks as he looked at her screen.

Despite typing in the details Vivian had on the smartboard four times, Marilyn could not make the machine do what it was meant to do.

writingclass@devonportlibrary . . .

'Did you put the dot after Devonport?'

She pushed her glasses down her nose and glanced up again at the smartboard. A stupid dot? She let out a long sigh and followed his instructions. The rest of the class was probably already filling in those online forms the teacher was talking about. When was it ever going to be morning tea?

Marilyn was grateful to see the back of the computers. After morning tea, Vivian got them to work on whatever writing they were interested in. She thought about her books and Cathy's encouragement. With a resigned sigh, she began to write down what she thought of the last book she'd read. It gave her space from the chat in the room and those damn machines. Although her hand got a bit sore halfway down the page, she kept going. Anyway, the teacher was flat out helping others to even get started. Oscar was still working on forms. When Vivian finally got a chance to come and ask how she was going, she was full of praise for the amount Marilyn had written and how much detail she could remember. She went to look away, not sure how to handle the praise, but Johnny caught her eye and gave her a wink. God, they'd just made her decision about continuing this course all the harder.

Chapter Thirteen

Marilyn got off the boat and walked the last stretch of her journey home. After several arguments with his father, Jamie was steering clear of the place. Ethan would be out at work. With any luck, Frank might still be round at his mate's which could mean coffee or a stop off at the takeaway shop, but which invariably included a trip to the bookies. She could run a hot bath and enjoy a quiet house. Thoughts of the warm soapy water on her skin almost made her forget the soreness in her feet and legs from tramping back and forth to the library. But when she spotted Frank's car parked in the driveway, the soreness returned, making her feel every step as she trudged toward home.

Inside, Keisha was sitting at the kitchen table, a schoolbook open in front of her. Hearing her come in, the child looked up and gave her a smile. Marilyn knew instantly all was not well, but like she did with most matters regarding her family, she'd wait to be told.

'Hello, darl. What you doin' here?'

Frank was sitting on the couch in front of the television. He glanced round and made a face that let her know he wasn't happy.

'Pop had to get me,' said Keisha. 'I got sent home 'cause of headlice.'

Marilyn closed her eyes before turning back to the child. This was the third time she'd had them. The teacher, Marilyn suspected, was trying to send a message to Brad and Julie that did not mean simply palming her off on her grandparents.

'That's no good!' Her fingers went involuntarily to her own head and she started to itch. 'Your brothers not got them?'

The child shrugged.

'You just give Nan a minnie to get some lunch for us and Pop, and we'll give those nits a dose of what's good for them.'

'Thanks, Nan.'

Marilyn sighed as she took the pot of soup she'd made the day before from the fridge and set it on the cooker to warm. Taking a loaf of sliced bread, she buttered several pieces and set them on a dinner plate, keeping one eye on the girl as she worked. She made herself a coffee and took one to Frank.

'Soup won't be long,' she told him.

His response was a grunt. If he had a problem with soup made from the veggies in his own garden and the chicken stock she'd made from the bones of their Sunday roast, he could suck it up. At least she was trying to make the kind of healthy meals the doctor recommended.

'You doing school work?' she asked as she came back into the kitchen.

Keisha leaned her chin into her hand and twirled a pencil between her fingers. So far, Marilyn hadn't seen her put anything on the page. She could see it was a workbook with boxes to be filled in. It occurred to Marilyn that, in seeing her grandchildren only on Sundays, or when it suited their mother, she missed out on most of what they were learning at school.

'Mind if I have a look?'

Keisha shook her head and pushed the book toward her.

'Let me get my specs.'

Taking her glasses from the handbag she'd hung in the hallway, Marilyn came back and sat down at the table. There were pictures and letters you had to unscramble to spell words. There was a man in a white coat with one of those things they listened to your lungs with around his neck, another man standing at a whiteboard like the one in the library, a woman in a space suit . . .

'Are they all job words?' she asked, hoping she'd caught on to the theme correctly.

'Yeah. Says it there.' Keisha pointed to the top of the page where it did indeed say, *Can you find the jobs?*

When the soup started to bubble, Marilyn shot up out of her seat to stop it from boiling. 'Just put the words in the boxes then. You have all the letters.'

After she'd turned down the heat and given the pot a stir, the boxes on the page were still empty and Keisha's chin was still leaning in her hand, her mouth twisting from side to side. The soup could wait. Marilyn sat down at the table and pulled her glasses back on.

'What's this fella do?'

'A doctor,' said Keisha.

'Starts with a *d* then, don't it?' She was in Grade 3 if Marilyn recalled. Surely, she'd learned to spell by now.

With her pencil gripped tightly in her fist, the girl put a *b* in the box. 'D–o–c—' she started to sound out.

'That's not a *d* though, is it?'

'I always do that!' Keisha slammed the pencil down on the page. 'My whole class think I'm dumb.' She folded her arms and sat back against the chair.

'Don't say that.' None of Marilyn's kids had turned out to be rocket scientists, but they were not dumb. They did dumb things, okay, but . . .

'It's true. Even the teacher said I was two grades behind.'

Marilyn felt her blood boil like the soup on the stove.

'When d'ya hear her say that?'

'She told Tamika Thornton's mum. That's our TA.'

Marilyn took a moment to push down thoughts of throttling the teacher and anyone else who trash-talked her granddaughter. There was a time she might have, but these days she'd leave that kind of drama to the young ones. She thought about those foreign ones in the library. Spoke three languages some of them, and yet they struggled to talk to each other. Marilyn thought how eager they were to improve their English. For the first time, she wondered how much it must take to put themselves out there. She'd be damned if Keisha couldn't read and write in her own language.

A strength of feeling welled up from somewhere deep inside. The kind of feeling she'd pushed down so many times and let others walk over her. They could roll over now, her and Keisha, or they could fight back. Didn't someone say something about the pen being mightier than the sword? She sat up a little straighter and looked squarely into the girl's eyes.

'Tell you what, if I help you with your homework, will you help me with mine?'

The child looked back at her, not understanding.

'See, *I'm* learning to write better an' all. Maybe we could . . .'

'We could be study buddies.' Keisha's beautiful big eyes were wide. It was the first time she'd looked happy since Marilyn had walked in.

Twenty minutes later, they'd unscrambled all of the words together. It had taken all the patience Marilyn could muster not to just do it for her, but she knew that wouldn't have helped in the long run.

'Any sign of lunch?' Frank appeared in the doorway between the kitchen and living room, hoiking his trousers over his belly.

Marilyn gave the child a wink and got up to serve their meal. Without being asked, Keisha packed away her school things and started to carefully transfer the bowls Marilyn filled to the table.

'Nan's helping me with my spelling,' Keisha told Frank. 'I'm helping her too.'

'Is that so?' He pulled out a chair and set himself at the table.

'So how was the Dim Sims today?'

Marilyn smarted at the remark.

'Dim sims?' Keisha looked confused.

Marilyn didn't respond, but when she turned to take her seat at the small table, Frank was pulling at the skin around his eyes and making their granddaughter laugh. She let him have his fun. At least it was only in the house. There'd be no harm done.

～

In the bathroom, Marilyn got Keisha to sit on the lid of the toilet so she could carefully undo the topknot that separated a section of hair from the rest of her long dark mane.

'Stay still,' she told the child who was turning from side to side to take in all the books that lined Marilyn's shelves.

'Did you actually read all of them?'

'Sure did. Some a few times.'

Keisha pulled in her stomach with a big breath and sat up straight, her eyes wide in amazement. Then, letting her torso slump, she said, 'Wish I could read them.'

Marilyn had to smile. 'I don't think your mum would be very happy with me if I let you read 'em.' She took the rubber showerhead from the bath and attached it to the mixer tap on the sink. 'Here, stick your head under there and I'll wash your hair.'

Keisha bent over the sink, hands on the porcelain edge, and let Marilyn run the warm water over her head.

'What books do *you* like to read?'

Face down, she took a moment to answer. 'I don't really read them . . .'

'What's that supposed to mean?'

'I take books home from school and everything. But mostly I look at the pictures.' Marilyn was grateful the child couldn't see the shock on her face. 'Sometimes Mum and Dad read them to me. Then I remember what they're about in case I get asked.'

Marilyn lathered Keisha's hair up with her special anti-nit shampoo. As much as she liked that Brad and Julie took the time to read to their daughter, she knew they were missing a golden opportunity to help her. Assistant or no assistant, the teacher would hardly have time to listen to them all read in the course of a busy day. Marilyn had always taken her granddaughter for a smart kid. Definitely smart enough to work out what those books were about, she realised. It would be enough to fly under the radar if she was asked to tell her class something about their stories.

She thought of the class in the library and how long it had taken for Vivian to get around everyone. At Keisha's school there were at least twenty-five in each class. But Marilyn knew she couldn't go poking her nose in. If Julie got wind of her interfering in the way she was raising her kids, she'd arc up and wouldn't let her see them for months.

After the painstaking task of fine-combing conditioner through the child's hair, Marilyn had dispatched a rake of ugly oval-shaped beasts. She rinsed her hair and wrapped Keisha's head in a towel, fashioning it into a turban and told her to go sit with her pop while she fixed them some afternoon tea. It would have been good to have left them reading one of the borrowed schoolbooks the girl couldn't decipher, but the only thing Frank read was the racing pages or the footy scores in the daily rag. Marilyn thought about it for a second. Maybe that wasn't a bad place to start.

'Your horse come in?' She tried to sound casual as she set a tray with two mugs of coffee and a hot chocolate on the coffee table they'd had forever. If she'd known the child was coming, she'd have bought a packet of Tim Tams or something from the bakery. At least she'd found the end of a packet of marshmallows from a previous visit.

'Damn mare never came anywhere.' Frank huffed and reached for his drink.

'Thought you might show Keisha what you been readin' in the paper.'

He eyed her over the top of his mug as he took a sip. 'Don't want to be giving our granddaughter any bad habits now, do we?'

'I won't bet or anything.' Keisha was earnest as she looked up at him, her eyes full of excitement.

'Just give her a look.' Marilyn winked at him. 'Might bring you luck.'

Frank shook his head but set down his mug and opened the paper all the same. By the time Julie arrived, he'd given young Keisha an insight into Tasmanian horse racing that left Marilyn wondering why they weren't millionaires.

Her daughter-in-law refused the offer of a cuppa. Said she'd left a friend watching the boys at the footy club. Marilyn told her what she'd used to combat the head lice.

'I could have done that when I got home.' Julie took the towel from Keisha's hair and shoved it toward Marilyn.

'It wasn't a problem. Done it that many times . . .'

'Nan helped me with my homework,' Keisha told her Mum. 'We're going to be study buddies.' With a broad smile, she squeezed her Mum's hand. 'Please let me come every Friday.'

Julie hesitated, but Keisha persisted.

'The boys get to go to the footy. I'm soooo bored waiting for them all the time.'

'I thought you did your homework there.'

Marilyn couldn't let the opportunity slip away. 'She's welcome here any time.' Lowering her voice, she added. 'Gives Frank a lift an' all.' She'd just used her partner's ill-health as a bargaining chip to spend time with her grandchild, but Julie had always got along better with Frank. She gave a resigned smile.

'If you're sure.'

Keisha jumped up and down. 'Your turn to do some work next week, Nan.'

Marilyn waved them off at the door. As the car pulled away, she let out a yawn. The library course might be taking her out of her comfort zone but if she could spend more time with Keisha it would be worth it. There was certainly no backing out now.

Chapter Fourteen

Week Three

Oscar joined the queue in the café on the ground floor of the library and ordered a large latte, triple shot. He'd already had a coffee this morning from his sister's fancy machine, sat out the back by her pool with Dog stretched out beside him, both needing a breather after an early bushwalk. The fresh air was doing him good, but it was still a struggle to keep up with the retriever. Turning to wait at one side of the counter, he noticed Vivian in the queue behind him.

'Morning, Oscar.' She gave her order and came to wait alongside him.

'Morning, Miss . . .'

She leaned her tall frame sideways so her head was level with his. 'Please, call me Vivian.'

'Triple shot latte!' the barista called.

He picked up the drink and came back to wait with Vivian. She nodded to his cup.

'Is my class that boring?'

It took him a second to realise what she meant. He laughed.

'No, no. I'd have no problem staying awake if it wasn't for this long Covid.'

She put a hand to her mouth. 'I'm so sorry. I shouldn't have . . .'

'Don't be sorry.' He shrugged. 'One of those things.'

He was grateful the barista rescued him from his least favourite topic.

'Skinny cap!'

Vivian collected the coffee and they fell into step toward the escalator.

'You're not local, are you?' she asked.

'I'm over from Melbourne,' he told her. 'House sitting for my sister and her husband. They're on a cruise.'

'Ah. Not sure if I'd be brave enough to . . .' He knew she'd stopped herself before mentioning the pandemic.

'They normally go on two a year.' He smiled, hoping to make light of it all. 'Making up for lost time, or so she tells me.'

'Morning, Vivian, young Oscar.' Cathy came along the corridor with her usual cheer. He left them to talk, anxious to sit and get the caffeine into him.

⌒

In the classroom, Oscar found a spot beside Johnny, the bloke from Iraq who'd helped him the week before when they'd had to fill out that sheet with their names and all that computer work. As he unpacked his pen and notebook from his back-pack, he noticed Johnny had brought in his own computer. Oscar didn't even own a computer. The Centrelink people said he could do everything on his phone. He preferred to go in there. Might mean long queues, but he had time to kill these days.

If writing wasn't his favourite thing, reading wasn't far behind. He'd been having a go at using the accessibility button Vivian had shown him on his phone. On a call with his son, Bobby, he learned he could use it in the supermarket to read things out to him. He could talk his shopping list into his phone too, Bobby told him. It was a backup, Oscar decided, saved time. He preferred to try working the words out before pulling the phone out. It just took so bloody long.

As Oscar chatted to Johnny about what they'd been up to in the intervening week, his classmate's easy manner made him forget his fears.

'Yeah, my boy lives in Japan,' he told Johnny. 'Very smart . . . like my sister. Got all the family brains those two.'

'Sounds like *my* sister,' said Johnny. 'Studying to be a lawyer. Born in Australia. Makes such a difference, I reckon, with learning English from the get-go and that.'

Vivian was at the front of the room, ready to make a start. As he watched the way she ran her fingers along the edges of her papers, Oscar realised he'd been right the week before when he'd suspected even she was a bit anxious. He wasn't sure whether to be relieved or worried, but so far so good.

'Another Friday!' she began. 'Thank you all for your efforts so far. We've spent the last couple of sessions getting to know one another a bit and talking about why and when we write, but today we'll be going across to the gallery . . .'

At the mention of getting out of the classroom, Oscar breathed a sigh of relief.

'When we come back,' Vivian went on, 'I'd like you all to have a go at writing a recount, so first I'll spend a little of our session showing you what I mean.'

For a moment, Oscar's fears returned, thinking he was back in school, but he sat forward and focussed on the board where Vivian began to draw one of her spider diagrams. As she invited their ideas, he remembered doing this kind of thing donkey's years ago when only the efforts of the clever kids stood out, the ones who'd be asked to read their work aloud, like essays, poems and these recount things. Last he'd heard, one of those fellas was a doctor in the Royal Alfred Hospital and another a published author. And here he was in his mid forties, hoping for a second chance to learn what had come so easily to them. He'd had plenty of ideas running around in his head. Just could never get them down.

Before shame got the better of him, Oscar opened his notebook and followed the others in jotting down the ideas from the board as best he could. At least it wouldn't be all bookwork today.

⁓

The gallery was literally across the way from the library entrance. Oscar couldn't remember if he'd ever been to a gallery. There were lots of them in Melbourne, of course, but it wasn't his thing. His son Bobby went to them. Him and his arty mates. Oscar used to like looking over the brochures he'd bring back from exhibitions and launches, but most of it went over his head. One of Bobby's pals painted big canvasses with thick lines that were supposed to represent the city. Sold quite a few of them too, according to Bobby. 'Money for jam,' Oscar's father would have said had he still been with them. But then, Willie Frost hadn't been big on fostering what he'd have termed 'soft leanings'.

Geraldine got all the educational opportunities like piano lessons and after-school tutors in the lead-up to exams. If his mother ever raised the possibility of Oscar doing anything other than playing footy with the local club, Willie shut her down. Oscar grew up thinking reading, playing piano and anything 'soft' was for girls. As he walked into the gallery, he allowed himself a small smile. If his old man could see him now.

In what their guide called the first exhibition room, they were met with the most vibrant display of women's clothes Oscar had ever seen. He stood in awe, taking in the sheer brightness of the space. Lots of bald faceless mannequins, the kind he'd seen in fancy shop windows, were dressed in dazzling outfits that contrasted with the simple black masks on the walls. It took him back to the days when Geraldine would make him play with her paper dolls, when going along with her favourite rainy-day activity was easier than getting into mischief and risking stoking the wrath of their mother. He was never a big fan of rain.

'A couple of women from Brisbane . . . museum archives . . . the global financial crisis . . .' He caught up with the guide as she mentioned how the designers outsourced the hand-crafting of the garments to countries like Vietnam and India. The rest of the group were already moving around, comparing their views on different outfits and posing for the photos the teacher encouraged them to take. Vivian appeared beside him.

'What do you make of this?'

'Never thought I'd be so fascinated by women's clothes.'

She laughed. 'I'm no fashionista, but this whole room is like a burst of sunshine. Would you look at that?' She pointed to the skirt of a sleeveless dress where what must have been thousands of sparkling yellow beads had been hand-sewn in layers.

'Wow!' He took a step closer and reached out to touch the garment, but her hand stayed his arm.

'We're not meant to touch them.'

When he turned, her cheeks were as red as his must have been.

'I was tempted too,' she said in a moment of mutual but not entirely uncomfortable embarrassment.

After admiring the various outfits, their guide invited them to go to the next floor. Vivian went to show Bjørn to where the women with babies were taking the lift.

'I'll go up with him,' said Oscar, hoping she'd think he was being helpful rather than needing the easy way up himself. The exhibition had made him forget he couldn't do things like he used to, but the thought of having to climb flights of stairs brought it all back.

In the lift, he tried to take a couple of surreptitious deep breaths. Rosa was oblivious, talking nonstop to Sienna about the alpaca knitwear she would like to import from Peru. Bjørn seemed to notice but didn't remark. Had enough of his own problems, Oscar reckoned as they reached the first floor. They joined the others in a long narrow room where photographs set at the same height lined each wall. Taking a slow wander, he recognised some of the places in Devonport: Geraldine's favourite brunch spot down one of the laneways off the main drag, a sea view toward the bluff and lighthouse, tree-lined streets that looked familiar.

'Do you like them?' It was the lady from China, Robyn.

'Yes, very much,' said Oscar, a little self-conscious. 'I recognise some of these places.'

'Me too.' She pointed to the café Oscar had recognised. 'I was there one time. Nice place.'

The previous week, she'd told them she'd been a tour guide back in China. He tried to imagine her leading a group in a place like this, talking fluently in her first language about the exhibits, knowledgeably, like someone who had the confidence to go wherever they pleased. When she'd walked into the classroom the first day, he'd presumed she was an Asian bride, keeping house for some Aussie bloke she'd met on the internet and providing whatever other services came with the role. Bobby would have given him a lecture about stereotyping, but he couldn't help it. He was old school.

A couple of his mates had met Asian women on the net and brought them to Australia. He'd been at barbecues where these women would produce bowls of delicious salads but could hardly string a sentence together, and he'd always wondered how they managed. He'd wished he had the courage to travel

overseas, even for a holiday, but all those signs in airports for
a start . . . He'd miss his flights for sure. Even the thought
of it made him sweat. No, Tassie was far enough for him.
He'd navigated the route from Melbourne enough times to
have made it almost stress-free. Bobby had asked him count-
less times to visit him in Japan, but he had enough troubles
with the English language without landing in a place where
everything was written in strange sketchings.

'We have one more exhibition for you,' their guide was
saying. 'If you'd like to follow me . . .'

Back in the lift, Bjørn gave Oscar a nod that he wasn't sure
how to interpret. He would like to have made conversation
with the man and indeed the two mums, but simply gave a
nod of his own and leaned against the side of the lift, happy
to let the oxygen return to the muscles that ached from all
the walking around.

In the top gallery, he took a seat beside Bjørn on a bench
where the Norwegian looked like he might be meditating.
Nearby, the guide explained the stories behind the pieces on
display and the mammoth task that had been involved in
transferring them from the old gallery. Oscar remembered
the converted church. He'd passed it so many times and never
gone in. Galleries were for educated people, he'd thought, and
yet here he was enjoying the creations of artists whose skill
and way of seeing the world had made him stare and wonder.
He had a feeling of having been allowed into a locked room.

As the guide spoke about award-winning paintings by local
artists, photos of the city in times gone by, ceramic bowls
in impossible shapes on plinths, he found himself equally

fascinated by the personalities he was beginning to get to know, people he would never have imagined spending time with. The South American woman was standing in front of a painting with Marilyn, stroking the fabric of her baby pouch with one hand while gesturing animatedly with the other. He wasn't sure Marilyn shared her enthusiasm. Robyn was quizzing the guide about the logistics of hosting the fashion exhibition. His mate from Iraq was doing his best to entertain the other baby who was squirming in the arms of the young mum called Sienna. He tried to imagine the parents who had named Sienna after the town in Italy where they'd got married. A pity they weren't around to mind their grandchild on Friday mornings, he thought. He'd sometimes wondered what it would be like to have grandchildren. If he ever kicked this long Covid, he was sure he'd be happy to look after them, take them on bushwalks, teach them how to make damper on a campfire. He might even share the poems and stories that sometimes popped into his head. He wouldn't be much good at reading them stories from books, that was for sure. But before today, he'd never have seen himself walking around an art gallery. Maybe there was hope for him yet.

'Can I join you?' Amalia didn't wait for an answer but plonked herself in the respectful space he'd left beside Bjørn. 'I guess she'll want us to write one of those recounts she was talking about next.'

'Ah!' Oscar gave a sigh. 'Just when I was beginning to enjoy this gallery lark.'

'It's not so bad,' Amalia countered. 'She explained it really well before. Especially for those other ones.' She made a vague gesture toward the middle of the room but Oscar knew she meant Robyn and Rosa.

'And me!' The zen Bjørn had been keeping up after all. 'I like the homework. Makes me think.' He tapped a middle finger to his head of once blond hair.

Oscar had nothing to add. Homework had never been his strong point.

As he turned into Geraldine's driveway, he saw the truck. T-O-T-A-L, Total Pool SER-VI-CES, the signage read. At the back of the house, he found a bloke in a high-vis shirt leaning over the side of the pool like a crocodile thinking about slipping in.

'G'day, mate.'

The pool bloke looked up. 'Just repairing the damage. Need to replace a filter and a few broken tiles. Will give it all a scrub while we're at it. Make it good as new.'

'Anything I can do to help?' Oscar asked. He used to do lots of maintenance jobs at his sister's house.

'Cleaning lady's asked, but all good.'

Oh god! Geraldine had mentioned the pool man, said something about phoning the cleaner. He'd completely forgotten to let her know. The tradie saw the look on his face.

'Don't worry, we gave her the heads-up when she got dropped off.'

Oscar left him to it and went toward the house, mortified at the thought of having to apologise to the woman. On previous visits he'd seen her in action, going through the house, flat chat, shooing them out of her way if they were foolish enough to enter a room with her in it. Geraldine found her so intimidating, she sometimes called her 'the boss'.

Oscar let himself in the laundry door, removing his shoes to limit the list of offences he'd be committing by invading her space. But instead of the earful he'd been expecting for his oversight, he was met by a woman hunched at the kitchen bench, loud sobs drowning out his footsteps.

'Hello there . . .'

Startled, she looked up. He took in the red tear-stained cheeks, the fine bones of her jaw. This wasn't Angie. The slim woman shot to her feet, and bringing her hands together, she bowed. She was younger than Angie. Mid-thirties, Oscar guessed.

'Sorry, I'm Oscar . . . Geraldine's brother?' In the awkward moment, he didn't know whether or not to bow back, but settled for a hopeful smile. 'I'm house sitting . . . looking after the place?'

As the young woman straightened, she took a tissue from her apron and dabbed at the corners of her eyes. She gave a nod and a small shrug. 'I work.'

Oscar went to say something about not knowing she was their new cleaner, to thank her for coming, make reference to the tradie, but as his mouth opened, she picked up the spray bottle and cloth from the bench and proceeded to clean the bar stools with a vigour that made him take a step back. Although he had no clue as to why she'd been so sad, and no right to know, it was clear she should be given the day off. The place couldn't have got that dirty in the last week.

'You don't need to clean today. I'm sure . . .' But she cut him off.

'I clean.' She gave a light laugh that sounded somewhat hysterical, but without missing a beat, her hand, cloth, whole body kept moving around the kitchen like her life depended on it.

Chapter Fifteen

After class, Sienna returned to the shelter to pack. It wasn't exactly a big ask. As she zipped the large sports bag she'd bought in an op shop, she took a last look in the drawers and wardrobe. The bag sagged in the middle. She'd way overestimated the amount of stuff she had to move to the new unit. Perhaps she'd been thinking of the suitcase she'd filled when they'd come from the mainland, the one Cole had sat on to help her close, teasing her about all the summer outfits he said it would be too cold to wear in Tassie. She wondered what he would do with them all now that she was no longer in the small weatherboard house they'd shared. Throw them in the fire pot one night and get stoned, watch them burn, fragments of fabric swirling in the orange flames before falling to a pile of ash? She thought of Robyn, the woman in the writing group who told them about her name. Could she become a phoenix, rising from the ashes of her relationship? She fed the straps of the bag over the pram and wheeled Daisy out of the room that had been their safe haven away from the world.

In the foyer, Jess was waiting to take her to what would become their new home. A shiver of dread tempered any excitement. Mandy came out from behind reception and gave her a hug.

'Good luck, darl.'

'Thank you.' Part of her wanted to fall in a screaming mess, but she knew she had to hold her nerve.

She caught the women exchange a look. They'd witnessed this kind of thing before; she had no doubt. There was a statistic she'd read about women leaving partners an average of seven times before leaving for good. Sienna had no intention of living that life, but in one of her nightmares, she'd seen a revolving door with Cole on one side holding a knife to her throat, threatening to kill her while on the other side, Mandy and Jess were smiling, welcoming her back to the shelter. Up to this point, she hadn't been able to imagine any other options.

'All set?' Jess pressed the button on her car key to unlock the doors.

Sienna nodded. As they drove away, she could see the African children playing four-square in the courtyard of the shelter. Their mother waved from where she sat in the shade in a swing chair, a swathe of bright fabric she was sewing in her lap. Waving back, Sienna wondered if she would ever see her again, if they would find a house with a garden where the children could play safely.

When they got to the unit, two men were unloading furniture from a large van. She recognised the logo on the vehicle and on the backs of their shirts. In Year 11, some of the students at her school had raised money for the charity. How innocent she'd been, never imagining herself at the receiving end.

Inside, the place looked completely different to when she'd come to view it with Jess. It was like something from one of those home reno shows she and her mum had liked to watch. The horrible carpet had been replaced with a light laminate floor covering that made the space look bigger. There was furniture too, thanks to the generosity of people she would never meet. Dead people? The thought gave her goosebumps, but she pushed it aside. More than anything, she was grateful. Holding Daisy close, she followed Jess on a tour. In the bedroom, a white cot was set beside a decent-sized bed. Jess was talking about taking a trip to Kmart to choose bed linen, but Sienna was quiet, taking in all the improvements that had been made since she'd agreed to take the place. A rundown laundry had been given a fresh coat of paint. Damage to the bedroom wall had been plastered over and repainted. There was no longer a drip from the shower and the bathroom sparkled with a just-cleaned look. She would love to keep it this way.

When they'd first moved into their house in Tassie, she and Cole had shared the housework. He'd talked about keeping their space clutter-free, prided himself on curating a selection of indoor plants they'd bought together, arranging their furniture to make their space look cosy. He'd come home in the early days with stylish storage baskets he said would be great for toys when Daisy arrived. But that was when the rot she hadn't noticed set in really began to take hold. She could see it for the jealousy it was after several counselling sessions. Once their daughter arrived, Cole no longer had her all to himself. He did a u-turn on wanting to be a father, said if she wanted a baby, she could look after it and 'all the shit that went with it'. 'It' was what Sienna had thought was going to be their lovechild. She thought he'd come round, put it down to the male post-natal depression she'd heard about, doubled down on her efforts to maintain the house the way he liked it. But he'd never comment, never offer a word of praise or gratitude.

She looked around at what would be their new home. Here, at last, she could make her own rules.

Not ready to be left alone just yet, she wished Jess could stay a while longer.

'Will you help me give Daisy her bath?'

Jess turned from where she was checking for smoke alarms. 'Sure. I'll be right back.'

When she went outside, Sienna heard her thank the delivery guys and make a call. 'Tell her I won't make the staff meeting today . . . yes, it's important I stay . . .'

As Daisy sucked on her chew toy, eyes searching her new surroundings, Sienna felt her shoulders relax. At least for the next hour or so they wouldn't be on their own. She went to the sparkling bathroom and ran the water into the tub.

Jess came back with a large carrier bag.

'I've got just the thing for bath time!'

Sienna couldn't believe Jess's kindness when she opened the bag and found a little seat to keep Daisy safe in the water and some plastic ducks. For a moment, she imagined how her mother might have showered her grandchild with gifts, how they might have shopped together for all the baby equipment she was now receiving from strangers. But she put aside the what-ifs and got on with the job of making Daisy's life as good as she possibly could.

Jess rolled up the sleeves of her cotton shirt, gathered her hair into a knot and got stuck in, soaping up a face washer and gently stroking Daisy's skin. She played a game where she'd hide one of the ducks under the bubbles and then release it to surface with a splash, sending Daisy into fits of contagious giggles. They sang 'Five Little Ducks Went Swimming One Day' until Daisy began to rub her eyes, and the soapy water made her cry. It was a joy to sit on the bathroom floor watching Jess soothe Daisy and wrap her in one of the two big fluffy shelter towels Mandy had let her keep.

'Do you have kids?' Sienna asked.

'One boy.' Jess smiled as she patted at Daisy's patch of fine hair. 'He's in high school.'

'Didn't you want any more?'

Jess shrugged, continuing to pat the towel over Daisy's skin. 'Wasn't to be.' She handed Daisy over and stood up, checking herself in the mirror over the vanity as she shook out her hair.

'Well, as nice as this has been, ladies, I'd really better get going.' She offered to hold Daisy again, but Sienna leaned one arm on the bath and pushed herself up. Since becoming a mother, one-handed manoeuvres had become her superpower.

'There's enough food in your cupboards to last until you're feeling up to going to the shops,' said Jess.

Sienna watched as she gathered her workbag and denim jacket from the new sofa and headed for the door. Before leaving she turned and touched Daisy's cheek.

'Be good for Mum.'

Daisy gurgled in response. When Jess put a hand on her arm, Sienna wanted to grab it and pull her into a hug, but she just stood wondering what the hell she would do when the woman walked away.

'You'll be okay, yeah?'

'Yeah.'

Tears welled in her eyes. Jess's face fell. She reached out and drew them both to her chest.

'First night's the worst.'

When they stood apart, she looked Sienna in the eye.

'I'll text you later to make sure you're okay, but please don't be afraid to call if it gets too much.'

Sienna sniffed back the tears and smiled. Jess had gone the extra mile, hanging around to help her with Daisy, but it was all on her now. She watched the car slow at the speed bumps that lined the shared driveway and disappear along the main road.

A dog in next door's garden who'd barked when they'd first gone to the door gave a lonesome whine. Sienna went to the fence that separated them from the next unit. She thought the poor thing might get stuck in the bars, such was the jumping and straining to reach her.

'Hello, neighbour.' She bent down, keeping Daisy a good arm's length away, just in case he was cross, but she needn't have worried. Like any staffy she'd met, he was a people dog. His hot tongue licked like crazy, as if her hand were covered in treats. When the front door of the house opened, a short heavy-set woman appeared barefoot on the veranda.

'Oi, Sandy.' The dog shot to the woman's side, sitting down on the concrete beside her and looking up with a pair of contrite eyes. 'Oh, you old sook,' she said, bending down awkwardly to give his smooth head a pat. 'Just moved in?' She was still looking at the dog, but Sienna nodded.

'I'm . . .' It occurred to her that it mightn't be a good idea to tell the woman her real name. 'Anna . . . and this is Elsa.' Okay, so she'd seen *Frozen* one time too many, but the woman would hardly get the reference.

'Tina.' The woman waved and gave Daisy a smile but didn't come any closer to the gate. 'Last one only stayed a couple of months.' She'd inclined her head toward their unit.

'Well, better get D—Elsa to bed.'

The woman was looking at her properly now. 'Ain't none of my beeswax how you two ended up here or how long yous'll be stayin', but Tina's my real name and I like to be a good neighbour if anyone round here needs me.' She reached under the neck of her washed out t-shirt and retrieved a phone from her bra. 'I don't want your number or nothin'. Just trying to find mine . . .'

Sienna added Tina to her contacts. She might never need her, but saving the number gave her a similar feeling to patting Sandy. She and Daisy weren't completely alone.

Later, as they lay in bed, the night-time sounds of the neighbourhood kept Sienna awake – the wind stirring up the bushes in Tina's garden, the occasional car travelling up the main road, a cat squealing out in fight or flight. She decided against watching endless TikTok videos as had become her habit. Instead, she tiptoed out into the small lounge room where a streetlight shed a swathe of silvery light on the vinyl floor. Finding her backpack, she took out the notebook and pen she'd been given at the library and curled up on the couch.

Opening the book in her lap, she thought about making a start on the homework, but it was late and there would be plenty of time to do that on one of the long, lonely days that lay ahead. Letting the pen play across the page, she started to draw the beautiful designer dresses they'd seen in the gallery. The blue ink pen didn't do them justice, but she was enjoying the freedom of putting exactly what she wanted on the page. She would buy some decent pencils and maybe some brush pens when she got a chance.

The photo of her parents' wedding came to her. She wished she'd brought it to Tassie. It was something she took from a drawer in her bedroom when Gary Stone had been particularly creepy, or she'd just retreat there to stay out of his way. With soft tentative strokes, she outlined the shape of her mother, stunning at twenty-four, her father as strong and lean as she always remembered him. More deliberate strokes let her define his tailored suit, then her mother's dress and veil, her pen sweeping off to one side to capture the lengths of snowy tulle. She drew in smiles, remembering how happy they'd looked standing against a backdrop of biscuit-coloured buildings with reddish tiled roofs, the bouquet picking up the baby blues and whites of a sky filled with scudding clouds. 'Best day of our lives,' they'd always said when visitors would remark on the picture that had hung in their lounge room until Gary came on the scene.

Tiredness taking over, Sienna packed the book away. What the hell was she going to do? Keeping Daisy safe was her top priority, but she couldn't live like this for the rest of her life. She'd blocked Cole's number, deleted him from Facebook and all her social media, but in a way, she wished she could keep track of him. Stay well away, for sure, but at least know where he was. For all she knew, he could be following her. The thought made her look over her shoulder, through the darkened windows where all she could make out were the shadowy shapes of the nearby units. She couldn't even see as far as the main road. If he was out there looking for them, she wouldn't get much warning. That ute he drove could block the narrow driveway; she wouldn't even be able to run. They'd be trapped. Abandoning her notebook, she jumped up and went round checking all the windows and doors, then climbed into bed beside Daisy. Despite the warm night, she pulled the doona up to her chin. Not for the first time, she cried herself to sleep.

Chapter Sixteen

Sienna woke to a scream. Reaching out an arm, she registered the warm but empty patch on the sheet beside her. Daisy wailed as she scooped her up from the hard floor, cradling her head and cuddling her in close. Lying her on the bed, she ran her hands over the child to check there were no broken bones. A lump was starting to swell on her left temple, but other than that, Sienna reckoned she was okay. Taking her in her arms again, she brought Daisy to the kitchen sink and let the tap run cold. Shushing and soothing her, Sienna held a face washer under the water, then squeezed it before setting it against the purpling skin. Big tears made Daisy's eyelashes clump together as she wailed.

'There, there, that's better.' Sienna remembered her parents' cold cloth trick. It had come to her automatically. A brief wave of pride was swept away by guilt. She knew she could no longer sleep with Daisy in the bed. They'd been given a perfectly good cot. From now on, Daisy would have to sleep in it.

She warmed a bottle and took Daisy to the sofa. As the child sucked hungrily, Sienna checked her phone. There was a text from Jess checking they were okay. She'd be round on Monday morning to take them to the childcare centre. Oh god, she'd see the bruise!

In the car, they talked about the incident. After two days of cold cloths and wishing it away, Daisy's forehead still sported the ugly purple lump. But if Jess was concerned, she didn't show it. She said most parents would have had a similar experience once in their parenting journey. As much as Sienna tried to feel reassured, she couldn't help wondering if it would be a black mark against her. Daisy was all she had. She vowed to take better care of her, starting tonight.

'I thought this might be a good place for the access visits too,' said Jess as they pulled into the carpark at the centre.

Sienna's mouth had gone dry. She couldn't respond. Jess turned in her seat.

'We knew there was every chance he'd apply to see his daughter.'

Sienna could feel the tremor in her hands as she listened, powerless.

'It's safe territory. The visits are supervised. Cole will only have an hour with her at a time.'

'Do I have to see him?' Her voice came out in a whisper.

'No. We'll work it out so you two don't meet.'

'Okay.'

Inside, Jess introduced her to the manager, a business-like woman who thankfully made no mention of the bruise and proceeded to give them a tour. Sienna did her best to keep up as the woman opened doors with a swipe card and took her through the daycare area. In one room, a care worker was putting a baby down for a nap in a cot with a beautiful mobile made of felt giraffes and elephants in soft pastels. The classical music surprised her, but she'd heard about the calming effects of it on one of the parenting pages she followed. In a larger room, toddlers and pre-schoolers looked busy with clean, colourful play equipment that made Sienna want to hang out for the morning. Daisy wriggled to get free from her hip, but the lady in charge was already ten steps in front, beckoning her to come and see the outdoor area where sandpits and water stations were shaded by triangular sails. They had the same ones over the barbecue area at home in Queensland. But she couldn't think about that now.

'Jess tells me you're taking a class at the library on Friday mornings,' the woman said once she caught up with her. 'We have a spot available, but you'd have to be quick.'

The thought of leaving Daisy gave her goosebumps but Sienna tried to be rational. It would be good for them both. Daisy would have some interaction with other kids and adults like any normal child, and she'd be doing something for herself.

'It would only be for a few hours,' she told the woman. 'I'd collect her straight after class.'

For a moment the woman slowed down, as if resting her business brain for a moment, and looked at her with a kind smile. 'It's not easy leaving our little ones, but it's good for us to do things for ourselves too.'

Sienna gave another sweep of the centre. On the lawn, a couple of boys jiggled on their toes with excitement as one of the workers emptied a box of building blocks onto a low table. A girl in a blue paint-splattered apron waved to them with a dripping paint brush. Beside her a worker sat looking patient on a tiny chair. Around her neck was the same type of key card the manager had used to let them in. This would be a safe and happy place for Daisy.

'I'll book her in if that's okay.'

'No problem.' The woman consulted her phone and tapped something in. 'She can start next week.' On the move again, navigating her way back through the rooms, Sienna followed her past the nursery where the baby in the cot was fast asleep. Sienna recognised the gentle sound of a harpsichord from somewhere in her school days.

In the bright open foyer, a group of women and toddlers were getting settled for the music session Jess had convinced her to join. She recognised Rosa from the writing class and gave her a wave.

Without a moment's hesitation, Rosa handed Camilla to the woman beside her and jumped up from one of the massive bean bags that were spread out in a semicircle.

'Welcome, my young friend.' She wrapped one arm around Sienna and rubbed Daisy's back with the other. 'This is Daisy, yes?'

Sienna nodded.

'You are so beau-ti-ful,' said Rosa, pinching Daisy's cheek.

Sienna thought her baby might cry, but instead she gave Rosa a huge smile and one of the gorgeous gurgles she reserved for people she liked. So far, that amounted to Mandy, Jess, Rosa and their African neighbour from the shelter. Other kids Daisy's age would be showered in love by grandparents, aunties, uncles and masses of cousins. Daisy didn't even have her Uncle Hugo around.

'Did she have . . . ac-cid-ent?' Rosa asked.

Sienna felt her face burn. How could she have come here with an injured child? Without looking round, she imagined the women judging her, thinking how she could have done this to her own baby.

'She rolled off the bed.' Tears welled in Sienna's eyes. She tried to hang on to Jess's words . . . this happened to other people too.

Rosa threw her hands in the air. 'It happen,' she said, with a shrug of her shoulders. Sienna breathed in her sophisticated smell that was a comfort in itself.

'Oh, you poor thing.' It was another one of the mums who looked a bit older, a baby boy in her arms and a little bird-like girl clinging to the leg of her jeans. 'You must feel terrible.'

Sienna smiled and sniffed back the tears. 'I do,' she said. 'I can't believe I let it happen.'

'Don't worry, sweetheart. Same thing happened to this one.' The woman looked down at the girl and placed a hand around the curve of her blonde head. 'That was the end of co-sleeping for me.' She smiled a reassuring, loving smile. 'Please stay and have a cuppa with us after.'

The musician who sat facing the collection of bean bags started to strum her guitar. Rosa bid Sienna to come and take the spot beside her. Settling into the brown corduroy fabric, she knew what she would write in her gratitude journal. Jess had been right to make her come here.

In one of the rooms off the foyer, Jess was meeting with the centre manager and a social worker to discuss Daisy's access visits. Sienna's stomach churned, but she turned her daughter toward the strumming, humming woman in the middle of the room and forced herself to put thoughts of Cole to one side. Daisy deserved to enjoy the session. Her baby didn't have any friends either. A stress-free session of rhymes and songs might be exactly what they needed.

⁓

Half an hour later, Daisy's cheeks were blotchy and Sienna's arms felt like they were going to fall off. They'd bounced, clapped, crawled, pretended to be every Australian animal from koala to kookaburra. She hoped the music therapist was well paid for the effort she put in to keeping up a smile for the infants while choreographing the mums. When Rosa asked her to join her at the centre's canteen, Sienna had to stop herself from responding in a singsong voice after being immersed in the actions and songs like 'Twinkle Twinkle Little Star'.

With a welcome mug of coffee in her hands and Daisy sitting happily in one of the highchairs, sucking on a rusk,

Sienna listened to the women chatting about their babies' routines. She wasn't the only one exhausted. She wasn't the only one doing it on her own either. By the time Jess emerged from the manager's office, the group were breaking up with friendly goodbyes and promises to see each other at the same time the following week.

'See you Friday,' Rosa called to Sienna as she wheeled Camilla away in her pram.

'You've made a friend?' Jess was beside her, taking a wet wipe to the soggy rusk bits on the highchair and Daisy's hands.

'Just someone from the library.' *Friend* was stretching it, Sienna thought, but someone to look forward to meeting again was a good start.

'I know it's a bit rushed, but we've organised a supervised visit for this afternoon.'

Jess might as well have let the air out of a balloon.

'There'll be enough time to make sure you're gone before he comes in,' she reassured.

'Here?' Panic gripped her in the chest like she'd been stabbed.

Jess looked her in the eye, her gaze steady. 'It will be okay, Sienna.'

Turning away, Sienna gathered her baby and her bag. She'd like to have run out of there and taken Daisy on the first flight off the island. But her mother and Gary Stone were hardly the kind of support network the legal people told her she'd need if she wanted to take Daisy interstate. They were stuck in Tassie. She would have to play by the rules.

Sienna kissed the soft hair on top of Daisy's head and whispered to her, 'Mum won't be long.'

Handing her to the social worker that Jess had met with had been one of the hardest things she'd ever had to do, but hard things were becoming commonplace for Sienna. Getting into Jess's car and driving away also went on the list. She couldn't speak. Jess suggested a trip to the shops or a walk on the beach, but when she didn't respond, Jess parked at a nearby café and suggested they sit tight and have a hot drink.

The skin around Sienna's nails was almost bleeding by the time the hour was up. Afterward, she wished they'd stayed there for a few minutes longer. It wasn't how Jess and the social worker had arranged it, but as they pulled up to the centre, Cole was only leaving. Her hand shot out to where Jess was putting on the handbrake.

'Oh god. I'm so sorry,' Jess began but trailed off as Cole's eyes found them.

He stopped in his tracks, his demeanour changing in a split second from man on a mission to someone in no rush anywhere. As they sat, essentially trapped in the car, Cole put his hand in his jeans pocket and retrieved a lighter and a roll-up cigarette. Standing there, he drew the cigarette to his lips and lit up, cupping his hands to shelter it from the breeze, then returned one hand to his pocket in what felt to Sienna like slow menacing motion.

'Hi Pamela!' Jess was on her mobile. 'I need you to move that father on. He's harassing my client.'

With the phone still in her hand, they saw the social worker emerge from the building and address Cole. With a shrug, he swaggered toward his ute and got in, but not before turning and looking directly at Sienna with a sinister sneer.

Chapter Seventeen

Tuesday morning found Marilyn sitting at the back of the sex shop, in for her usual catch up with Georgie. She'd had the weekend from hell. Again. Ethan still hadn't found a place of his own and his father had threatened to cancel his twenty-first birthday party if he didn't move out. 'Bloody poof,' Frank called him before storming out of the house, revving the car and backing onto the main road at a speed that could have killed a pedestrian. Shoot first, ask questions later, that was Frank.

'Your Ethan okay?' Georgie asked.

Marilyn took her time to respond as they flicked through the magazines Georgie claimed she only looked at to know what her clients were after.

'Ah, he'll live.' Marilyn winced at a photo of a semi-naked couple that left little to the imagination: the man's oiled, rippling torso met the V of a groin obscured by one of the woman's cellulite-free buttocks. She put down the magazine and took a drink of her tea.

'How'd Friday go?' asked Georgie.

'Oh, it was all right.'

Marilyn was grateful for a change of subject but wasn't keen to gush. She'd gone all enthusiastic when she'd shown Keisha the photos she'd taken of the beautiful clothes from the gallery, their bright colours making the child's eyes light up. Her hundred questions had been great prompts for that recount or whatever their teacher called the story they were supposed to write. But she didn't want to remind Georgie of a time when they could go wherever they damn well pleased and art galleries weren't off limits to the likes of them. Their little class excursion had reminded Marilyn of how set in their ways the two friends had become. How partners and families had squashed them into boxes they'd just gotten used to. But she wasn't going to lump Georgie with that depressing insight. The woman had enough to do, keeping her own shit-show on the road.

'Dawnie phoned ya?' Marilyn kept the conversation to immediate matters, like trying to corral wayward kids like Georgie's estranged daughter for a night.

Georgie shook her head and continued to stare at the magazine. 'No, and I ain't phoned her neither.'

'I'd like her at the twenty-first . . . for Ethan's sake. He's saved up . . . insisted on paying for most of it himself.' Marilyn wanted the whole family to be together – immediate, extended, old friends like Georgie who may as well be family.

Georgie sighed, but still didn't look up. 'I hate that kinda thing.'

As she held the pages a little away from her, Marilyn saw the picture she was referring to, with two men in bondage outfits, shiny leather caps and trousers that showed so much skin they couldn't really be called trousers.

Tiring of the porn pictures, she flicked to the back where the adverts for products and people were set out in neat squares, three in a row, three rows to a page, like some kind of puzzle. Their teacher had asked them if they ever did the like of crosswords or word searches, if they read much. She'd probably be horrified to find out what Georgie considered 'reading material'. But then who knew what those library ones got up to in their spare time.

'You still haven't answered me,' she told Georgie.

'I did answer ya.'

'I mean about the twenty-first.' Marilyn was starting to get tired of their conversation. In fact, after she'd reported to Georgie on how things had gone in the library that first Friday, their normal conversations had begun to annoy her. Messed up kids, quick-tempered partners, porn paraphernalia. Was this it? Closing her magazine, she drank what remained of her tea and stood.

'Better get on,' she said. If Georgie was aware she'd cut their catch-up short, she didn't say.

'Should be right for the party,' Geogie said. 'I'll see if I can ask someone to get Dawnie along.'

Marilyn walked out into the late morning sunshine. It occurred to her that her chats with Georgie were no longer the highlight of her week. She wouldn't have gone as far as to say they'd become a chore, but Friday mornings at the library and afternoons with Keisha were what she'd come to look forward to most. Still, if it hadn't been for Georgie, that would never have happened. The writing class would soon be over, and another winter would set in where she'd be grateful for any escape from her house. Ethan's twenty-first couldn't come quick enough. She'd broach the subject of him moving out after the party. He was old enough. Earning enough money of his own to afford to maybe rent with a couple of his friends. As much as she hated to think of the house without him, he needed to get away from Frank, make a life of his own.

At the ferry stop, she breathed in the fresh sea air that was blowing in at the mouth of the Mersey. There was enough sun to warm her bones and brighten her road home. The house would be quiet. She'd give Frank his lunch and sit down to do her journalling.

Looking forward to taking that black notebook and settling in for the afternoon, she walked up the steps to the front door. Turning the key, she heard a groan.

'Frank?' He was lying half in, half out of the bathroom, trousers around his hips like he'd started to pull them down as he'd gone for a pee. She threw down her keys and went to him.

He groaned again. 'Get the ambos!'

Fumbling in her handbag, she found the phone and dialled triple zero. 'Ambulance . . . my fella's havin' heart attack . . .'

Kneeling beside him, she spat out the answers the call centre lady was asking. 'Yes, *East* Devonport. Fifty-three. Breathing, yes. Can you hurry up?'

She texted Ethan. Frank reached for her hand and squeezed. They'd been here before. He hadn't wanted to let her go then either.

Ethan arrived just before the ambulance, quick enough to help her pull Frank's trousers on properly and shift his head away from where he'd vomited. The ambos were great, talking to him as they worked.

'We'll soon have you in the Mersey Hospital, mate. They'll look after you.'

Marilyn and Ethan stood aside to let them get Frank onto the stretcher and wheel him out. Curtains twitched at a neighbour's window across the road. The bush telegraph would be buzzing, but Marilyn didn't care. Emergency services were regulars on the street. Although her neighbours kept mostly to themselves, a few gave the whole place a bad name. Old mate across the road wasn't nosey, just careful.

Marilyn hopped into the ambulance and looked out at Ethan. 'Grab yourself a sandwich before you go back to work, son.'

The most reliable of the three of them, and Frank treated him the worst. He gave her a wave but didn't move from where he watched them drive away. If Frank carked it one of these days, she hoped Ethan would look after her. No matter what his father thought, it was a comfort to know she'd raised one decent bloke.

Chapter Eighteen

Week Four

In the library, Marilyn sat in the classroom and watched the others file in, happy to give a smile or word of acknowledgement now that the room and its personalities had become familiar.

They'd moved Frank to the Launceston General for tests. Jamie had gone with him, which meant she didn't have to miss class. Besides, it would give their son a taste of responsibility. There was a slim chance Frank might even appreciate his help. She could have rushed off and been the dutiful partner, but she didn't want to let Keisha down either. If she were honest, she'd thought more about getting home to spend time with her grandchild than she had about looking after Frank.

'Morning,' she said as Oscar took a seat beside her.

'G'day, Marilyn.'

As they opened their notebooks, she registered a funny feeling that made her smile. He'd called her by her name. She shrugged it off but took a furtive glance toward the pages he'd opened. The writing was all in block letters with wide spaces between, but there was a lot more of it than a few weeks ago. Her own had improved too. She'd written so much for homework, it made the page all textured to the touch.

'Okay, Week Four,' Vivian announced. The noise settled to a low hum. 'No excursion today, but before we get into the nuts and bolts of our pieces, can we do a round of gratitude? Perhaps you've managed to write something in your books?'

Marilyn kept her head down, hoping someone else would begin. She gave an inward sigh when the woman from China piped up.

'I am grateful for the opportunity to learn,' Robyn began, consulting her notebook and reading from what looked like a carefully written list. The others too had noted things down in their own time and followed Robyn's example with snippets about healthy children and the qualities of their island home. Yes, Tassie was a beautiful state, Marilyn knew, but didn't most people think that about where they lived? She hadn't written it down, but it occurred to her that she was grateful she and Georgie had got to see some of the outside world.

'What about you, Oscar? You always have something to add,' said Vivian.

Beside her, Oscar shook his head and sat back, folding his arms.

'I'm not much of a writer, but I wrote . . .' He put on his dodgy glasses and read, 'I am grateful for a free holiday at my sister's, to be getting better at writing, and for walks on the beach with Dog.'

Marilyn eyed his notebook and was sure that today what he'd said was actually on the page.

'Dog?' Vivian's eyes narrowed, making the lines in her forehead stand out.

'That's my dog's name,' said Oscar.

Vivian wrote it on the board. When she turned back, she was beaming at him. 'Great name,' she said. 'Does anyone have any thoughts on how Oscar's dog might have got his name?'

'Maybe you got him from someone who didn't give him a name,' Sienna suggested.

'Your imagination went on strike that day?' Johnny joked.

Oscar laughed.

'Footrot Flats, in'it?' Marilyn hadn't meant to attract the attention of the room but was happy to see Oscar's smile.

'It's a cartoon,' Marilyn explained as she caught the quizzical looks on some of their faces. 'Comic kinda books from the seventies.'

'And a movie,' said Oscar. 'They're my favourite books of all time.'

As the others conferred about whether or not they'd heard of them, Oscar leaned over to her and whispered, 'Only bloody books I ever read.'

She gave him a nudge and stifled a smile.

'They have them here in the library.' Robyn was looking at her phone. 'I can see on the app.'

'Fantastic,' said Vivian. 'Looks like you have a few books on there, Robyn. Any favourites?'

The woman gave a nervous laugh. 'I can't read English books very fast, but I try.' She turned the phone toward Vivian. 'I read this to my son.'

'*Wonky Donkey*,' Vivian read. 'Oh, that's a funny one! All that lovely rhyming – a great way to help children read and spell. What about you, Marilyn? Any news, books or otherwise?'

Marilyn sighed. In the small group, there was no escaping audience participation. 'Didn't get much journal writin' done this week. My partner had a heart attack. Ended up in the Launceston General.'

There were a few gasps.

'Is he all right?' Vivian asked.

Marilyn shrugged. 'Tough as old boots, my Frank.'

'Can't keep a good man down,' said Vivian.

That Irish lilt was growing on her, even if the comment was misplaced. *Good man*. She didn't think so.

Vivian had turned to the board and was writing '*Footrot Flats*.

'As we've mentioned favourite books,' she said, 'does anyone else have one they'd like to share?'

Marilyn could hardly believe her own ears as she joined in the discussion, telling them about her romances and other books she'd loved over the years. Hearing herself talking to a captive audience made her want to pinch herself. At the mention of the outback and cattle stations, she had their interest. The romantic elements and happy endings had them smiling and joking.

'How very Australian,' said Robyn.

Marilyn gave her an appreciative nod. She doubted these foreign-sounding women around the table would ever pass for Aussies, and yet they chose to live here, bringing up families, cooking tea with groceries from the same supermarkets. Weren't they all just trying to stay healthy and keep out of trouble? She thought of Jamie's girlfriend. She'd been so busy trying to keep the peace with Frank, she hadn't even asked the girl where she was from. In getting to know her classmates a bit better, it had begun to bother her that Frank was passing on his racist attitude to Keisha and the other grandkids. Nothing would change if she didn't make more of an effort to teach them something different.

'Do you prefer print books, Marilyn,' Vivian was asking her, 'or do you read on your phone or listen to audiobooks?'

'Real books,' she answered, visualising her collection in the bathroom and another in the bedroom.

'Audiobooks are real books too,' said Vivian, 'but I know what you mean.'

'I like listen books,' said Rosa. 'In eh-Spanish mostly, of course.'

'Any favourites we might know?' asked Vivian. 'There are so many famous books translated from Spanish . . .'

'You know Isabel Allende?'

Vivian nodded and told them about a book called *The House of Spirits* that took her months to read and that she still hadn't finished. Marilyn liked her honesty. When she'd first started the course, she thought the teacher was a bit up herself, but she realised now she was just quiet.

With her courage growing she asked Vivian, 'What's your own favourite?'

'*The Bridges of Madison County.* It was made into a movie with Clint Eastwood and Meryl Streep.'

'That was a while ago.' Marilyn had it out before she could stop herself, but Vivian laughed.

'These young ones wouldn't have seen it,' she said.

Amalia asked them to repeat the title and said it into her smart watch. Marilyn wished she could afford one of them. Frank would no doubt think it was a waste of money, but she would have to keep up to date with technology if she was to help her granddaughter navigate the world.

Chapter Nineteen

Vivian was delighted her students were so willing to share insights into their daily lives, and the enthusiastic discussion about books, although a little off piste, had given her a real boost. She was beginning to feel like the capable knowledgeable teacher she used to be. Teaching adults was no scarier than teaching kids and with their different motivations, these students were making her work hard but also giving her unexpected rewards.

Looking at her session plan again, she turned to the task of editing recounts. As she took them through her COPS technique about looking out for errors and omissions, there was good-humoured banter. 'Call the cops,' was Johnny's reaction, which gave them an easy way to remember the acronym. The students had even become comfortable enough with one another to agree to let her make copies of their recounts so they could edit each other's work. She divided the class into pairs to mix the non-native speakers with those with English as their first language and gave Robyn, who'd become her unofficial assistant, the job of handing out the copies.

As she did the rounds, it became apparent that some of their recounts had come closer to the mark than others. Robyn herself had managed to go off on a complete tangent, ending up with something that looked more like an advertisement for Tourism Tasmania than a recount of a visit to a single attraction. She was pleasantly surprised to find Sienna doing a great job of explaining to her where she'd gone off track. Despite having to simultaneously tend to Daisy, the girl was kind enough to discuss ideas with Robyn and help her get her thoughts down on paper. Hadn't Cathy said Sienna had a chance to study teaching? Vivian stored that one away for a later conversation.

Marilyn's recount was a revelation, full of detail, but she didn't fare as well as Sienna on the helping front. Rosa had her bamboozled with questions about grammar, but Vivian took a pew beside them and lent a hand.

Oscar was the one she was most concerned about. He had written the least and had the most work to do, but Vivian was filled with admiration for the guts of the man who she suspected had to work at least twice as hard to get anything on paper. He seemed to enjoy working with Johnny, who had a problem with run on sentences. She showed them how to use breathing to see where to put punctuation marks. It suited both men to work slowly through their writing, allowing Johnny to practise the breathing technique and giving Oscar more time to follow what was on the page.

Amalia and Bjørn worked well together. To his credit, Bjørn had no problem with being corrected by his young classmate. In fact, he welcomed all suggestions for improvement. When he dropped small words like articles, Amalia was ready with tips on how to make his writing sound more fluent. As well as helping, Amalia diligently edited her own work, insisting she turn over a new page and write the entire piece out neatly again.

At morning tea, Vivian noticed the alliances that were starting to form. Sienna and Amalia sat together with their phones out, exchanging numbers and adding each other to social media. Robyn and Rosa chatted without letting their levels of proficiency in English get in the way of a good giggle. As she turned from her papers to get herself a drink, she found Marilyn hovering at the edge of the desk waiting to speak to her.

'I was wonderin' if you could give me some advice,' she began. 'It's about me granddaughter.'

'Let's get a cuppa and have a chat, will we?'

Vivian listened as Marilyn described her granddaughter's difficulties which, in her experience, sounded like undiagnosed dyslexia. She gave what advice she could, knowing that intervention was really needed in the school. What struck her most, was the wider impact their course might have. She hadn't given the idea much thought before now.

After break, the students continued to work on their own writing projects. Cathy agreed to lend a hand, giving her a bit of extra time with Oscar who was having difficulty putting pen to paper. At the back of the room, they had a little privacy which Vivian thought he might need.

'You've mentioned your dog a few times,' she said, trying to find something to inspire him. 'Do you have a picture?'

Oscar scrolled on his phone and turned it to show her a handsome golden retriever.

'He's a beauty,' she said. 'I thought he'd be a border collie after the Footrot Flats discussion.'

'Ah, I called him Dog for a different reason.' He smiled, but Vivian detected a sadness he hadn't wanted to share with the room. She waited a beat to let him decide if he wanted to share with her.

'He belonged to a homeless bloke,' Oscar said, his voice low, eyes on the photo. 'Used to lie in the stairwell of my building in Melbourne . . . Found the dog whimpering beside him one morning when I went to do my shopping.' He paused, still smiling at the photo. 'Thought the fella was asleep, but I went to check on him. He'd passed away. Had an empty coffee cup beside him with "Dog" written on it . . .'

Vivian's breath caught in her throat. She drew a hand to her mouth, aware of tears smarting in her eyes.

'Oh, Oscar,' she said softly. 'If you have the strength to write that down, it would make for a beautiful story for our book.' She looked again at the picture and smiled. 'Along with that photo of course.'

'Thanks for your help today,' Vivian called to Robyn when the session was finished. The pocket rocket slung the strap of her handbag over her shoulder and waved as she swept out of the room, last to leave as usual.

'No worries,' she replied. 'See you next week.'

'Well, you've certainly made some inroads today,' said Cathy, who was packing away the tea things onto one of the library's book trolleys.

'You mean with Robyn?' asked Vivian, not sure if her earlier difficulties with the woman hadn't gone entirely unnoticed.

Cathy grinned. 'Amongst others.'

'Some of them seemed a little despondent when we were panning for errors. I was trying to talk up the good stuff and emphasise being clear . . .'

'You worry too much,' Cathy interrupted. 'I've had lots of positive feedback. You're doing a great job.'

Vivian breathed a quiet sigh of relief as she gathered her bag and went to hold open the door.

'Much planned for the weekend?' Cathy asked, pushing the trolley past, mugs jiggling against the metal bars.

'Haven't thought quite that far ahead,' said Vivian in another practised reply to one of her least favourite questions. But as she left Cathy to get back to her office and walked out into the midday sunshine, it occurred to Vivian that she never asked Cathy what she might have planned herself.

Cathy was married to Lee. She knew that much as she'd always spoken of him so fondly in the staffroom. Outside of school, they'd moved in different circles, kids at different ages and stages . . . But as she climbed into her car and took a moment to check herself in the rear-view mirror, Vivian thought she might take just a moment longer when the students disappeared next week and ask Cathy what she was up to for a change.

Chapter Twenty

When he got back to his sister's, Oscar found the cleaner hard at work. Not wanting to get in her way, he took a walk around the pool, checking the workmanship on the recent repairs and giving Dog some attention to pass the time. With the warm day and the caffeine worn off from the coffee he'd had at morning tea, he craved one of the bottles of cola he had stockpiled in the fridge. Through the windows he could see the woman leaving the kitchen and took his chance to nip inside. As he took a glass from the cupboard above the worktop, he wondered if she too might appreciate a cool drink. He poured for them both and went to the door of the dining room where she was going about her work like a machine. He hadn't been in there since he'd arrived in Tassie, but that didn't seem to make a difference to the effort she was putting in to keeping the place dust free.

'Would you like a drink?' he asked, holding a glass toward her.

She stilled her hand and for a moment he thought she would decline, but in what looked like a deliberate gesture, she tucked her cloth into the pocket of her apron and accepted the drink with a bow. He opened the double doors that led onto the decking and bid her take a seat in one of the Adirondack chairs beside the pool.

'It's okay to take a break, you know,' he said, hoping she would relax a little. It was obvious she took her job seriously, but there was something manic about her movements, and after seeing her sobbing the previous week, he wondered if she felt under pressure to get the house to a certain standard or have it done in record time.

She smiled and took a sip, keeping her eyes low. As she moved the glass around in her hands, Oscar noticed the patches of dry chapped skin, pale against the cola.

'Thank you for all your hard work,' he began. 'You have the place sparkling.' It sounded inane but he couldn't just sit there and say nothing. She shook her head and her silky black ponytail swished at her neck.

'I'm sorry. I don't even know your name. I'm Oscar . . .'

She nodded again like she remembered from the week before.

'Siraporn,' she said, still not meeting his eye.

'What does that mean?'

She looked at him then, surprise in her dark eyes.

'I don't mean to be rude or anything,' he said. 'You see, I'm doing this course at the library . . . with students from all over the world . . . we had to share something about our names.' He shrugged wishing he hadn't asked.

She took a moment before speaking.

'It's Thai. It means blessing . . .'

'You're from Thailand?'

She nodded and took a quick drink.

'I have mates who've been there. They say it's a great place for a holiday.' Oscar heard himself trot out the only thing he knew about Thailand and felt inadequate. What did he know of the world when he could barely make it from Melbourne to Tasmania?

She took her phone from her pocket, swiped it with her thumb and showed him her cover photo. He saw a long wooden boat bedecked in coloured flags, an older man, weatherbeaten from the sun, smiling at the camera, a backdrop of sea and sand.

'My father,' she said, 'take tourists around . . .'

'That looks amazing.'

He waited, hoping to learn a little more about her, but she drew back her phone and stood, head bowed, keeping her gaze on the drink in her hands as the bubbles hissed to the surface. Unsure what to say, Oscar stood as well. He'd been so delighted not to have to deal with the old cleaner, he'd forgotten to ask about arrangements.

'I'm so sorry, Siraporn, do I need to pay you? I didn't give you anything last week . . .'

She shook her head. 'My boss . . .' She gave a furtive glance toward the front of the house. 'I get back to work now.'

As she went back inside, Oscar wished they could have talked for longer, but the opportunity had passed. Time was money, he supposed, and no doubt she had other houses to

be getting on with. It was none of his business, but something about the woman made him feel he'd crossed a line by
talking to her at all.

With Dog pestering him to take him for a walk, he went
back to the kitchen where Siraporn was washing her glass,
a cloth squeaking against its edges to give it a perfect shine.
She reached for his. He drained the last of his drink and
handed it to her.

'Thank you.' Then thinking better of it, he said, 'I could
have done that . . .'

'It's my job,' she said, a note of strength back in her voice.

He left her to finish her work and gather her things. As
he heard her leave, he went to see her out.

'Might see you next week,' he said, raising a hand to wave.
But she didn't respond.

From the road, a horn beeped. He watched as Siraporn
quickened her step, her chin to her chest as she headed toward
a vehicle parked on the nature strip opposite the house. The
same black transit van had been there the week before. He'd
assumed it was someone visiting the neighbours.

Later, when the cola kicked in and he managed to amble
through Dog's favourite bush trail, Oscar was still thinking
about his sister's cleaner.

Chapter Twenty-One

After lunch, Marilyn went through her pantry, reorganising the chaotic collection of food items she could never seem to keep in order. Today she wanted Keisha to be able to open the pantry door and easily retrieve the ingredients for the cakes she'd decided to bring to the hospital. Frank had survived the heart attack, but they were keeping him in for observation and further tests. It would be tomorrow before Ethan could drive her down to Launie to see him. Turning up the volume on the radio, she joined in with Dolly Parton in the chorus of 'Jolene'. She was loving these Friday afternoons with her granddaughter, and having Frank out of the house would mean she'd have her all to herself.

It was Vivian who had given her the idea of baking together. She was glad she'd managed to summon up the courage to ask her teacher for some tips on how she could help Keisha with her reading and spelling. Vivian had made it easy for her, grabbing a cuppa and sitting with her like they were just having a yarn.

'That's wonderful,' Vivian had said when Marilyn told her about her and Keisha being 'study buddies'. 'Teaching someone else is the best way to reassure yourself that you know something about a subject.'

Marilyn wasn't convinced she knew a whole lot about reading and writing, but she'd enjoyed the morning's session and was beginning to think she wasn't as bad as she'd thought. When Cathy helped the women from overseas, she'd told her how all that grammar stuff came naturally to her because she'd been surrounded by English her whole life. There were plenty mistakes in her own piece about the gallery, but Cathy showed her how it flowed better than the others'. When they read aloud, she could hear the way Rosa got things back to front or put in the wrong word, so it didn't make sense. She'd learned it was because Rosa was translating directly from Spanish. Thinking about Rosa and Robyn now, she was a little ashamed of how she'd let her frustration show when they'd asked for her help. Hopefully she'd have more patience with her granddaughter. She shook her head as she hummed along with the Dolly special.

'Nan!' Keisha was standing behind her by the time Marilyn registered the child had come in.

'Oh, Keisha,' she said, backing out of the pantry with a tidy bag full of packets and containers of out-of-date food. 'Turn down that radio and get yourself an apron from the drawer.'

'I thought we were going to study,' she said, sounding far too grown up for a nine-year-old.

'All in good time,' said Marilyn. 'Baking first.'

Keisha's apparent disappointment at not getting stuck into bookwork was short-lived. She reached to the radio on the kitchen bench and ran her eye over the baking things Marilyn had set out.

'What are we making?'

Marilyn tied the bag and went to the back door to set it in the wheelie bin outside.

'Wash your hands, put on your apron and then we'll decide.'

There was no hesitation. Keisha skipped off to the bathroom and returned to pick out one of the spare aprons, a beautiful smile on that oval face Marilyn loved. If Vivian was right, they'd kill two birds with one stone: a cake for Frank and a little reading practice into the bargain.

After they'd pored over a couple of those free supermarket magazines for inspiration and still couldn't agree, Marilyn showed Keisha her nan's old cookbook. She'd thought the child would be turned off by the musty smell and the stains of use on the pages, but the fact that it had survived this long and belonged to someone the child had never got a chance to meet seemed to capture her imagination.

'I'm holding a book that she held in her hands, Nan. How cool!'

Marilyn smiled. When her mother was too busy out partying to parent, it had fallen to her nan to step in. She'd been the one who'd taught her how to bake. Liked to read too. Pity she couldn't have defended Marilyn against the brothers who used to lie in wait after school with their toy guns and use her as target practice, but that was history. She'd make sure Keisha didn't have to put up with that kind of bullying as best she could.

They began by looking at the contents page and flicking to the cakes and desserts section. When a page slipped out, Marilyn deliberately lost the place where it came from and helped the girl insert it back in the right spot, thinking her numbers might need checking too.

'We'll sticky tape that in later,' said Marilyn. 'But let's find Pop's favourite in the back here.'

'I know, I know,' said Keisha, jiggling on the spot, 'vanilla slice.'

'Okay, you find it then.' Marilyn showed her how the index worked and watched as Keisha used her finger to navigate down the first page.

'Everything starts with A,' the child huffed.

Marilyn wished she could remember everything Vivian had said . . . something about knowing the sounds with your eyes closed. She took a breath and decided to try it hoping she wouldn't make the girl feel dumb like she did in school.

'Close your eyes for a sec.'

Keisha rolled her eyes but set her chin on her hand and did as Marilyn said.

'What does Vanilla sound like in slow motion?'

'Van-ill-ahhh?' Keisha didn't sound sure, but Marilyn kept going.

'What's at the start, veh-ah-nnn,' she hinted.

'V,' said Keisha.

Marilyn moved closer to look at the book alongside her granddaughter.

'Can you run your eye over the pages and find the Vs?' she asked. 'You don't have to read all the words. You can jump to the letter you want and skip the others.'

Not looking convinced, Keisha moved her finger from side to side and down the page quicker than before.

'Vs are at the end right?'

Marilyn didn't say anything but watched as Keisha flipped over the pages and found the bold black V on the last page of her grandmother's book.

'Van-ill-ahhh,' Keisha followed, eyes on the page. 'Here, Nan. That says vanilla, don't it?'

'Sure does.' Marilyn turned to a drawer to retrieve the measuring cups. 'Now move your finger across to see what page we have to look up.'

Keisha's brow furrowed in concentration. 'One hundred and seventy-three.'

'Right then. Let's find that page.'

The girl hesitated. It was a big book and Marilyn knew she was challenging her granddaughter to step out of her comfort zone, but she had few enough opportunities to spend time with the child. The thought of her falling behind or thinking she wasn't smart enough broke her heart.

'Let's see.' Marilyn came in close again, glasses on, and drew her finger down to the corner of the page. 'This says two-hundred and twenty, so we don't have to go back too far . . .'

Keisha began to flick backwards, calling out numbers as she went and stopping to double-check she hadn't gone back too far.

'We're getting close,' said Marilyn as they got to the hundred and eighties.

'Found it!' Keisha beamed as she showed her the tempting photo of Frank's favourite treat.

'Good job,' said Marilyn. 'I think I have everything we need. Let's see.'

As though she had forgotten the hard work associated with reading for a moment, Keisha began to sound out the ingredients and together they looked through the pantry. Marilyn blamed poor eyesight and getting old for any delay in finding the necessary items, allowing Keisha to catch up on reading packaging and labels.

Once they got down to following the steps of the method, Marilyn could see Keisha's confidence grow. It was no longer about sounding out and finding her way around the words and numbers. This was about laying out the sweet biscuits on the greased tray lined in baking paper, heating the milk with vanilla, then mixing the cornflour, caster sugar, butter and cream together with the egg yolk they cracked carefully that would give the custard its yellow glow. Taken back to those days as a young girl with her nan, Marilyn felt a tear slip from her eye, but she wiped it away quickly, happy to see her granddaughter getting the same pleasure out of being with her. There had been good times in amongst the bad.

'You could come with us to the hospital tomorrow if you like, share this with Pop . . .'

'I'll ahks Mum.'

Seeing the glum look she knew only too well, Marilyn decided to park that one. No point getting the child's hopes up if her mother would disappoint her later.

'Guess what I found while I was tidying the pantry?'

Keisha shrugged but a spark of enthusiasm returned to her eyes as Marilyn went to the cupboard and pulled down a couple of mugs and the packet of Tim Tams she'd been surprised her boys hadn't discovered. The child wrapped her arms around Marilyn in a rare and unexpected hug. They didn't go in for all that soft, touchy stuff in her family, but she reached a hand round the girl's shoulders and planted a kiss on her head.

'Let's get the jug on.'

As they sat in the peace of the kitchen, vanilla slice safely in the fridge to set overnight, Marilyn sipped her tea and watched as her granddaughter nibbled either end of her Tim Tam before dunking it in her tea and using it as a straw. She thought of the writing class and if those ones from overseas had ever tried the classic Aussie move.

'I should take you and them Tim Tams to the library,' she thought out loud.

Keisha looked up from where she was sucking carefully to get the cream out from between the sandwiched biscuits, chocolate melting in her fingers.

'Get you to show 'em how to be an Aussie.' Marilyn laughed. In the quiet of the kitchen, just the two of them, no TV blaring out horse racing commentary, only the country music on low in the background and the sound of Keisha sucking on her biscuit, Marilyn felt lighter than she had done in some time. She shook it off, thinking her age was making her go funny in the head, but it was there, something alongside the peace, maybe pride.

Chapter Twenty-Two

Determined not to let another week go by without dealing with the bags and boxes sitting in the boot of her car, Vivian drove to the small shopping centre near her home. With two of the refuse sacks nearly pulling her arms out of their sockets, she entered the charity shop hoping to make the job quick and get home without running into anyone.

'Good afternoon, stranger.' Petronella shot out from behind the counter and gathered the drawstring handles of one of the bags, the knees of her pedal pushers either side as if her entire frame might be required to move it. For a second, Vivian thought the woman might buckle under the weight of the load.

'I didn't know *you* volunteered here.' She hauled the other bag after her, proceeding to the counter despite wanting to retreat to the safety of her car.

'Plenty of time on my hands these days,' said Petronella. 'Always nice to give back a little, don't you think?'

Vivian managed to respond with a tight-lipped smile.

'Whatever have you got in here?' Petronella made to lift one of the bags off the ground. 'This all Dave's junk?'

There was a pregnant pause as Vivian thought she might lose it or run out of the place. Their eyes met over the concealed collection of items which Vivian had in fact deemed junk.

'Sorry, Vivian.' Petronella shook her head of salon-managed hair. 'I shouldn't have said that. Not very professional of me.' She gave a light laugh. 'Professional.' She laughed again. 'Not a very professional volunteer, am I?'

Vivian would happily have had the ground open and swallow her, but she kept smiling. 'I'll just leave these with you, then.'

'Righto. I'll look after them.' There was another awkward moment before she went on, 'Do anything on Sundays?'

Vivian thought she might have run out of excuses for all the times she'd been asked that kind of question, but Petronella wasn't giving her a chance to make one.

'We're getting together in a week or so . . . It's on Facebook. "Any Excuse for a Luncheon?" Have I invited you? Don't worry, I'll add you.'

'Thanks.' Vivian started to back away from the counter. 'I'll see if anything's clashing and let you know.'

The rest of the donations would have to sit in the car for a bit longer. There was no way she was going back in. Maybe she'd take them to Ulverstone on her next shopping trip. A job for next week. Right now, all she wanted to do was retreat to the comfort of home and have a quiet weekend. The phone that hardly rang chimed and pinged in her bag. Probably Petronella, she thought as she took the scenic route around the bays and beaches, grey clouds gathering over choppy waters where the estuary widened out to meet the sea. She imagined having to spend winter on her own, lighting the wood fire on cold nights and climbing into a cool bed. *Buy an electric blanket*, she told herself, her inner voice stern. If Dave wasn't coming back, she'd have to toughen up.

When she saw the gate open, Vivian's first thought was whether or not the man from the electricity company had come to read the meter. In an effort to give themselves privacy from the road, Dave had planted a row of native bushes along the curve of their driveway, which had grown to such a height as to occlude all cars from view. Ready to remind the meter man to close the gate when he left, she rounded the corner.

'What the . . .' She slammed the brake. The camper van was parked in the driveway. Only one other person knew where the keys were kept.

Her first thought was to do a U-ey and drive somewhere, pretend she'd never been home, buy herself time to prepare for the uncertain reunion. But as the front door opened, and the tall shape of him appeared, there was no way of avoiding her husband. *Big girl's pants*, she told herself.

She checked her phone. Four missed calls from Dave. Pulling the strap of her handbag over one shoulder, she stepped out of the car and made for the door, laptop bag thrust out in front. As his arms began to lift, palms out to embrace her, she side-stepped into the house and marched down the hall away from him. Did he really expect a hug? What the heck was he planning? Moving back in like nothing had happened? Loading up the camper and taking off again?

By the time she'd deposited her accoutrements on the kitchen bench and started to fill the kettle, he still hadn't said anything. Looking up from the sink, she saw he'd sidled in after her in his sock soles, hands in the pockets of his jeans, a new shirt tucked in and that belt she'd given him in '93, Clodagh's first Christmas. Was it tied a little tighter? He'd definitely lost a few pounds. For a moment, she thought he might burst into tears.

Her brain wrestled with the emotional train wreck he'd caused: guilt, anger, frustration, confusion; until he told her why he hadn't come back before now, she couldn't decide how to feel. Would he tell her he was leaving permanently or hoping to stay?

'Rory doing better?' Whatever about her own pain, the man she'd met however briefly was in a worse state than any of them.

'He's doing as well as can be expected,' Dave replied. 'The doctors are giving him a year.'

He shrugged, eyes down, hands still in his pockets. She took a deep breath, switched the tap off and roughly set the jug in its cradle.

'You want tea?' It seemed like such an inane way of breaking the awkward silence, but someone had to go first.

He nodded. 'That would be nice.' He moved closer to the bench, touching the surface with a tanned hand, running his fingers lightly over it as though it might burn his soft skin. 'How have you been?'

How do you think I've been? teetered on the edge of her tongue, *mortified, reclusive, going out of my mind,* all backing up behind.

The boiling water got louder. She reached into a drawer and took out two mugs, nothing fancy, cheap mismatched ones she'd never give a visitor. The force she set them down with surprised her. This was so raw.

'Tell me, Dave, when you waltzed in here, what did you think I'd say? Welcome home, love. How was your little break from our marriage?'

The eyebrow arched slightly over his left eye.

'You know I was helping a mate,' he said. When she didn't respond, he added, 'I thought the break might do us *both* good.' The words were said in a low voice as if to not ruffle any feathers. *Too late for this angry bird,* she thought as she stood, arms spread wide, the heels of her hands leaning into the worktop to steady her.

'I feel terrible about your friend's diagnosis, but three months, Dave! You've been gone three months.'

She whipped round to take a teabag from the canister and made them both a drink, dunking the bag in and out of the mugs more times than was necessary. He'd have preferred her to make it in their favourite teapot, she knew, but he was lucky to get anything at all.

'If this *break*, as you call it, was to do us both good, shouldn't I have been consulted before *we* took it?'

She squeezed the teabag on a teaspoon, dropped it into the sink with a clatter and nodded to the fridge next to him. He could get his own milk. If he noticed the low level of supplies, he didn't comment. She waited as he poured the milk into both their mugs in a practised move, to exactly the level they liked; his a centimetre from the rim, hers almost overflowing. So many tiny conveniences sabotaged by his unexplained absence. She waited for him to speak again. He'd never been able to multitask.

'I've missed you, Viv.'

She'd missed him too. But the loneliness, the utter sadness she'd endured these past months was on him.

'Have you any idea what it's been like for me, people asking after you, thinking god knows what about what's going on . . .'

'Since when did we ever worry about what . . .'

'Don't you dare come back at me with that platitude.' She leaned toward him, almost spitting her words. 'Let's just recount the facts here. My husband abandons me at an event in another state and leaves me to make my own way home with friends who have no clue what to think either. Why, Dave?' He went to speak but she wasn't finished. 'Couldn't you have mentioned to me at some point that you wanted this *break*, given me some kind of heads-up, not the humiliation of being abandoned.'

He gave a tut and went to say something again, but she needed to get this out. God knows, she'd been keeping it under wraps for long enough.

'I'm mortified! Every time I see someone we know, I cross the street. I've been food shopping in Ulverstone for Christ's sake! "When is Dave back?" If I had a dollar for –'

'Okay, Viv.' He made a quick stop sign to interject. 'I hear you. You're right. I should have explained myself before now.'

She drew her mug to her lips but didn't take a drink.

'Rory's an old friend,' he began. 'We go back a long way. That night at the festival, we opened up, shared stuff . . .' She stared at him, wondering where this was going. He hadn't touched his tea. 'Okay, there was drink involved . . . but it felt good, like the lifeline I needed to hang on . . .'

She set her mug down, careful not to let the tea spill over, careful to rein in the anger. 'Were things that bad?'

His chin dropped to his chest, eyes down. In the silence, she could hear him exhale.

'What about me?' She hadn't wanted to turn this into self-pity, but this surprise return had left no room for rehearsal. 'Couldn't you have turned to me?' Another breath, another silence. 'Or was this something you'd already planned?'

He turned toward the table, but she stood where she was. If this was a longer story than the one she'd been telling herself about a chance meeting with an old friend, she didn't want to settle in for a cosy heart-to-heart about why she'd been rattling around alone in some kind of separation arrangement that was not of her making. The man standing in her kitchen might be her husband of over thirty years, but right now, he felt like a visitor she wanted to give short shrift.

Turning back to her, he didn't meet her eye, but went on, 'We'd reconnected on social media . . .'

Newsflash! When she and Dave had had little enough to talk about, he'd been messaging this Rory. Why hadn't he told her?

'He was in a local choir too. Said he'd be at the festival, but I had no plans beyond meeting him there. It was as if the years fell away . . . When he said he had cancer, I . . .'

There was a tenderness to his tone, a look in his eyes she couldn't read, but it was all about Rory, not the kind of contrition she might have expected. She thought back to the night of the festival, the warbling in the hotel bathroom as he got ready that night, the better form in the days leading up to the trip. She'd thought it was a sign he was emerging from his funk, looking forward to spending time with her and their friends. What if it was the prospect of meeting Rory that had perked him up? Were there signs of something she'd completely missed?

'Dave.' She spoke in a low voice. 'Were you ever in a relationship with Rory?' Her question sounded like something better suited to the courtroom case of Bill Clinton and Monica Lewinsky than any discussion that might have occurred in what she'd believed, until recently, to be a fairly normal home.

With a sigh, Dave pulled one of the stools from under the bench and eased himself onto it, elbows resting on the worktop. He waved a hand to dismiss her question like an annoying fly. 'That was all a very long time ago.'

As she took in his response, she recalled that night again, the image of the pair of them heading to the bar, the familiarity, how happy she'd been for him to have run into someone from home. Surely there was nothing in that scene she could have picked. Dave cleared his throat.

'Rory and myself were in college together.' He gave a shrug, looking down as he spoke. 'We experimented, I suppose you'd say. Became lovers for a short period.' He kept his eyes on the bench. 'It was the eighties. Not the kind of thing you'd broadcast. At least not in the circles I moved in.'

Not in the ones she'd moved in either, but in thirty-odd years, hadn't he thought to tell her? With the blood threatening to drain from her head, Vivian dragged a stool to her side and slumped onto it. Up to that moment, she'd have said her husband was a terrible liar. And yet he hadn't actually lied, more withheld the truth. Either way, the shock was enough to silence her. Dave took it as a cue to continue.

'I swear to you, Viv, it was the only relationship I've ever had with a man. We didn't suddenly get back together in Queensland or anything like that . . .'

'And yet, you've spent the past three months with him.' The words came out staccato like the line of a song he'd taught the choir.

He sighed, that exact exasperated sigh he emitted whenever they argued and he didn't get his way. It infuriated her now as it always had, that way he made her feel like a child, a little woman who didn't know what she was talking about. They'd never been able to fight properly. But this was no time to roll over. He was talking again.

'I've been honest with you, Viv. I said I needed time to sort myself out . . . Rory was grateful for the support . . . I owed him . . .'

'Owed *him*? Jesus Christ, Dave!' She'd heard enough about Rory. This was about them now. 'Did you expect to turn up and slip back into our old life like nothing had changed? Walk completely over me?'

He went to respond but she cut him off.

'I retired for you, Dave. I wanted to help you "sort your-self out", whatever that even means. God knows, I'd hope I could support a friend with cancer too, but I can't imagine that involving leaving you.'

'Viv, I'm sorry.' He stood up then and started around the bench, arms opening up to embrace her, but she couldn't bring herself to fold, to fall into those familiar limbs, let her spinning head lean against that broad chest where she would inhale the scent of him, the smell of what had always been home. Whatever version of him had just returned, she wasn't even sure she knew him anymore.

'Dave!' She slid down from her stool, backing away from him. 'I don't know what you're expecting me to say, but I can't go on like it's all fine . . . You've hurt me.'

For a moment, they stood in silence. She knew he was processing what she meant.

'I could stay in the camper . . .'

She nodded. 'Yeah, stay in Winnie, for a while anyway.'

They'd liked the idea of travelling round Australia in a vehicle with a name that sounded like a reliable friend. She'd never imagined the van becoming some kind of doghouse.

'I'm sorry I didn't let you know I was coming home, Viv. I just thought . . .'

She put up a hand to silence him. 'This is your house too, Dave, but I'm not ready to share it with you right now.'

He stood, understanding in his eyes. She took their mugs to the sink, turning the tap on full bore, drowning out the sound of his socks shuffling along the tiles as he left.

Upstairs, Vivian ran a hot bath. In the back of the vanity, she'd found the remains of a packet of bath salts she'd picked up on a pre-Covid holiday to Bruny Island when they'd tried out the van for the first time. Dumping what was left of them into the water, she watched the salty crystals sink and dissolve. A bit like her marriage – capable of changing state, their relationship, once rock solid, in danger of fizzling out.

Lying in the soothing water, she ran a sponge over her body, noticing the wrinkles on her ageing hands, the round bulge at her tummy several diets had been unable to shift, the nicks and scratches from her efforts at gardening that seemed to take forever to heal. Not so long ago, she'd thought herself fit and attractive. On Bruny, they'd found quiet coastal campsites, rising early for long bush walks before returning to make love in the afternoons like their twenty-something selves. Dave had told her she was still beautiful. Despite the ravages of middle age, she'd believed him. Letting the soapy water wash over her, she sobbed into her hands. Right now, she didn't know what to believe.

Chapter Twenty-Three

Week Five

First to arrive at Home Hill, Vivian parked the Subaru in front of the white weatherboard house that had been home to Tasmania's only prime minister. *So far,* she mused, as she took in the modest home that reminded her more of something from *Out of Africa* than the more famous white home of American presidents. Set back from the road, the house was half hidden by a beautiful garden, where deciduous trees were beginning to lose their leaves and bursts of colour still clung to vibrant bushes before winter thinned them out.

Checking herself in the rear-view mirror, Vivian ran a hand along her chin to check for those pesky bristles that plagued her. Clodagh used to take the tweezers to them, overcoming her disgust to prevent the embarrassment of anyone else seeing them. Vivian could have predicted her daughter would turn into a helicopter parent. God knows what she'd do when Max became a teenager. No doubt, she'd have him using a hundred-dollar-a-jar vegan answer to acne and, knowing Clodagh, applying it for him. She'd tried FaceTiming during the week, but to no avail. Clodagh was busy, as usual. Although she hated to think about it, since this business with Dave, she feared she had become surplus to requirements.

Sitting waiting for her students to arrive, she took a few deep breaths and thought about their gratitude journalling. Top of her list today was getting out of the house. The past few days had been foul, the kind of weather that reminds you summer is well on the wane. A typical Tasmanian March, blowing hot and cold like a moody friend. When the heavens opened and the gloomy weather mainlanders hated settled in for a few days, she'd embraced it as weather fit for the near recluse she'd become. But with Dave out in the camper van, binge-watching *Bridgerton* and devouring a brilliant crime novel didn't come with the peace she might have otherwise enjoyed. She couldn't shake the guilt at the gap in their levels of comfort; she with the whole family home to herself and him rattling around the rectangle of floorspace between the bed and kitchen-cum-everything-else, rain battering against the windowpanes and wind threatening to lift the camper off its wheels.

On breaks for copious cups of tea and the ensuing trips to the bathroom, she'd found herself going to the laundry window from where she could get a hazy look at the Winnebago that was parked not too far away along their boundary fence. He had easy access to the house through the side door they rarely locked, but for the most part he'd steered clear, at least when she was around. She'd felt more than a little disingenuous as she'd listened to the rain drumming on the tin roof. It was one of the things they'd loved about their home, especially on a cold winter's night when they'd cuddle together under their thickest duvet, lulled to sleep by the sounds of nature and the comfort of being together. There'd been several times when she'd just wanted to text him and tell him to come in, but the pain from what he'd told her about Rory wouldn't go away.

Her phone pinged in her handbag. A Facebook notification. Any Excuse for a Luncheon were inviting her on a picnic. She pressed 'Going'. With Dave on the property, the quiet weekends she'd gotten used to had lost their appeal. By Sunday, she'd need any excuse to get away from the place.

An old Land Rover was turning in off the main road. She grabbed her bag and got out, ready to welcome her writers. Despite assurances from Cathy that they'd all had the address and maps emailed to them, Vivian couldn't help worrying that one or two of them might get lost. There'd been some confusion already caused by the language barrier, with students asking her to repeat instructions on more than one occasion.

She gave a wave as Bjørn parked beside her and wandered a little away to give the man space and privacy to extricate himself from the driver's seat and organise his belongings. When she turned back, he was pulling the strap of a satchel over one shoulder, one hand steadying himself with the crutch.

'Good morning, Bjørn. You're good and early.' She smiled, hoping to sound encouraging. He smiled back, but she thought it might be more of a grimace through the pain.

They were spared any awkwardness when Rosa pulled up in an SUV, emerging resplendent, if overdressed, in a fur-lined hooded jacket. She waved to them before unloading Camilla and her pram into the fresh autumnal air.

By the time the lady from the National Trust appeared from a side entrance, the group were assembled and ready to begin their tour. Only Sienna hadn't appeared. Amalia offered to message her while they waited a few more minutes. Vivian hoped it wasn't all too much for the girl having to leave Daisy at childcare. The idea of the single mum having some time to herself seemed great but it wasn't always that simple when it came to saying goodbye.

As they gathered at the large fireplace in what their guide called 'the volunteers' room', Vivian was pleased to see a large table with plenty of chairs taking up one part of the L-shaped space. An easel with a flip chart and a small whiteboard had been brought in for their use. This would be their classroom later in the morning. As the students chatted, she breathed in the smell of old house and silently delighted in the surrounds. Black-and-white photos lined the walls. An old cathode-ray television sat across one corner. Ornaments and memorabilia adorned the mantelpiece of the wide fireplace. Rays of fine dust danced in the bright sunlight washing over the wood floor. It was a setting worthy of Hemingway. She fancied she might get creative herself.

'That was the first television in Tasmania.' The guide was pointing to the antique in the corner. Vivian was glad someone had had the courage to ask about it. In fact, for a group with such a range of ages, languages and backgrounds, they were becoming a united bunch. Tuning in to the woman's voice, Vivian followed as she led them into the adjoining room to begin their tour, grateful these Friday mornings were giving her some respite from the nagging fears about the future that kept her awake at 3 am.

The house turned out to be a shrine, not just to Joseph Lyons, but to his wife's many and varied talents. Apart from being first lady of the state and the first woman to be elected to the Australian parliament, Enid Lyons was an artist and home improvement nut. Every room held evidence of her handiwork. She'd knocked out walls, put in walls, turned doors into bits of wall, cleverly fitting shelves under glass to showcase tea sets and other precious items they'd been gifted by dignitaries from around the world. With twelve children, Vivian marvelled at where she might have found the time, but at each turn, was amazed at the ingenuity of the woman who took DIY to a whole new level. She'd sewn cushions, made bedheads, painted over cracks in the plaster with a magnificent mural, dug out rocks to pave an area outdoors . . .

As the guide opened drawers and cupboards, they were treated to a close-up look at some of the hats and dresses Enid had hand made. In the grand dining room where a long table was set with a dazzling array of dishes and silverware, there was a photo of her wearing one of the dresses at the coronation of King George VI. A lucky daughter had

accompanied her on the trip. The juxtaposition of elegance
and grandeur with the ordinariness of a large Aussie family
had the group enthralled as they went from room to room,
listening intently to the guide and commenting to each other
with awe and admiration. How Vivian had lived in the area
for so long and never been to Home Hill left her wondering
what she'd been doing with her life, but that was one of the
upsides of retirement – time to explore what was on your
doorstep. She wouldn't think about having to do it alone.

They were in the office of Joseph Lyons hearing about the
first ABC radio broadcast made from the phone on his desk
when Sienna made an appearance. Vivian gave her what she
hoped was a welcoming smile, but it wasn't until they recon-
vened in the volunteer room for morning tea that she got a
chance to speak to her. With their guide handing out slices
of a gorgeous-looking apple cake, she caught her eye.

'I'm so sorry I was late,' said Sienna, moving toward her
and pulling off that baseball cap she always wore. 'Had to
drop Daisy off at daycare.'

'No problem.' Vivian tried not to look worried. 'Did she
settle okay?'

Sienna shrugged. 'Not too bad, actually. She's only used
to being with me lately so I thought it would be much worse.'

'You're very brave,' said Vivian. Sienna's response was a
thin smile that told Vivian she didn't feel brave at all.

'Will you join me for a tea or coffee?'

When she agreed to a cuppa, Vivian made for the sideboard where an urn and cups and saucers had been laid out
for them. Although Cathy hadn't given her too many details

about how this young woman had ended up in Tasmania, she'd been on the button about her lacking confidence. Vivian had seen her journalling and her recount. There was nothing wrong with her writing, but something deep inside Vivian, maternal instinct perhaps, made her glad this girl was part of the group.

'I wanted to compliment you on your part in the group-work last week. You were very patient,' she said. 'Cathy mentioned you wanted to go to university.'

Sienna shook her head of fine dark hair and looked down at her cup. 'I'm not that smart,' she said in a low voice that made it hard to hear her.

'We're not always the best judges of our own abilities,' said Vivian, matching her volume so as not to embarrass the girl. 'Give yourself a chance, sweetheart. Maybe this course will help you explore the possibilities.'

Sienna nodded but didn't meet her eye. What or who had made this lovely girl doubt herself, Vivian wondered.

'Okay if I call on you if I need some help?' she asked.

Sienna looked up. 'If you think I can help, I will.' She didn't sound convinced but at least she'd agreed. Maybe they could get her to believe in herself just a little by the time the course was finished.

'Right.' Vivian tapped her cup with a teaspoon. 'If everyone has had a chance to grab a cuppa and something to eat, I'd like to invite you to have a seat and we'll get into our workshop.'

Chapter Twenty-Four

Oscar snaffled a last piece of cake as the tour guide made quick work of clearing away the morning tea things to give the class an extra table. When Vivian asked them to form two groups, he was content to sit in the warm sunshine, opposite Marilyn and flanked on either side by the other men in the group. As they awaited further instructions, he thought about Siraporn and whether or not she would be there when he got home.

'Okay, let's see what we remember from our tour.' Vivian stood at the whiteboard, pen in hand. 'Everyone got their journals with them?'

There were nods of agreement. By now, they knew the drill. Everything was to be written into the black notebook they'd received on the first day. Opening his book, Oscar put thoughts of Siraporn aside and focused on Vivian's voice.

'I'd like you to choose one of the rooms you've been in this morning and draw what you saw.'

A murmur of surprise rippled round the group. Someone scrabbled in a pencil case, sending others searching for pencils and erasers. Oscar was lucky to have remembered his free pen and his glasses, let alone the kind of stationery supplies some of them brought along.

The bedroom with the huon pine chest of drawers came to him. A rough sketch would suffice, Vivian assured them when Marilyn said she couldn't draw to save herself. She was funny, but Oscar didn't think it would do him any good to laugh at her. He kept his eyes on his page. The hardened middle-aged Marilyn could protest all she liked; he for one was grateful for not having to write down words he couldn't spell. Drawing would bring a welcome change.

Despite initial doubt as to what they had to do, a pleasant silence fell over the group as each of them got to work on their task. As he sketched, Oscar remembered how the strong smell of huon pine hit him the moment their guide opened the drawers of the heavy piece of furniture. There'd been a special slim insert where an ostrich feather was laid out in tissue paper. He attempted to draw the feather, remembering the loving way the guide had handled the object. Her passion for her job and great reverence for the family had been evident at every stage of the tour.

'So, if you've all had a chance to get something on paper ...' In a low voice, Vivian broke into the quiet, 'can you have a chat with a couple of people around you and talk about what you drew?'

Marilyn, whose efforts had been accompanied by a series of audible sighs, pushed her book away and sat back in her chair.

'Mine ain't up to much. What you lot got to show for yourselves?'

'Better than mine.' Johnny laughed as he invited them to take a look at his drawing of the old dame's bedroom. 'A bit sad she slept in there in a single bed after her husband died.'

It was a detail that made Oscar pause for thought. His ex-wife had accused him of being too soft. Catching Marilyn's eye, he imagined he saw a tear. He smiled to himself. Even the toughest bird in the room had a heart.

Oscar turned to take in Bjørn's drawing of the dining room. *Smart man*, he thought as he noticed details like the number of place settings and the layers of crystal in the chandelier. An odd sort of bloke, keeping himself to himself, Oscar thought, although Marilyn wasn't having any of it.

'What made you sign up for the course?' she asked him straight out. Oscar could only be grateful she hadn't asked *him*.

'My children and grandchildren, all Aussie now . . .' Bjørn moved a hand over his phone with a flourish. 'They have apps. Always tapping into these things.'

Marilyn rolled her eyes. 'Tell me about it.'

Bjørn smiled then, as if grateful for an ally. 'I must keep up, improve my writing in English, how you say . . . keep up to date.'

Oscar pulled out his phone and showed them how he sometimes used voice to text.

'Only one problem with that, mate,' Bjørn gestured to his mouth, 'this Norwegian accent.'

Oscar found himself involved in a conversation about things he'd never thought about. Johnny, who spoke multiple languages, talked to or texted his parents every day in Arabic. At first, he seemed a bit shy about showing the group, but when Marilyn put on her glasses and leaned over his phone, demanding a look, he pulled up some recent messages that looked like a collection of curls and dots. Oscar felt admiration but also a renewed shame at his own limitations. If these men were operating in other languages as well as trying to improve in another, why couldn't he even master one?

After doing the rounds, Vivian was back at the whiteboard. Standing to one side, she read her words back to the group. 'Draw, talk . . . We've all drawn a room in the house, we've talked to our groups about our reflections on the tour . . .' She turned and wrote another word before continuing. 'Now it's time to *write* about our experience, a written description perhaps. Some of you may even like to create a story . . .'

There was almost a comfort in the shared writing anxiety that seemed to pervade the room each time Vivian set them a task. At the same time, Oscar sensed a stronger willingness amongst his fellow learners to have a go. Memories of his school days bubbled up inside. For a second, he imagined Vivian outing him as the dumbest in the class with some caustic comment. He had an urge to disappear but breathed deeply and reminded himself that this was nothing like school. In a way, there was no hiding place. But neither was there a need for one. Even though he was sitting at what might be termed the back of the room right now, he felt very much included, not one bit overlooked as he had been in school. From a young age, he'd been highly aware of the power the loud ones wielded over teachers, where large class sizes necessitated much crowd control. If you were quiet and bright, you had some chance of learning by putting your head down and getting on with the work. But if you were slow, or in his case, confused by words from the get-go, you had no chance. He'd never been able to get ahead, shake the feeling of falling behind. He'd begin every year with a good attitude, try and behave himself, but it never made a difference. Nobody expected any different either. The scars hadn't gone away.

'You okay?' Vivian caught his eye, bringing him back to the moment.

She'd mouthed more than spoken the words. Appreciating her tact, he nodded and started to write. It may not be much good, but at least he wouldn't be judged.

Chapter Twenty-Five

Sienna checked her phone. No messages from the childcare centre. No need to worry. She'd enjoyed this morning, but with her writing task completed, she was ready to be reunited with her baby. Beside her, Rosa was bent over her notebook, her pen moving over the page in neat deliberate letters. Every so often, she would pause to read over what she'd read, cross something out and continue the script, speaking in a barely audible whisper as she wrote. Sienna suspected she was mumbling half in Spanish, loving the sound in any case.

Rosa and the others had given her lots of compliments about her drawing. She'd chosen the library where they'd stood listening to stories about the Lyons family. She'd tried to visualise a sick Joseph Lyons sprawled out along the couch, one leg resting on the cushions Enid had so lovingly sewn. And the way he'd read to her aloud while she'd ironed. She couldn't imagine what it must have been like to iron for fourteen. There was no mention of help, but she imagined children pitching in.

When Vivian had come round to their group, she'd told Sienna she had a gift. 'I could sit on that couch myself,' she'd said in that cool Irish accent. 'You've made it look so soft and real.'

Sienna thought she'd struggle to get the perspective of all the items in the room, but as she'd sketched, she'd found herself enjoying the challenge. She'd even tried to include the books that lined the bookshelves with the most amazing collection of classics and other books she'd love to have had longer to peruse. 'A waste of time,' Cole had said when she'd brought a John Green novel with her from Queensland. It had disappeared soon after they'd arrived. She'd asked him if he'd seen it, but he'd shrugged, suggesting she hadn't brought it at all.

At least her welfare payments had been sorted out. Another step in the process of getting away from Cole. Jess had helped her open an account in her own name so she could access the money that was rightfully hers. It had been almost surreal downloading the bank app and seeing the balance. She must have checked it twenty times that first day to make sure it was still there. Despite her happiness at having her own money, the fact that it had been earned by people with actual jobs who paid tax had given her more than a moment's guilt. When she'd shared her concerns with Jess, the case worker explained how it wasn't meant as a handout but rather a hand up. She'd also reminded her of how wrong it was of Cole to keep control of her money, spending it how he saw fit and not providing properly for her and Daisy.

'Hey,' Amalia whispered, leaning in beside her. With Rosa and Robyn still working hard on their pieces, she spoke softly.

'We're having a few friends round next weekend if you'd like to come.' As Sienna hesitated to respond, Amalia's eyes widened with her usual enthusiasm. 'My daughter would *love* to meet Daisy. She's great with small kids.'

A gathering . . . in someone else's house . . . It had been that long, she hardly knew what to say, but how great would it be to just go out, have a few drinks at a friend's, even non-alcoholic ones? Maybe she should branch out. Do something normal. She hesitated for a moment. *Stuff it*, she thought. There'd been too many nights stuck inside, obsessing about Cole. She and Daisy deserved better.

'Thanks. That would be awesome.'

'Cool! I'll message you the deets later.'

As they fell quiet again, Sienna added a few finishing touches to her drawing, aware of Vivian sweeping quietly around the room in one of her lovely loose tops over dusky pink jeans. She reminded Sienna of her mum and the designer lounge sets she'd taken to wearing in the early days of dating Gary Stone, back when he'd thrown money at her. She remembered the day he'd given her his credit card and they'd gone shopping together, flopping down in a nail salon, the collection of paper carrier bags from all the best shops at their feet. High on the thrill of having been in some of those shops for the first time in their lives, her mum had used her free hand to book high tea, swapped hands and started to search up over-water bungalows.

Things changed after Gary moved in. They'd never made it to the Maldives or wherever it was she'd wanted to go. At least not while Sienna was still living with them. She realised now that she didn't and would possibly never know if they'd gone after she left.

At the end of the session, Sienna was first out the door. The childcare centre was a twenty-minute bus ride away. She wished it was closer but was grateful the bus would take her almost to the door. If it ever arrived. She pulled on her cap and tucked the loose strands of hair in underneath. Wrapping her arms around her big notebook, she took some comfort in the warmth it provided against the stiff autumnal breeze. It would be balmy on the Gold Coast today. She'd checked the forecast. Did so every day. Cole had been right about one thing. She hadn't needed all those strappy dresses and crop tops.

Hearing the loud rumble of the bus approaching, she stepped closer to the edge of the pavement. So focused on getting on the bus, she didn't notice who was in the queue behind her.

'Sienna?'

At the sound of the male voice, she turned to find Cole's mate, Josh. Thinking she might pee herself with fright, she gave him a weak smile before scooting into the nearest seat. But she wasn't getting away from him that easily. As the bus lurched onto the road, he sat his broad bulk down beside her, like someone twice her weight getting on the opposite end of a seesaw.

'Where you goin?'

'A friend's.' *Vague*, she told herself, *keep it vague.*

'She mindin' Daisy for ya?'

Sienna nodded.

'I seen Cole, you know.'

Sienna thought she might gag at the strong smell of tobacco mixed with the remains of a meal, a meat pie maybe, judging by the smudge of ketchup on his top lip. 'Said you broke up.'

She went to say something, but he didn't give her a chance.

'Looks like shit, ya know. Not sleepin'. Missin' you and his daughter so bad . . . Says he'll kill himself if he don't get back with you.'

As the bus took a tight corner, Josh's arm shoved in closer. When they were back on a straight stretch of road, he hadn't moved it. For the next fifteen minutes he kept up a spiel about his poor mate and how sorry Cole was for causing her to leave.

'My stop.' Sienna barely got the words out in time. He made a production of moving his knees to one side, forcing her to squeeze past his man boobs before she could escape to the aisle.

'I'll be seein' ya,' he called after her. She mustered a small wave, hoping to look like she was fine with the prospect. This wasn't her stop, but Josh didn't need any information that might bring her closer to realising her worst fear: bumping into Cole.

Chapter Twenty-Six

Oscar took the turn off to the road of bush blocks where sea changers and climate refugees had moved in alongside the original inhabitants of the long cul-de-sac his sister and brother-in-law called home. The black transit van was parked on the nature strip again. As he slowed, he saw a woman in the driver's seat, head angled toward a phone propped on a stand near the steering wheel. Although he couldn't see her face, he recognised a Netflix show playing on the screen. Siraporn's friend? Her boss? Instead of turning into the driveway, he continued to where the woman wouldn't see him do the u-turn that would let him get a better look. Almost back at Geraldine's, he caught her glance up briefly before returning her attention to the phone. The scowl, the thick set eyebrows . . . unless his eyes were deceiving him, it was Angie in the driver's seat of the van.

He parked in the driveway and let himself in the side gate where Dog greeted him with enough enthusiasm as to nearly bowl him over.

'Come, Dog,' he said when the jumping and panting calmed down. 'There's someone we need to check up on.'

The dog bounded round the back ahead of him.

'Steady now,' he said. 'This lady is a bit shy.'

Unsure whether his words were for his own benefit or the dog's, Oscar scanned the windows for signs of life. Upstairs, he saw the slender shape of her, cloth in hand, dusting over a bedside table before turning to attend to the windowsill. When she saw him, she stood and waved, a swift movement that seemed to stop in midair before her hand returned to her side and the spontaneous smile disappeared. She turned to look over her shoulder. Was there someone else in the house?

'Wait!' Dog would have happily followed him in, but today he would have to be content to sniff around the garden. Closing the door behind him, Oscar proceeded through the laundry with more than a little caution.

He reckoned she must have slid down the banister, such was the speed with which she appeared in the open plan kitchen. There was the bow she'd greeted him with before.

'Siraporn, hi! I just saw our old cleaner, Angie, out there . . .'

As she glanced out the wide bay window at the front of the house, her whole body seemed to stiffen. He took in the dark top and jeans, the puffy pouches of skin under her eyes, the hair tied back but unkempt all the same. Although he doubted her clothes were a uniform, she'd worn the same ones each week she'd been here.

'Are you okay?' He sighed, all too aware of the dip in his own energy levels after the full morning. 'I was going to make a coffee if you'd like a break.'

He'd hoped they might expand on the short conversation they'd had the previous week. It had been nice to sit with her and not come home to an empty house. But as she shook her head and rushed toward the kitchen bench to grab a spray bottle, he wondered if he'd overstepped the mark, offended her in some way. Without looking up, she began to spray the liquid, swiping at the patches where it had landed on the granite worktop, the strong, sweet smell of scented Ajax filling the space between them.

'I work now.'

He raised a hand in defence. 'Yes, of course.'

Unsure of what to do with himself, he took a step back and dug his hands in the pockets of his jeans. For a moment, all he could hear was the swish of the cloth as she cleaned. He turned to where she'd looked before and saw the van. It may have been unrelated, but he found himself wondering if Angie's presence had something to do with the fact that Siraporn hadn't been able to give him the time of day.

He went to Geraldine's hall table and took a pen from the small pottery planter she used to hold the collection of free pens she got on her travels. On the notepad beside it, he wrote down his phone number. Returning to the kitchen, he tried to stay out of sight of anyone that might be looking in from the front. Despite the fact that he had every right to be here, something about the whole bizarre situation made him uneasy.

'I'll let you get on, Siraporn,' he said. 'My number is in the hallway. If you need anything . . . Ring me any time.'

She nodded but didn't look round from where she was dousing the glass cabinet doors and ridding them of any speck of dust that might have dared lodge there since the week before. He let himself back out through the laundry.

'Come here, Dog.' The retriever lolloped toward him, feathery tail wagging, a balm for the pain Oscar felt on Siraporn's behalf but didn't understand. When he came back inside after dozing off in a chair beside the pool, she'd left. He went to the hallway. The piece of notepaper with his number was gone too.

Chapter Twenty-Seven

On Saturday night, Marilyn sat with her family in the private room they'd hired for Ethan's twenty-first, a glass of cheap bubbles in hand, ready to toast her youngest son. Frank had been discharged from hospital with an altered prescription and a fresh dose of cautionary lifestyle advice she knew he'd ignore. But despite his threats to derail the event, they'd all enjoyed a special three-course meal and the company of their nearest and dearest, who were happy to play by the Aussie rule of paying for themselves. Except for the cake of course. That had been ordered from their local bakery and was occupying centre stage on a table at the top of the room. Marilyn had decorated the venue with a Happy Birthday banner, balloons and lolly bags the children could take home with them. Beside her, Keisha jigged her legs about, eager for the cake to be cut. Ethan had promised to let her 'help'.

'Not long now,' Marilyn told the child.

She'd had a lovely night so far, catching up with folks she hadn't seen in forever. There'd been comments like, 'Where you been hidin'?' and people saying they'd missed her at other events, but she'd smiled and made the usual excuses about Frank not being well. She could hardly tell them he hadn't wanted to go to what he called 'their stupid get-togethers' and she couldn't exactly have gone without him. Still, it was good to see them all. Georgie's brood were taking up a whole table with Dawnie in the mix, she was glad to see.

If Frank ever got round to making the speech he'd insisted on, they could all enjoy a slice of the two-tier chocolate cake that sat tempting them. Marilyn had tried to catch his eye once he'd scoffed down his meal, but he'd acted like she wasn't there and headed straight to the bar. He and his mates had been on the beers since the afternoon when they'd guzzled their way through a slab of Boag's well before it was time to go out for the birthday tea. Taking Keisha by the hand, she went out to the bar and confronted him.

'You making a speech or what?'

He turned to his mates and gave them a wink. Once he'd hoisted his trousers round his belly, he took what must have been his tenth or twelfth drink and staggered toward the dining room. Standing to one side of the top table, he raised his beer bottle.

'Here's to the last of my brood of sons, addicts the lot of them . . .' Shocked, Marilyn could only look on. 'Sex, drugs . . . wastes of space, 'specially this one.'

He pointed the bottle toward Ethan who she could tell was squirming in his seat. A few laughs went up from guests who probably thought he was fooling around before getting to the serious fatherly part. She put her arms around Keisha who stood in front of her, trying to shield her ears.

'Nothing but a no-good poofdah . . .'

Brad was on his feet, lunging forward to take a swing at him. Turning to avoid the blow, Frank stumbled and fell onto the table, his neck and shoulder plunging through the creamy, spongy layers of chocolate cake. Keisha turned in to Marilyn, hiding her face in the flowy shirt she'd borrowed from Georgie, and started to cry.

Her eldest son might have ended up in the cop shop had his brothers not taken an arm each to restrain their father. As Frank swiped at the gunge on his face and tried to wriggle free, the guests looked on in disbelief.

'Settle down, Frank.' One of his mates tried to play it down with the kind of laughter Marilyn knew only covered up fear. Frank might have mellowed as he'd grown older and his heart weakened, but if he was riled up, he could still floor someone with a punch. Like Marilyn, his mates knew better than to cross him. When he stormed off back to the bar, the atmosphere was like one of the big balloons waving slowly in the corner, half deflated.

In the aftermath, Marilyn and Georgie sat together in the empty function room going over the ugly scene. With the last of the bubbles, they took a moment to themselves after they'd done their best to tidy up the mess with the restaurant staff. By ten thirty, all the young ones had headed into Devonport while the older friends and relatives had long gone home to their beds. Someone had bundled Frank into a taxi when he'd drunk so much he was out of it.

'You did an awesome job organising everything,' Georgie said, breaking the lull in their conversation. 'Wasn't your fault it ended in tears.'

'Mostly Keisha's,' said Marilyn. Even Julie had been disgusted with Frank's behaviour. When she and Brad had rounded up their three kids, they'd come to tell her they were heading home.

'Will you be okay, Mum?' Brad had asked her.

She'd nodded and set a hand on his shoulder. 'Thanks for standing up for your brother,' she'd said.

As a waitress came to let them know their taxis had arrived, Georgie repeated the question. She placed a warm hand on her arm. 'Sure you'll be okay, darl?'

Marilyn nodded. 'Okay as I'll ever be.'

Chapter Twenty-Eight

On Sunday, after having raided her wardrobe and dug out every possible item of appropriate beachwear, Vivian packed a small esky and tote bag and jumped in the car before she could back out. It was one of those pet days when summer reappears, and everyone scrambles to squeeze in a last outing or two before putting away their summer clothes. From where she'd parked near Petronella's Porsche, Vivian could see a couple of families enjoying the afternoon on Freers Beach, one playing cricket, another huddled around the makings of an ornate sandcastle. The sky was a cornflour blue, and the sea sparkled with sequins of sunshine. She'd only put on her bathing costume because the lycra managed to suck in her stubborn fatty fold and looked better with shorts than the numerous tops she'd tried on. The pink floaty overshirt was meant to draw attention away from her cellulite and wrinkles. At least that's what she'd hoped.

'Hey, Vivian! Over here!'

Standing at the top of the walkway surveying the strand, she turned to find Petronella waving from under a blue and white cabana and took in the clutch of silver-haired ladies in jaunty sunhats, some in light open shirts that billowed in the sea breeze. Pulling on a jaunty hat of her own and slinging a respectable towel that used to be her daughter's over one shoulder, she held her swim bag and esky a little tighter and went to join them. As her Birkenstocks scooped up the hot dry sand with every step, she thought it would have been easier to walk into a restaurant. But staying focussed on the group, she slapped on a smile as thick as her sunscreen.

'Hello, ladies,' she said.

'So glad you could come.' Petronella reached up to give her a hug.

Vivian thought the woman had shrunk until she realised Petronella was in bare feet. Pushing off her own shoes and letting her skin adjust to the warm sand, she tried to keep up with the introductions.

'Of course, you know most of the gang . . . Lyn, Dianne and Gloria already . . .'

Yes, there were the choir ladies, Lyn, Dianne, Gloria, faces all too familiar, but Vivian kept smiling. This was exactly the kind of social gathering she'd been desperately trying to avoid in recent months. These, the very people she'd hoped to never run into, the ones who made shopping out of town preferable to nipping into the local supermarket. All witnesses to her abandonment on their trip to Queensland.

But here on Freers Beach, those women were nothing but kind. She was met with reassuring compliments on her outfit and comments about how well she looked. It occurred to her that they may all just be on their best behaviour, but she was here now. She'd give them the benefit of the doubt.

'Shall we have something to eat?' asked Petronella when she'd done a round of introductions to the women Vivian didn't know.

'I brought something to share,' said Vivian. She bent to where she'd set her esky and retrieved the cheese platter she'd put together.

'Do you have a glass?' someone asked.

When she looked up, she saw Dianne twisting the wire off the top of a bottle of Jansz and pulling at the foil wrapping.

'Now you're talking,' Gloria piped up.

Vivian smiled at the Irish accent and the memory of Gloria telling her she was only in the choir for the après sing.

'One of your lot, of course,' said Petronella, smiling as she handed Vivian a spare plastic glass that looked like cut crystal. She made a mental note to get some. A water bottle had been the only beverage she'd taken as she was driving, but a small bubbles wouldn't hurt. *Might even help*, she thought.

A cheer went up as the cork was popped and Dianne began sharing the fizz around. As the women raised their glasses, Vivian stood at a loss as to what was about to happen. It was Gloria who made the toast.

'To Any Excuse for a Luncheon,' she said.

'To Any Excuse for a Luncheon,' the chorus went up.

Vivian raised her glass and downed a good gulp of the drink before she had time to prevaricate. Clinking glasses with the woman beside her who was new to the area, she couldn't help wondering if *she* knew about the whole Dave debacle, but she remembered what it was like to be new and started to ask a few normal questions. The woman had bought a doer-upper in Shearwater, so far loving her project and the change of pace from Sydney. They sat together on the vast picnic rug Vivian could have happily installed in her living room as plates of food were sent round.

'You've got to try some of Sharon's pâté,' said Petronella.

Vivian was sure Petronella was deliberately reminding her of the woman's name as well as making sure she got enough to eat. In fact, as the bubbles and conversation flowed, she was seeing a different side to Deb's sister. Before her best friend had moved, Petronella had been the social butterfly. Older than Deb and a lot better off, Vivian had always seen her as somewhat ditzy with what her mother would term 'more money than sense'. But watching her today and listening to the commentary about how everyone was doing and what those who couldn't make it were up to, Vivian realised Petronella was more social glue than anything frivolous.

'Anyone for a swim?' Gloria got to her feet and reached into her bathers to fish errant crumbs out of her cleavage.

'Anyone for a nap?' Lyn asked as she made a pillow with her towel and eased back down on the sand.

'I'll come for a paddle,' said Vivian.

'Good on you.' Petronella removed her sunhat and popped it on her tummy as she lay down beside Lyn.

Vivian smiled at the supine women. How lovely to be living in a beautiful part of the world and able to enjoy a nap on a spectacular beach amongst friends. She'd been hiding herself away, ashamed to stand in the sun and be seen. Maybe she could start again. Join in? When she'd set down her glass and hoisted herself off the comfortable spot on the rug, Gloria was already striding toward the sea, cap and goggles dangling at her side. With an energy she didn't know she still had, Vivian trotted across the warm sand and caught up with her.

'Do you swim here all the time?' she asked.

Gloria didn't take her eyes off the water, but answered, 'If I can swim in Galway, I can swim here.' She held out a hand and gestured at what was the incredible vista before them.

'We're so lucky aren't we?' asked Vivian. She didn't need a response. Two Irish women walking in half-nothing on a beach in late March, sun splitting the stones, knew exactly how lucky they were.

As her compatriot swam in a comfortable crawl parallel to the shore, Vivian and a couple of the others walked along the water's edge. The women made to bring her in to the conversation, but she was happy to half-listen, nodding now and then. Mostly, she marvelled inwardly at Gloria and the strong consistent strokes that made it look like she was gliding through the shimmering sapphire that stretched out into the bay. This was on her doorstep and yet, since Dave had retired, she hadn't been down here, hadn't thought to come without him. This had been the beach where they'd spent so many happy days with Clodagh and Finn as children, as teenage surfers, and latterly just together for a Sunday stroll.

When Gloria finished her swim, the others called out words of praise.

'We don't call her Glorious Gloria from Galway for nothing,' said Lyn with good-humoured laughter.

She and Dianne walked on, but Vivian stood, looking out to where the small islands sat in crops of green bush and beige sand. Watching Gloria stride back through the shallows, she wished she could just strip off and run in.

'Ah, that was only marvellous,' said Gloria, taking off her cap and mussing her tangle of whitish hair.

'I'll take your word for it,' said Vivian.

'You should come in with me one day.'

Vivian smiled, non-committal, and noticed the shamrock tattoo on Gloria's left shoulder. The faded green ink made her wonder where and when she'd had it done.

'How have you been getting on?' Gloria asked.

Vivian hadn't expected the question and immediately thought to give one of the default answers she'd perfected, but there was genuine concern in Gloria's voice and in the way she'd moved in close, her white head bent like a priest in a confessional.

'Oh, okay, I suppose,' Vivian began. 'It's been harder than I realised.'

Oh god, she'd let the guard down. This was Glorious Gloria from Galway, the afternoon-drinking Old Woman of the Sea she was talking to, not some shrinking violet.

'It takes time,' she said with unexpected calm. 'No one can walk your road, *a chara*.'

My friend. Somehow the sound of the accent and the Irish dropped in so easily gave Vivian goosebumps. As they walked back toward the shelter, a couple on bicycles pedalled across the wide stretch of sand still wet from a previous tide. The sight made her breath catch in her throat. They'd taken bikes to beaches on camping holidays, done just the kind of lazy loops the couple were doing now, no hurry on them, soaking up the sights and sounds under Tasmania's brilliant sunshine. Her foot faltered as she went to walk on.

'You all right?' Gloria asked.

Vivian had bumped into Gloria as she'd been busy staring at the couple.

'Sorry, Gloria. I just . . .'

If Gloria was aware of what had put her off her stride, she didn't let on.

'Why don't you and I have a swim and coffee one morning next week if you're free?' she asked.

It was as though someone had thrown her a lifebelt. *Grab it,* she told herself and before thoughts of sharks, jellyfish, cold or anything else could sabotage her, she turned to Gloria.

'I'd love that.'

Chapter Twenty-Nine

Still only Tuesday, but it was shaping up to be Vivian's busiest week in months. The physio appointment she'd finally got round to making was first on her list. Later she would catch up with Gloria for that swim. Her sore shoulder had settled down, but she'd kept the appointment anyway, deciding that at her age it might be best to err on the side of caution as any pursuit of a physical nature was likely to incur injury.

'Got much on for the rest of the day?' the physio asked.

'Hoping to have a dip at Little Beach after this if my arm still works,' she told him.

'You won't be playing in the Australian Open this year,' he said, smiling at her, 'but you'll be fine to have a gentle swim.'

When asked how she'd hurt her shoulder, she'd told him she'd been playing tennis. It had seemed like a better reason than decluttering her home after the hiatus in her marriage. Something about the physio's good posture, the confident way he looked her over as he put her through the exercises, had Vivian wishing she spent her extensive leisure time doing something more athletic than just walking up and down the road at an hour that ensured her neighbours were inside having their evening meal or asleep.

She'd lain down on her back for the soft tissue massage he prescribed, self-conscious in her bra and hoping to get it over with. But when he began to rub in the cool camphor-smelling cream, his touch was hypnotic. Even as he worked his hands into the muscle he called the deltoid, finding a tightness she didn't know she had, the pain was overridden by the sense of connection. Apart from a couple of hugs from Petronella, how long had it been since anyone had touched her?

'I think a swim will help loosen that up for you,' the physio said as he washed his hands at the sink and left her to pull up her bra strap and put her top back on. She'd heard of skin hunger in neglected babies and old people wasting away at home with no visitors, but as she walked to her car afterwards, she realised she'd been experiencing it firsthand.

⌒

Gloria was standing on Little Beach, a Bohemian sarong tucked into the straps of her bathers, head of snowy hair making her unmissable as she looked out to sea. A couple of mums with toddlers were setting up a bright green beach shade and unloading buckets and spades from a pull-along cart. Vivian and Deb had once thought they'd end up doing that as grandparents, but that was before their daughters had chosen to move away and bring their children up elsewhere. That *uaigneas* came over her again, but she thought of her

Friday students and willed herself to be grateful. She was here, and someone had cared enough to invite her.

'Gloria!' She cast her off her sandals and placed them with her bag beside a rock before trudging over the sand.

'You made it!' Gloria turned and put an arm out to give her a quick hug.

'I did,' said Vivian. 'Not sure if I'll even remember how to swim, it's been so long, but I'll get in anyway.'

'*Maith an cailín.*'

It was idyllic. Once the water got to thigh-height, Vivian hesitated briefly, then followed Gloria's lead and dived in, water covering her hair, her whole body immersed, weightless. They swam out for about thirty strokes before taking a break.

Vivian turned over on her back and took in the vast expanse of powder blue sky, a patch of shaving-foam clouds off to the east and nothing but pure open water between. She had been right to talk herself into this, drag the bathers up over the orange peel of her cellulite and make herself get in the car as she had done for the picnic. There'd been no sign of the van when she'd left. Dave had taken to leaving the property early in the morning. She had no idea what he did with his days. It had felt more important to get on with her own, try and build herself back up as best she could. This was a step further. She'd actually got in.

'Ready for a bit more of a swim?' asked Gloria.

'I'll catch my breath first,' said Vivian, keen to hold onto the feeling of being held. As Gloria swam away, she stroked the hair back off her face and felt the gentle rock of each incoming wave. There was a freedom in lying there, a freedom even her own four walls couldn't provide. It reminded her of 'The Seal Lullaby' the choir had practised for hours and hours. She tried to lean into the comfort of the present and not let her mind go to her worries.

'Enjoying it?' Gloria had returned and was standing beside her, chin above the water line, no sign of exertion.

'I can't believe it's so warm.'

Gloria lay back, hands sculling at her sides. 'My happy place,' she said. 'Just beyond the shallows. Deep enough to have a decent swim without being too far away to get help.'

Vivian's feet found the bottom as she checked how far out they were, the water coming up to her breasts. She looked back at the women and children on the shore. She didn't feel unsafe.

'You're not thinking of carking it on me, are you?'

'Ha!' Gloria laughed. 'Not any time soon. I'm more worried about you.'

'Oh, thanks!' They laughed and lolled in the water for a few more minutes, lost in their own thoughts under the infinite sky.

⌒

'Good morning, ladies.'

There must have been six beaches he could have chosen, but no, Dave had to pick this one. She leaned into Gloria as they walked up the shore.

'Of all the bars in all the world . . .' she murmured as they returned Dave's wave and watched him dive into the incoming tide and stroke away in the opposite direction.

'He's in a hurry,' said Gloria.

'We're not exactly getting along,' said Vivian. She had to face up to it sometime, and while she'd been lucky enough to escape any questioning at the picnic, she couldn't avoid the subject of her marriage forever with people that knew it was in trouble.

'I'm not going to wheedle it out of you, Vivian,' said Gloria, 'but I'll listen if you choose to tell me.' She took the Bohemian sarong and made a tent of it, pulling down her bathers and dressing faster than Vivian could decide whether to dress here on the beach or find a bathroom.

'Spot the Irish,' she said.

She took Gloria's lead, but not before glancing round to where Dave was doing a steady freestyle out past the collection of rocks that divided the beaches. Was he out a tad far, she wondered, thinking of Gloria's rule of thumb. But he was a grown man, well able to make his own decisions. She dressed as quickly as she could manage, not wanting him to see her. The fact that he had seen her naked on a regular basis for more than half of her life seemed irrelevant. He'd crossed a line to where lots of things were off limits. This, she realised, was one of them.

⁓

Gloria had chosen the perfect time to swim. The day had warmed up by the time they got to the café that doubled as a homewares store. People sat in the outdoor area where a dog dozed in the sunshine and a couple of small children played in the cute cubby house under the sails. They had a wander through the shop before ordering at the counter. A book on indoor plants caught Vivian's eye. Clodagh and her Oliver had all the air-purifying species imaginable in the house they'd bought in Hobart. Even Max was trained in their care. Vivian could hardly look after the peace lily they'd gifted her at Christmas that wilted on a weekly basis. She thought to buy the book for herself, but coffee would be treat enough now that she'd begun to watch her pennies.

In the outdoor area, they found a table under shade. Vivian went to a sideboard at the far end to get a bottle of water and a couple of glasses.

'Hello there.'

When she turned, it took her a second to recognise the face. The bright-eyed retriever at his side gave him away.

'Oscar!' Trying to get past the *what are you doing here?* note in her voice, she bent down to give the dog a pat. 'Hello, Dog.'

When she returned her attention to its owner, she saw the poor man was glowing with embarrassment.

'How are you?' she asked. 'Everything okay with your sister's house?'

In the moment it took him to respond, she wondered if the dreaded Covid brain fog had affected his memory.

'Yes. All good. How are you doing?'

She smiled and touched a hand to the wisps of damp hair that were curling at her forehead. 'We've just been for a swim.'

'You're braver than me,' he said, smiling back at her.

'This is my friend, Gloria.' She gestured to where Gloria waved from the nearby table.

'Are you staying out this way?' she asked.

'Squeaking Point.' He motioned in the direction of the area where so many bush blocks had been bought up in recent years by city folk in search of a sea change.

'I'm just up the road here in Shearwater,' she said. 'I love it out here.'

'Great spot.' He nodded toward Gloria. 'Best let you get back to your friend.'

'I'll see you Friday,' she said with the most encouraging smile she could muster.

'Looking forward to it,' he said.

'Bye, Dog.' She stole another pat and was rewarded with a sideways lick of her wrist.

When she sat down opposite Gloria, she was struck by the normality of what she'd already achieved this morning. An appointment, a swim in the sea, coffee with a friend, running into someone she knew and not being too anxious to stop and talk.

They thanked the waitress who set down their coffees and two of the morning buns the café was known for.

'Ah, one of life's simple pleasures,' said Gloria.

'Mmm.' Vivian took a bite of the piece of sticky pastry she'd broken off and dipped into her long black. These buns were a real treat, but what was even more of a treat was sharing the experience with someone for a change, not sitting alone in cafés up the coast away from her community. Not that she was ready to throw herself back into everything she'd done before. Far from it. But the small steps she'd taken these last few weeks were progress. Even with Dave blindsiding her with his revelation, she'd managed to stay on track. There was reason to hope the shut-in phase was past. She wanted to reach out. Reconnect.

Oscar and the mums and bubs had gone, leaving Vivian and Gloria with the undercover area to themselves in the mid-morning lull.

'Not a bad looking bloke.' Gloria made eyes toward where Oscar had been sitting.

Vivian smiled. 'I could put in a good word for you if you want.'

'Alas, those days are well and truly behind me,' said Gloria. 'But what about you?'

Vivian shook her head but couldn't help a smile. 'Gloria, have you gone mad?'

'I'm only codding.' Gloria leaned over her coffee cup and smiled. 'At least we can have a laugh. Gets us Irish through a lot, let me tell you.'

Vivian was in no doubt her companion was speaking from personal experience.

'You must all be wondering what's going on now that Dave's back in town.' Vivian sat back with her cup in both hands having devoured the bun.

Gloria did the same. 'I will admit there are a few rumours going around as to why he's going about in that van, and of course, we were all a bit shocked the morning after the gala ball when there was no sign of him at the airport.' She looked pensive, as though choosing her words. 'It's all a bit awkward,' she went on. 'We're friends with you both. God knows we're all long enough in the tooth to have seen a thing or two in our time. We just want the best for both of you.'

'I was completely knocked sideways that morning,' said Vivian, not ungrateful for the chance to talk it out, but feeling again the shock of it, the confusion and knowing it was only the half of it. 'I'm not sure if I was the only person to not have read anything into Dave and his friend catching up, but when he came home, he told me they'd been in a relationship before we met.' Gloria's brow furrowed, but she didn't say a word. With her full attention, Vivian went on. 'Things hadn't been great before our trip, but I'd put it all down to the challenge of retirement.' She cast her eyes down to her plate where her fingers absently pushed around at the flaky crumbs. 'His friend, Rory, has cancer. Dave said he wanted to spend time with him, have a break from us into the bargain.' She shrugged and sniffed back a tear that threatened to undo her in public. 'He says they're not in a relationship now, that it was all a long time ago, but I'm not sure I believe him, or even want things to go back to normal.'

It sounded strange, her thoughts spoken so clearly into the open air, into the space between her and the woman sitting opposite who she didn't know all that well. It occurred to her that, apart from Deb, close friends hadn't featured much in her Australian life. She'd been busy raising children, working full time, being a kind of personal assistant to her husband, organising their calendar around his performances, his travels, packing in as much family time as possible when he was home, keeping to a strict routine when she was parenting alone.

'There's no shame in that,' said Gloria, matter of fact. 'Middle age can bring all sorts of change in a relationship.'

Vivian listened as Gloria offered an example.

'I was at a friend's twenty-fifth wedding anniversary just before Covid. Huge expensive do. The original wedding guests, or most of them, and the friends they'd made over the years, all the kids, grandkids . . .'

'What happened?'

Gloria turned up a hand and shrugged. 'A female colleague confronted my friend, and she realised she had feelings for her too. Said life was too short not to be honest and mature about it.' She looked at Vivian over her coffee cup and added. 'I'm not suggesting that's what's happening to you. Quite the opposite if Dave is back to stay, but . . .' She gave a sigh. 'I have to admire my friend in a way. I know you're hurting after what Dave did, but I'd hate for you to have regrets down the track. Only you and he can decide how to go forward.'

Vivian sat with the sage advice. Right now her life was stretching out ahead of her like a barren plain. As much as she didn't feel ready to make any decisions with Dave, it felt good to have her feelings validated, her story understood.

Not everyone had been so supportive. Clodagh had surprised her most. Dave had got to their daughter first. Not entirely his fault, or hers. Clodagh had been trying to get in touch with them on the Sunday she'd travelled home from Queensland. Vivian hadn't been able to face the weekly family video call, and in typical Clodagh form, she'd forgotten they were away and kept ringing until Dave picked up. Finn didn't always manage to connect, but it was their way of letting him know there would be a regular catch up even if their youngest was too hungover or too busy with his mates to answer. Turned out, he was available that Sunday. At least he'd had the grace to phone her afterwards and show a bit of empathy.

'I know it's a shock, Mum,' he'd said. 'To be honest, I'm trying to process it myself. I'll leave you two to sort it out. Not sure what to say, but you know I love you and I'd do anything for you.' It had been all anyone could say, and yes, it was up to the grown-ups to sort it out. But her children were adults too. Clodagh didn't need to hammer her with her views.

'Dad told me he's staying on with his friend for a while,' she'd texted. 'I'm sure it will do him good.'

When they spoke, it had disappointed Clodagh to hear her mother wasn't of the same mind. She'd always been a Daddy's girl, but that was the limit.

'You must be missing Deb something terrible.' With the mention of her best friend, Gloria brought Vivian back to the moment. She shook her head.

'Oh god, yes. Deb was such a great support. Still is. We call and text, of course, but it's not the same. The timing of their move couldn't have been worse.'

Gloria set her cup down and moved her chair closer to the table. 'Have you thought about what you're going to do?' she asked.

Vivian shrugged. 'It's a bit ridiculous living in a house on my own with my husband parked in the driveway.' She smiled. It was the first time she'd been able to see the crazy set-up for what it was. In the silence Gloria was allowing her to process her thoughts, it became clear what she needed to do. 'I should really talk to Dave.'

Gloria nodded. 'He's a reasonable man. I'm sure you two can have a good talk about what's best for both of you.'

When they'd finished the last of their drinks, they stood to go. Vivian put a hand on Gloria's arm.

'Thanks for getting me out . . . and for the chat.'

'No bother at all,' said Gloria. 'Hit me up for a swim any time. We live in a beautiful place, but it's nicer sometimes to share.'

Vivian noticed a vulnerability in the strong Galway woman's eyes.

'I'd like to make it a regular thing if you wouldn't mind me tagging along.'

'Same time next week?'

Vivian got in her car and drove home at her usual speed. No dawdling or drifting today. Even if there were tough times and difficult conversations ahead, at least she had things to look forward to.

Chapter Thirty

When they met on Tuesday, Marilyn and Georgie didn't have an awful lot to say to each other. Normally irritated if a customer dared enter the shop and interrupt their catch up, this morning Marilyn found herself willing someone to walk in the door.

She hadn't been able to speak to Frank. Nursing his two-day hangover helped. She'd brought his meals to him in bed and left him to it, taking to sleeping in the boys' room. Ethan still hadn't returned home. He'd texted to let her know he would be staying at Brad's.

In what was now the empty nest she hadn't been prepared for, Marilyn found herself rattling around like a bird who'd had its flight feathers clipped. But they'd been clipped a long time ago.

Georgie brought her chair closer and held out her phone.

'Wanted to show this to you before but didn't want to upset you.'

It was a picture of a horse tied to a plastic chair just like the ones they were sitting on. Marilyn took the phone and held it while the reason her friend might have thought of her started to sink in. She was tethered to a situation she could easily get away from? Did Georgie really think it was that simple?

Without a word, she stood up and left the shop.

On the bus home she called Ethan.

'You plannin' on comin' home any time soon?'

In the silence, she could hear him step out of the workshop.

'I've been wanting to talk to you, Mum.' She waited as she heard him take a deep breath. 'I can't live with him, but I don't want to upset you neither . . . If I'm honest, I've only been staying there for you.'

'It's okay, son. You shouldn't have to put up with . . .'

'Same goes for you, Mum.'

'Okay, I'll let you go. I know you're at work but I had to . . .'

'Call me any time, Mum. Love you.'

She squeezed her eyes shut and sniffed back the tears. Her baby was all grown up. She was so proud his brothers had stood up to their father for him. He didn't need her the way he used to. The only one who needed her now was Frank.

'I'm home,' she called as she let herself in.

The house was quiet. Frank would be lying in bed, waiting for his lunch, or maybe he'd made it to the sofa today. No sign of him. Ten minutes went by, and he hadn't called out an order. She turned from where she'd been drying the morning's dishes. With the house still, she could hear birds chirping in the trees outside, a neighbour's radio blaring as they hung out their washing. Drying a last plate, she set down the tea towel and went to the bedroom.

Frank lay there, mouth open, drooling into the pillow, his bare chest rising and falling, like a wild boar grunting with every snore. Even asleep he was scary. She thought of Georgie's horse. She could stay mad at Georgie, at the whole world, at the lousy hand of cards life had dealt her. Or she could think of Keisha, her sons, those folks with their struggles in the library . . .

With calm, quiet movements, she slid open drawers, the door of her wardrobe, gathering clothes into a bundle in her arms. If he woke, she would tell him she was doing a laundry load. In the bathroom, she added a few essentials and set her bundle down on the toilet lid. She ran a hand over her beloved books, stopping at one she hadn't enjoyed. Taking it from the shelf, she opened to where she'd hollowed out a section and stashed a year's worth of bingo winnings. Hiding the wad of cash in amongst her bundle, she went to the hallway and piled the lot into a shopping bag. With no idea where she would spend the night or indeed the rest of her life, she slung her handbag over her shoulder and left.

Chapter Thirty-One

Week Six

In the paranaple building, Vivian collected her coffee and turned to take the escalator to the first floor. Ahead of her, Amalia was striding up the moving steps to catch up with Sienna.

'Hey, Sienna. Wait on,' Amalia called.

Vivian had to smile at the latest hair configuration, a set of tight braids, the ends of the pink dye intermingled with a bright aqua worthy of a mermaid.

'Cool colour,' said Vivian as they all walked along to the classroom.

'Mum did it for us last night.' Amalia pulled her phone from the depths of her tote bag and turned it round to show them a photo with her seven-year-old. Through the goofy cat-ear filters, Vivian recognised the child from pictures Amalia had shown her a couple of weeks before.

'Looks great!' said Sienna, taking in the long silky locks in the same aqua as Amalia's. 'I can't imagine Daisy with that much hair.'

Their shared laughter was infectious. Vivian walked into the room with a genuine smile and none of the unwanted butterflies she'd experienced in the early weeks.

⁓

As she took out her notebook and opened it on the table in front of her, it occurred to Vivian that all her students were there, on time. Such a good sign, she thought.

'Good morning, everyone. How has your week been? Write anything?'

When she glanced in Sienna's direction, the girl didn't look away or bend her head down. Vivian took a chance.

'What about you, Sienna? Anything inspire you to write since last week?'

There was a shrug, but also a shy smile. At least her efforts at rapport building had paid off, Vivian mused.

'You should see her drawings,' said Robyn, who was sitting beside Sienna. 'They are something special.'

When Robyn turned toward Sienna, she was rewarded with a roll of the eyes, but also a beautiful smile that spread across Sienna's reddening cheeks. Although she knew the girl didn't want to attract the attention of the whole group, Vivian suspected she didn't get much in the way of praise outside of class. She gestured for permission to have a look. Sienna pushed the notebook toward her, then sat back in her chair, arms folded.

'Wow! These are great.'

Vivian turned the pages slowly. The girl had done an amazing job of the living room at Home Hill. She'd added colour to her original sketch of Joseph Lyons stretched out on the sofa, propped up by the cushions his wife had hand-crafted. Bringing their guide's descriptions to life, Sienna had drawn Enid standing at an ironing board, holding one of those ancient irons, steam rising from it, while she reached to take a shirt from a vast pile on the armchair beside her. Flicking back to a page she'd skipped, Vivan's eyes widened.

'Who are these happy folks?'

'My mum and dad.'

'So beautiful, Sienna. These will go in the book.'

Sienna's face burned as she pulled the sleeves of her hoodie over her hands, but Vivian turned the picture round so the others in the room could catch a glimpse of the girl's talent before she handed the book back.

'Well done, Sienna. Not everyone can draw like this. Me, for instance.'

There were nods and gasps of awe at what Sienna had produced, but the girl herself seemed doubtful. Vivian wondered how someone with that kind of talent hadn't pursued a course in visual arts. That drawing of her parents . . .

'We need more pictures for our book,' she told the group. 'Photos of places you love, of items in your homes maybe that mean something to you, your drawings . . .'

Robyn started to scroll on her phone.

'Got anything, Robyn?'

Vivian returned Sienna's notebook and went to take a look. A tall glass vase held a trio of bright sunflowers, their dark centres like faces encircled by bonnets of yellow bunting.

'That's stunning, Robyn. Where did you get those?'

'We took a drive to a farm near Penguin,' she said. 'You should go. It's so beautiful.'

Vivian nodded. She and Dave had taken their family to that very place, but she didn't mention it now. How to share memories that included the four of them was just another difficulty to navigate. 'Have you written something about it?' she asked.

Robyn shook her head. 'Only journal.'

She showed Vivian where she'd been writing what looked like a short paragraph each day. Taking a closer look, Vivian realised she'd written about the small things, like a neighbour's child leaving a handmade card in her mailbox, hanging out washing in the sunshine, leaving the back door open to let in the fresh Tasmanian air. The sentence structure would need tweaking, but that was why they were here. This she could work with.

'You've done a great job of the journalling, Robyn.'

'I try to be grateful,' she said. 'Enjoy life. Make my father proud.'

Returning to the front of the room to start the day's topic, Vivian was sure she'd heard a hint of something that suggested Robyn's life wasn't all flowers and sunshine. Who's was? But her attitude had made Vivian think this gratitude practice could really be something to aspire to in her own life.

Chapter Thirty-Two

After a restless night, Oscar arrived later than usual and made for the last spot available on the table nearest the door.

'Sit, sit,' said Rosa, smiling at him from where she was cradling Camilla in her arms. 'I learn from you.'

He gave a self-deprecating laugh. 'You ladies are the clever ones,' he said, looking from one to the other. 'How many languages do you speak?'

Rosa pinched her thumb and forefinger together. 'For me it's just eh-Spanish and a little English. This is smart one.' She gestured to Robyn.

'In Guangdong, we speak Cantonese, but we also know Mandarin.'

He shook his head. 'I have only one language and I'm still learning it.' His comment was rewarded with a smile. He tried to imagine Siraporn sitting in the classroom with them all. Her English was good, but he knew nothing about where she was from in Thailand or what she'd done before coming to Australia.

He parked thoughts of his sister's cleaner as Vivian enquired about what they'd been writing, doing the rounds for an update before turning to the smartboard to introduce the morning's topic. Drawing a line down the middle of the board, she made two headings, Formal on one side and Informal on the other. Giving each of them some sticky notes, she asked them to write down ideas and place them on the board. Forms for an insurance claim he'd had to do for Geraldine when the tree came down hadn't seemed worthy of the class, but Oscar was grateful to have something to contribute.

Rosa had been a revelation when it came to ideas, giving formal examples from her work: reports, emails, databases. When he'd asked her what she did, she'd told him she was a marketing executive in Peru. Robyn too had great suggestions, like visa and passport forms. He'd heard about the letters migrants had to write about why they wished to live in Tasmania to support visa applications. Robyn had hers on her phone. Vivian asked if she'd mind sharing. In her quiet voice, she did her best to read about her fondness for Tasmania, how she would like to volunteer to help homeless people and that she was studying for a certificate so she could work in aged care. It sounded almost like a begging letter. He'd had no idea of the hoops folks from other countries had to jump through to stay in Australia.

At the end of the session, he hung back and took the opportunity to speak to Vivian and Cathy when the others left.

'How did you go today?' Cathy asked him as he packed up his backpack and pulled it onto his shoulder.

'Good, thanks. I'm learning heaps . . . Even getting better on the computer.'

He tried to sound upbeat, but he'd spent most of the morning tapping at the keyboard with his two fingers, heavily relying on Johnny and prompts from the laptop about how he could write better. It was a bit hit-and-miss, whether to believe the computer or not. He'd overheard Vivian mention to someone how a dictionary wasn't much use for finding out how to spell a word if you didn't know the first few letters. If dictionaries and computers couldn't help him, he was stuffed.

'So you're getting something out of it?' asked Cathy.

'Definitely.' There was a moment's pause where he thought they expected him to say more, but Vivian rescued him.

'We've only got a few of weeks left,' she said, 'but is there anything in particular you'd like help with?'

Before this course, Oscar might have considered himself a lost cause, but here he was being offered assistance with the one thing that had kept him back all his life. He'd be foolish to pretend he didn't need it.

'My spelling is shocking,' he said. 'Don't suppose you could fix that in a couple of weeks?'

Cathy was straight in with the problem-solving he'd come to recognise. 'We can always match you up with a tutor if you want some one-to-one sessions.'

He shrugged. 'I'm only in Tassie for a few months.'

'That's right. You're housesitting,' said Vivian. 'For your sister?'

He nodded, grateful she remembered their exchange at the café.

'I've got a bit of time these days if you'd like the extra help.'

Oscar knew she was going above and beyond, but this was a chance he couldn't pass up. A chance to really get to grips with this beast of a handicap that had him hamstrung at every turn.

'Okay,' he said, too embarrassed and tongue-tied to make a more appropriate response.

'You're welcome to use a room here in the library,' Cathy suggested. 'I'll put in the paperwork once you've agreed on a time.'

'Cathy tells me you used to work in a printers',' said Vivian.

'Most of my life,' he said, embarrassed to have been the subject of discussion.

'We're looking for volunteers to help organise the layout of our book. Would you be up for helping?'

'Sure.' Oscar wasn't convinced he'd be any good at the kind of work the graphic design crew did at his old workplace. He'd been more hands on with presses and packing. But he wasn't about to say no to these kind ladies who had given him a space to learn and distract him from his aches and pains.

Pleased with his morning's work and grateful for Vivian's offer of help, he drove straight home, too tired and sore to hang around town. As much as he didn't wish to get in Siraporn's way, something told him he should keep an eye on her.

Chapter Thirty-Three

'Thanks for volunteering to give Oscar a hand,' said Cathy as she packed up the pens and papers onto her trolley.

'I think he needs it,' said Vivian. 'I've noticed he hasn't written much apart from a few sentences that day we went to Home Hill.'

'Ah! Could be a confidence thing,' said Cathy.

'Or shame.'

Vivian had seen it before; students, especially boys, who'd acted out in class, doing everything to distract themselves and everyone else from their struggles with reading and writing. Schools too stretched to put measures in place, like more support staff. She'd seen the consequences playing out in kids being excluded, getting into all sorts of mischief.

Cathy began steering her trolley toward the door. 'Well, have a nice afternoon,' she said.

Vivian remembered her promise to ask Cathy about her plans for a change.

'Got much on for the rest of the day?' she asked.

Cathy turned. 'For once, I have a meeting-free afternoon. Might even have time to go out and grab lunch.'

'I'm going to that place on Oldaker Street if you want to join me,' said Vivian. 'The service is pretty quick.'

Cathy smiled. 'Let me get these put away and I'll join you downstairs.'

Vivian gathered her laptop bag and stuffed her pencil case and notebook inside. The room was empty, but the buzz of the morning's discussion still reverberated between the huge window and soundproofed walls. It had begun to feel like her zone. She walked out slowly, calm in the face of leaving the classroom behind for another week, already looking forward to coming back next time.

Cathy had beaten her to the front door of the building. A curtain of grey hung overhead as they took the laneway through the marketplace and reached the café just before the downpour.

'Four seasons in one day,' said Cathy.

'Just like home.'

They had a quick look at the specials board before settling themselves at a corner table in the conservatory at the front.

'Funny how you call Ireland home when you've been here so long,' Cathy remarked.

Vivian sat back, holding the menu but letting her eyes assess the scene outside. A couple were trying to cross the road, jaywalking to save themselves from getting soaked. A young man in shorts and a t-shirt seemed oblivious to the rain, while others had their Tassie tuxedos on, ready for anything autumn threw at them. It rained a lot in Ireland. That she remembered.

'Maybe it gets worse as you get older,' she began, 'but lately, I've really felt a longing to go back.'

Cathy's eyes were full of questions, but she let her go on.

'Not getting any younger,' said Vivian, laughing to lighten what was a heavy topic of conversation. She was here to learn about what Cathy did in her spare time, not to be maudlin.

'I've been thinking of taking a trip there myself,' said Cathy.

Vivian's mouth opened at the unexpected comment. She knew Cathy had Irish roots, like so many Australians, but had forgotten the details. She'd heard so many stories over the years. Names of small towns she might have heard of but never been to. Surnames mentioned with an implied hope that she would know the whereabouts of long-lost relatives. It had taken her years to understand the deep connections people felt to her homeland.

'Tell me more.'

'Let's order first.' Ever the pragmatist, Cathy caught the eye of the waitress and ordered the soup and a mug of coffee.

'I'll have the same,' said Vivian, eager to hear of Cathy's plans.

'Ah, I've been doing a bit of the family tree,' she began. 'Found I have living relatives in County Meath. Near the Hill of Tara?'

'Oh my god, that's a spectacular place. So much history ... and what a view ... It's not far from Dublin.'

'Hold on.' Cathy took her phone out of her bag and started typing into an app. 'How far from Dublin?'

When the waitress left them to their meal, Vivian told her as much as she could remember from a visit to the historic site many years ago.

'The high kings of Ireland were crowned and buried there. So much myth and legend attached to the place. And that view. Oh my god, you can see over about four counties . . . on a clear day.'

Cathy rolled her eyes. 'I'll have to get the cousins to watch the forecast for me.'

'When are you guys planning on travelling?' asked Vivian.

'Oh, it would be just me.'

Vivian raised her eyebrows as she brought a spoon of the soup to her mouth. 'Would Lee not go with you?'

Cathy shook her head. 'His days of travelling are over I'm afraid.'

Vivian took in the news with a sense that she'd missed out on so much of what had been going on in other people's lives, too wrapped up in her own grief to even register that of others. Holding eye contact with Cathy, she willed her to go on.

'His back is worse since the operation. We thought they'd fixed it . . .'

Cathy gave a resigned sigh before replacing the momentary glum look with her signature smile. Not for the first time, Vivian saw through the facade. She'd been the same when they'd worked together at the school. Always appearing to bounce back from challenging situations, like student stand-offs or staffroom conflict. She had no doubt the woman sitting in front of her could travel independently to Ireland and poke out her rellies. But to have to do it without her husband was so unfair.

It was something Vivian had never had to contemplate before now. It had been a good few years since she'd done so, but when she'd travelled home it was always with Dave or one of the kids. She still had immediate family there to trot her round to relatives' houses, and old friends to catch up with for coffee or a pint in old haunts. But it struck her that, even if she was serious about going home for a while, it would be so different without Dave's involvement. No sharing in the mix of excitement and apprehension, bouncing ideas around, him invested in the journey as much as she was. Seeing the shine in Cathy's eye at the mention of Lee's troubles, she felt a sudden awareness of her own mortality and wished she could talk to Dave about how the Shannons were faring.

It would have been nice to have gone home, put the kettle on and relayed her news to him over a cuppa. As she motored down the sweep of the Port Sorell Road, taking in the familiar views she loved, the rich greens of the land and the glimpses of blue sea rimmed by slivers of sandy beach, she considered initiating the conversation. But when she pulled into the driveway, there was no sign of him or the campervan. For the first time since he'd moved back, she cared about where he was gone.

Chapter Thirty-Four

On Saturday, Sienna booked a taxi to take them to Amalia's. Grateful she didn't have to try and squeeze Daisy into any of her old outfits, she chose a denim pinafore and white long-sleeve top from a donation from the family centre. The lady in charge had come to her with a big striped carrier bag, its zipper almost busting at the seams.

'Just a few things for Mum to make life a bit easier,' she'd said as she'd carried the load out to Jess's car. 'And some things to make this little one feel extra special.'

Sienna wasn't sure second-hand clothes were the antidote to living hand-to-mouth and not having friends, but she swallowed her reservations and thanked the woman. When she'd got back to the unit and emptied the contents of the bag onto the bed, she was ashamed she'd been so skeptical. There were enough toiletries, including tampons, to last her months, baby food and nappies that would save her heaps at the shops, clothes for Daisy and a few things she wasn't too proud to wear herself.

Sitting Daisy on the bathroom floor in the bouncy chair she'd bought from the Salvo's, Sienna hopped in the shower and gave her hair a good wash with the coconut shampoo and conditioner that made her imagine a tropical island. Singing a few of the baby group songs to keep Daisy entertained, she realised she hadn't sung in the shower in forever. At home, her Mum would bang on the door and tell her she was using up all the water, but her dad would join in with words he mostly made up to drive them both mad. The singing stopped when Gary moved in. She'd learned to keep quiet and lock the bathroom door when he was around. But she shook off the painful memories. No getting sad. They were going on a night out.

As she pulled on black jeans and a cotton top with a rainbow motif, her heart began to pound. It was so nice of Amalia to invite her, but the butterflies were going into overdrive. Would Amalia's friends and family judge her? What if they thought she was weird and didn't speak to her? Or worse, asked her awkward questions? She took a deep breath and blew it out in a long 'whooh' sound. None of that mattered, she told herself. It wasn't like she wanted to hook up with anyone, and besides, Daisy would be on her hip for most of the night. She looked at her daughter, so beautiful in her 'new' clothes, her tufts of hair brushed back, that smile. Everyone would love her, and if they didn't, that was on them. As she slipped her hoodie over her head and fixed her baseball cap in position, she wished she wouldn't always feel she had to hide. The taxi driver beeped the horn. Before she could change her mind, she picked up her daughter and went outside. Tina and Sandy were on the veranda next door. She went to wave

as they drove past. Tina gave the barest nod. It was obvious
the neighbour wished to keep her distance, but at least she'd
got an acknowledgement.

⌒

At the address Amalia had texted her, balloons bobbed above
the mailbox. Sienna double-checked her phone. There'd been
no mention of a party. With the meter clocking up the fare,
she thought to back out. She hadn't even brought a plate to share,
let alone a present. But before she could tell the driver to put
his pay machine away and turn around, her phone pinged.

Hope you find us. Can't wait to see you both, then four
love-heart emojis.

Reaching out her card, Sienna paid, gathered Daisy and
the baby bag into her arms and thanked the driver. They were
here now. She couldn't deny Daisy the opportunity to play
with Amalia's daughter and any other children who might be
there. She'd have to suck it up and try to behave like an adult.

Following the sound of a Childish Gambino song, she
walked down the side of the house toward the backyard.
Amalia saw her the moment she rounded the corner and came
with arms outstretched, squealing at them.

'Thank you so much for coming,' she said, pulling the
two of them into a hug.

'I'm so sorry, I didn't bring anything . . .' Sienna began.

Amalia shook her head of gorgeous hair, now coloured
white with blue and pink layers like a unicorn.

'You look so different!' Sienna hoped the comment hadn't
sounded off.

Amalia pulled at a few strands of her hair. 'Gave myself a little treat.' She winked. 'I didn't tell you, but it's actually my birthday.'

'I would have brought something . . .'

Amalia put up a hand to shush her. 'Your presence is my present.' Putting an arm around Sienna's waist, she led them to a trestle table where a selection of salads and snacks were laid out. 'Let's get you a drink and I'll introduce you to everyone.' She pointed to a big bucket of ice. 'Bubbles, beer, cruiser, soft drink?'

'Just a Coke if you have it.'

Feeling a prickle of cautious excitement, she cuddled Daisy in close and kissed her head, breathing in the smell of her, taking comfort in the soft blonde down on her skin. The little girl in her arms was the reason she'd made the decision to avoid alcohol like the plague. Cole had tried to derail her time after time, party after party, until he stopped bringing her along. But she was here with their beautiful daughter, and he wasn't. It was all that mattered. As Amalia fetched a plastic cup and poured from the two-litre bottle, Sienna took a furtive glance around the crowd. No one she recognised. She removed the baseball cap and shook out her freshly washed hair.

'Thanks.' She took the cup from Amalia and followed her to a group who were standing around the barbecue.

'This is Sienna,' said Amalia, 'and this cutie is Daisy.'

There were nods and smiles as Amalia rattled off names. Sam, cooking the snags, was her partner, Sienna got that much, but the two couples with him had names she'd already mixed up.

A young girl ran between them, chased by another girl and a boy, all of a similar age. Amalia called to them, 'Kids, come here for a minnie.'

The first girl ran to her side, hugging her and jumping up and down. Amalia put an arm around her shoulders.

'This is Charlie,' Amalia told her. 'Charlie, do you think you could show Daisy some of your baby toys?'

Charlie looked around and beckoned to her friends. 'Come on.' Like a captain with her shipmates, they all ran toward the house. Daisy's smiles disappeared as she strained to follow them.

'Don't worry, Dais,' Amalia reassured her. 'They'll be back to play with you as soon as they find those toys.'

Minutes later, they reappeared with armfuls of furry animals and a plastic Barbie car.

'Here, let's put this down on the grass.'

Amalia and one of the women shook out a picnic blanket and set it down for the children. Daisy couldn't wait to get out of Sienna's arms, wriggling and bouncing to let her know she wanted to play.

'Who's this cherub?' The woman who looked like an older version of Amalia knelt down on the blanket beside Sienna and offered Daisy a purple teddy bear. She introduced herself as Patti, Amalia's mum, and chatted as though Sienna had known Amalia for years.

'Amalia tells me you go to the writing class in the library,' she said. 'How is that going?'

Sienna smiled. 'Really good, actually.'

She told the woman about Home Hill and the gallery visit, grateful to have something to talk about that didn't involve running away from home or escaping an abusive partner. Neither Amalia nor her mother seemed the type to pry. Instead, they made her feel they were genuinely glad to have her there.

By the time she'd eaten all the sausages and salad she'd been able to fit in, Sienna had begun to relax. The children were as fascinated by Daisy as she was by them. The adults talked and joked over beers and bottles of wine that flowed freely but didn't dominate the event. It reminded her of nights at her parents' when her dad was still alive. Nights with family friends gathered around the pool, sharing a long meal with lots of banter. Sitting here, mingling with people she'd never met, she longed to be around that pool with Hugo and her mum and dad, paying each other out about the small things that bonded them and made them laugh. It had never been the same once Gary had wheedled his way into their home.

When Daisy grew sleepy, Sienna left her with Amalia and went to the bathroom to call a taxi. The baby was already asleep when she got back. The other kids had also started to fade. Charlie was curled up on Sam's lap, settled back against his chest, eyes drooping as she tried to play a game on his phone. He seemed oblivious to the child in one way, chatting to a mate beside him, yet his body language said otherwise. As he gave an absent-minded stroke of her hair, Sienna was reminded again of her own father and how, when she thought he was ignoring her, talking to grown-ups, he'd stretch his arm out for a fist bump. A small check-in to let her know he wasn't forgetting her. She'd have liked one of his fist bumps or bear hugs right now.

'Can I give you a run home?' Amalia's mum broke into her thoughts.

She shook her head. 'No, it's fine. I called a taxi, but thanks anyway.' It would have been cheaper to accept Patti's offer, but they'd already been so generous. Besides, it wasn't like she'd been going out every weekend.

Basking in the normality of the evening, Sienna sat in the taxi, watching Daisy sleep in the child seat beside her. Exhausted from the effort of getting out and talking to so many new people, she joined in for a snooze. Back at the unit, the driver had to wake her.

'Hey miss, this you?'

As her eyes opened, Sienna took a second to recognise the driveway and set of units of their new address. She paid, unbuckled Daisy and went round to the other side of the car to lift her out gently without waking her. From next door's veranda, Sandy gave a low whine. Not exactly his usual greeting, but it was late. He was only doing his job. With Daisy still fast asleep in her arms, she went to take the house key from the pocket of her hoodie.

'Uhh!' she gasped. Pinned to the door was a photo of Daisy. Cole would have to have taken it the day of his first access visit at the centre. He'd photoshopped a red arrow pointing to the bruise on her forehead and text that read,

I could have her taken off you for this, or you could come back. Love heart.

Holding Daisy close with both arms, Sienna scanned the sleepy side street. Shoving in the door and locking it behind them, she went around the unit to check every door and window was shut tight. How the fuck had he found out where they lived? Her mind raced. Only Jess knew her address. Okay, it would be written on official documents. The police, the daycare staff. . . Could someone have left it on a table or somewhere Cole might have seen it? Mistakes were made all the time, even by people with the best intentions. She texted Jess.

Manic with terror, she couldn't bear the thought of putting Daisy in the cot. Even the half-metre of space between them would keep her awake all night. Trying to calm the shaking in her hands, she lay the baby down on the bed, grateful to hear her barely grizzle as she pulled a blanket from the cot and spread it over her. With every ounce of strength, she heaved the nightstand from its position in the corner to the opposite end of the room, then pushed the bed into the space so it was flush with the wall. As she lay down fully dressed beside her daughter, she realised it wasn't just her hands, but her whole body that was shaking. After hours of anxious waiting, she gave up on the hope of hearing from Jess.

⌒

She thought she had just drifted off to sleep when a knock on the door woke her. Beside her, Daisy was sleeping – a long sleep, judging by the bright sunshine that peeked in through the crack between the curtains. As the nightmare came back to her, Sienna sat bolt upright. What if Cole was on the other side of the door? Taking her phone, she tiptoed to the kitchen and went to take a knife from the drawer.

A woman's voice called out, 'Are you there?'

Sienna set the knife back and went to the door. Through the glass panel, she saw the short wide shape of her neighbour, the familiar staffy at her side.

'Tina, is that you?'

'Yes, love. Are you okay?'

Heart pounding in her chest, Sienna undid the lock and opened the door a fraction. She let out the breath she'd been holding like she'd been underwater and opened the door wider. Sandy jumped up to greet her, a fresh cut over one eye.

'Are you okay?' Tina asked again.

From behind her she could hear Daisy starting to cry. Leaving Tina on her doorstep, she ran to the bedroom.

'Come in,' she told Tina when she returned with Daisy on her hip.

Tina didn't move. 'I don't get involved in my neighbour's business,' she said, her face serious. 'Just wanted to tell you someone came round here last night, shoutin' and bawlin'. He was pretty mad you wasn't home. Even threw a rock at me dog.'

Sienna looked down at Sandy and gave him a pat, taking a good look at the cut as Tina went on.

'I wanted you to know I'll be callin' the RSPCA Monday mornin' to report him.'

Looking from Sandy to the door, Sienna felt everything she'd eaten at the party swirl in her stomach. Beads of sweat broke out on her skin like she'd been for a run. Tina's face was replaced by stars, spinning in front of her eyes. Staggering backward, she tried to point to where the photo had been the night before. But it was no use, as she tried to cradle Daisy, she felt she was being sucked into a black hole.

—

Tina was holding Daisy when Sienna came to. Trying to sit up, she felt the room revolve.

'Easy now, hun.'

The older woman's hand felt warm as she helped her sit back against the sofa. Her instinct was to reach out and take Daisy, but all the energy had leached from her body. It took any strength that was left to focus and wait for her mind to stop racing for long enough to think straight. How could that photo have been there last night and not this morning? What time was it, anyway? Could she even trust her neighbour?

'Is there a bottle in the fridge?' Tina leaned on the sofa and strained to stand up as she balanced Daisy in her arms.

The baby's cries shot through Sienna. She reached an elbow behind her and pulled herself up.

'Yes,' she said, but as she took a step forward, her knees went to jelly again. Tina held an arm out and steadied her.

'Sit,' Tina ordered. 'I'll look after this one.'

Stunned at the turn of events, Sienna could only watch as Tina took Daisy to the kitchen and listen as the crying ebbed away with reassurances from their neighbour that everything would be okay. Her phone rang in her pocket.

'Jess!'

Her case worker was full of apologies saying she'd had her phone on silent.

'I'm so sorry,' she said. 'What's happened?'

'Can you come?' It was all she could say as tears began to stream down her cheeks.

'Give me twenty minutes.'

By the time Jess arrived, Tina had fed Daisy and was changing her on the rug. She'd told Sienna she'd raised four kids of her own and two grandkids, but the details were lost on her as she could only think about the photo and the fact that Cole had been here. The dog heard Jess arrive before either of them. He gave a bark and ran to the door.

'Sienna?' Jess called.

Tina shot her a look. 'Not Anna then?'

With a weak smile, Sienna got up from the sofa and went to let Jess in.

'Thank you so much for coming.'

Jess surveyed the lounge room where Daisy and Tina were having a conversation of sorts on the floor, toys and baby changing supplies everywhere.

'This is Tina, my neighbour,' Sienna told her.

Tina looked up and nodded. 'I'll leave you to it.'

Sienna felt a pang of guilt, hearing the woman's knees creak as she got up.

'I'm not sure what I'd have done if you hadn't been here,' she began.

'Like I told ya, you know where I am if you need me.' Tina shuffled toward the door, looking sore. She turned as she was about to leave. 'The RSPCA will be getting that call tomorra.'

Sienna gave Sandy a last pat, fresh tears welling in her eyes. 'Sorry, mate.'

⁓

In the kitchen, Sienna made Jess a cuppa and explained what had happened. With both hands around her mug, Jess took a few moments before saying anything, deep grooves settling on her brow.

'You've had no contact with him?'

Sienna shook her head. 'I swore to you I wouldn't.'

'That's good. But how did he find you?'

Sienna wasn't sure it was a fair question. She'd thought *Jess* would have the answers. 'Would someone have told him where we live?'

'God no!' Jess set down her mug. 'More than our jobs are worth to do something that stupid.'

She waited as Jess twirled a strand of the beach-blonde hair round an index finger.

'We should report the incident to the police,' she said. 'They'll interview Tina. She might have seen the car, be able to identify the intruders.'

Intruders. Surely, he'd come alone. Meeting Josh on the bus came back to her.

'Jess, I have to tell you I met his mate . . . on the bus . . . I was going to collect Daisy.' With her heart racing in her chest, she couldn't get the words out fast enough. 'I got off a stop early, tried to lose him . . . but what if he followed me . . . told Cole we were here?'

Jess took out her phone and began dialling the police. 'If this happens again, you have to call the police straight away.'

The thought of it happening again sent a shiver down her, but Sienna nodded. Jess believed her, she could take some comfort in that, but without evidence, this stuff wouldn't stand up in court. Cole could potentially continue to terrorise them and get away with it.

Chapter Thirty-Five

At home on Sunday evening, Vivian gave the duvet a good shake before taking its cover from the pile of linen and turning it inside out. Bringing the corners together, she fed the crisp yellow fabric over the duvet, cursing the fiddly task she used to prefer to do with Dave. They'd had a habit of leaving it until just before bed. On a sunny day, with wind enough for good drying, they'd strip their bed with every intention of dressing it in good time. Distracted by the day's events, they'd inevitably go to brush their teeth and see the unmade bed, grumbling at one another about why they couldn't be more organised and do it earlier. It was another part of the minutiae of their lives she never imagined she'd miss. She could do what she liked with their bed. It was all hers, it seemed. But she'd tackle changing that another day. Today she was making Clodagh's bed with no idea why or for how long the girl was coming home.

When Dave had messaged to say he would be back on Sunday, she'd been torn between relief at knowing he was okay and worry as to why he would be returning with their eldest child. There was no explanation. No direct word from their daughter. Phoning her might have been misconstrued as prying, and not phoning her, uncaring. In an ideal world, a daughter should be able to pop home whenever she pleased. But Vivian was under no illusion that her family relations were far from ideal. She'd decided to make the place look as homey as possible and wait until they were face-to-face to find out what was going on.

It was after eight o'clock when they arrived. She'd long covered over the salads she'd made, set them in the fridge and stacked away the cutlery and good plates she'd laid on the table. Having steeled herself to sit down and talk in a civilised manner about whatever it was that had prompted the visit, she was exhausted by the time they arrived. Seeing Winnie's lights, she went out to welcome Clodagh as she stepped down from the camper. Her quirky, independent daughter, always youthful and super fit, stood in front of her now looking shook.

'Hello, darling,' said Vivian, her hands moving like robots as she tried to gauge if this was a hugging moment. She could never be sure with Clodagh.

Vivian stood, taking her in: hands in the pockets of a pair of oversized denim overalls, chin almost at her chest, dark hair that looked in need of a wash covering her eyes.

'Okay if I stay for a few days, Mum?'

Vivian reached out and drew her daughter into an awkward hug. She didn't need to wait for an explanation to know Clodagh needed one.

'I'll take the gear in.' Dave had jumped out of the driver's side and retrieved a small travel case from the back of the camper.

She put an arm around her daughter's shoulder and led her to the house.

'Smells great,' said Clodagh, taking in the scented candles lighting the hallway.

Vivian smiled. At least she'd done something right.

In the kitchen, they stood for a moment before any of them spoke.

'Would you like a cup . . .' Vivian began.

'Is it okay if I go straight to bed?'

The dark circles under Clodagh's eyes suggested sleep was a good idea. Vivian didn't try to persuade her to stay up. Whatever her daughter was doing here, she was sure it could wait until they were both rested. There was only one thing she wanted to know.

'Max okay?'

'Yes, Mum.' The slight tone of annoyance was countered with an embarrassed smile. 'I'll tell you all about it in the morning, yeah?'

'Will I put this in the room?' Dave nodded toward the stairs, holding the travel case.

'Sure . . . thanks, Dad.'

What in the name of god? Vivian could only look on as the pair of them climbed the stairs to Clodagh's old room.

When they'd gone inside, she went to the bottom of the stairs and listened.

Ever the peacemaker, Dave spoke in low reassurances,

'Don't worry about Maxie. His dad will do a great job looking after him. He'll be fine.'

Vivian shook her head and strode to the cupboard where she kept the Baileys for the occasional drink. Setting a glass on the worktop, she poured a nice measure and went to the fridge for ice. When he came back down, Dave eyed the glass. If he thought she was about to offer him one, he could think again.

'What's up with Clodagh?' she asked.

He glanced away, looking sheepish. Vivian wasn't sure if he felt guilt, embarrassment, or both.

'I'd rather we didn't let on to be talking about her,' he said.

'Please yourself.' Vivian put the drink to her lips.

'We could have a drink outside,' he said.

A cool wind had come in from the east. There was rain forecast. They could hardly sit outside on the veranda. She raised her eyebrows.

'In Winnie,' he clarified.

'All right.' She gathered her cardigan from the coat stand, pulling it on to stave off the chill in the night air.

⌒

The camper van smelled of him. Intensely, like everything in it was part of him. Living in it would do that, she reasoned, as she set her glass down and pushed a pile of sheet music out of the way so she could take a seat at the booth-style dining table. He closed the door and stood in the muted moonlight, pouring a glass of red wine from an already opened bottle. Not much over sixty, he was fit and lean, but there was a greyness to him, like he'd aged without her noticing. Perhaps the same had happened to her from where he was standing, looking at her now like a timid child, anxious about speaking up. She waited as he turned on the heating, impatient for him to sit. The sooner he told her, the sooner she could go back inside and get some sleep.

'Are you going to tell me why she's here?'

He brought his glass to the table and slid into the seat opposite, taking a moment before he spoke. He'd never been good at conflict, always taking the fastest route out of an argument – backing down or walking away. They'd never actually fought. It occurred to her now that maybe they should have.

'Oliver and Clodagh haven't been getting along for a while.'

Vivian drew a hand to her mouth. 'Why didn't she tell me?'

Dave looked at her, the steady green eyes, the set of his strong jaw saying, *Why do you think?*

She closed her eyes tight with shame, regret and fear. When she opened them again, he looked as crestfallen as she felt.

'How long have you known?'

He shook his head. 'Don't turn this into a "good cop, bad cop" thing, Viv. I only found out today.'

She bristled at the remark, but this wasn't about her. Their daughter was navigating a rough patch without them. How could they have become so disconnected? Any discord between her parents needed to be pushed to one side.

'What's happened?'

She followed his gaze out the window to where stars twinkled between the slender giants of a stand of gum trees. Suddenly too warm, she pushed back the shoulders of her cardigan and reached for her drink. The cool creamy liquid bought her time, a moment's distraction before she might have shouted at him, demanded he stop his stargazing and tell her in detail what the heck had been going on. She took another sip.

'So are you going to tell me or . . .'

'I'll let *her* tell you.'

He was looking at her in that way he had of warning her without words. It was a look that had spared many an argument when the kids were teenagers. She'd loved him for it, but their children were all grown up. They didn't need to pussyfoot around each other anymore, and yet she couldn't bring herself to have the conversation they needed to have. After hearing about Clodagh and Oliver, all she wanted to do was forget about herself and help. She nodded and knocked back her drink.

As she made to get out of the seat, he touched her arm. 'What about us?'

She stood frozen to the spot, her head spinning. 'Us?'

He let go. 'I just want to talk it out.'

'Your actions spoke volumes, Dave.'

'Can't we at least have an adult conversation?'

It was true. No matter how painful this whole situation was, putting up walls was like putting a band-aid on a gaping wound. She slumped back down.

'I'm listening.' Feeling all of her fifty-eight years, she wished she could climb into bed, but after her conversation with Gloria, she'd promised herself she'd talk to him.

'You have to tell me what you want. I can't keep living like this, Viv.'

He turned and gestured to his cramped if cute billeting arrangements.

Seeing Winnie at close quarters for the first time in so long, she felt the loss of him, the loss of the future they'd imagined together. In the last few weeks, she'd regained some of her self-esteem. The writing class had done that for her. She'd even reconnected with friends – not close ones, but friends, nonetheless. She hadn't thought to look too far ahead, but here in the van, sitting opposite him, she knew the future would have to be faced sooner or later.

'What about Rory?' she asked.

He shook his head and took a while to answer.

'In those first weeks I was away . . . it was like we were twenty again . . . at least for some of it . . .' The kind twinkly eyes that had made her heart skip all those years ago were wet with tears. 'The cancer's advanced.' The weight of it sat between them. 'The family were around him, ex, kids . . . after a while, I wasn't helping . . .'

As much as this was not what she had signed up for when she'd taken her marriage vows, the utter sadness in his eyes could not be avoided. The loss, the passage of time . . . and Rory, by the sounds, was running out of time.

'What do *you* want to do, Dave?'

He wiped his tears with the back of his hand and sniffed back fresh ones.

'I missed you, Viv. I don't want to waste any more time.' He took a moment to gather himself before going on. 'We have a good marriage, you and I . . .'

'You weren't honest with me, Dave. Never once did you tell me about your sexuality. And when things got tough for you, when I retired for you and you found yourself living twenty-four seven with your wife, you avoided me. You sought out Rory . . .'

It was getting far too hot in the camper van. She needed fresh air. She stood and took her glass in her hand.

'I didn't lie to you,' he said. Without turning from the table, he added, 'I chose you.'

Chose. The word fizzed in her head like he'd added vinegar to baking soda. So many connotations to those five simple letters. She needed to get out of the van that felt like it would close in on her. 'I can't do this tonight. I have to face Clodagh in the morning. She's my priority.'

He came toward her. 'Can we at least put on a united front for her sake?'

'Sure,' she quipped. 'We're good at that.'

Chapter Thirty-Six

Clodagh might as well have been in her late teens, such was the sleep-in she was having. Vivian was about to have her second cup of coffee by the time she appeared in the kitchen, an old jumper of her brother's over a pair of short pyjamas.

'Hey.' She pulled a stool out from under the bench and perched herself on top of it.

'Coffee?' Vivian asked, raising the cafetiere.

'That would be great. Any chance I could have a couple of Panadol first?'

Vivian went to her handbag to retrieve the pills and got her a glass of water. It was like going back in time to mornings or middays where her children emerged from their bedrooms, half the day gone, with hangovers and hazy stories from the night before. But no party preceded this, no fun times to justify the sore head, the long face. 'Will I put on a bit of toast for you, love?'

Clodagh shook her head. 'Coffee's fine. I'll eat something later.'

Without arguing, Vivian took a couple of her beloved Irish pottery cups and poured for them both.

'Thanks, Mum.' Clodagh placed both hands around the cup. Despite the warmth in the kitchen, she looked cold.

'Did Dad tell you what happened?'

Vivian took a breath before answering. 'The what but not the why. You know Dad.'

They both sipped their coffee. Clodagh usen't to take it black.

'You and Oliver not getting along?'

Better to leave this wide open for Clodagh to fill her in than presume anything. She liked Oliver. A simple, easy-going lad from Cygnet, a quiet seaside place south of Hobart that reminded Vivian of home. They'd been together for years. Both committed to environmental activism. Always off somewhere to save an endangered species or stop the clearing of a clutch of prehistoric trees. *United*, Vivian would have called them, often envious of their shared purpose. She'd get to the apology she owed Clodagh later. For now, she needed to listen.

'Understatement of the year,' said Clodagh, her eyebrows arching over her lovely green eyes, just like her father's. 'We can't agree on what to have for tea, let alone how to spend the rest of our lives together. He thinks I can't do anything right.'

Vivian suspected it was a case of the pot calling the kettle black, but she reserved judgement and waited for her to elaborate.

'I'm just trying to be a good mum,' said Clodagh. The jumper slipped from one shoulder, but she didn't seem to notice. She was in full flow. 'I read all the up-to-date articles, follow the experts on Instagram . . .'

It took Vivian all she could do to hold her tongue.

'I had Max in a good routine.' Clodagh's tone was indignant. 'Oliver was no help. He used to be so conscious of everything we brought into the house. Now, he can't even make a healthy meal.' Her voice rose as she went on. 'He's late home every night, always breaking promises . . . then wants to do stupid stuff like take Max to the playground at seven o'clock, just when he should be having his bath and winding down.'

Right now, Clodagh sounded like she was the one needing to wind down, but Vivian let her rant. By the time she'd been given chapter and verse on their daily routine, she was exhausted, but she knew her daughter well enough to go thin on advice. This was the child who'd needed to work things out for herself, fall far enough to realise she might do well to accept a hand up. No one could tell Clodagh what to do. It was a lesson Vivian had spent years learning.

'We were so perfect before Max came along.' She gave a frustrated sigh. 'That came out all wrong. Max is perfect too.' She pulled the jumper back up on her shoulder and cradled the cup between her hands. 'We end up fighting all the time. I'm so exhausted . . .' Her breath caught before she continued. 'I can't cope with both of them.' As tears tumbled down her cheeks, Vivian went to her.

'Oh, Clo, you've been carrying all this on your own. I should have been there for you.'

Clodagh shook her head. 'You've had your own troubles, Mum. I couldn't land this on you as well.' She wiped away her tears with the end of a sleeve only for a fresh lot to leak out. 'When Dad told me what's been going on for you both, him living in the van and everything, I just wanted to come and help the two of you sort it out.' She shrugged and looked into her coffee cup. 'Ironic, I know.'

'Clodagh, love, you don't have to worry about anyone but yourself.' Vivian stroked the lock of hair, wet from tears, back off her face. 'Whatever's going on for myself and your father, we're here for *you*.'

Clodagh sobbed and tucked her head into Vivian's shoulder. It was as though she were a child again, but that was the thing about being a parent, she thought. They never stopped being your children.

When the tears subsided, Vivian kissed Clodagh on the top of the head and drew her a little away. She heard the growl of her stomach.

'Why don't you go up and have a nice hot shower, sweetheart, and we can have a bit of brunch when you come down.'

Clodagh hopped off the stool. 'Thanks, Mum.'

Vivian looked in the fridge to where her salads from the night before sat waiting to be used. But salads weren't the kind of comfort food she clearly needed. Pancakes were in order. She set to work, hoping she had the ingredients to make good on her idea. Eggs, milk, butter, a half a bag of flour gone out of date. Only by a month, she'd throw it in. Having promised to support their daughter together, she texted Dave.

Pancakes in 20

Emojis were too cheery. Full stops too cold. He arrived just as Clodagh was coming down the stairs, a bunch of fresh flowers in his hands. Vivian recognised them as being from the local supermarket. He would have to have ducked out just then to get them. Clodagh went to him, her wet hair covering his face as he took her in to his arms. Dave gave the best hugs, even with one arm. He held the flowers out and gave Vivian a tentative smile. As tears pricked at the corners of her eyes, she turned to the oven where she'd stacked a plateful of pancakes and took them out to add another couple from the pan.

'Can someone make a fresh pot of coffee, or tea if you want?'

She sensed the moment's hesitation behind her as they worked out what to do with the flowers and who would invade her space in the kitchen.

'See to these flowers, love. I'll give your mother a hand.'

If it felt awkward to be occupying the space with her husband, she tried not to show it. He was on automatic, scooting back and forth between cupboards, drawers and the table, where she'd laid a gingham cloth, worn from years of wear. As Vivian cooked up the last of the batter, Clodagh took a vase from a display shelf and filled it at the sink. At the table, she arranged the vibrant gerberas and dahlias, setting them as a centrepiece beside the cinnamon and maple syrup

Vivian had found in the pantry. When they sat down to eat, there was an odd Christmassy feel to the room.

'These look amazing, Mum.'

It was a joy to see Clodagh devour a pancake and tuck into another.

'Mmm. They're really good,' said Dave.

With her mouth full, Vivian could only nod her acknowledgement. It was at once strange and pleasant to be sitting down with the two of them. A thaw seemed to settle over her, the presence of two of her closest kin banishing the emptiness that had pervaded the house for too long.

Dave made himself scarce for the rest of the day, saying he had jobs to do in Devonport. He'd offered to clear up after breakfast, but Vivian declined. They'd managed to be civil toward each other, but playing happy families wasn't on her agenda. With no clue as to how long Clodagh planned to stay, Vivian thought she might need to spread out the family sit-downs. She was grateful for a call from Deb but took the phone to the bedroom to avoid being overheard.

'I ran into Oliver,' Deb told her. 'He looked a bit glum.'

'Did he say anything about how they're travelling?'

'No,' Deb answered. 'Just that Clodagh was spending some time with you.'

'I think she's hoping to help myself and Dave work things out, but she has enough on her own plate. Part of me thinks she came for a rest.'

'Well, now you know why she was so hyper at Christmas.'

'Yes,' Vivian was thoughtful. 'The two of them must have been putting on a front, trying to keep it together but really wishing the holiday was over the whole time.' She let out a long breath. 'I wish I'd seen it.'

'Don't be too hard on yourself,' Deb soothed. 'You've raised a lovely girl. She may have her feisty side but there's a very caring young woman on the inside.'

Vivian wanted to cry. 'I should have been there for her.'

'You're there for her now, Viv. She came home. That's all that matters.'

As she went to go downstairs after the call, Vivian heard sobbing from behind Clodagh's door. Knocking gently, she waited for permission to go to her.

'Deb was asking for you.'

She took a tentative step inside. Clodagh nodded from where she was staring at her phone, a box of tissues beside her on the yellow duvet that was wrapped around most of her as she sat up in her old bed.

'He's doing all the things I've said we shouldn't be doing.'

Inching closer, Vivian inclined her head so she could see what Clodagh might be using as evidence against the father of her child. Clodagh turned the phone so she could see the slightly blurred photo of a beaming Max halfway down a slide, Oliver smiling into the selfie.

'What a great photo!'

Her reaction was met with a huff. 'Do you know where they were?'

Without her glasses she couldn't see beyond a happy father and son in a playground.

'K-F-C!' Clodagh spat out the acronym like a set of swear words.

Vivian brought her hands to her mouth to stifle a laugh.

'I know, right?' said Clodagh.

Vivian interlocked her fingers under her chin and took a breath before asking, 'Is it so bad?'

'Mu-um!' Clodagh sat up straighter in the bed. 'We agreed. No fast food. I packed plenty of healthy meals for Max when I left. Even snacks in those stacking boxes . . .'

Her hands were working to reinforce the effort she'd gone to. Vivian could well imagine. An image of the inside of her daughter's fridge came to mind. When she'd been there for Christmas, she'd eaten about as much leftover nut loaf as she might need for the next decade. She'd been torn between admiration for her daughter's fastidious meal prep and sheer exhaustion from having to adhere to it. Relations had been so strained after Clodagh's reaction to her father's absence, Vivian hadn't had the strength to suggest she relax a little. But here in her own home, having had months to try to come to terms with her predicament, she couldn't watch her daughter judge her marriage on the basis of disagreements on things like how they fed their son.

She gestured to the side of the bed. Clodagh moved her legs across to let her sit down.

'What's really going on, Clo?'

Realising her mother was digging a bit deeper than diet, she flung the phone onto the bed and tucked her knees closer to her chest. This girl hated to fail. Vivian had watched her try and fail, try again, and grow into the beautiful strong smart woman she'd become, but tonight the battle scars were laid bare. As a memory of her daughter in the swimming pool came to her, she smiled.

'What?' Clodagh looked ready to accuse her of laughing at her. Vivian shook her head.

'I just remembered the time you were training in the Devonport pool and those older girls were trying to stay in front of you in the lane.' Her face softened. It was one of those family stories that had and would be retold over and over as the years went on. 'Little Clodagh wasn't going to let those big slow ones stand in her way. No, you freestyled up the middle of that lane for all your worth and got in front. I can still see old Arnie Bascombe smiling at me from the poolside, trying to keep in the laughing. Rocket fuel, he said you had . . .'

'I wish I had some of that rocket fuel now.'

The face was still glum. Vivian reached an arm around her duvet-covered knees, aware of the rarity of the moment, of how lovely it was to be comforting her girl.

'You're doing a brilliant job with Max,' she began. 'You both are.'

Clodagh frowned at her from under the fringe Vivian thought did nothing to enhance her broad Irish facial features. In the silence, she waited. Perhaps her fiercely independent Clodagh would work this out on her own, but she was here. Something more than frustration with her parents' predicament must have driven her to come home, but she sat patiently giving it another moment for Clodagh to share.

'It's like no one sees me,' she began.

'Oh, sweetheart . . .'

'No.' Clodagh put a hand up in a stop sign. 'I know you and Dad have your own problems, one big problem obviously . . . but, Jesus, it's like I don't exist.' Her voice rose as she went on. 'Oliver's no help and I'm just left to my own devices, working and trying to be a good mum to Max.' Spent from the energy it must have taken to offload, she turned away from Vivian, slamming her head into the pillows.

When had things got so bad that Clodagh couldn't call on her to help out? Vivian let the comments settle.

'I thought you didn't want me in your way,' she began.

Clodagh turned back, an indignant look in her eyes, but sitting up again, she reached for Vivian and pulled her into one of those hugs that had bound them as the mother and daughter they once were. When had Vivian stopped feeling her daughter needed her, or stopped believing she did?

'I'm sorry, love. I'm so ashamed. I've let you go through all this alone.'

'No, Mum.' Clodagh leaned her head into Vivian's. 'I didn't think you needed me either and just left you and Dad to get on with it. But you haven't done a very good job of it, have you?'

Vivian let her hands slip from their embrace and dipped her chin. 'I'm not sure you understand . . .'

'Try me.'

This was painful, but Vivian realised that in not discussing her problems with her daughter, she'd shut her out.

'That weekend in Queensland, I felt so abandoned. Well, I was. Your dad and I hadn't been getting on, barely speaking if I'm honest.' She took a breath. 'When he said he needed time to sort himself out, I was devastated. I retired for your father. We should have been able to face any issues he had together.' With Clodagh listening carefully, she wondered if Dave had told her about Rory, but they were adults, the girl deserved to know. 'Your father and the friend he stayed with had a relationship years ago, before he met me.' As Clodagh nodded, she could feel her soft hair brush against her cheek. This wasn't the kind of conversation she'd ever imagined having with her baby girl, but she kept going. 'I got the shock of my life. I can't stop thinking about whether he would have preferred to be with a man than with me . . .'

'Mum,' Clodagh interrupted, sitting up, 'do you even know what bisexuality is about?'

Vivian waited, hoping she wasn't going to be lectured, but she let her go on.

'Sure, it means you can be attracted to both men and women, but it doesn't mean you can't live a long monogamous life with someone you love.'

Vivian nodded. Clodagh's explanation made sense, but it did little to reassure her.

'I know you must think I'm old-fashioned. I'm not really. I just wish he'd told me when we started out, not thirty-odd years later.'

Clodagh shook her head. 'Do you think we'd be here now if he had?'

It was as if her daughter could see through her. How had she raised two children who were so 'woke' and been so conservative herself? She had no answer.

'I can't tell you what to do, Mum. I don't know what Dad was thinking when he left you up there, that was unfair, out of character. But he does love you and only you. Why do you think he's back?'

Vivian took her daughter's earnest face in her hands.

'Whatever about me and your dad, I want you to know that I love you, sweetheart, and I am so sorry for not being there for you . . . and Oliver and Maxie. Such a beautiful little family . . .'

'Oh, Mum. You're such a softie.'

Vivian drew back a little. 'I always thought I was the hard parent.'

Clodagh smiled. 'Compared to Dad, anyone would look like the tough guy.'

As they sat together, Vivian thought about what Clodagh had said about her dad's behaviour. 'Unfair', definitely. 'Out of character'? Yes, it was.

Clodagh gently twirled a strand of Vivian's hair between her fingers as she'd done as a child.

'You look sad, Mum. Come in here.'

Vivian pulled at the duvet and scooted in beside her. Clodagh snuggled into her. The warmth and closeness felt so new, rare and wonderful like a gift of something given after a long period of going without.

'Oh, Clo, I wish life could be easier for you,' she began. 'But don't you think you're being a little hard on Oliver?'

Clodagh pulled away and looked at her. Vivian smiled.

'Before you tell me I have no idea, can I just point out that he's given you a few days off, and despite your reservations, I'd say he's doing his best.'

Clodagh huffed, about to refute the argument, but Vivian went on.

'You said he's no help, but he's helping you right now. Couldn't you have a talk, let him know what you need from him? How you two could work together, make parenting a bit more fun?'

Clodagh was quiet as she processed the notion.

'Maybe you two could talk it out,' Vivian pressed in her most gentle tone. 'Let him know how you're feeling.'

'Sounds easier than it is, doesn't it, Mum?' Clodagh looked up at her.

'Touché!' Vivian gave a wry smile. How did her small girl ever get to be so grown up?

'You and Dad are painful to watch. You're like characters in a Jane Austen novel, politely skirting around each other, completely avoiding the elephant in the room.'

'Oh god,' said Vivian, 'we agreed to put on a united front. You obviously saw through *that*.'

Clodagh shrugged and cuddled in close again. 'I suppose without a decent conversation, nothing ever gets resolved.'

Vivian lay back and let the words sink in. Clodagh was right, of course. If Dave had told Vivian about Rory back in the eighties, she'd have gone elsewhere. She'd seen young people in her school struggling with their identity, done courses on inclusion, gender diversity. It was so easy to be open-minded when she was dealing with someone else's family, but when it had come to her own, she'd been rattled. Wrapped up in her own troubles, she'd alienated her daughter, the girl who set herself the highest standards and needed only to be reassured when she felt she was falling short. By the time they fell asleep, she and Clodagh hadn't solved any of their problems, but like the old adage of 'a problem shared is a problem halved', Vivian was sure they both felt lighter for having opened up.

Chapter Thirty-Seven

Over breakfast the following morning, with no sign of Dave or the van, Vivian and Clodagh agreed on a mother–daughter day that would take them along the north-west coast. Vivian smiled in delight at having Clodagh in the car with her. As she bypassed Ulverstone, it felt good not to have to turn off for what had become the thankless job of grocery shopping alone. Instead, they tripped along the highway, stopping off at Penguin and sitting in the light-filled bakery, indulging in thick slices of carrot cake and mugs of good coffee. Clodagh told her about Max's latest antics and how he was pestering them to get a dog, which sent them reminiscing about former family pets and their various personalities. At the foreshore, they stood with the large penguin statue and took selfies Clodagh insisted on sending to Finn. By the time they were back on the highway, Finn was video calling them from Sydney.

'I thought you'd be in work,' Vivian said, glancing at Clodagh's phone screen where her handsome son was smiling at them. She felt a wave of pride at the sight of him in a smart business suit.

'Just stepped outside, Mum. Don't stress. They won't fire me!'

Clodagh laughed. 'Hope you're not falling short of the family *standards* there, bro.'

Vivian shook her head. They'd always ribbed her about what she accepted were fairly high and possibly somewhat outdated standards, but she couldn't help the way she was.

'How's Dad?'

There was a pause before Clodagh answered.

'He's good. Isn't he, Mum?'

'Yep, he's good.' She was grateful to have her eyes on the road and not have to witness the look she knew was passing between her offspring.

'So where are you two off to?'

Vivian heard the deliberate change of subject and thanked her children inwardly for respecting her privacy.

'Wynyard next, I believe,' said Clodagh.

'All the hotspots,' Finn joked.

'You're just jealous,' said Clodagh.

'Have fun. Some of us have work to do.'

They rang off, promising a group call with all four of them before Clodagh went home. Vivian wasn't sure she'd be able for it but managed a smile in response for the son she sorely missed.

After spending the afternoon trawling the homeware shops in Wynyard, Vivian and Clodagh took an early dinner of fish and chips to a picnic spot at the riverside.

'Have you spoken to Oliver yet?' Vivian asked when she thought the moment was right.

Clodagh shook her head. Vivian waited as her daughter leaned back on her hands and looked out to where the Inglis River wended its way along the grassy banks beneath the almost imperceptible movement of clouds.

'I've decided to accept his offer of "help", as you said, Mum.' Her eyes narrowed into that determined look Vivian recognised. 'I'll spend some quality time with my parents and return to Max refreshed.'

'I thought we decided conversation was the way to go?' Vivian ventured.

Clodagh turned and sat up a little straighter, leaning over her crossed knees. 'Would this be a case of the pot calling the kettle black, as you'd say, Mum?'

Vivian had to smile. As much as she hated to admit it, she knew Clodagh was right. There'd been enough trying to be civilised and act normally.

'Let's make a pact,' she said. 'By the end of this week, we will have faced our fears and talked things out like the grown-up women we are.'

Clodagh reached her hand out to Vivian with her little finger poking out.

'Pinky promise?' she said. They joined fingers in what had been a childhood ritual. 'Love you, Mum.' Clodagh wrapped her arms around her in a hug Vivian wished she could bottle.

The weather gods were kind over the next couple of days, allowing Dave to take Clodagh waterfall hunting, but Vivian had felt strange being left out of the excursions. Retreating back into her solo routine didn't come as easily as she had thought it would. Thankfully, she'd arranged to catch up with Gloria on the Thursday and was grateful when it came.

With the sea temperature holding, Vivian managed to enjoy twenty minutes of immersion, mostly marvelling at her indefatigable compatriot, ploughing the persistent waves of an incoming tide. Vivian did a few slow laps between rock lines in shallower water, and by the time she and Gloria regrouped, she actually thought her fitness might be improving.

Afterwards they settled into the coffee shop and ordered the popular morning buns they'd had last time. As they waited, Vivian found herself touching the sides of her still wet hair, wondering how she'd managed to front up in a public place looking so unkempt.

'So how is the co-parenting going?' Gloria smiled.

'Mmm,' Vivian murmured. 'I'm afraid the jury's out on that one.'

The waitress set their coffees down and promised their buns were being warmed and weren't far away.

'It's very weird,' said Vivian, resuming their conversation.

Gloria nodded, encouraging her to go on.

'It's the small things, like watching them fill water bottles and pack old schoolbags with cereal bars and sunscreen . . .'

Vivian paused as the waitress returned. Breathing in the sweet smell, she was glad she wasn't alone. Having Clodagh and Dave in the house had reminded her of how she'd missed the sheer togetherness of family life. Being on the outer of their recent arrangements had only served to reinforce her memories of family outings, tramping around the Tasmanian country-side, discovering the wild and beautiful places of their island home, collecting stories of encounters with leeches and tiger snakes to add to the anthology of their lives. They would throw away so much if they couldn't find a way forward.

'Brings it all back, doesn't it?' said Gloria.

'I suppose it's knowing that things may never be the same,' said Vivian.

Gloria looked up from where she was pulling a curl of pastry from her bun. 'Doesn't mean they can't be of course.'

Vivian studied her face, unsure what Gloria meant. 'Are you suggesting I take him back like nothing's happened?'

Gloria made a tutting sound. 'I'm not suggesting anything, *a chara*. Just putting it out there that we have choices. You and Dave are reasonable, mature people. I have every faith you'll do what's best.'

Vivian didn't respond, but as they ate, she let Gloria's comment slip down into her thoughts, tucking it away for later analysis.

Chapter Thirty-Eight

Week Seven

By Friday, despite being sleep-deprived, Sienna was glad to be out of the house. Each night since Amalia's birthday party, she'd lain awake in fear. In the daytime, she'd napped when Daisy napped, never venturing too far from the unit, hoping Cole wouldn't come near them in daylight. She may not have done her body clock any favours, but for now at least, she'd managed to keep them safe. Tina had dropped round a pot of soup and a loaf of bread. She'd wanted to ask her neighbour about the previous tenants, if they too had suffered at the hands of abusive partners, and if so, where they had ended up. Instead, she spent the next few days living on the woman's generosity, grateful to have been able to avoid the supermarket.

Jess had checked in every day and even given her a run to the library that morning. When Sienna had suggested giving the session a miss, Jess had convinced her to go. But she hadn't been able to part with Daisy who, none the wiser, was being spoilt with all the attention. Marilyn had taken the seat beside them and was talking to Daisy in a weird high-pitched voice that sounded very un-Marilyn. She was even smiling.

'No childcare for bub today?' she asked, looking at the baby but meaning the question for Sienna.

'I thought she was getting sick.' Sienna surprised herself with the excuse.

'Your place damp?' asked Marilyn, glancing up at her.

Sienna shook her head. 'Don't think so. Just moved in and it's all freshly painted.'

'What you got? A unit or something?'

'Yes.' Sienna imagined she could strike Marilyn off the list of people she suspected of letting Cole Sutton know where they lived. 'We're in a unit a couple of streets away. Handy for everything.' *Too handy*, she thought, but Marilyn was still talking.

'Where were ya before that?'

Sienna took a breath, unsure of what to tell this woman who looked a similar age to her mum but with lines that suggested she'd had a much harder life.

'The shelter.'

Marilyn eyed her with a seriousness that made Sienna shrug with embarrassment. She was grateful for the distraction as Rosa joined them at the table, some luxurious scent wafting over them as she shook off her jacket while balancing her baby in her lap.

'Ah, Camilla, you have friend today.'

As the baby began to squirm, Rosa pulled up her top, and in that practised move, latched Camilla onto her breast.

'I never done that with mine,' said Marilyn in her normal voice. She turned to Sienna. 'You ever done it?'

Sienna held Daisy a little closer. 'My partner wasn't for it,' she said.

'Nor mine.'

There was a silence between them, filled only by Camilla's vigorous sucking and the background noise of other students chatting as they took their places for the session.

'Men can be cruel bastards,' Marilyn murmured. 'And the bad ones don't change neither.'

Sienna took in her words while across the table, Rosa looked oblivious, content, watching her baby fill her tummy with the milk her mother's body had made without any sterilising or mixing. If things had been different, Sienna might have happily breastfed her newborn, could have pulled Daisy close in the middle of the night to feed and soothe her without having to leave the bedroom. She sometimes imagined what her life would have been like if she'd never met Cole, if a baby like Daisy hadn't come along until well into a future where she would have qualifications, a career, not to mention a supportive family who would encourage her to give her babies the best start in life and be there to help out.

At the front of the class, Vivian was about to start.

'Do you want me to take her?' asked Marilyn.

'I think she'd like that.'

Daisy sat happily in Marilyn's arms, sucking on the rusk Sienna had given her. Marilyn didn't seem to notice the soggy crumbs that fell onto the baggy t-shirt she always wore.

'How about I give her back when she plays up?' asked Marilyn. 'Haven't had a bub to cuddle in a while.'

Sienna smiled. She was right beside her daughter, and Marilyn sounded like an old hand. There were good people in Tasmania, she thought, as she felt her shoulders relax and her mind scale back from high alert. As long as the teacher didn't look in her notebook this week, everything would be fine.

Chapter Thirty-Nine

Marilyn breathed in the soapy smell of the little girl in her lap. Vivian was doing the rounds, asking if they'd written anything since their last session, how their ideas for the book were coming along. With Daisy reminding her of Keisha, Marilyn plucked up the courage to speak up about what she'd written that week. She didn't mention she was couch-surfing.

'I'm grateful to yous all,' she began reading from the page in front of her. 'I only came to this class to get Cathy off me back . . .' The laughter from around the room made her smile. 'Anyway, Vivian gave me a few tips a couple of weeks ago and I've been helping me granddaughter with her readin'. For the book, I'm writing about the books I'm reading 'coz I reckon books are my "special space".'

Aware of every pair of eyes on her, she stopped there. As she popped her glasses back on her head, Daisy made a grab for them.

'Well done,' Sienna whispered as she leaned across and managed to prise the chubby fingers from around the frames.

'That's wonderful, Marilyn,' said Vivian. 'Glad I could help. Anyone else?'

As some of the others spoke, Marilyn sat feeling a kind of pride she realised she hadn't felt in a long while, a pride she only remembered feeling on others' behalf, like when Keisha spelled a word right in her homework, or Ethan got a bit of extra money from his boss, or indeed when Jamie told her he'd managed to stay off drugs since he'd come out of jail. It had only been a few weeks, but that was a record for her middle child.

'Recognise anyone?' Vivian asked when she showed a collection of familiar faces on the smartboard screen.

'Winston Churchill.' The normally quiet Bjørn was first off the rank. In an earlier session, he'd mentioned his Norwegian grandparents had harboured resistance fighters in WWII. She'd liked history at school, but never imagined she'd have much use for it.

'British Prime Minister, middle of the last century,' Vivian added for anyone who had no clue, which thankfully didn't include Marilyn.

'Is that Jane Austen?' asked Sienna in a timid voice. *Of course*, Marilyn had thought she'd recognised her too.

'Yes,' said Vivian, 'famous for books like *Pride and Prejudice, Sense and Sensibility* . . .'

'Mister Darcy?' Marilyn had thrown in the comment before she could stop herself, but Vivian looked pleased.

'Great character,' she said.

'Einstein.' It was Johnny.

Marilyn listened, fascinated, as Vivian took them through some of the other historical figures who she told them were poor spellers. Leonardo DaVinci was thought to have been dyslexic. Agatha Christie had said she was the 'slow one' of the family. That had raised a few eyebrows, as books and movies like *Death on the Nile* and *Murder on the Orient Express* were mentioned. As Vivian flicked through slides with celebrities like Jennifer Aniston, Whoopi Goldberg, Steven Spielberg, Marilyn could hardly believe her eyes but took some comfort in knowing Keisha was in good company.

Vivian asked the class to split into groups again, to talk about their experiences of learning to read and write before feeding back to the class as she called it. There were people with university degrees in the room alongside those who had never finished school. The ones from other countries shared stories of challenges in learning English. Robyn said she'd had a useless English teacher back in China who she blamed for her poor pronunciation.

'They gave her a job in the school canteen after discovering she'd faked her qualifications, but the damage was done,' she told them.

'In Peru, we had one English teacher from eh-Scotland,' Rosa told them. 'Very good looking, but when he spoke quickly, we could not understand him.'

Marilyn imagined schoolwork had come easy to their teacher. Somehow, she felt brave enough to ask.

'Vivian, you must have been one of the smart ones at school,' she said when the others had finished sharing.

'I was lucky,' said Vivian. 'And besides, the nuns in the good Catholic school I went to had us in fear of the metre stick.' There were murmurs of acknowledgement as their teacher mimed a good crack of the long wooden ruler Marilyn herself had been on the receiving end of once or twice. 'But you've got me thinking,' Vivian went on, 'about a girl who used to bully me into doing her homework. I wonder now if she had difficulties with reading and writing and was only covering it up by pushing us around.'

Marilyn was glad she'd asked. Vivian was like any of the rest of them when it came down to it – smarter than her, for sure, but not the stuck-up woman she'd imagined she was at the start of the course. As she pressed on with the basics of spelling, assuring them that eighty per cent of English words followed a pattern, Marilyn took notes. They began with prefixes, another throwback to the school days that were well behind her. Working in a group with Robyn and Oscar, she took more time about helping today. Spelling had always come easy to her, but she could see their struggles. It wasn't just children like Keisha that needed help. Cathy and Vivian had been patient enough to help her get things like punctuation right. Even those laptops she'd hated weren't so scary anymore. By the time Vivian announced break time, she was ready for a cuppa, but instead of her usual clock watching, she was looking forward to the next half when she would work on her latest book review.

Chapter Forty

When Vivian spent the first half of the morning on spelling, Oscar didn't share that he'd arranged to have private sessions with their teacher on the subject. It was enough to know he was no longer alone in this frustrating world of words. There were no clocks now, no school bells, tests or exam times. Students who seemed to finish tasks quickly were given others while he was never hurried. Vivian put him in a group with Robyn and Rosa and gave them counters and small whiteboards. She asked them to pay attention to his pronunciation, listen for sounds and syllables. They had fun, something Oscar had never associated with spelling before.

After break, he'd worked on his story about Dog. As sad as it was, it felt good to get it down on paper. Maybe it was the story itself or the attempt at remembering the homeless man who others may have forgotten, but there was a point to it, something deeply personal that made him want to write it well. He'd been so absorbed in it, he'd been the last to leave.

Back at his sister's, he hugged and stroked his beloved Dog and told him he was going to be in a book. There was no sign of Siraporn. Once the retriever settled down, Oscar went to the hallway and dropped his keys into the abalone shell Geraldine had brought home from one of her cruises. Not sure why, he ran a finger over the small table. Not a speck of dust. The mirror above, spotless, his reflection sharp and clear. The kitchen he'd left a bit untidy that morning as he rushed out the door was pristine, the bench gleaming, the sink empty of dishes, the aluminium sparkling. Siraporn had definitely been here.

He took a drink from the fridge and slumped in the Adirondack chair out the back. In the paddock behind the property, an echidna ambled oblivious through a patch of native grass. A butcher bird sang out in what reminded him of Harold Faltermeyer's *Axel F*. It was peaceful, as had always been Oscar's impression of Tassie. He imagined Siraporn's experience of the state might be quite different and resolved to try and get her to speak a little more when he saw her next.

⌒

Oscar spent the afternoon ambling through the bush trails around Geraldine's property. He'd done most of them before, but today he must have covered the whole four-leaf clover shape of them, ending up at a stretch of shelly beach where the creek meandered toward the sea. Dog didn't need any encouragement to get wet, bounding in until he was out of his depth and paddling happily in the current of an outward tide. Oscar stripped down to his boxers and joined him. It was his first swim since arriving in Tassie. Stroking into the deepest part of the creek, he marvelled at the feeling of weightlessness. He'd avoided the water for so long; afraid the exertion might be too much, that his lungs would let him down. There'd been nights when he'd woken in a sweat after nightmares about all sorts of scenarios where he couldn't save himself, like the one where he'd been unable to pull himself onto a raft way out to sea.

After swimming over and back across the creek, he sat on a rock in the sunshine and watched as Dog gambolled in and out of the water, immersing his whole head in search of stones, then racing up the beach to find a spot where he could lie and lick the salt from them. With the cloudy autumn sky starting to grow dim, Oscar thought about his ex-wife. They'd been married on a beach not far from here. He'd been so hopeful, so in awe of his smart and beautiful bride. She'd run their household, paid all the bills, opened all the letters. Cleaned him out when it came to the divorce. But the bile that rose in his guts when he thought about it was no longer there. Had he finally moved on? Had this trip been more than a break from the mainland?

Dog came and shook himself beside him.

'Come on, boy. Let's get you home and dry.'

He pulled on his shorts and t-shirt and picked up his walking shoes. Vivian was onto something with the gratitude stuff. He did indeed have much to be grateful for.

Chapter Forty-One

The smell of baking wafted toward the front door as Vivian walked in after class, happy to find Clodagh up to her elbows in soap suds at a sink full of baking dishes.

'Mmm, smells great in here, Clo. What you making?'

For a second, she suspected some dairy-free, sugar-free, grainy slice that would resemble birdseed.

'A chocolate cake I saw in one of your magazines.'

Vivian eyed the recipe open on the far bench beside a bowl of what looked like very decadent icing.

'Any special occasion?' she asked.

Clodagh took an audible breath but didn't turn from her task. Vivian could see the smile spreading across her face, but still didn't get what she was supposed to remember.

'You're worse than Dad!'

Vivian set her bag down on a stool and held up a hand. 'No, wait, wait . . .' She thought to herself, the date, the sixth . . . 'Oh, sweetheart, it's your wedding anniversary.' She wasn't sure whether the cake-making was for celebrating or comfort-eating.

'I phoned Oliver.' Clodagh did a dance on the kitchen tiles like someone desperate for a pee. 'They're coming tonight, Mum. When Oliver finishes work, he's collecting Max from his mum and dad's and driving up.'

Vivian went and hugged her. The relief and excitement reminded her of all those other milestones: Clodagh's Year 12 results, her acceptance into university on the course she wanted, exam results, graduation day, telling them she and Oliver were engaged, the wedding day . . . so many wonderful, joyous occasions she and Dave had shared with their daughter. As they pulled apart, she brushed at the side of her face to hide a tear.

'Oh, Mum, how do you cope with my dramas?'

Vivian laughed. 'I love you,' she told her, 'and always will. No matter what.'

They hugged again, Vivian inhaling a long breath of the daughter she loved for all her highs and lows.

Clodagh held her tight and spoke into her hair, 'I love you too, Mum. No matter what.'

❧

They spent the afternoon preparing dinner together. Although Vivian had avoided eating with Dave and Clodagh the past few days, Clodagh had asked if they could all have dinner together tonight. She couldn't deny either of them the family reunion. Besides, they had enough food for two families. Vivian couldn't remember the last time she'd had to perform a juggling act to manage closing the door of the fridge that was full to capacity.

'So tell me more about your writing class?' said Clodagh as she started on what she assured Vivian was the final dish.

'Oh, I have an amazing group,' said Vivian. 'When Cathy asked me to take it on, I wanted to run a mile, but I'll be sad to see it finish. It's been an eye-opener.'

Vivian was only too happy to tell her daughter about the personalities that made up her Friday mornings. They'd all had backstories she'd been fortunate enough to have glimpsed through their exercises. Some were awe-inspiring, like Robyn, their phoenix, honouring her father's hopes for good fortune, coming to Australia from a poor family and working hard to build a prosperous life for herself. And Oscar, who might have had the lowest level of literacy but possibly the biggest heart.

'I'm worried about a young girl from Queensland,' she told Clodagh as they took a cuppa to the sofa for a brief rest before the house would be overrun by their favourite two-year-old. Clodagh listened as she went on. 'She sometimes brings her baby to class. A gorgeous smiley child, but they both have a neglected look about them like you'd love to bring them home and give them a bowl of soup.'

'Your answer to everyone's problems, Mum.' Clodagh laughed but was eager to hear.

'She shocked me today, actually,' Vivian went on. 'She's quite the artist, drawing really detailed sketches, able to bring a room to life . . . but today I saw something sinister.' Vivian paused, remembering how Sienna's notebook had been held partly open by her chunky pencil case. 'I couldn't see the whole page, but she'd drawn part of a pair of scissors with drops of red dripping down the page.'

Clodagh gasped. 'Is she dangerous?'

'God, no!' Vivian explained the little information that Cathy had shared with her about Sienna, that she'd first come with a case worker who seemed to be going the extra mile for the girl. Said she'd come down from the mainland with an abusive partner and only recently managed to get away from him.

'Is he living in town, like still around?' Clodagh's face was full of concern.

'I don't think so. I haven't heard many details but can't help wondering what made her draw that.' She took a drink and thought for a moment. 'It's like something's changed for her.'

'Oh, Mum, that's terrible. I just want to cuddle Max right now and never let him go after hearing that.'

Vivian reached out and stroked her daughter's arm. 'Any word of them?'

'If they left Hobart at four . . .' She looked at the time on her phone. '. . . not far away now, I reckon.'

As Clodagh scrolled to find the latest photos Oliver had shared, Vivian thought of Sienna's mother, the grandmother of that cute, cuddly Daisy, and where she might fit in what sounded like the scary story of their lives. It was one thing to respect the girl's privacy, but maybe they should be doing more. She resolved to speak to Cathy before next Friday.

Vivian only realised she'd dozed off when she woke to the sound of Clodagh squealing beside her as she jumped off the couch.

'They're here!' Clodagh ran to the window where a layer of orange sunset sat between the darkened gums of their front yard.

Before Vivian could extricate herself from the deep cushions, Clodagh was outside opening the back passenger door and lifting her beautiful son into her arms.

'I missed you,' she told a bemused-looking Max.

He looks so cute, thought Vivian, as his head fell onto his mum's shoulder, a finger in his mouth, the gorgeous blonde curls of hair that hadn't yet been cut, flattened on one side where he'd been sleeping.

She held back to let them have their reunion. Oliver got out, his tall frame hunched somewhat. Weary from a week of being Mum and Dad, Vivian suspected. His face had a worried expression as he waited for Clodagh to make the first move. *Go on, Clodagh.* She willed her daughter to go to him. The boy had proven he wanted to do better. He'd promised to come home from work earlier, wait up to really talk with her when Max was down. He'd given her a few days away from the exhausting task of trying to be super mum. What more proof did she need? As Clodagh walked around the front of the car, he met her halfway, pulling both her and Max into a huge hug like he never wanted to let them go.

Vivian turned away as they kissed, not just to leave them to their making up, but because she caught sight of Dave looking out the window of the camper van, highly aware he was feeling the same but not able to share. In a previous life he'd have put an arm around her, and they'd have strolled back inside, saying how happy they were for their daughter in gestures rather than words: a smile, a rub of her shoulder, a squeeze of her hand.

⌒

They kept up a show of solidarity at dinner, taking turns to entertain Max and pass round bowls of the food she and Clodagh had prepared in the afternoon. When the small fella grew sleepy, Vivian suggested they hold dessert until after he'd had a bath and they'd put him to bed. As Clodagh followed Oliver and Max upstairs, she turned and gave her mother a look that said, 'Talk to him.'

Dave had started to stack the dishwasher.

'That was a fabulous meal,' he said. When Vivian didn't comment, he wiped his hands on a dishcloth and turned to her. 'I'll leave you in peace so.'

She nodded. Despite rehearsing how to broach the subject of their future, she stood there, listening to those sluggish steps going down the hallway. *What a coward!* After multiple conversations with her daughter about the importance of talking problems out, not letting them fester, she'd not been able to take her own advice.

From upstairs, she could hear laughing and splashing. It seemed like yesterday that she and Dave had been the ones bathing small children, reading bedtime stories, tucking in their darlings. They'd been so happy.

She grabbed her cardigan from the set of hooks in the hallway and pulled on her rubber ankle boots. This nebulous future had to be faced, some way forward agreed upon. She couldn't keep pushing Dave away, skirting round the issue of how to live the next phase of their lives. It was time to talk this out.

Chapter Forty-Two

The door of the camper sounded tinny as she knocked, the whole home on wheels a shell in comparison to their sturdy double-brick house. That Dave had been willing to make Winnie his home, for however long, spoke of his patience. He'd given Vivian time and space. Whatever had gone on in the lead-up to the Queensland trip or in the aftermath, he'd come back. He'd wanted to come home. Together they'd helped get Clodagh over one of what would be the many bumps in the road of her life. They'd been a good team even if they had somehow lost their way.

'Viv, hi, come in.' Dave held the door open and stepped back.

Standing in the galley, she glanced to one end of the van to where the lovely, big double bed that had sold it to them lay unmade. The day's dishes were still piled around the tiny sink that made the one in the house look like a bathtub. He followed her gaze.

'Have been a bit slack on the tidying up front,' he said.

In the yellow light from the slim fluorescent bulb above the dining table, she took in the stubble she'd noticed at dinner. He'd always prided himself on being clean-shaven, resisting her attempts at persuading him to grow a beard. She'd loved when he'd shave less in the holidays and he would rub his hirsute chin against her neck when they made love, the short whiskers round his lips brushing over her skin, heightening the delicious sensations of being close to him.

'I thought we should talk.'

'Sure, sure.' He turned to the dining booth and bent to sit down at one side. 'Have a seat.' He gestured to the other side.

She hesitated. Part of her didn't want to have this conversation, but in her heart, she knew they must. Still, the last thing she wanted was to have to eyeball him over what was going to be a difficult discussion.

'Can we drive this somewhere?' she asked.

He got out of the seat. 'Of course. I've only had that one glass of red with dinner.'

She'd had a drink as well, hoping the pinot noir their son-in-law had kindly brought with him would ease the tension she'd felt at having Dave in the room. Clodagh had appreciated the gesture too. The bottle was from the vineyard where they'd married five years ago. She texted Clodagh and told her to have dessert without them.

'Hopefully those two will get a chance to finish the red in our absence.'

When Dave was belted into the driver's seat, she manoeuvred herself into the passenger side. The sheepskin cover felt warm and soft as she got as comfortable as sitting beside her husband would allow.

'Where to?' he asked as they came to the T-junction at the top of the road.

'We can just park at one of the beaches . . . Sankey?'

There was no talk between them as they drove the ten minutes to one of the suburb's sandy stretches of coastline where the kids had spent so many sunny days on boogie boards and skimboards with friends. The best of the local beaches for waves, a couple of surfers were waiting out beyond the breakers, silhouetted in the diminishing daylight where an amethyst haze settled over the national park.

Dave sat mute, like someone who would have happily let the moment linger indefinitely. It had always been left to Vivian to break the ice, take the first steps in coming back from an argument. Now was no different. She clicked open her seat-belt, pushed it away and turned toward him. He let his hands fall in his lap, fingers interlocking like he was about to pray.

'I thought we'd try to navigate where to go from here,' she started. 'Work out what we want to do. If we should stay the course or call it quits.'

He turned and looked at her, eyes shining in the low light, his features dark.

'Is that what you want? To finish everything?'

She looked away. It was what she'd thought she'd wanted from the moment her world was rocked by his disclosure.

Dave slowly shook his head. 'I never meant to hurt you, Viv. We could just . . .'

'What?' She looked at him, incredulous. 'Just go on as we were?'

He looked down at his hands. It took a minute for him to speak.

'I know I abandoned you, Viv, but I want to come home.'

'I've had plenty of time to think about it, Dave.' She tried to look him in the eye but couldn't bear to see loyalty where she wanted love, the kind of unconditional undying love they used to feel for one another. 'If you need something or someone else, something I can't give you . . .' Tears threatened to stop the flow of her words, but this needed to be said. 'You need to let me know. Be honest. We weren't happy for a long time before the choir trip. I know I tried to charge on, keep going when what you probably needed was to stop and talk about it. But you wouldn't let me in either.'

His eyes were wet with tears. 'I never meant to hurt you . . . I'd moved on from Rory when I met you. We were happy, Viv. I didn't need anyone else . . . Never have.'

'But you've lived most of your life, our life, sacrificing part of yourself for us . . . Don't you think you could have brought it up?'

Dave's shoulders relaxed a little as he took a moment before answering.

'Vivian, one of the things I love about you is that you're so compassionate and tolerant. But everyone has their limits.'

She could hear Clodagh in her head. This must have taken up Dave's thoughts, but she was the last person he could share it all with.

'Were you afraid of losing me if you told me?'

Dave gave a low huff.

'And I brought us to Tasmania!' She let out a bitter laugh at the irony. 'Most homophobic state in the country.'

'At the time it was,' said Dave. 'Things have thankfully moved on.'

They sat silent for a moment, enveloped in the relentless rumble of the waves tumbling toward the shore.

'Viv, I need to tell you about Rory. Something I've been carrying my whole life. The real reason why I stayed on with him for so long.'

She sat up straighter in her seat and stared at him. What truth was he about to tell her? An affair perhaps? He'd mentioned owing Rory in that first conversation after he'd returned unannounced. She'd cut him off. Whatever it was, she wasn't sure she had the capacity for further hurt, but they were here now, she'd hear him out.

'It's a lifetime time ago now, but something I had to revisit, make amends for, I suppose.'

They sat for a moment with only the wind ruffling the branches of the she-oaks breaking the silence.

'Rory was my best friend,' Dave began. 'Sure we experimented, but it went deeper than that.' He took a long breath and looked out to where the silhouetted surfers were catching their last waves for the night. 'I let him down, Viv. With time to think in retirement, more time than I wanted, it all came back to haunt me.'

She listened as he recounted the gruesome story of the night he and Rory alighted from a bus to the north side of their hometown after one of their dates. Rory had walked on a bit ahead of him while he'd hung back for a few words with the bus driver who was a friend of his dad's. As Dave went to catch up with Rory, he heard the taunts. Poofter, faggot . . . nothing they hadn't heard before, but as he got closer, the gang pushed Rory to the ground.

'Jesus Christ, lads! Leave him alone!' Dave had started to jog toward them, but when a big lump of a lad turned to him, he saw the knife.

'Get away, college boy,' he'd shouted. 'Unless you want a dawk of this.' As he came at him with the knife raised above his head, Dave ran.

'I fucking ran, Viv.'

She sat taking it in. The perpetrators were known to him: neighbours, classmates who'd joined the dole queue like generations before them, not privileged like him and Rory, the 'college boys'. What had started with insults ended with part of Rory's ear hanging off and too many broken bones to talk about. In the comfort of his parents' hallway, Dave had called the police.

There was a moment when she wanted to reach out and hold him, but the question that entered her head and pushed past all the shock and hurt on Rory's behalf pinned her to the spot. When she'd thought they'd grown into the kind of couple who could discuss anything, why had he never been able to tell her?

Rory emigrated soon after the incident, first to England then Australia. They'd lost touch. Deliberately, Dave admitted. He told his family about the incident but stopped short of mentioning their relationship. They said things like, 'Isn't that awful,' and, 'Those fellas will get their comeuppance,' but there was enough unsaid to let him know they didn't want him to have been anything other than the victim's friend. He'd been terrified, stopped going out, decided he'd prefer to be straight and safe than live in fear of being found out by the wrong people. His brother, Paudie, had kept him going, he said, got him out, encouraged him to keep playing music, date women, but he'd carried the guilt of that night all his life.

Her mind cast back to the night they'd met. It was her higher diploma year, when she and her friends had taken to meeting on Thursday evenings in the college bar. Her friend, Breda, was going out with Paudie, the lead singer in one of the regular bands. Dave played keyboard and saxophone. When he took the sax solo in Baker Street, Vivian was mesmerised. After the show, Breda introduced them. From then on, Vivian found herself living for their Thursday nights in the small intimate venue. Being personally acquainted, it fell to Vivian and her friends to keep the thirsty musicians supplied with drink. Every time Dave gave her a nod or a wink of thanks, her heart skipped a beat.

He hadn't asked her out straight away. Rather, they met for lunches in the company of others, but their conversations always ended up including just the two of them with the right mix of talking shop, fun and solving the world's problems. He had a quiet way about him that set him apart from the loud, self-assured fellas. 'Still waters run deep,' her mother had warned. She'd had no idea how deep.

'Some friend I was,' he went on. 'Never followed up. Never reached out to see if he was okay.'

They sat in silence, Vivian pondering the enormity of what Dave had been reliving in those days when the study grew quiet and she could only offer suggestions around keeping to their eating and walking routine or going to the GP. The guilt, the shame. It all made sense now. How he must have been mulling over the event, drinking down his pain. Caring for Rory was a kind of atonement.

'You've been a terrific partner to me,' she said, her voice about to break.

It was true. The man beside her was a great father. When all was said and done, he had been a loyal husband, her best friend. In the nights she'd been alone, when she wasn't cursing him, she'd imagined what it would be like to never share the magic of love-making again, to be forever alone, not attractive to anyone, not important enough to share a bed, a home, a life with, and worse, imagining that her life had been a sham. She reached out and pulled his hand toward her, holding it in both of her own. It was the first time she'd touched him in months. The cool of the wedding ring, the warmth of his skin, the soft hairs . . . she savoured every detail.

'I want you to spend the rest of your life being true to yourself,' she told him. 'I want you to be able to talk to me.'

He squeezed her hand. 'I have been true to myself, Viv. That's why I came back. I need you . . .'

She reached out a hand and put it to his lips. He held it there for a long moment before moving it to his cheek, the stubble bristling against her skin, sending a tingle through her. Without a word, she scooted closer and held his face in both hands. As they kissed, the longing of the past year welled up inside, but hearing the surfers heading back up the sand toward the nearby ute, she drew a little away. He read her mind. Together they scrambled into the back of the van, quickly closing the curtains as they made their way to the messy bed, slowing down to silently undress each other with the intensity of overdue connection. For the first time in so long, she felt fully alive, everything awakened as Dave's hands stroked her neck, her breasts, his fingers sliding down over her belly, between the curve of her thighs. Heart pounding, breaths short, she came within moments of him touching her vulva, and again as he entered her, strong slow pulses gaining speed as they climaxed together. Overcome with emotion, Dave let out a sob. 'Forgive me,' he said, closing his eyes and holding her close.

'I love you, Dave,' she told him. 'How about we start again?'

Chapter Forty-Three

Week Eight

On Thursday evening, Oscar sat in Geraldine's mini-cinema, legs stretched out on one of the reclining ends of the leather sofa where he usually spent hours watching the eighty-two-inch television. Tonight, he'd surprised himself by doing a little writing homework instead of turning on the device straight away. He'd managed to do his gratitude journalling and finish his story for their book. With Dog snoring beside him, he flicked through the TV's apps. Instead of relying on the pictures, he made an effort to decipher the titles. He was about to start *Lost for Words*, a series Vivian had mentioned, when his phone buzzed in his pocket. It was a text from Siraporn.

Can you help me?

Oscar's head spun. Where was she right now? Was she in some kind of trouble? He tried to type but his fingers seized over the phone. It would have been easier to record a message like Bobby had shown him, but then she'd have to play it. All sorts of scenarios raced through his mind as he willed himself to think logically. The crying, the manic cleaning, the furtive glances out the front window to where that van had been parked each Friday. Was he making assumptions about her just because she was Asian, because she was a cleaner? Maybe she needed help with something quite ordinary, like her English or maybe where to buy a car. He gave himself a mental shake. If he didn't reply, he'd never know. He looked at the screen and began to type.

How can I help?

The reply came quickly.

Meet me at house after class if you can.

He typed *ok*. Her reply was an emoji. Hands in prayer, like the way she bowed. He waited, watching his phone, but there were no further texts. Whatever she wanted help with, she wasn't going to ask him about it over the phone. There was nothing for it but to honour her wishes and get home straight after class.

⌒

The next morning, Oscar reckoned he might have been more nervous than on the first day of the course, as he navigated the revolving doorway and stepped into the foyer of the paranaple building. Except it had nothing to do with writing and everything to do with Siraporn's request. The girl in the café smiled at him, oblivious to the hammering in his chest or the cold clamminess of his palms as he approached the escalator. He waved and said something about grabbing his coffee later, then turned to ascend before he could hear her reply. The fact that he'd been able to forego his usual caffeine hit registered with him as a possible sign of progress on the health front, but he told himself it was probably adrenaline that was keeping him going today.

Upstairs a couple of older women chatted as they ambled along toward the library entrance in front of him. Willing them to hurry up, he heard his name.

'Oscar, aren't you the early bird?'

He looked round to find Cathy coming toward him, cheery as ever, her slim laptop tucked under one arm.

'Oh, hello.' Trying not to look too agitated, he managed a smile.

'Week eight, can you believe it?' she asked without waiting for an answer. 'I'm so glad you decided to join us.' There was an awkward moment where he wished he could get going, but she held him there with that laser look she gave people. 'Actually, I'm glad I ran into you before class. I've got a favour to ask.'

Oscar had met her type before; the kind you couldn't say no to. He nodded, waiting for her to hit him with her request.

'Would you be around later to chat about the layout of the book? I'd love you to be part of . . .'

Uneasy with having to do so, he cut her short.

'I'd love to, Cathy, but today is tricky for me. Would next week do?'

If he detected a flicker in her gaze, it didn't last. She beamed at him. 'Absolutely. Let's lock it in for next Friday. Best get to my meeting.'

She rolled her eyes in exaggerated displeasure as she strode off, her free arm swinging at her side. 'Have a great session.'

In class, he took a seat beside Amalia who sat with her head of funny-coloured hair bent over her phone, thumbs going a hundred miles an hour. Oscar wondered if he should mention voice messages, but from where he was sitting, he was sure she could probably type as fast as she could speak.

'Hey,' she said as she brought her phone to her chest and leaned back in her chair.

He nodded. 'How're ya going?'

She let out a sigh and looked down at her device. 'Trying to get my employment mentor off my back.'

Oscar wasn't sure he wanted to be party to the girl's problems but felt he might know exactly where she was coming from.

'They want me to apply for a gazillion jobs a fortnight.' She huffed.

'I'm on the lookout for work too,' he said.

Amalia looked at him as if seeing him for the first time. 'What kind of job are you after?'

As much as he might have wished to avoid talking about himself, her question was so direct it deserved a straight answer.

'Not sure I have many options,' he said. 'Got retrenched when I had Covid. Still don't feel a hundred per cent, I'm afraid.'

She glanced up to where Vivian was writing on the whiteboard and reached out a hand to give him a gentle nudge.

'This might help,' she said, eyes still on the front of the room.

Res-um-es, Cov-er let-ters, job app-lic-a-tions . . .

Before today, these belonged to Oscar's long list of things other people did. As he sat up, pen poised in his hand, he was aware of Amalia doing the same. She was an unlikely ally, but an ally all the same.

At morning tea, Oscar checked his phone. He hadn't heard from Siraporn. Best stick to the plan and get back to the house asap after class, he thought. After their break, Vivian instructed them to each take a laptop from the trolley. When he logged in on the first attempt, Oscar shot up his hand in a fist pump. 'Yes!'

Beside him, Johnny huffed as he navigated his own device.

'Sorry, Johnny. That might be a small thing for most people, but that was a big win for me.'

'On ya, mate!' Johnny smiled and gave him a high five. 'You know, Oscar,' he told him, 'my baby sister got all the smarts. Just not fair, is it?'

'You said she's a lawyer, didn't you?'

'Immigration lawyer,' Johnny clarified.

'I got the same kind of sister. Made a lot of money with her brains too,' said Oscar.

Johnny made a face. 'Looks like you and me have a bit of catching up to do.'

Once they'd nutted out how to get to where Vivian was guiding them, they got their heads down and began to type. As he tapped out his efforts from the past few weeks, despite the snail's pace, Oscar felt a growing sense of pride in his progress. Now and again, he was distracted by thoughts of Siraporn. As he battled to type out a short email, he hoped she wouldn't ask for his help with any paperwork. But the thought didn't fill him with the inadequacy that had consumed him before. He had found people who were willing and able to help and there was reason to hope that he mightn't always struggle so much.

⌒

After class, when Vivian tried to engage him in conversation about getting the book printed, he'd made his apologies, saying he'd already made arrangements with Cathy. As he drove out of Devonport, he hoped he hadn't sounded rude, but his priority was honouring his agreement to meet Siraporn at the house. It must have something to do with her cleaning job, he reasoned. In any case, he wasn't about to let her down.

There was no sign of the van when he got to his sister's place, but in the kitchen, he found Siraporn cleaning cupboard doors. Geraldine would come home to a near-new house at this rate. Noticing she had earphones in, Oscar gave a loud cough. As her head snapped round, he saw fear then relief in her eyes. She smiled at him, a soft smile. She hugged her cleaning cloth to her chest and bowed.

'Thank you for coming, Oscar.'

She cast a glance to the front window and beckoned him to follow her to the back of the house.

'I can't be long,' she began. 'I need to clean. My boss text me already. Say me hurry up.'

Oscar sat on one of the poolside chairs and gestured for her to sit.

'You're not cleaning today, Siraporn. Whatever is bothering you is more important. The house is perfect. You're doing a fantastic job.'

She bowed again and sat down at the edge of the seat next to his. In halting English, she told him a story that made the hairs stand on the back of his head.

She'd travelled to Australia just before the pandemic. Her family were poor, but their cousin was doing well in Australia and had promised to help her find a job. They'd arranged a visa, helped with flights. Her plan was to send money home and maybe even save enough to see the Great Barrier Reef and Uluru, places she'd heard about as a child in school. When Covid hit, her cousin reassured her, said she could stay with her and wait it out. The early weeks were idyllic. Even in lockdown, she was able to go for long walks and explore the local area with its beautiful natural surroundings. Her cousin, Angie, and her partner seemed welcoming, making delicious meals for Siraporn and spending evenings talking about everyone back in Thailand and watching television together. She wasn't sure exactly how long it had taken for things to change.

At first, it was small chores like cleaning the house. That was fair, she'd thought, given her extended stay. Then it was cleaning houses, doing Angie's work for her. When Siraporn asked if she might be paid, her cousin lambasted her with a tirade about how ungrateful she was. The unpaid cleaning job was only the half of it. There were other favours asked of her, demeaning ones like massages and sleeping with one of Angie's friends.

'My family not like that,' she said with tears in her eyes as she looked away.

Oscar remained quiet, as much in sympathy with the girl as embarrassed on his own behalf. How isolated she must have been to reach out to him. Why hadn't the family back home helped her out? It was an obvious question, but one he had to ask.

'My cousin say she show pictures of me with her partner and friend. Bring dishonour to my parents, my brothers . . .'

Oscar wasn't exactly sure how he could help, but he was certain he couldn't handle this on his own. There were organisations who dealt with this kind of thing. The library people would surely know.

'She take my passport . . . see my phone,' she told him.

'How did you text me?'

'I say I texting my mother. I text you. Delete.' She made a cutting gesture with her hand.

Good god! This was like something from a documentary. The kind of thing you couldn't imagine happening in your own neighbourhood.

'I want to help you, Siraporn, but I might need a little help myself.'

She looked into his eyes, fear outweighing any hope.

'I know some good people where I go to class. Can you trust me to take it to them?'

'I have to trust,' she said, her voice low. 'I need to escape this life.'

A horn beeped from outside. Her face stricken, Siraporn turned toward the sound and then back to him.

'She beat me if I take too long.' She waved her cloth. 'I come next Friday.'

Oscar already had his phone out and was searching the library number.

'Thank you. Thank you.' She brought her palms together and bowed again before grabbing her small backpack and running from the house.

Chapter Forty-Four

On Saturday, Sienna woke before Daisy. She had an *actual* brunch date with Amalia, who she hoped was becoming an *actual* friend. In the eighteen months she'd lived in Tasmania, the only people she'd had anything to do with were Cole and his associates, or the people who were paid to help her get away from them. A voice in her head told her to stay home, not to risk being seen by anyone who would go dobbing to Cole. She told it to shut up, made a coffee and tidied round the unit while she waited for her beautiful baby to wake up. If she listened to that voice, they'd never set foot outside.

When she arrived at the mall, Amalia was waiting as promised. Her mother and Charlie, she explained, had gone off to get their nails done so they could catch up without Charlie getting bored. Sienna suspected Amalia meant they could have an adult conversation but laughed off the comment as they went to find somewhere decent to sit down.

In what Amalia told her was a newly renovated café, Sienna looked over the menu, paying as much attention to the prices as to what was on offer. Cole never took her anywhere that didn't serve hot chips and meat pies. Her face gave her away.

'Are you okay with this place?' asked Amalia.

Sienna nodded. 'Been a while, that's all.'

'What? Since you've been in a coffee shop?' Amalia's eyebrows narrowed as she said it.

As Sienna sat Daisy on her lap and peeled off her little denim jacket, the warmth in her cheeks was enough to answer Amalia's question. She turned Daisy toward the table and wrapped her arms around her belly. The waiter came to take their order before she could decide how to explain.

'The bruschetta . . . and a chai latte,' said Amalia.

'I'll have the same.'

She took a rusk from the lunch box she'd packed for Daisy. Across the table, Amalia looked like she had twenty questions on the tip of her tongue.

Finally, she asked, 'Are you sure you're okay?'

Sienna took in Amalia's nice top, the layer of makeup well-applied to her skin. Despite having chosen the best top in the pile and brushing her own hair out, Sienna felt dull, like a shadow in Amalia's light. How could she ever be normal like this girl, have a job, a supportive partner, a family who loved her? Was trying to be Amalia's friend even realistic? She shook her head.

'I'm fine. Just a lot on lately.' She forced a smile. 'How have you been?'

Over brunch, Amalia told her about her week, the family dramas, her partner's promotion, the childcare course she'd applied for. Sienna began to relax as she listened, but when there was a lull in conversation and it was her turn to share, she couldn't think of much outside of what she and Daisy had been watching on TV. *Peppa Pig* and *Married at First Sight* seemed a bit lame, but she opened with the latter. Thankfully, Amalia was a fan, and by the time they'd finished their food and decided on a round of iced coffees, Daisy had fallen asleep in her arms, and this was feeling like a semi-normal day out. They talked about the personalities in the writing class and how they were going with their pieces for the book. Sienna told Amalia she would probably choose what she'd written about Home Hill and that she'd thought to go back to the piece about the gallery. Amalia told her she was amazing, but she was the clever one, with lots of ideas for stories she could make up about rooms in her own house. Sienna didn't share her thoughts about the lack of safe spaces in her life.

When it was time to leave, Sienna knew she wouldn't make it home without peeing herself. As she looked round for the toilets, she realised it would be quicker not to have to steer the pram through the tight gap between the tables. Amalia read her mind.

'I'll watch Daisy if you need the bathroom.'

As Amalia had already been, it would be idiotic for Sienna to pretend she didn't need to go after all the caffeine and the tall bottle of water they'd shared over the meal. With a queue of women in the ladies' room, she almost backed out.

After her turn, she washed her hands without drying them and jogged back to the table.

The pram was gone. There was no sign of Amalia.

Searching past clutches of customers for signs of her baby, she pushed past a man who held the door open for her. Without even a nod of thanks, she sped past him. He didn't matter. All that mattered was finding Daisy.

Outside she looked both ways, scanning the afternoon crowd, her breaths coming in short audible gasps. To her left down the street, a dark-haired man was pushing a pram at a jog. Why was he in a hurry? Sienna started to run.

'Hey!' she called out. 'Hey . . . stop!'

As she got closer, the shape of his head told her it wasn't Cole. Maybe he'd sent a mate. She kept running. Across the street, a woman was waving at them. Sienna slowed and drew up beside the pram. Glancing in, she saw a baby boy giggling up at the man as he bounced the pram along.

'We're going to see Mumma Bear,' the man half-sang to the boy. With air pods in, he hadn't even noticed her. As she stopped to catch her breath, her phone buzzed in her pocket.

Just up the street in the nail bar.

An urge to grab Amalia by the throat and impress the severity of the situation upon her threatened to overwhelm Sienna. She needed to regulate, be rational about this. Her baby was in the care of someone who wanted to be a child-care worker, a mother for god's sake, an ordinary Tassie girl living an ordinary Tassie life. They all trusted one another here. Left doors unlocked, walked out of coffee shops with each other's children . . .

At the door of the nail bar, Sienna stopped to gather herself. Up the back, beyond the rows of foot baths, Amalia's mother and daughter were deep in manicure mode. Amalia had taken a vacant seat beside them. With one hand pushing the sleeping Daisy back and forth in her pram, she was trying her best to talk Charlie out of acrylics in a shade of shocking pink she told the child she would get sick of.

Hoping not to sound like she'd just run the length of the mall, Sienna willed herself to calm down. Her baby was safe. As she stepped through the centre of the shop, Patti turned and waved. She imagined her mother sitting there smiling at her, happy to be spending an afternoon of pampering together with her daughter and granddaughter. The thought of her mother and Daisy never having the kind of easy relationship Patti and Charlie shared rattled her, but she somehow managed to keep it together and sit down with them all, pretending to be cool.

⌒

It was almost time to think about what to have for tea by the time Sienna and Daisy walked back from the town centre and turned into the driveway that was starting to feel like coming home. Maybe it was the scent of jasmine from the unit on the corner with the neighbour who was always tending his garden, or perhaps it was Sandy's usual greeting, stubby tail wagging and tongue lolling as if he were smiling at them. But today there was no sign of the dog. Sienna glanced up to the veranda, expecting him to be dozing beside Tina while she had a cigarette, but they were nowhere to be seen. She searched in her bag for the key, laughing inwardly at the thought that she might be turning into a nosey neighbour. The phone chimed in the bag. She turned the key and walked in.

Later, she would wonder why she hadn't bolted, just backed out pulling the pram with her. But in the moment she entered the lounge room, hearing the door click shut behind them, Sienna froze. At this point she couldn't know the window in her laundry door had been smashed and shards of glass were lying across the tiles, the clothes she'd gathered that morning while her baby was sleeping, covered in shiny slivers she'd never pick out. She couldn't know the chiming of her phone was her neighbour trying to warn her.

'I don't get it. I just don't get it.' Cole stood up from the couch with that smug smile she'd come to read as the calm before the storm. She glanced round but it was too late to even think about escaping. He was up close, the back of his hand stroking the side of her face. When he turned his attention to the pram, she realised she'd been holding her breath.

'You leave her alone,' she told him, trying to sound in control. She was anything but. On the inside she felt like a leaf trembling in the autumn breeze, teetering on the edge of safety, but she would focus on Daisy, try to stay calm for both of them.

The baby looked out from where she was buckled into the half-reclined pram, eyes wide, her silence speaking volumes. Not yet a year, and she had learned to stay quiet around her father.

Cole took a step back and gave a cackle, that low laugh Sienna hated, another trick from his repertoire of put-downs. He brought a hand to his chest, a look of mock hurt on his lined face. To think she once saw him as hot.

'Me, leave my daughter alone?' He cackled again, pointing a grubby index finger at her face. 'I'm not the one who hurts our baby or abandons her with strangers.'

Her mind raced. The photo on the door, the day in the childcare centre, the bus trip when Josh had bailed her up. What about today? Had he seen them in the mall? Had he seen Amalia take Daisy up the street? As her heart hammered in her chest, she prayed for the shaking to stop.

'That's why you need me, Si.' He curled a lock of her hair round his finger, bending his head so close she could feel his sour breath on her ear. 'I wouldn't mind if you had a friend . . . went out for coffee . . . had your nails done once in a while . . .'

She made fists to hide her fingernails. Had he noticed the smooth aqua shellac that matched Charlie's? Could he have seen them all in the nail bar, Amalia persuading her to stay and have a manicure? She replayed the scene in her head, Patti lifting Daisy out of the pram, bouncing her on her knee while Charlie made her giggle, acting out 'Incy Wincy Spider'. *Oh god!* He must be stalking them.

Sienna tried to give Daisy a smile. The child kept her gaze on her from where she sat gnawing on her little fists, tiny feet pushing at the handbag Sienna had left resting at the end of the pram. Her phone. If Cole would only turn away from her, she could grab it.

'Do you want a coffee or anything?' It was a vain hope to distract him.

'All nicey-nicey to me now, are we?' he said. 'I looked after you, Si, did everything for you and Daisy . . .' He grabbed her and pushed her toward the kitchen, shoving her against the bench and rifling through the drawers. 'You like some pampering, eh?'

'Don't, Cole. Don't do anything you'll regret.' Her whole body shook. 'We can sit down and talk.'

'Oh, I think we've done too much of that old talking, haven't we, Sienna?'

'Please!'

Her breath caught in her throat as she felt the metal of the scissors slide along the back of her neck, his knuckles digging into her skin. The first snip at the base of her hair confirmed her worst nightmare. This could be the day he killed her. As Daisy began to wail, he tugged Sienna back toward the lounge room. Tears streamed down her cheeks. She wanted to scream, but seeing Daisy's distress, she did her best to give the child a reassuring smile.

'I should go to her,' she said as calmly as she could.

'I don't fucking think so.'

Snip, snip. He shoved her to her knees, dropping to the floor behind her, pressing against her.

'Oh yeah. I could take you right here. Like old times . . .'

Jesus Christ, she was trapped. If she cried out, he could slit her throat. If she didn't, he'd rape her again, just like before. So many times before, always apologising, always saying she made him do it.

Daisy was wailing louder now, squirming in her pram, her arms and head reaching over one side. Sienna made to go to her, but Cole gripped her waist tighter. She struggled to breathe, imagined her ribs might crack if he didn't let go. There was a low thump as the scissors hit the floor, then the glide of a zip as he undid his jeans and started to tug at hers.

A noise from the back of the house made him stop. Amongst his ragged breaths, she could hear footsteps.

'Help me!' she screamed, finding the voice that left her in dreams.

There was a shove at the front door.

'Police! Open up!'

He went to scramble away, but caught by his loosened pants, he stumbled, hitting the deck beside her. Cole had said she was slow, dumb, that she'd never amount to anything. She'd stopped trying to believe it wasn't true, until she'd gone to the library where people showed her she was smart, that she and Daisy had a chance. In the quickest move of her life, she reached the scissors before he could recover.

'You bitch,' he shouted. 'I'll kill you.'

As he lunged to grab the scissors from her hand, she swung round. It all happened so quickly, the buzzing electrical sound of the taser just as the scissors connected with his jaw.

'Aaahhh! Cunts!' He writhed around, clutching his leg.

Sienna backed away as a police officer pinned him to the ground. Another stood, holding the taser, her body shielding the pram where a terrified Daisy was rubbing her eyes, her face purple from crying. Sienna caught the eye of the police officer who nodded in permission, waving a hand to tell her to get behind her. She scooted across the floor to her daughter, almost falling on the small girl as she went to comfort her.

'She's bashing my kid, man,' Cole told the officers as he was dragged to his feet and his clothes pulled roughly up around him.

Sienna could hear the siren. Back-up, an ambulance, she couldn't tell. She didn't care. They were safe for now. As she sat cradling her daughter in her arms, stroking the soft hair, damp from her own tears, she knew there could never be a next time. The next time, they'd be dead.

⌒

Tina and Sandy appeared in the doorway as one of the officers made them a cup of tea.

'Thank you.' Sienna shivered despite the warmth of Daisy asleep on her chest and a fleece blanket draped over them as they lay on the sofa. The officer had told her it was Tina who'd phoned for help. If only Sienna had answered the phone before putting the key in the door. If only she'd looked inside and not barrelled into the house on a stupid high from her first proper day out in years. Tina came and sat beside them, Sandy staying close to her, tail between his legs.

'Hope you're keepin' him behind bars,' Tina said to the police officer.

'We'll do our best.'

The young man handed Sienna a mug of milky tea. At the taste of the sugar-laden drink, she wanted to gag, but a memory of something her mum used to say about shock and sweet tea came to her. It was enough to help quell the chattering of her teeth and the terror in her stomach, as she held Daisy close and drank the tea in long grateful gulps. God, she missed her mum.

Chapter Forty-Five

Week Nine

After Vivian and Dave's night in the camper, Dave had come back to the house. It had felt so good that first morning, to wake up beside him, to feel the warmth as she slipped her arm around his belly. She'd breathed in the manly smell of him, grateful. She held firm to the feeling. *I am grateful for Dave. I am grateful for Clodagh. I am grateful for Rory.* Yes, even Rory had played his part in bringing them back together. He'd urged Dave to return home, to explain, to find a way back to his true love. It had taken the help of her supports. Clodagh, Deb, Gloria and, even in their own ways, her writing class and the ladies from Any Excuse for a Luncheon, for her to be brave and honest with herself. Dave was the love of her life. She knew now she was the same for him. For the first time in a long while, she felt she was enough.

In class, it would be business as usual, starting with a review of all the writing they'd explored over the course of the previous sessions. They would spend the remainder of their time finessing their submissions for the book. She gave Oscar a nod as he came in and took a seat beside Johnny. Cathy had taken her aside and tipped her off as to what was ahead of him later today. Broad strokes of information, as was her way. Thin on details, like this course had been at the outset. She'd learned to keep the faith in her old colleague.

She would have thought the fate of Oscar's enslaved cleaner would have been enough drama for one morning, but when Sienna arrived at the door with a blonde woman who was beckoning to her, Vivian was completely blindsided.

'If everyone could get going on their project pieces,' she told the class, 'I'll be back in a minute.'

'Hi, Sienna,' said Vivian as she walked into the hallway and closed the classroom door behind her.

Sienna looked exhausted, eyes like two burnt-out holes in a blanket. Without her babbling baby, Vivian thought the girl had a hollow look about her. She only managed a weak smile as the blonde woman introduced herself.

'Hi, I'm Jess, Sienna's case worker.' She looked around and asked, 'Is there somewhere we can have a private word?'

Vivian invited them to take a seat in one of the small tutoring rooms she and Cathy had used for their meetings. She had no idea if this was okay, but she could justify her instincts later. As Sienna went to sit down, the hood slipped from her head. It took Vivian a moment to take in the cropped hair. Sienna went to quickly put the hood back up, but Jess stayed her arm.

'You don't have to do that,' she told her.

With Sienna worrying at the skin along her fingernails, Jess explained how the ex-partner had attacked the girl. As Vivian listened, the drawing of the scissors came back to her. She knew Jess was giving her the abridged version, but she had enough experience to fill in the gaps. Sienna said she wished to come in to class, but they agreed Jess would be contacted at the first signs of a panic attack.

When Vivian asked Sienna what she would like to work on, she asked if she could sit in a quiet spot and write a letter to her mother. After Vivian had gone round to each of the others to make sure they were all on track, Sienna caught her eye. She held out her notebook for Vivian to read the handwritten note entreating the girl's mother to let her back into her life.

Dear Mum,

I'm not sure if you will read this after all I've put you through, but I would love you to read to the end before you throw this paper in the bin. Also, if you can, please don't show it to Gary. You can make up your own mind about what I have to tell you.

When I met Cole, I was in a very low place. I had no close friends in high school. It wasn't like I didn't try to fit in. I just wasn't cool enough, smart enough, or maybe I was too smart, I don't know. The only real friends I had were you and Hugo, Mum. I know you were going through your own stuff and I'm sorry I wasn't there for you as much as you needed me to be. I tried to like Gary, but I couldn't relax around him. When you were out or having a sleep, he'd come into my room or follow me into the bathroom, try to touch me. That's why I couldn't come home.

After I met Cole at the end of year party, none of the girls would talk to me. Word got round he was a bit older, and they didn't want anything to do with me. I believed him when he told me they were jealous, when he told me I was pretty and interesting. I wish I'd never listened to him.

I have a daughter now. Her name's Daisy. She looks like Dad, the same squished nose, but she has your eyes. Don't tell Hugo, but she farts like him!

I'm in a writing class here in the library in Devonport. The teacher is very understanding. They even let me bring Daisy, but she's in childcare today. I've made a friend here. A cool kind-hearted girl called Amalia. She has a daughter too.

I've missed you so much, Mum. I'm afraid I'll never see you again and you won't get to meet Daisy. Last Saturday, Cole tried to kill me. The police came and he's in custody, but I don't know how long for. Maybe he'll come for us when he gets out. I think he will. Anyway, if the worst happens, I want you to know I love you. Tell Hugo I miss him. It wasn't the same after he left for the army, but I know he wants to be like our real dad. He was a legend.

If you've got this far, thank you for reading. I'd love Daisy to meet you and Hugo, but that may not be possible. I'm sorry I couldn't stay with you.

Love
Sienna

'Oh, Sienna!'

Vivian couldn't stop tears leaking down her cheeks as she handed back the notebook. She went to the box of supplies that Robyn organised every week and found an envelope.

'If you put an address on that, we can get it in the post today.'

Their eyes met. For a moment, Sienna looked like she would say no, but she turned her attention to the page and carefully ripped it from the spiral binding.

Vivian gathered herself and turned her attention to the rest of the group. Marilyn was in flow, typing on one of the laptops, oblivious to the conversation between Oscar and Bjørn about using AI. Amalia, her favourite crazy-haired tattooed girl, was writing acrostic poetry with Johnny. They'd both chosen names of loved ones and were bouncing around adjectives to describe them. They'd already written fictional stories, Amalia's a simple one about children's toys coming to life and Johnny's, a Tassie-based adventure involving motorbikes. Vivian was highly aware that this group had probably learned as much from one another as they had from her in recent weeks.

When Cathy came in toward the end of the session, she asked, 'What will you do on Fridays now?'

'I'm not sure,' said Vivian. 'What will you do?'

'Oh, there are no shortage of projects to work on around here.' She paused, giving a wistful glance over the bent heads of their busy students. 'I'll miss you and this bunch though.'

Before Vivian could respond, she noticed Robyn had her hand up for help. Despite having mentioned on the first morning that they could call her by her first name and just sing out if they needed anything, Robyn had always been extra respectful and addressed her as 'teacher'.

Cathy went to help Robyn out and Vivian took a seat beside Rosa.

'Can I have a hold?'

Rosa handed over Camilla without hesitation. The soothing smell and the warmth from being in her mother's arms made Vivian smile. She'd like if Clodagh had another child. She loved the baby stage. Finn might even surprise them one day. He was great with Max but adamant he wasn't ever having children of his own. Perhaps she'd visit him soon or invite him home. Have those long conversations they only had face to face, over a cuppa. Hear about his hopes for the future.

'I love that you breastfeed her in class,' said Vivian. 'I'm sorry I didn't feed my babies for longer. In too much of a rush to get back to work.'

'Do you know,' said Rosa in that way that made Vivian feel she was being let in on a well-kept secret, 'my grandmother fed my father on the breast for five years.' As Vivian's eyes widened at the thought, Rosa leaned a hand on hers and moved in close. 'And she had seven children!'

Vivian had to stifle a belly laugh so as not to startle Camilla, who was content in her arms. As they looked over Rosa's writing and photos, she was transported to Piura in northern Peru. It was a far cry from the images she conjured up when the nuns would go round her school, rattling a tin can and asking them to donate their pennies to the Peruvian missions. Rosa had written about the things she missed, like the cocktail made with the fruit of the algarroba tree and how they would mix a black honey with milk for the children. There were photos to match her pieces, like the one of the colourful three-wheel moto-taxi she'd hail to get to work and one of a bench in the Plaza de Armas where she sometimes ate lunch.

'Your family?' asked Vivian, pointing to a photo of a large group outside an imposing cathedral.

'Easter,' said Rosa. She waggled an index finger. 'No eggs! We visit seven churches.' She pointed to where she'd written about it in the text.

'Sounds like my childhood,' said Vivian. 'My mother always traipsed us around churches in the holidays.' She laughed. 'At least we had Easter eggs.'

'Vivian, have you got a minute?' Marilyn called.

'Okay to take Camilla with?' she asked Rosa.

'Of course. She loves you, like *abuela*.'

Vivian took the comparison to a grandmother as a compliment rather than a reminder of her age and went to help Marilyn.

'Maybe it's not great, but have a read of this.'

Marilyn passed the notebook where she'd written one of her book reviews. *Dawn at Clear Mountain* didn't sound like something she'd read herself, but by the time she reached the end of the second page, where Marilyn had drawn five stars, Vivian thought she might google the author.

'That's amazing, Marilyn. You've given just enough to make me interested but not too much to spoil it for me,' Vivian told her, 'unlike movie trailers . . .'

Marilyn blushed, but behind the hand-waving to brush off the praise, Vivian could tell she was pleased. 'Yeah, them new trailers nearly give away half the story,' she agreed. 'They make you not want to watch the movie anymore.'

With Camilla dozing in her arms, they put their heads together to add in the punctuation Marilyn had skipped over and talk about how Marilyn could include a paragraph about how her love of reading developed. She agreed to type it all up and email it to Cathy, who was collating submissions. Vivian allowed herself an inward smile as she continued on her circuit of the room, handing Camilla back before proofreading Bjørn and Oscar's pieces.

Mindful of the time, Vivian called the group together and thanked them for all their hard work. There was one week to go, but arrangements for their book were underway. Cathy had already begun organising their celebration. Guests were to be invited. Family members would be welcome. Vivian left Cathy to the last of the announcements while she took

Sienna to one side. She had addressed the envelope. Her hand shook as she gave it to Vivian like she was entrusting something precious into her care. Indeed, she was. Vivian could only hope the girl would get a response.

Chapter Forty-Six

D riving down the scenic sweep of road toward Geraldine's, Oscar hardly registered the rolling hills and ripening vines as he focussed on saving Siraporn. Today was D-day. Oscar would return to his sister's as normal with specialist detectives ready to move in. As he neared the turn-off for the house, he saw the unmarked car and remembered the instructions the police had given him. He was to drive in at his usual speed, park, keep to the routine of previous weeks. *Easier said than done*, he thought as he drove past.

Angie sat in the van, scrolling on her phone. Dog barked at the sound of his car. *Good boy, stick to the program,* he thought as he got out and went round the side of the house to greet him. Through the windows he saw Siraporn wiping down the kitchen benches. When he went inside, she gave him a half-smile as she bowed, but turned quickly to check that the woman in the van wasn't looking in at her.

'In a minute or two,' he said, 'follow me out to the pool.'

They might have been some of the longest minutes of his life. The responsibility of what he was part of weighed heavier with every second. He heard the door open. Siraporn appeared with the cloth in her hand. She looked so thin, so vulnerable.

'I've sent a text to the police,' Oscar began. 'They are nearby.'

Her head bobbed in understanding, but her eyes shone with fear.

'It will be okay,' he said. 'There are good people who will look after you.'

As she hesitated to move, he could see tears welling in her eyes. He took a step closer to her and caught her hand.

'You are very brave.'

'Thank you . . . Oscar.'

⌒

They stood in the kitchen counting the minutes on the clock. Nine, ten, . . . thirteen . . . the police siren went off. He didn't need to be there to know the police were doing their job. When two uniformed officers came to the house and informed them Angie had been arrested, Siraporn fell to the floor, still shaking with fear. Oscar went to her and gently pulled her to her feet, guiding her to the lounge room where he sat on the sofa beside her while the officers explained the procedure. She would be taken to a safe house. The Red Cross would take things from there. As they led her to the police car in the driveway, she looked back and waved. Oscar still saw fear, but also gratitude in her eyes. He hoped it wouldn't be the last he'd see of her.

All he could do now was hope Siraporn could pick up the pieces of her life and heal from her ordeal. One of the detectives had mentioned she might not have a valid visa. Immigration would be involved. She might need a good lawyer. He took out his phone. Now that Angie had been apprehended and Siraporn rescued, he could call Johnny. His sister's smarts might come in handy.

That evening, with a strange lonesome feeling over him, he decided to give Bobby a call.

'How have you been, Dad?'

At the sound of the familiar warmth in his son's voice, the breath caught in Oscar's throat, and he thought he might sob instead of speak. 'Good . . . good, son,' he managed.

'You been going to that course in the library?' Bobby asked. His son had a knack for remembering what they last spoke about even if several weeks had passed between calls.

'Yes, mate. What about you? Work treatin' you okay?'

Bobby filled him in on the latest project before bringing the topic of conversation back to Oscar.

'Everything okay with you, Dad? You sound a bit down.'

Oscar sighed, but instead of brushing off his own worries as he had done with Covid and losing his job, he shared his news of learning to read and write better at the library and how he'd helped Siraporn.

'Jeez, that's a lot, Dad,' said Bobby. 'Sounds like you need another holiday.'

Oscar laughed off the comment, but Bobby's tone became serious.

'Dad, I'd really like you to come to Japan. I'm thinking of staying on. I've met someone.'

Oscar thought he'd had enough excitement today, but his son had invited him to visit enough times to know he was genuine. It was great to know the boy needed him, but the thought of travelling overseas was terrifying. As he listened to Bobby's reassurances about collecting him at the airport and showing him around, he thought about Vivian. Maybe he could ask her to help him with reading all that travel stuff.

'I'll come,' he said, interrupting Bobby's efforts at persuasion.

They agreed dates. Bobby had annual leave coming up. There were so many experiences he wanted to share with him. By the time they rang off, Oscar was still partly terrified, but mostly excited. He thought of Siraporn and how she was faring tonight; in amongst the uncertainty of what the future might hold for them, at least there was hope.

Chapter Forty-Seven

Week Ten

When he'd volunteered to help with the layout of the book, Oscar didn't realise it would involve a trip to a local printers'. Keeping his reservations to himself, he agreed to drive there with Cathy to meet the woman who would oversee the work of turning the fruits of the writing course into something they would all get to keep and, in his case at least, treasure.

Cathy's contact greeted them in the foyer.

'I hear you used to work in a printers', Oscar,' she said, shaking his hand. 'My name's Mel. I can show you round if you like.'

She didn't wait for a response but took off toward the back of the building with long, determined strides. Cathy gave him an enthusiastic smile and marched after her. Despite his trepidation, there was nothing for it but to follow her.

'We'll come back to the art room,' the woman was saying, 'but come in and see the boys.'

Through glass panels, he could see the machines and a couple of fellas at their stations. As she opened the door, he was transported back to his old work in Footscray. The *thunk-ah-thunk* of the presses, the smell of ink solvents . . . It was like stepping into a pair of old boots that no longer fit. While Cathy marvelled at a machine from days gone by, Oscar wondered how he used to cope with the long hours, standing on his feet all day long, breathing it all in. If he'd been in any doubt that those days were behind him, this brief visit had convinced him his working future would have to look very different.

Back in the art room, Mel logged on to a computer. Across a wide curved screen, she showed them her ideas for the book that would incorporate the drawings, photos and pieces of writing the class had produced. Although some final drafts were still to be agreed, Oscar registered a special buzz at seeing his classmates' creations on the screen. The copies of Sienna's drawings had come out so well. The written pieces, longer stories like Johnny's and Amalia's, interspersed with the shorter ones, like Robyn's gratitude journal entries, all looked so professional. Even his own short piece about the *Spirit of Tasmania* looked good beside the photo he'd taken one evening as he'd watched the ship sail out of Devonport. Vivian had insisted that he have two pieces in the book, the same as everyone else. When he'd thought his struggles to get Dog's story on paper had been enough, she'd raised the bar. Inwardly, he told himself he was glad she had.

'Gorgeous shot of *The Spirit*,' Mel remarked. 'You could sell that.'

Cathy gave him an encouraging nod. He'd thought anyone could take good photos now that phones were so smart, but maybe he'd give the idea some thought. If Covid had taught him anything, it was not to look too far ahead. Today he would take the wins around being able to contribute to the book, give back for all the help Cathy, Vivian and his fellow classmates had given him. Geraldine and Malcolm would return soon, but he had them to thank for a much-needed break. His long Covid symptoms were starting to wane, and although helping rescue a woman from a horrible situation might have been a bit unexpected, he was glad to have been useful.

∽

When they got back to the library, the other students were writing what Vivian called their bios and putting the final touches to their pieces. They'd all produced way more than him, but he didn't mind. They had their own learning journeys. Something told him he was only getting started on his.

Vivian gathered them to share a final read-through. He smiled at Robyn as she took the seat beside him and read aloud from her journal entries. He loved how she was taken by the ordinary; a cool breeze in summer to air the house, a wave from a neighbour's child when she was feeling low, a zucchini flower to decorate her food. As he listened to the others read, his thoughts turned to Siraporn, hoping she would be free to find her own small joys wherever she ended up. Cathy assured him she was being looked after.

Johnny's sister was proving another much-needed ally. When the police discovered Siraporn had been coerced into working to pay off a bogus visa application, they contacted the organisation she worked for. They were doing their best to find longer term accommodation and secure a visa for the traumatised Thai woman. Oscar and Siraporn had promised to stay in touch, but he would give her a bit of space. She'd have a lot on her plate.

Oscar felt his world was opening up. Johnny had helped him look up flights to Japan. Bobby would have to do all the translating, but for the first time, Oscar could imagine himself getting there. His reading and writing were improving. Vivian's help was making a difference. Words he'd never been able to decipher were starting to make sense to him. There was still heaps to learn, but he was in the right place to get the help he needed.

They would all meet again at the book launch in a few weeks. Geraldine and Malcolm would be home by then. If it didn't mean overstaying his welcome, he'd ask if he could stay on. He'd lasted the course with all its challenges. It would be good to be part of the celebration.

Chapter Forty-Eight

On an early morning beach walk, Vivian slipped a hand round the arm of Dave's puffer jacket and updated him on the library event. He had an online meeting at nine but promised to try to make an appearance.

'Will you miss it?' he asked.

'You mean the teaching?'

Dave nodded. 'I wondered if it made you feel you retired too early.'

Vivian hesitated. Had she made it that obvious how much she liked getting out of the house? But they'd made a pact, agreed to be honest and not make assumptions about what each other was thinking or feeling. She'd remembered an interview where the Irish writer, Cathy Kelly, revealed her recipe for solving marital problems; 'Stay up and fight,' she'd said. Although Vivian had avoided conflict for most of her married life, she was determined to put those words into practice. Dave agreed. They'd spent far too much time side-stepping their issues. She told him what was on her mind.

'Cathy's been asking if I'd like to do some more work at the library, but we have our big road trip and . . .'

He stopped and turned to face her. Taking both her hands in his, he looked into her eyes as if there was no one else on the beach.

'Would you like to do the work?' he asked.

She looked away to where the tide was inching its way up the shore. They were so lucky to live in this beautiful place. In time they would grow old here, but that was for the future. She wasn't ready to quit. Dave had been getting calls from his contacts. There were offers of short gigs. She'd recognised the twinkle of enthusiasm in his eye as he'd told her. She looked into those kind eyes now.

'Yes. Part time. Maybe with a break in winter to let us get away.'

He folded her into his arms.

'I just want to make you happy, Viv,' he said, holding her close.

'You do,' she said, slipping her arms around his waist and tilting her head up for one of the long lingering kisses they'd been sharing in private.

'Oh, would you look at you two!'

Vivian disengaged from what was shaping up to be something more suited to the bedroom and turned to see Petronella emerging from the bush path and striding over the sand toward them, her smile as bright as her sporty sun visor and designer gym wear.

'Morning, Petronella,' said Dave from where he was standing behind Vivian, leaving her in no doubt their little moment had been one of intense passion.

'I won't stop,' said Petronella. 'Have to get in a few steps before my shift at the shop. Good to see you both!'

She winked as she went past, arms swinging at her sides.

'Oh god, that could have been embarrassing,' said Dave once she was out of earshot and the two of them could crease over with laughter.

Near the smartboard in what had been their classroom, Oscar was introducing Geraldine and Malcolm to Johnny when he caught sight of Siraporn. He had to do a double take as he watched her walk in with Cathy, wearing a simple yet stunning green dress and sparkly black flats, so different from the crying woman he'd met that day at the house. He was glad he'd worn a good shirt.

'Excuse me, guys,' he said to the others. 'I'll be back in a minute.'

As he approached, Cathy beamed at him. 'Ah, young Oscar,' she said warmly. Siraporn bowed politely, but there was a smile too, a smile that went all the way to her beautiful dark eyes, eyes that held no fear. He could only half-listen as Cathy enthused about the lessons and projects she was lining up that would include Siraporn.

'I'm sure you have a lot to work out,' he said, still looking at Siraporn.

'Oh, we'll take it steady,' said Cathy. She turned to Siraporn. 'Thought I'd invite you here to make you feel welcome.' She took a breath and looked back at Oscar. 'Besides, I thought it would be nice for you two to catch up.' And leaving them with the comment, she swept off to mingle with some of the other students.

'You look beautiful, Siraporn. Are you well?'

Siraporn nodded.

'I'd like you to meet my sister,' he said. He beckoned to where Geraldine had tactfully waited to be invited. She'd been blown away when she'd heard what had unfolded under her roof.

'I always thought of Angie as a demon, didn't I, Oscar?' she'd said.

They got along well, Geraldine and Siraporn. As they chatted over the generous spread put on by the library, a warmth filled his heart. Was it a case of being in the right place at the right time, that day he'd found Siraporn in his sister's kitchen? Perhaps.

When they got a moment to chat alone, she asked how he'd been. He told her about his plans to visit Bobby in Japan in a few months, how he and Dog would head back to Melbourne to tie up a few loose ends before returning to Tasmania. He even found himself telling her how Vivian would continue to help him get to grips with reading and writing and about the photography course Cathy had found for him at the local college. As they stood chatting about their plans, Oscar hoped Siraporn would also be part of his future.

Sienna was beside herself with anxious energy as she and Daisy moved around the room, catching up with her classmates. Keeping one eye on the door, she couldn't wait for her mum to walk in. Vivian and Cathy had been so supportive, even organising a lift for her mum from the airport. Michelle had read her letter and called the library straight away. On their first video call, they'd hardly been able to speak, so overcome with emotion as they both tried to explain how things had got so out of hand. Hugo messaged soon after. He had leave coming up in a few weeks. They would all be together in Queensland, far away from Cole Sutton who was on remand. Her mother had plucked up the courage to tell Gary Stone to pack his bags. Turned out, she wasn't very happy with the man either. She didn't know all of the details yet, but Sienna was grateful they'd have lots of time to heal together.

'Sienna, this is my husband, Enrique.' Rosa appeared beside her with a gorgeous man who made Camilla look like a doll in his arms. Leaning in, she whispered, 'I brought the speaker.' She'd felt a bit special when Rosa suggested they keep her plans for the salsa lesson a surprise.

'Anyone as nervous as me?' It was Amalia. She'd come with her mum and Charlie.

'Me,' said Sienna, 'but not just about the book.'

When she turned round to check the door again, there was her mum, looking beautiful as ever but older, Sienna thought. She went to her and hugged her in close until she could feel Daisy squirm, squashed between them.

Still breathing in the scent of her, Sienna felt her mum touch her cheek and hold her gaze for a moment where no words were needed. Turning to look down at Daisy, her mum's face broke into the widest smile.

'Hello, little one,' she said gently.

Sienna handed over her bub without a moment's hesitation. Daisy was exactly where she belonged. She introduced her mum to Amalia and her family. Patti and Michelle chatted easily about their granddaughters. Daisy had taken her first steps that week, managed to get herself from the coffee table to the sofa all on her own. Two teeth had come through to boot. It had been such a joy to share the milestones with her mum. Looking round the room, she remembered the anxiety and loneliness she'd felt when Jess had brought her here a few months ago. Everyone she'd shared this space with had helped replace those feelings with the anticipation she'd felt walking in here Friday after Friday. This group had become her tribe, the library, a place where she belonged. When she moved back home to the mainland, this was the kind of place she would do her best to find.

As Cathy summoned the students to the front for presentations, Jess appeared at the door, holding it open for a man her own age in a wheelchair. Sienna went to help.

'Sienna, this is my husband, Sam,' Jess raised her eyebrows, 'the wise man I once told you about.'

Sienna wasn't sure what to say, but the man rescued her.

'Oh god! You and me might need to have a talk later, Sienna.' He smiled at her from where she was sure the only thing he might be able to move was his face.

Their chat would have to wait, but as Sienna showed them
to a suitable spot in the audience, she could only imagine what
her fabulous case worker and her husband had been through.
Little wonder she'd put her trust in Jess from the start.

⌒

Vivian checked her phone as people started to take their seats.
She'd hoped Dave could have attended but with his meeting
delayed, he probably wouldn't make it. She nodded to Cathy
who began the formal proceedings with her calm efficiency. As
each participant's name was called out, the library manager,
who'd been drafted in to do the honours, presented them with
a certificate and a copy of the book. Extra copies for family
and local worthies lay fanned out on a table, the cover boasting
Robyn's vibrant sunflowers and the words, Special Spaces,
appearing at the centre in English and surrounded by their
translation in Norwegian, Cantonese, Arabic and Spanish. It
had been Oscar's idea. Vivian couldn't have been prouder of
the way her students had embraced all she'd brought to this
writing course. She'd given a lot of herself, but in doing so
had received so much in return.

On behalf of the class, Cathy presented her with a bouquet
of flowers to a round of appreciative applause. Before she
could cry, Rosa surprised everyone by taking the floor with
her handsome husband and announcing that they should all
join them in the open area at the front. Sienna, who seemed
to be in on whatever Rosa was scheming had set a Bluetooth
speaker on the serving table and was scrolling on her phone.
When the music came on, Rosa and Enrique began to dance

in the practised moves of a salsa. It was pure joy to see young and old join in with what Rosa had jokingly promised the very first week.

Sienna's mother held Daisy close as she stepped in time to the music. Robyn and her husband took no time to get moving. What Robyn might have lacked in coordination, she made up for with her indomitable enthusiasm. Johnny was a revelation, whisking Cathy into an energetic back and forth that had her whooping in delight. Amalia had her mother getting in amongst it. Beside them her daughter and Marilyn's granddaughter were carefully trying to match Rosa and Enrique's footwork. Vivian watched as Oscar bent his head and held out a hand to Siraporn. Those two would make a lovely couple, she thought, as the shy woman accepted and stepped into the mix. A smiling Bjørn took in the show from the comfort of his chair. She hoped his operation would let him dance again soon.

Marilyn looked like she might leave the dancing to the others, but just as Vivian thought to stand beside her to keep her company, a grey-haired woman about her own age took Marilyn's hand and began to lead them in a slower version of the dance. Vivian thought there was something especially gentle and loving in the way the women moved together with the kind of understanding that made words surplus to requirements.

Thinking she could slink off to the side, she felt a hand reach round from behind and relieve her of the flowers. She wished she'd seen him, but there was no time to gather herself.

'Are you dancing?'

She turned to find Dave looking and indeed smelling resplendent. The smart blue jacket and chocolate brown chinos took years off him, and that scent, Aramis, she knew . . . God, he hadn't worn that in years.

'Are you asking?'

As he slipped a hand round her waist, she smiled inwardly at the thought of all the shabby worn clothes she'd emptied from his wardrobe. She hadn't salsaed in years, but after a few awkward steps, they found a rhythm. If the last few months had taught her anything, it was that life was better when you said yes.

At the end of their celebration, Vivian had the sense that the students didn't want to leave. Marilyn, who usually couldn't get out the door fast enough, came over to introduce her granddaughter and her friend Georgie. The friendly woman reached out and squeezed Vivian's hand.

'And you must be Keisha,' said Vivian to the child with the most beautiful raven hair tied in neat braids. 'I hope the morning tea was as good as your baking.' She was rewarded with a shy smile. The fact that she was missing school wasn't lost on her, but Vivian was honoured to think Marilyn had deemed the celebration important enough to bring her grand-daughter along.

'What are your plans for Fridays now, Marilyn?' Cathy asked.

Marilyn rocked back and forth on the high heels that had surprised them all. She was like a different woman today in a bright silk blouse and classy trousers.

'Not sure what to do with myself . . .'

'Well, I would love to talk to you about helping out here in the library,' said Cathy. 'There's a job I think you'd be perfect for.'

Marilyn looked dumbstruck. She held Keisha close and rubbed her arm. 'Do you hear that, Keisha? Your nan might be getting a job.'

In the sex shop, Marilyn sat opposite Georgie, her notebook from the library open in front of her where she'd started a bucket list. It was Jamie of all people who'd encouraged her to make one. He was like an advert for rehabilitation. At night on his lounge room sofa, when he and Neha had gone to bed, Marilyn had taken to gratitude journalling, silently thanking his girlfriend, his parole officer and her son for staying off the drugs. Technically, she was homeless, but it wasn't the version she'd dreaded. She had family around her and she was useful, cooking and cleaning, even learning the Nepalese recipes Neha showed her. Frank had steered clear. After the night of Ethan's party, he knew better than to provoke his sons.

'You know what we need, Georgie?' she asked her friend.

Georgie looked up from a leather lingerie catalogue. 'And what does my writer friend think we need?'

Marilyn looked her square in the eye. 'A holiday.'

Georgie was about to laugh, but Marilyn could see it dawning on her that she was serious.

'You mean you and me, go somewhere?'

Marilyn nodded. 'Yeah, somewhere on the mainland.'

Georgie raised an eyebrow. 'You've only just managed to leave your house. What makes you think you can go to the mainland?'

Marilyn sat up straight and flicked her newly dyed hair off her face.

'You know that job Cathy at the library was on about?' she asked.

'Mmm.' Georgie waited.

'Well, I got it *and* I've opened my own bank account . . .'

Georgie's face broke into a smile. 'You beauty!' She cackled as she reached forward and gave Marilyn a playful whack of her catalogue.

As Marilyn relaxed back in her plastic chair and let the enormity of what she'd done sink in, she could almost hear the cogs turning in her friend's brain.

'Stuff this place and all,' said Georgie. 'We've been kept down for long enough. Let's go!'

'You and me, Georgie. We deserve a holiday as much as anyone!'

Chapter Forty-Nine

In the conservatory of a beautiful Federation home, Vivian found herself basking in the company of her Any Excuse for a Luncheon friends. Petronella had secured an invite for them all to what was the home of one of her arty connections. Surrounded by original seascapes and pretty cake stands packed with triangles of crustless sandwiches and petit fours, Vivian relaxed into easy conversation with the women whose regular gatherings she'd come to look forward to. She'd even invited Cathy to join them. No longer the newbie, she was able to reach out to someone she thought might enjoy the gatherings too. Only a few months ago, she'd felt completely alone. Her best friend had left town and her husband gone AWOL. Although she hadn't realised it at the time, Cathy and Petronella had thrown her lifelines.

After lunch, they took a wander in the lush gardens, marvelling at the work and care that had gone into them. By a patch of kangaroo paw and other natives, she caught up with Cathy.

'There's been something I've been meaning to ask you,' she began.

'Ask away,' said Cathy as they walked along the path.

'I've been wondering . . . if I hadn't agreed to take the writing class, what would you have done?'

The corners of her friend's mouth curled up in a smile.

'I'd have done it myself,' Cathy answered.

Vivian shook her head. 'So that morning you ran into me, why did you ask?'

Cathy stopped walking. 'It's a small place. I'd heard about Dave, that you weren't doing so well . . .'

'Are you allowed to tell me who told you, or is it a state secret?'

'Oh, I think it might have been a team effort.'

Vivian didn't press. It was enough to know that even though she'd felt so alone, there'd been people batting for her.

'Thank you,' she said. 'It really made a difference.'

'And how are you and Dave now, if you don't mind my asking?'

Vivian smiled as she answered. 'Never better.' It was true. She'd always thought a good marriage could be measured by happy kids, a comfortable home, mostly harmonious relations, but she'd learned not to take happiness for granted. She and Dave had committed to loving each other for the rest of their lives, to being more open and willing to face conflict. There would be no more stonewalling. They'd agreed that even when they didn't see eye to eye, each would listen to the other's voice.

Her phone pinged in her pocket.

Date night reminder.

Inside, she fizzed with excitement. She hadn't been on a date in years. They might be fifty-eight and sixty, and together for over thirty years, but instead of the end she'd envisaged, their marriage was getting a fresh start.

Acknowledgements

At some point just before the madness of the Covid pandemic, I was asked to deliver a ten-week writing program at Devonport Library in Tasmania. When the project was put on hold, I started to turn the idea into a novel. My thanks then must firstly go to Kerrie Blyth for giving me the opportunity to do two of the things I love, teaching and writing. Rebecca Saunders, my publisher, thank you so much for your response to my proposal, your belief in my story about literacy and other subjects close to my heart, and for your patience which I must have really tested with this book. To my editors, Ali Lavau, Meaghan Amor, Dianne Blacklock, thanks to each of you for your insights. Special thanks to Bec Hamilton for your thorough copy edit and for understanding my story. Dear readers, whether you've purchased, been gifted, or borrowed this book from a friend or a library, thank you. I hope you love the cover as much as I do. The team at Hachette Australia do an amazing job throughout the process, but bringing the book together at the end is very special after all the 'crossings out' of rewriting.

This book allowed me to draw on my teaching experience and to remember the adult learners I've had the privilege of working with over many years. In particular, of course, I wish to thank the members of the writing class which did indeed eventuate at Devonport Library post Covid. Special thanks to Marjorie Ng for permission to use your Cantonese name in honour of your father. To all the staff at the library, Birgitta Magnusson-Reid at Devonport Regional Gallery and Ann Teesdale at Home Hill, thank you for your part in this journey.

Marcella Walsh, thanks for the story of the three-legged stool. Mariana Farfan, thank you for sharing insights into your life in Peru and to Julie Good, thanks for a tour of the Impress printing works in Devonport. Dr Shirley Patton, thanks for your generous sharing of your academic research into domestic violence and your encouragement to pursue the storyline of Sienna which was the most difficult for me to write. Teresa White, thank you also for your professional insights in that regard. Liz Tangney, for all the life lessons, not least those on dyslexia and parenting.

I am blessed with the friendship of booklovers in my local community who continue to cheer me on. Special thanks to Helen Dick, and to Sue Chapman for your kind permission for me to use the name of your group, Any Excuse for a Luncheon. Mardie Loone, thanks for a lovely day out on the water when *The Spirit of Devonport* was still running on the Mersey River.

The encouragement and support of my family and friends, near and far, means everything to me. Thank you all for keeping me going.

Finally, to Tommy Watson, we have lost touch, but if someone reading this knows you, I hope you come to know the huge difference that helping you to read and write better many moons ago has made to my life.

Author's Note

The Writing Class is a work of fiction but it deals with issues faced by many.

If you or someone you know is experiencing violence or abuse, you do not have to face it alone.

You can call 1800RESPECT on 1800 737 732.

If you are under 25, you can call Kids Helpline on 1800 55 1800.

If you are an Aboriginal person or a Torres Strait Islander person, you can call 13YARN on 13 92 76.

If you live in New Zealand, you can call the Family Violence Information Line on 0800 456 450 or Shine on 0508 744 633.

If you need crisis or mental health support, you can call Lifeline on 13 11 14.

If you would like to improve your reading, writing, maths or computer skills, you can call the Reading Writing Hotline on 1300 655 506.